SEXTON BLAKE

SPY STORIES

A Collection of 3 Classic Tales

The Case of the King's Spy
The Case of the Strange Wireless Message
The Mystery of the Turkish Agreement

W. W. Sayer

ROH
PRESS

The Golden Age: Volume 1
Sexton Blake: Spy Stories

A Collection of 3 Classic Tales

W. W. Sayer (1892-1949)
The Case of the King's Spy, The Sexton Blake Library #110, January 1920
The Case of the Strange Wireless Message, The Sexton Blake Library #125, May 1920
The Mystery of the Turkish Agreement, The Sexton Blake Library #135, July 1920

Cover: Judge, #2420, James Trembath, 1927.

Illustrations: Arthur Jones

Biographic information on W. W. Sayer sourced from "I Meet W.W. Sayer" an interview Mr Sayer had with researcher and author W. O.G. Lofts.

ISBN: 978-1-998879-11-3

Typos and Text
Each story has been meticulously edited to give you the best reading experience possible. However, sometimes the odd typo or two may have slipped through. If you spot one, please let us know and we'll fix it immediately. You can contact us at: rohpress@gmail.com.

www.rohpress.com

A Note from the Publisher

The Golden Age #1

An Anthology of 3 Complete Tales of Mystery, Detective Work and Adventure.

Featuring: Sexton Blake, Tinker, Pedro James "Granite" Grant and Mademoiselle Julie

"Mr. Blake, no doubt you are wondering why I have sent for you. I admit that it is rather an unusual course for a man of my position to adopt, but there are strong reasons for it."

With those words, Sir Vrymer Fane, head of the British Secret Service, invited Sexton Blake into the world of international political intrigue. In the many cases that followed, the great detective would find himself allied with two of the most popular characters in the Blake canon: James "Granite" Grant, The King's Spy, and Mademoiselle Julie of the French Secret Service.

Grant was renowned for his fearlessness and dogged determination, and reputed "the brains of the British Secret Service." Mademoiselle Julie was a multi-skilled, highly intelligent agent whose uncommon beauty "could cast its spell over the strongest of men." Together, the two would feature in some of the most popular tales of the Roaring Twenties. *Sexton Blake: Spy Stories* collects their first three adventures: *The King's Spy, The Case of the Strange Wireless Message* and *The Mystery of the Turkish Agreement.*

This is the first title in a series of anthologies that collects tales from Sexton Blake's Golden Age. We'll draw from a wide list of authors: John W. Bobin, Andrew Murray, William Murray Graydon, G. H. Teed, William J. Bayfield, and many others. Enjoy!

Nico Lorenzutti
Editor
www.rohpress.com

Author Spotlight

Walter William Sayer was a popular writer of the twenties and thirties, who wrote under the name "Pierre Quiroule." He was considered by many to be one of the most brilliant of all pre-war authors of Sexton Blake stories. He is best remembered for his creation of "Granite" Grant, the King's Spy, and his French counterpart Mademoiselle Julie.

Born in 1892, he began his professional life as second cashier at the Midland Bank in Fleet Street. His clientele included G. H. Teed and William Murray Graydon, two Blake authors who brought in weekly cheques of £100 each from the Amalgamated Press. Witnessing firsthand that a prolific author could earn fifty times his weekly salary, it is little wonder that Sayer turned his hand to writing. His first stories were for *Pluck*, featuring Blake friend and ally Detective-Inspector Will Spearing. He also wrote for the *Tubby Haig Library*, *Titbits*, and penned numerous 'girl stories' under the penname Madge Crichton.

During the First World War he served in France and on his return he set up a small office in Fleet Street as a free-lance writer. In 1920, he wrote his first Sexton Blake story: *The Case of the Criminal Scientist* published in *Union Jack* #850. It was followed by *The Case of the King's Spy*, published in *The Sexton Blake Library* #110. It featured Granite Grant, a character of his own creation, the first title in this anthology. Sayer thought the tale "a very poor effort," and had no intention of continuing to feature Grant in later stories. But readers clamoured for more and Grant soon reappeared in *The Case of the Strange Wireless Message* in *The Sexton Blake Library* a few months later. His second story introduced Mademoiselle Julie, a French Secret Service agent, and for the next six years she and Grant worked with Blake in various cases at home and abroad. The two made a final appearance in *The Ethiopian's Secret* in 1926 then did not return to fight alongside Blake until the 1930s. Many of the original stories were then republished, or rewritten to meet reader demand.

In 1936 Mr. Sayer joined the British Lion Film Co. as a script writer, and, two years later his tale *The Mystery of No. 13 Caversham Square* was adapted for the screen. Entitled *Sexton Blake and the Hooded Terror* it starred George Curzon as Sexton Blake, Greta Gynt as Mademoiselle Julie and David Farrar (who played Sexton Blake in later films) as Granite Grant.

Sayer also wrote several novels under the name of Pierre Quiroule. These include *The Hour of Recognition* (1932) *The Silhouette Symbol* (1935) and *The Painted Death* (1936). In the 1940s he published three novels under his own name: *Sellers of Death* (1940), *The Nemesis Club* (1946) and *Mine Sinister Host* (1948) the last of which was his final work.

THE GOLDEN AGE #1
SEXTON BLAKE
SPY STORIES
A Detective Romance Specially
Written to Appeal to All Tastes,
All Ages—Either Sex.
FRANCIS H. WARREN.
Illustrations
by
"VAL,"
and
FRANCIS
H.
WARREN.

Our Anthologies
Collections of Classic Works of Fiction

The Golden Age

Sexton Blake: Spy Stories
Sexton Blake: The Ferraro Files #1
Sexton Blake: The Three Murrays
Sexton Blake: The Claire Delisle Files
Sexton Blake: Spy Stories #2

The Teed Files

Sexton Blake: Yvonne's Vengeance
Sexton Blake: Rymer and Wu Ling
Sexton Blake: Wu Ling Strikes Again
Sexton Blake: Cunning Schemes
Sexton Blake: Palmer and Beauremon
Sexton Blake: Dawn of the Great War
Sexton Blake: Schemes and Scandals

The Criminals' Confederation Series

Sexton Blake: The Bat Files
Sexton Blake: The Bat Files #2
Sexton Blake: The Bat Files #3
Sexton Blake: The Bat Files #4
Sexton Blake: Confederation Rising
Sexton Blake: The Sinister Island Saga
Sexton Blake: Yvonne Joins the Fight
Sexton Blake: Beware the Shadow
Sexton Blake: Plots and Intrigues
Sexton Blake: Reversals of Fortune
Sexton Blake: The Rival Presidents
Sexton Blake: Reece's Republic
Sexton Blake: Twists in the Trail
Sexton Blake: Final Curtain

The Great Ladies of Crime

Moriarty's Rivals: 12 Female Masterminds
The Exploits of Fidelity Dove
Miss Brandt Adventuress
Nelson Lee: The Black Wolf Files

THE SEXTON BLAKE LIBRARY.
4d
THE CASE OF THE KING'S SPY.
A Clever Detective Story, Introducing Examples of Brilliant Deduction and Skilful Investigation.

The Greatest Sexton Blake Epic Begins Here...

The exploits of a talented cracksman. The deadly schemes of a nefarious criminal mastermind. These are the first tales leading to the formation of The Criminals' Confederation, a union of thieves and crooks that spanned the globe.

Available in ebook and paperback.

ROH PRESS

Four New Volumes of the SEXTON BLAKE LIBRARY are issued on the first Friday of each month. Please give your Newsagent a Standing Order for them.

THE
Case of the King's Spy.

A Remarkable Complete Novel of Detective Adventure, Introducing a Wonderful New Character, " Granite" Grant.

Chapter 1
"Granite" Grant

JAMES GRANT, known throughout the Embassies of Europe as "Granite" Grant, the King's Spy, strode thoughtfully along the glistening pavements of Whitehall. It was one o'clock in the morning, and the great boom of Big Ben had just chimed out over the sleeping city.

The famous thoroughfare, ordinarily so full of bustle and life and scurrying throngs of people, was deserted. Not another solitary figure or vehicle could be seen on the broad, sweeping highway as far as the eye could reach.

It had been raining hard: the pavement glistened beneath the long line of street lamps.

Granite Grant had been summoned to a private meeting in Whitehall Court. Momentous issues had been discussed; on his shoulders rested grave responsibilities of worldwide importance to the British Empire.

They had been entrusted to his able hands, for he was the only strong man capable of seeing them through.

By his resourcefulness and enterprise many a skilful diplomatic venture had been brought to a successful issue. Now he was to be again tried.

The Government had reposed infinite trust in his ability to see this thing through. And not without reason, for it was because of his iron will and courage that he had earned the name of "Granite" Grant.

He had dismissed his chauffeur some time before. Granite Grant was not the sort of man who keeps his employees hanging about half the night; with his great courage went also a simple kindness of heart which endeared him to those who obeyed his commands.

As he strode thoughtfully along the pavement, a thousand and one questions crowded into his active mind. He was to go abroad again on some secret mission. There was no time to lose; the matter was urgent. It seemed to be his fate to be exiled from the land he loved so well—to be mixed up in some great adventure or other over on the Continent, or in more remote foreign parts.

No sooner had he returned from settling one big question, than another would appear to demand his attention elsewhere. It was too bad!

He thought of the charming Miss Laura Valentine, the famous actress, whom he was shortly to make his wife. The wedding had been already arranged. Their photographs had appeared in the papers that very day.

However, duty must come first. His country had need of his services, and he was not the man to shirk his duty for his own private ends. His wedding must be put off once more.

With a start, Granite Grant suddenly pulled himself together. His mind had been wandering. That was not usually a failing of his, for his work was too full of unknown dangers to allow him to indulge in dreams.

He glanced furtively around him. He was in London—the safest city in the world—and yet no city or place was safe to him.

He smiled grimly to himself. After all, he was quite prepared to take care of himself in a scrap. He had been something of a lightweight in his time, and on many an occasion since his knowledge of the pugilistic art had stood him in good stead.

He reached the top of Whitehall, and crossed into Parliament Street.

"Good-night, sir!"

Granite Grant looked up quickly. It was the policeman on point duty. He stood in the shade of a lamp-post, and Grant had not noticed him as he was passing by.

"Good-night, constable!" he said pleasantly, and continued his way across the road.

The constable watched him until he vanished in the darkness.

"I could do with his screw," he muttered to himself; "but I'm blowed if I'd like to take on his job. Bit too big for me."

He shook his head and turned towards Whitehall as a big limousine, with shaded head-lights, glided swiftly towards him, and passed on in the direction taken by Granite Grant.

"Out late!" he muttered. "Wonder where he's been? Hallo, it's pulling up. Now what's the game?"

The policeman was right. The car had slowed down in the shadow of the Abbey Gardens; the door was flung open, and two men sprang out and crept silently and swiftly after the retreating figure of Granite Grant. The car hid them from the view of the watching policeman.

Suddenly, the King's Spy heard the patter of footsteps immediately behind him.

Instantly he was on the alert. He swung round to face his unknown assailants, clenching his fists, and bracing his muscles with the knowledge of some impending danger.

But it was too late. The headlights of the car shone full in his face, and blinded him for the moment. The next instant a blow from a sandbag hit him full on the forehead.

He staggered back a few steps, with his hands raised above his head, then crumpled up into the arms of his adversary.

Quickly the two men lifted him up and carried their unconscious victim into the waiting car. The next moment it was speeding toward Victoria Street.

The policeman had hurried to the spot; but all was silent. He stood in the middle of the road, staring after the tail-light of the car until it vanished round the bend to Victoria Street.

"Well, that's a rum go!" he said. "Sure I heard a sort of rumpus. Wonder what the game was? Funny it should pull up like that. However, it's no use running after trouble."

So saying, the policeman scratched his head, and began retracing his steps.

He turned the matter over in his mind for the next half-hour, and, having arrived at no solution of the problem, he straightway forgot all about it.

Chapter 2
The House in Kennington

THE big limousine swung up Victoria Street at a great speed, and, turning to the left past the station, sped on over Vauxhall Bridge. After threading its way for some distance in and out of a number of narrow turnings, it at length entered a mews, and pulled up at the rear of a gaunt-looking house in Kennington.

The door of the car was flung open, and two men leapt out, carrying the motionless form of Granite Grant between them.

Without a word to the driver, they entered the yard door of the building and closed it behind them. The big limousine moved silently off into the night.

The two men stumbled heavily across the yard, cursing below their breaths at the weight of their unconscious burden.

Reaching the back door of the house, they laid their victim on the ground and one of them gave a peculiar rap at the door.

The house appeared to be in darkness and untenanted; not a glimmer of light showed at any of its numerous windows.

But their visit had evidently been expected, for the door opened immediately, and, without a word, they picked up their burden and passed inside.

"Is that you, Dykes?" asked a voice, in a low, gruff whisper.

"Of course it is," grumbled the man addressed as Dykes. "Who else do you think it would be?"

"Is everything all right?" said the same gruff voice again, with a marked foreign accent.

The man named Dykes gave vent to a stifled oath.

"Are you going to keep us standing here all night?" he muttered angrily. "Why the devil don't you strike a light?"

The foreigner gave vent to a low, excited chuckle.

"One moment, my friend," he said, "we must take no risks. Don't be impatient. Now, follow me."

A beam of light from a pocket torch shot across the empty passage and hovered on the door at the further end.

"This way," said the voice again.

The three men stole silently down the length of the passage, and the foreigner gently opened the door of the room facing them.

A flood of light immediately shone out into the passage. The room was luxuriously furnished. A thick Axminster rug covered the floor, the walls were lined with hunting pictures and trophies of the chase, and innumerable bric-a-brac stood about the room on quaintly carved tables.

The two men deposited their unconscious burden on the floor, while the foreigner locked the door. Then, turning to a burly looking ruffian, with thick, shaggy eyebrows and big, prominent teeth, he said nervously:

"You are sure, Mister Dykes, that everything is all right?"

"Why," blustered Dykes irritably, "ain't I got him here in this very room, with a punch on the brain-box that would have knocked out Joe Beckett?[1] What more d'yer want?" He kicked the prostrate man contemptuously with his boot. "If that ain't Granite Grant, well, then I'm a Dutchman!" he added.

The foreigner glanced round furtively.

"Hush!" he said. "Not so loud. Well, Mister Dykes, I congratulate you. So far everything has worked splendidly. Now, there is one more thing for you to do."

"Look here, guv'nor! And how about the swag?"

It was Dykes' companion who had spoken. Up to now he had kept silent, but it was fairly evident that he didn't quite relish the job in hand, and wanted to make sure of his share of the spoil and clear out.

He was a spare, hunchbacked little man, and even more villainous-looking than his friend Dykes.

For years these two men had lived on the fringe of the law, earning a living by all manner of shady transactions, and prepared even to go to the length of serious crimes provided they held out hopes of big rewards and a fair chance of going undetected.

But it was evident that their present job was a bit out of the ordinary, and both men betrayed a feverish anxiety to get well rid of it.

"Quite right, Crick," said Dykes eagerly. "That's the stuff to give the troops! What about it, guv'nor? We ain't seen much of the brass yet."

The foreigner's face suddenly underwent a change. He turned swiftly on the two men like a wild cat.

"Confound you both!" he hissed fiercely. "We agreed on the terms. You know what they are—five hundred pounds[2] between you when you've finished your job. And until it's finished you don't get a penny. Understand?"

The two men cowered back before the other's fierce onslaught. Like all bullies of their type, they were very brave when it came to creeping behind a man in the dark and knocking him senseless.

---

[1] Joseph 'Joe' Beckett (1892–1965) was an English professional light heavy/cruiser/heavyweight boxer of the 1910s and early 1920s.

[2] £500 in 1920 is worth about £29,000.00 in 2023

But it was quite a different matter when it came to facing a man who was as unscrupulous as themselves, and who knew how to use his power.

"All right, guv'nor!" said Dykes humbly. "Keep yer hair on; we'll see the job through."

"Very good, my friend!" said the foreigner pleasantly. "Now just help me to undress Mister Grant, and then we can get the job finished with."

For the next few minutes the three men were busily engaged on removing every article of clothing from the unconscious man on the floor.

Soon they had him absolutely stripped. The foreigner took a blanket from the table, and flung it over the naked form.

"Now, Mister Crick," he said, "you remain here and see that he doesn't come round. If he does, tie him up with that rope over there. Come on, Mister Dykes. There is another Mister Granite Grant anxiously waiting to put on his clothes in the next room."

He gave vent to a sinister chuckle, and led the way to a door on the other side of the room, with Dykes following at his heels.

The room which they entered was just as luxuriously furnished as the other. Another thick Axminster rug covered the floor; the dressing-table and wardrobe were made of solid oak. Everything betokened refinement and wealth.

Over in the further corner was a bed, and sitting beside it, in a comfortable armchair, was a man, dressed in evening clothes, reading a book.

He rose to his feet as the two men entered the room, and came silently towards them.

"How goes it, Dulac?" he asked pleasantly.

The foreigner answered the stranger in a respectful manner.

"Everything is all right so far, Baron," he said. "The plan has worked without a hitch."

"Good!" said the man in evening dress.

He turned towards the bed.

"Our friend is sleeping peacefully," he said. "We must wake him up."

The form of a man lay across the bed. He was breathing heavily and irregularly. His left arm was sprawled across his head so that his face was hidden. The stranger shook him roughly by the shoulder.

"Now, Mister Granite Grant the second," he said jeeringly, "it's time to get up."

The sleeping man shook himself wearily, and, raising himself, sat up.

"Phew! Well, that's the limit!"

The exclamation came from Dykes. He was staring in fascination at the man's face; he rubbed his eyes as if he were dreaming.

"Well, I'm blowed!" he said. "But it's the same chap. Are there two of them?"

The Baron gave a low, amused chuckle.

"That'll put your confounded secret service agents off the scent," he muttered, and rubbed his hands gleefully.

Dykes was right. The man on the bed bore a wonderful resemblance to James Grant, the King's Spy. The man had the same crisp, short beard, cut in the naval fashion, the same dark moustache.

His thick head of hair was tinged with grey at the sides, and brushed straight back over his forehead, as was Granite Grant's.

In all respects he was the double of the famous Secret Service man—in height, age, and general build.

But his face was not keen and alert and healthy as was Granite Grant's.

Instead, the marks of long dissipation were clearly discernible. His eyes were dull and lifeless, as if he were suffering from the effects of drugs, and a strange pallor hung over his features.

The Baron bowed mockingly in front of his strange guest.

"And how are you feeling tonight, Mister James Grant?" he asked sarcastically.

The man gazed stupidly at the suave-mannered Baron, as if he did not understand the question. Then he muttered, in a toneless voice:

"Why do you call me James Grant? I am Jones—that is my name, as I keep on telling you."

"Pardon me," said the Baron, in suave tones. "You are forgetting. You are now Mr. James Grant, known throughout Europe as Granite Grant. And for that you are to have one thousand guineas. Just think, my friend, one thousand guineas[3] all to yourself!"

The Baron suddenly bent closer to the other man.

"Listen!" he whispered earnestly. "There is no time to lose. You must get into these clothes. Everything will be all right; the car will take you to Chelsea. You need do nothing. You will simply be found by the police wandering in the street, and suffering from loss of memory. You need say nothing, or, at least, very little. You must not remember anything. Your resemblance, and the fact that you wear these clothes, will be enough. For one brief fortnight you will be James Grant, and for that you will receive one thousand guineas. Do you understand?"

A flush of excitement passed over the man's pale face. He roused himself with an effort.

"Yes; I understand," he said.

"Good!" said the Baron. "Then get into these things immediately."

The three men helped him into the clothes of Granite Grant, and in a few minutes the change had been effected. The resemblance was now amazing.

Strong as the likeness to Granite Grant had been before, it was now so extraordinary that it would have been difficult for Grant's most intimate friend to have discovered the impersonation.

At length the Baron stood back, with an exclamation of undisguised triumph.

"Ah!" he said. "That is indeed excellent. And now, Mr. Dykes, just see if the car is outside."

As Dykes left the room, the Baron drew a wad of notes from his pocket.

"There, Mr. Grant," he said. "There are five hundred pounds for you. And the remainder you shall have, at the end of a fortnight."

---

[3] £1,000 in 1920 is worth about £57,000.00 in 2023

The other man took the notes eagerly, and thrust them into his pocket just as the door opened and Dykes re-entered.

"The car's outside, sir," said Dykes.

"Very good!" said the Baron. "Well, you know what to do. Take him to Chelsea, and drop him outside Grant's house. I needn't impress upon you the necessity of secrecy. If you bungle the job, it will be the worse for you. Remember that!"

Chapter 3
Sir Vrymer Fane Sends for Sexton Blake

IN an apartment on the second floor of a great block of buildings just off White-hall, Sir Vrymer Fane strode agitatedly to and fro in front of the fire that flickered in the large, open grate.

The great statesman, whose name is so familiar to the ears of all English-speaking people, and, indeed, throughout the civilised world, was plainly suffering from a severe attack of nerves.

He paused a moment by the mantelpiece, and, taking a cigarette from the box, hastily lighted it.

After two or three puffs, he flung it in the fire, and rang impatiently at the bell.

A grave-looking man, of clerical appearance, answered his summons.

"Has anyone called to see me yet, William?" he asked.

"No, sir," his private secretary replied.

"I am expecting a caller at any moment." Sir Vrymer glanced at the clock. "He should be here by now. Show him up directly he arrives, please; and on no account am I to be interrupted."

"Very good, sir!" said the secretary, and silently withdrew.

Sir Vrymer began striding up and down the room again, the look of anxiety deepening on his face. A moment or two later a knock sounded on the door.

"Come in!" called Sir Vrymer expectantly.

In response to his request, the door opened, and Sexton Blake, the famous detective, was ushered in.

"Ah, good evening, Mr. Blake!" said Sir, Vrymer Fane, as he hastened to meet his visitor with outstretched hand. "I have been anxiously awaiting you. Pray be seated."

Blake took the proffered chair, and glanced curiously at the minister. It was a habit of the great detective always to make a rapid calculation of the character of the man he was meeting for the first time.

He was an adept at reading faces, for long experience and a keen perception had taught him to draw certain conclusions from the flicker of an eyelid or the twitching of a lip.

Many a time had he been able to anticipate events, and to forestall carefully laid plans, by this well-developed faculty of his of reading a man's thoughts.

Whatever his surmises were, however, on this occasion, he kept them to himself. His own imperturbable features, at any rate, were too well under control for them to betray the thoughts that flashed through his active mind.

He waited for the other to speak, watching him narrowly through half-closed eyes.

The minister cleared his voice, and began again, with evident embarrassment.

"Mr. Blake," he said, "no doubt you are wondering why I have sent for you. I admit that it is rather an unusual course for a man of my position to adopt, but there are strong reasons for it."

He gazed keenly at the detective, and carefully chose his words.

"You understand," he said, "that what takes place between you and me is strictly confidential."

"The warning is unnecessary, Sir Vrymer," said Blake quietly. "It is an assumption without which I am never prepared to offer my services."

"I beg your pardon, Mr. Blake!" the minister said quickly. "I should have taken that for granted. Listen carefully. I will be very brief. Last night, in this very room, I had a private interview with Mr. James Grant. I need not tell you what Mr. Grant's official capacity is; you are doubtless well aware of that. Certain matters of a highly confidential and secret nature took place between us, and a certain course of action was decided upon. Mr. Grant left this building at five minutes to one this morning. Everything had been arranged. He was to catch a train at eight o'clock—the Continental express. By this time he should have been travelling overland on the Continent."

The minister paused a moment, and looked at Blake intently.

"Early this morning," he continued, "some two hours after he had left me here, Mr. Grant was discovered wandering near his chambers, at Chelsea. His manner was strange; he could give no account of himself. He was taken to his rooms, and a doctor was sent for. We have since been informed that Mr. Grant has been suddenly stricken with total loss of memory."

Again the minister paused, and glanced at the detective inquiringly. His manner was self-possessed now, but a tremor of his fingers denoted the high nervous tension under which he was labouring.

"Mr. Blake," he said gravely, "the task which Mr. Grant had undertaken must be accomplished within fourteen days of today. There is only one man who can possibly see it through with any chance of success, and that man is Mr. James Grant."

The minister got up from his chair, and began pacing up and down, with his hands behind him and his head bent in thought. Suddenly, he stopped in front of the detective, and, speaking in a low voice, said:

"Do you understand now, Mr. Blake, why I took the somewhat extraordinary course of sending for you?"

The detective met the other's gaze unflinchingly. Very coolly, he took the cigarette from his lips, and flicked the ash on to the carpet. Then he leant back in his chair again.

"I will answer your question," he said quietly, "by asking you another. Do you understand, Sir Vrymer, that you have really told me nothing?"

The minister's thin lips contracted in a flicker of amusement.

"Precisely, Mr. Blake!" he said. "As you say, I have told you nothing. You understand? I must not tell you anything. The authorities have the matter in hand. If it were known that I had approached you in my official capacity, it would be absolutely fatal. You see, I am trusting you implicitly.

"Mr. James Grant, to all intents and purposes, is suffering from loss of memory. It is not an unusual occurrence, yet I cannot help thinking that there is something mysterious behind it. That is why I have broached the subject to you. I am more intimately aware of your wonderful powers of unravelling things than you may possibly think, Mr. Blake. I have told you nothing, as you say; and yet I am hoping that out of nothing you may possibly discover something. Of course, my fears may be perfectly groundless. That remains to be seen."

The two men regarded each other narrowly for a minute or two, both trying to read the thoughts that were surging through each other's minds. Then the minister held out his hand.

"Well, good-bye, Mr. Blake!" he said. "You understand that to the outside world this meeting has never taken place. Whatever you do—that is, if you do anything in the matter at all—will be done on your own initiative."

The detective wrung the minister's hand.

"I understand, Sir Vrymer," he said. "Good-bye!"

As he reached the door, the minister called him back.

"Just one thing more, Mr. Blake," he said. "You understand that the secret service funds do not have to be accounted for. Should you require any money——"

The detective nodded his head.

"Quite so, Sir Vrymer," he said.

The next moment Sexton Blake had gone.

Chapter 4
Blake Makes His Preliminary Investigation

HELLO, Tinker, my boy! You're back early. I thought you were going to a show!"

It was Sexton Blake who spoke. He had been back from his interview with Sir Vrymer Fane some two hours or more, and was seated in his room at Baker Street, reading a book by the circle of light thrown by the green-shaded reading-lamp.

"So I have, guv'nor," grumbled his assistant, flicking some dust off his patent leather boots: "but I came away after the first piece."

"What on earth for?" asked Blake. "Dud show, Tinker?"

"Yes," said Tinker mournfully. "As a matter of fact, guv'nor, I only went to hear Miss Laura Valentine; and she was off. Some Johnnie came on the stage, and said she was indisposed, or some rot or other."

Blake glanced up at his young assistant with an amused expression on his face.

"You young dog, Tinker!" he said, in a bantering tone. "So that's why you've got yourself up like a fashion plate. Rather sweet on the fair Miss Valentine, eh?"

Tinker coloured up with confusion.

"You're pulling my leg, guv'nor," he said. "Nothing doing there. Why, she's engaged to somebody or other. Photographs were in the papers yesterday."

"Ah!" said Blake. "Well, you know what the saying is, Tinker, 'Only the brave deserve the fair.' So it's up to you, my boy!"

So saying, Blake settled himself again to his book. Tinker gave a grunt of disgust, and began looking over the daily papers.

"Here's the photo, guv'nor," he exclaimed suddenly. "There you are! The chap's name is Grant—Mr. James Grant. Quite a decent-looking chap."

Blake glanced up, quickly.

"What's that?" he said, taking the paper from Tinker's hand and gazing intently at the photograph.

"Yes, of course," he said, at length. "I had forgotten that."

Tinker observed the look of interest on his master's face, and decided to get a little of his own back. He was a little sore over Blake's remarks; perhaps there was more in them than he cared to admit.

"You were rotting me just now about the lady, guv'nor," he said; "but it seems to me that you're very interested in her yourself."

"As a matter of fact, Tinker, I am," said Blake drily. "You don't happen to know where she is staying, I suppose?"

"I expect it's in the telephone directory," said Tinker. "But why on earth do you want to know?"

"Well, to tell you the truth, Tinker, I'm seriously thinking of personally paying my respects to the lady," was Blake's response.

"Oh, I say, guv'nor!" protested Tinker. "That's coming it a bit too thick! Why, you don't know her!"

"Neither do you, Tinker!"

This cute shot went home; Tinker had nothing to say. But he looked distinctly upset all the same. He got the telephone book down, and found the number.

"Gerrard 004," he said rather glumly. "But you're only kidding, aren't you, guv'nor?"

"We'll see about that!" muttered Blake, and, reaching for the telephone, put the receiver to his ear.

"Gerrard 004, please miss!" he said, and waited.

"Hello! Is that Gerrard 004? Yes! Is Miss Laura Valentine there? Right, thanks!"

He waited a moment or two, and then began again. Tinker stood by, with his mouth open wide, and a bewildered expression on his face.

"Hello! Yes! Is that Miss Laura Valentine? My name is Sexton Blake—ah, yes—that's very nice of you to say so. I should like to see you, if I may. Can you spare me a few moments, if I come along now? Thanks, awfully. I'll come straight away. Good-bye!"

Blake replaced the receiver, and got up from his chair. Tinker watched him in amazement.

"Well, if that ain't the limit?" he gasped.

"Sha'n't be long, Tinker," said Blake, as he put his hat on and strode from the room.

Tinker watched his master as he closed the door; then, crushing his new velour hat in his hands, he flung it violently into the corner of the room, and dropped into the chair which Blake had just vacated.

"Well, if that ain't just the blooming limit!" he gasped again, and settled down to brood over his grievance.

Meanwhile Blake had hailed a passing taxi, and had driven off to Miss Valentine's flat. He was shown straight up to her room.

"Good-evening, Mr. Blake!" she said, hastening to meet the famous detective. "I am so pleased to meet you."

"The pleasure is mine," said Blake, bowing gallantly to the beautiful and accomplished actress.

"Please sit down, Mr. Blake, and make yourself at home. Perhaps you will smoke; I don't mind in the least. And there are some cigars in that box over there."

Blake helped himself to a cigar, and, biting off the end, lighted it. Then, leaning back in his chair, he knitted his brows, and looked keenly at the charming lady of whom he had heard so much.

"I ought really to apologise, Miss Valentine," he said, "for troubling you at this late hour."

"Not at all, Mr. Blake," the actress replied smilingly.

Then, leaning eagerly towards the detective, she asked, in a low voice:

"Tell me, Mr. Blake, it is about my fiancé, Mr. Grant, that you have called—is it not?"

"You are quite right, Miss Valentine," said the detective.

"Ah, I am so glad, Mr. Blake! I have been very anxious and worried, and I have absolutely nobody on whom I can rely."

"But surely Scotland Yard is in close touch with the matter?" asked Blake.

"Yes, yes! But you do not quite understand. You see, the police think it is simply a case of loss of memory, and so there is not much for them to do. They are quite content to leave the matter in the doctor's hands."

"Would you mind, Miss Valentine, telling me all you know about the matter?"

"Not at all, Mr. Blake. But there is so little. I saw Jimmy—that is, Mr. Grant—yesterday afternoon. We had tea together. You have heard, no doubt, that we are to be married very shortly. He came to the Jollity Theatre with me, and stayed through the first act. Later, he left to keep an appointment of a rather important nature.

"He was to have called for me at the end of the performance, to take me home, but a message arrived just before the last act to say that he could not possibly see me again that night, and would call in the morning. That is all I knew until mid-day today, when an inspector called here to say that he had been found wandering about the street early in the morning, and could give no account of himself."

"Thank you, Miss Valentine," said Blake quietly. "Have you been along to see Mr. Grant since?"

"I went over immediately, Mr. Blake, of course. But——"

The young woman hesitated a moment, and seemed about to burst into tears. Blake saw that the actress was somewhat distraught; he felt very sorry for her.

Her vocation was harder than that of most people. She had to face crowded audiences every night, and listen to their well-meant applause, masking her own private grief and sorrow with a smiling face.

"Tell me, Miss Valentine," said Blake gently, "just one thing more. Did Mr. Grant betray the slightest sign of recognition when he saw you today?"

"No, Mr. Blake; not the slightest. He pretended he did, to a certain extent, out of mere politeness; but I am certain that he regarded me as a perfect stranger."

The actress thought for a moment, then went on excitedly:

"Do you know, Mr. Blake, it is extraordinary. I cannot believe it is the same man. Of course, it is stupid of me to say that; but there is some remarkable change that I can't quite make out. I was absolutely dumbfounded."

Blake was silent for some moments. Suddenly he looked up.

"You are aware, I suppose," he said, "that Mr. Grant was to have caught the train to the Continent this morning?"

"No; I did not know that, Mr. Blake."

"Well, perhaps I ought not to have mentioned it, but I know you will keep my confidence. After all, we are working together on this job. Yes; Mr. Grant was under orders to proceed on some secret mission this morning. It was concerned with his appointment last night."

"It is the first I have heard of it," said Miss Valentine. "But I am not a bit surprised. He is always going away again at the shortest notice. This time he was very sanguine of being able to stay in London several weeks; but I thought it seemed too good to be true."

Sexton Blake did not answer for some time. He was thinking deeply, trying to piece some slender chain of reasoning that would throw some light on the strange affair.

"Well, good-night, Miss Valentine!" he said. "There is just one thing that I should like to ask. Will you allow me to accompany you to see Mr. Grant tomorrow?"

"Certainly, Mr. Blake. If you will call here at about eleven tomorrow morning, my car will be waiting ready for you."

"Thank you very much!" said the detective. "Good-night!"

"Good-night, Mr. Blake!"

Chapter 5
The Quarry in Sight

WHEN Sexton Blake got back to Baker Street that night, he found Tinker still sitting, as he had left him, brooding sulkily over the events of the evening. His own manner was somewhat preoccupied, and his brows were contracted thoughtfully, as was generally the case when some specially difficult problem was occupying his mind.

Tinker immediately noticed the familiar signs of what he termed "something doing" on his master's face, and sprang quickly out of his chair.

"Well, guv'nor!" he exclaimed. "Anything the matter?"

Blake did not answer for a time. He sat down in the easy chair, and proceeded to fill his pipe.

"What's the time, Tinker?" he asked suddenly.

Tinker looked at his watch.

"It's a quarter past eleven, guv'nor," he said.

"You can get to bed if you like, Tinker," Blake said. "I sha'n't be turning in for two or three hours yet."

"Can't I do anything, guv'nor?" asked Tinker despondently.

"I'm afraid not, Tinker; not just yet. I'm going out to make a few inquiries later on."

"But surely there's something I can do?" insisted Tinker.

"Look here, Tinker," said Blake, "there's nothing you can do just yet. Perhaps there will be nothing at all in this business; I don't know now. But I may be able to find out something tonight. That remains to be seen. If there should prove to be something behind the scenes—as I think there is—well, then, I shall certainly want your help. It may be something very big, so you just toddle off to bed, and have some sleep while you can get it. Do you understand?"

"Right-ho, guv'nor!" said Tinker, with a twinkle of excitement in his eyes. "Good-night!"

"Good-night!" said Blake.

Tinker left the room with a pleasant thrill of expectancy. He had forgotten all about his early disappointment at not hearing the beautiful Miss Valentine sing at the Jollity and his subsequent chagrin at Blake's leg-pulling. The prospect of something doing filled him with feverish anticipation.

He knew that look in his master's face, and, if he were not deceived, it presaged some exciting work in the near future. In the meantime, he was quite content with Blake's assurance to obtain his assistance if he should require it.

Meanwhile, the detective had made himself comfortable, and, had settled himself down to a good hour's silent enjoyment of a book on criminology, in which he was soon immersed.

At 12.30 Blake suddenly closed his book and got up. He busied himself with one or two details for the next five minutes, and then silently let himself out into the street.

It was a fine starlight night, and the air was invigorating. Blake plunged into some side-streets, and, after a walk of some twenty minutes or so, arrived in the vicinity of White-hall.

He made his way to the building in which he had had the interview with Sir Vrymer Fane earlier on in the day, and soon reached the flight of marble steps.

He took out his watch. It was just five minutes to one—the exact time that Granite Grant had left the building on the night before.

Everything was wrapped in silence; nobody appeared to be abroad. Replacing his watch, Blake began to walk in the direction of Whitehall.

As he turned the corner, the great boom of Big Ben floated out over the silent city. Blake, continued his way slowly up Whitehall, glancing alertly about him all the while.

Although he did not expect anything to happen of a dramatic nature, nevertheless he thought that by putting himself in the position of Granite Grant he might stumble across some small factor that would not be so easily seen in the ordinary course of events.

As he stepped into the road to cross Parliament Square, he noticed the policeman standing there on point duty. A sudden idea flashed across Blake's resourceful mind. He strode quickly up to the policeman.

"Good-evening, constable—or, rather, good-morning!" he said.

"Good-morning, sir!"

"Do you happen to recognise me, constable?" asked Blake.

The policeman came a little closer.

"Good gracious!" he exclaimed. "Why, it's Mr. Blake. I didn't recognise you at first, sir. It's rather dark, and I couldn't see your face."

"Did you happen to be on duty here last night?" asked the detective.

"Yes, Mr. Blake. As a matter of fact, I'm on this beat all this week."

"Good!" muttered Blake. "Now think carefully before you answer my question. Do you recollect seeing a man pass by here in the direction of Victoria Street about this time last night?"

The policeman thought for a moment or two.

"Why, yes!" he said suddenly. "I do. As a matter of fact, it was Mr. James Grant, from the Foreign Office. I remember him well because he said good-night as he passed."

"He said good-night!" repeated Blake, deeply interested. "And did he appear to be quite normal?"

"Why, bless you, yes, sir!" exclaimed the policeman, somewhat surprised at the question.

"His manner did not seem a little strange?" insisted Blake.

The policeman gave a curious glance at the detective.

"No," he said; "I can't say as he appeared to me to be anything out of the ordinary."

"I see," said Blake. "And did you notice which way he went?"

"Yes; he crossed the road there, and went past the Abbey Gardens towards Victoria Street."

"And that's all?" said Blake.

"That's about all, Mr. Blake," said the policeman.

"You're quite certain of that?"

The policeman puckered his brows and scratched his head.

Suddenly he gave a start.

"Oh, just a bit, sir!" he said. "I was forgetting one thing. Just after Mr. Grant had crossed the road, a big car came gliding towards me from Whitehall, and crossed over in that direction. Just over by the grass there it suddenly pulled up. I thought it was rather funny at the time. Then I heard a sort of fuss, so I ran towards it. But it suddenly started up again, and was off down Victoria Street before I could get more than a dozen yards."

Blake was not the sort of man to give vent to his feelings, but he could hardly restrain a start at hearing this piece of news.

"Think carefully, constable," he said. "Now, do you recollect seeing Mr. Grant after the car had gone off again?"

"Oh, no, sir! I expect he had gone some distance. It was too dark to see very far."

"Just one more question, constable," said Blake. "When you saw that car pull up, how far do you think Mr. Grant had got?"

"Well, he had only just passed by, sir. The car must have pulled up quite close to him."

"And there is absolutely nothing else that you can remember?"

"No, sir. That's about all."

"Thanks very much, constable!" said Blake. "Good-night!"

"Good-night, sir!"

Blake walked slowly over in the direction of the Abbey Gardens. He could not over-estimate the importance of what the policeman had told him.

Although, as yet, he had no clear idea of what he was up against, he knew now that Granite Grant's sudden loss of memory was no natural occurrence, but that behind the whole business there was some deep and cunningly laid plot.

By a stroke of luck, which was really the result of his own quick intellect, he had stumbled right up against an important clue to the mystery at the outset.

Well, if any man could unravel it, he was the one. This was a tough proposition which he was up against this time, but he did not doubt his resourcefulness in seeing it through.

Suddenly Blake became aware of a shadow moving away from the darkness of the building in front of him. It was a man who seemed to have appeared from nowhere in particular, and he was going away at right angles to Blake.

Something in the man's attitude made the detective suspicious. He began to stride rapidly in his direction. The man glanced over his shoulder; then began to quicken his steps.

Blake suddenly came to a standstill. The other man immediately slowed down. Suddenly, Blake leant forward and broke into a quick run. The man gave one glance over his shoulder, and was off like greased lightning.

Blake slowed up, and leant against the railings, breathing heavily.

"That's strange!" he muttered to himself. "That fellow seems to have been dogging me. Wonder what his game was! Just an ordinary pickpocket, I should think."

He began retracing his steps the way he had come. Big Ben had just struck the half-hour. Blake thought he had done enough for one night; he was beginning to feel a little tired.

But there was just one other surprise in store for the detective that night. As he was crossing the road to Whitehall, he saw a man slouch away from the entrance to the underground subway.

Blake wondered what the man was doing there, for he knew that the subways had long since been closed for the night.

He stopped by the entrance to make sure that the gates were locked. To Blake's surprise, the man on the other side of the road also stopped.

Determined to get to the bottom of this strange business, Blake suddenly sprang across the road, and rushed straight at the stranger. With an exclamation of dismay, the man turned to bolt.

But it was too late; Blake was already upon him. With an angry snarl, the stranger turned upon the detective, and aimed a savage blow at his head.

But Blake was not to be caught like that. He ducked swiftly, and at the same time his left shot out and crashed, with a jarring blow, full on the chin of his unknown assailant.

Gasping with rage and pain, the man staggered back, with the detective pressing him closely. Then a stunning blow descended on his head from behind, and Blake went down all of a heap.

***

"Steady on, guv'nor! There you are! Just put your arm around my neck!"

It was Tinker who spoke.

Blake put his hand to his head, and gazed round about him in a dazed fashion.

"What has happened? Where am I?" he asked vaguely.

"You've had a nasty crack on the head, guv'nor," said Tinker. "But don't worry; just hold on to me. That's right; now we'll get a move on."

Hanging heavily on his young assistant, Blake began to stagger slowly back along Whitehall.

"How did you get here, Tinker?" he asked presently.

"I followed you, guv'nor. Hope you're not ratty with me; but it's a good thing I did. Unfortunately I came up a second too late."

The detective gave a dry, painful sort of chuckle.

"Better too late than never, Tinker," he said quietly.

Chapter 6
Dykes Gets the "Wind Up"

AH, Dulac! And how is our guest tonight?"

It was the Baron who spoke. He had just returned to the house at Kennington, and was removing his coat in the luxuriously appointed billiard-room.

His opera-hat collapsed with a snap as he flung it carelessly on the table. He took off the silk handkerchief that hid his white collar and shirt-front.

As unscrupulous as the desperadoes he had gathered about him to aid him in his nefarious schemes, the Baron also moved in the tip-top ranks of society.

His manners were exceedingly polished and refined, and it was evident that he was used to holding a position of undisputed authority.

Tonight he had been attending some society function, as his clothes indicated, and from the amused smile that flickered over his sardonic features, one could see that he had had quite an enjoyable evening.

He turned again to his companion who had just come from the adjoining room, and repeated his question again.

"He is quite all right, Baron," said Dulac gravely. "He has been sleeping quietly, and has hardly moved all the evening."

"Good!" said the Baron. "And he has asked no questions?"

"No, he has not said a word."

The Baron nodded his head pleasantly, and stood humming a tune.

Presently he looked up.

"I think I'll have a chat with him," he said good-humouredly. "No doubt he feels rather lonely."

He strode to the door, and gently pushed it open. The room was in darkness. The Baron turned to Dulac with an expression of irritation on his face.

"Why," he muttered, "the room's in darkness! Why did you switch off the light?"

"But I didn't," whispered Dulac. "I've only just come out. It was on when I left."

The Baron stepped into the room, and put out his hand for the switch. As he did so, there was a sudden movement from behind the door. He turned his head swiftly, but just too late.

Two hands, manacled together with chains, swung down on his head. With a groan, the Baron staggered back into the arms of Dulac.

With an angry cry Dulac thrust the unconscious form of his chief aside, and, whipping out a revolver from his pocket, sprang through the half-open door and switched on the light.

He turned and faced Granite Grant as the latter made a sudden leap towards him.

But the chains round his feet prevented him from moving quickly enough. Dulac quietly stepped aside, and the next moment Grant felt the cold snout of the revolver pressed against his forehead.

"Don't be a fool!" hissed Dulac. "I've got you numbered. If you move an inch I'll put a hole through your carcase, and nobody'll be the wiser."

For a moment Grant looked as if he would leap at the throat of his jailer, then, realising that the odds were dead against him, he dropped his hands in front of him with a gesture of despair.

"I guess you've got my number this time," he said; "but I've weighed you up, my friend, and my time's coming. Just you sleep on that. I've plugged better men than you in my day, and next time it will be my turn to peep behind the six-shooter."

A look of fear came into Dulac's face. He glanced nervously at the tall, athletic figure in front of him.

What Grant said was true. Dulac knew of Granite Grant's methods of dealing with his enemies; when it was a question of "plugging," Grant was all there.

The Baron uttered a groan, and began to raise himself from the floor.

"Go over there!" said Dulac threateningly, covering Grant with his revolver. "No tricks, mind; I'll shoot if you attempt any of your games."

Grant hesitated for a moment, then, seeing that resistance was useless, he dragged his manacled feet over to the bed, and flung himself upon it.

Dulac helped the Baron to his feet. He was still dazed from the blow Grant had dealt him, and drew his hand painfully over his head.

"What has happened?" he asked wildly.

"Let me help you to a chair, Baron," said Dulac. "You'll be all right in a moment."

He put his arm round the other man's waist, and, half-supporting him, led him to the chair. Then, keeping his eye furtively watching Grant, he took a bottle, of brandy from the table, and poured out a stiff tot. The Baron gulped down the fiery liquid.

"I'm all right now," he gasped. "By gum! That was a nasty crack."

He turned to where Grant was sitting, with an evil glint in his eyes.

"Foul blow, that, Mr. Grant," he sneered. "You evidently don't quite appreciate my solicitude for your welfare."

Granite Grant leant towards the Baron. In his eyes there shone that dangerous look of cold anger.

"I know you, Baron Rodanoff," he said quietly. "We have met before. For the moment I give you best; but I've got you in line. We're in London now, not Russia; and our men will soon be after your body. Don't you forget it."

The Baron laughed scornfully.

"You're quite a good bruiser, Mr. Grant," he said, "but acting's not in your line. I should give it over. You think your Scotland Yard will be on my tracks; but supposing I've covered them up!"

"You can't!" said Grant.

"Well, just listen, Mr. Grant," the Baron rejoined suavely. "You think your men are at the present moment hunting for you. Well, as a matter of fact, they're not. For one thing, they're not clever enough; and for another, they happen to know where you are."

"Know where I am?" repeated Grant, in surprise.

"Precisely, Mr. Grant. You happen to be in your rooms at Chelsea, suffering from loss of memory. Just you think over that."

Granite Grant looked at the Baron with an expression of puzzlement.

"But I don't understand," he said.

The Baron gave a harsh chuckle.

"You just puzzle it out," he said.

As he finished speaking, the sound of a door being hastily slammed came from the rear of the house, and a moment later heavy footsteps sounded in the next room.

Dulac sprang to his feet, and hurried from the room. An anxious look came into the Baron's face; he sat listening intently to the sounds of excited voices that came from the next room.

Presently Dulac poked his head round the door.

"Will you come in here a moment, Baron?" he said.

The Baron rose unsteadily to his feet. He was still somewhat dizzy from the blow he had received. He poured himself out another stiff tot of brandy, and gulped it down.

He turned to Grant as he opened the door.

"No tricks, mind," he said threateningly, and went out.

Dulac was in earnest conversation with Dykes and Crick. He turned to his chief as the latter appeared.

"Sexton Blake's on our tracks!" he muttered nervously.

Baron Rodanoff started violently; it was evident that the name of the great detective was only too well known to him. He turned to Dykes with a look of great concern.

"What do you mean?" he demanded. "What the devil has Sexton Blake got to do with it?"

Dykes removed his hand from his chin, and showed a big red lump on his jaw.

"Don't know what Blake's got to do with the business, Baron," he said, "but he landed me a knock-out like a kick from a horse, curse him!"

The Baron looked from one man to the other.

"How did it happen?" he asked, frowning. "Come on, out with it."

"Well, boss," said Dykes slowly, "we hung about the lady's flat, as you ordered, just to see who went in. Then, who should come along but this feller Blake; I recognised him directly I saw him. Take my word for it, boss, it ain't healthy for somebody when Blake gets his nose on the scent."

"And what happened?" demanded the Baron irritably. "Hurry up, man! Don't stand there gaping like an idiot!"

"I'm just telling yer, ain't I?" muttered Dykes testily. "Well, after a long time Blake comes out, and we shadowed him back to his rooms in Baker Street. We were feeling rather nervy, I can tell you. That chap Blake is the very devil for nosing out trouble. Well, we didn't half like the look of things, so we took it in turns to watch his house.

"Just when we were thinking of chucking it, out comes Blake, as large as life, and starts walking off as if he were taking his morning's stroll. We couldn't just rumble his game; seemed as if he were taking a moonlight walk for his health—not for anybody else's, you bet. We shadowed him to Whitehall Court."

"What was the time?" asked the Baron quickly.

"Big Ben struck one just as we were walking up Whitehall," said Dykes.

The Baron gave vent to a low whistle.

"Go on!" he said curtly.

"Well, this fellow Blake goes up to the policeman and has a pow-wow. Then they both point to the place where the car stopped last night and we hit that cove in the next room. Then Blake goes off, and I missed him for a time. But Crick had got round the other side——"

"Yes," broke in Crick excitedly, "he nearly stumbled upon me. Never seed such a chap for smelling you out. I had to run for it."

"Well," continued Dykes, "I was just wondering where Crick had gone, when who should I see coming straight at me but this fellow Blake. I slipped across the road, hoping that he hadn't seen me; but the next thing I remember is him charging across at me like an angry bull. Gave me a nasty jar, I can tell you. Then, before I could get his measure, he had plugged me one on the jaw.

"If Crick hadn't come up in the nick of time and hit him over the head, I should have been in clink by this time. 'Tain't healthy, boss, I tell yer!"

The Baron cast a look of withering contempt at Dykes and his companion, but it was clear that he didn't quite relish the turn events had taken.

"Why," he sneered, "there were two of you to one man; why didn't you put him out of the way? That would have saved further trouble."

"We might have done," growled Dykes surlily, "but another bloke came up at that moment and started landing out. We thought it best 'to alley toutsweet.'"

"Pah!" muttered the Baron. "You've both got the wind up. Have a tot of brandy, and pull yourselves together."

Baron Rodanoff drew Dulac aside.

"I don't like the look of this, Dulac," he said. "Sexton Blake is no thick-headed clod."

He pointed over his shoulder to the next room.

"We've got to get G. out of this," he said, "and quickly, too!"

For some time the Baron and Dulac spoke together in whispers. At length they seemed to have arrived at some agreement.

"Better let these two men sleep here for the rest of the night," the Baron said to Dulac.

"Yes," said Dulac, "we shall want them tomorrow. They can sleep in the room below."

Chapter 7
Blake's Suspicions

AT eleven o'clock promptly next morning, Sexton Blake stepped from a taxi outside Miss Valentine's flat. His head ached badly from the blow he had received the night before, but his active mind would not let him rest while there was work to be done.

The car was already waiting outside the house, and as the detective entered the gate the front door opened, and the actress came down the steps.

"Good-morning, Mr. Blake!" she said, holding out her hand. "You are very punctual, but I am quite ready, you see."

He helped her inside, and followed after, closing the door behind him.

After a run of about ten minutes through the busy London streets they pulled up in front of the house in Chelsea and both got out.

"This is Number 12," said the actress. "If you will wait downstairs, Mr. Blake, I will call you in two or three minutes."

"Certainly, Miss Valentine," said the detective. "Pray do not hurry. I am entirely at your service."

"I shall not be long, Mr. Blake," she said.

Blake sat down in the hall, and rested his chin on his hands. He had a slight swimming feeling in the head, but he tried to think clearly.

He could not help feeling that he was up against one of the toughest propositions of his long career; yet at that moment he had to confess that he was completely baffled by the task that confronted him.

That Granite Grant's sudden loss of memory was connected in some way with the strange events that had occurred the night before, and the brutal assault that had been made on him, he felt certain.

But where the connection arose, and what was the motive behind it, he could not even hazard a guess.

However, one thing at least was certain, and that was that he was in this business now with both feet, and he would not leave it until he had dragged it to the light of day.

He was roused from his speculations by the entrance of Miss Valentine. He could see from her face that the meeting with her fiancé had greatly distressed her; her voice trembled a little as she spoke to him.

"Will you come up now, Mr. Blake?" she said. "But I am afraid you must not stay long."

"Thank you, Miss Valentine," said Blake. "I shall not require more than a few minutes. And please talk as much as you can, and ignore me altogether. It will help me in my observations."

He followed her up the stairs, and waited while she entered a room on the right of the passage.

"Come in, Mr. Blake," she said.

The detective strode into the room. The doctor was standing by the window. He turned and nodded pleasantly to the detective as he entered.

The actress was standing by a man who was huddled in a chair by the fire.

"This is Mr. Blake, Jimmy," she said.

The man half rose from his seat, and eyed Blake furtively.

"How do you do?" he asked, holding out his hand.

Blake shook hands with him; but he was quick to notice how clammy the other's hand was, and how limp the grasp.

"Good-morning, Mr. Grant!" he said, sitting down in the vacant chair beside him. "Miss Valentine is a friend of mine; she has been good enough to bring me along to see you."

"Oh, yes," muttered the other man. "I am very pleased."

He subsided into silence, and for a moment the detective felt slightly embarrassed. He glanced swiftly at the actress; she took the hint, and began to talk idly about passing events.

Blake did not add much to the conversation; every now and then he chipped in with some remark, but he was watching the man narrowly, nothing escaping his keen observation.

He could see that the man was very ill at ease, and was anxious for him to go. He noticed that there were heavy rings round his eyes, and that his face was puffy and inflamed. His hands also were trembling, and he constantly twisted his fingers together.

Suddenly Blake turned quickly towards him.

"Do you remember, Mr. Grant," he said quietly, "reading in the papers about a fortnight or so ago that extraordinary case of a soldier's sudden loss of memory?"

"Ah, yes," said the man. "It was in——"

Suddenly he stopped short, and cast a suspicious look at the detective.

Blake stared back at him coolly, not taking his eyes from the other's face.

He could not stand up against the detective's steel grey eyes; beads of perspiration started out on his forehead.

"I was going to say," he continued, recovering himself with an effort, "that I was reading it in the paper only today; it was an old paper I found on the table."

The detective made no reply, but behind that impassive face of his a number of quick thoughts flashed across his brain.

Was the man right? Had he read it only that day in an old newspaper, or was he lying? The detective eyed his companion narrowly, without appearing to do so.

The pseudo Grant was clearly struggling hard to hide his feelings, but Blake could see that he was in a state of tension. He fumbled in his pocket, and drawing forth a pair of small scissors, began nervously chipping at his nails. Blake took no notice for a while. Presently he idly picked up something from the carpet, and slipped it into his pocket.

"I think I must go now," he said, suddenly getting up from the chair.

A look of relief swept over the other man's features. He put out a limp hand and wished the detective good-day.

Outside on the passage Blake met the doctor.

"Just one moment, doctor," he said. "Has Mr. Grant been reading the newspaper this morning?"

The doctor shook his head decidedly.

"No, he hasn't," he said. "I have recommended a complete rest. He must not undergo any mental effort, it is best in these cases not to."

"Thank you, doctor," said Blake.

As the detective went downstairs he could hardly repress a smile at the doctor's professional manner.

It was evident that to him his patient was suffering from a simple loss of memory, which he had no doubt could be cured by the usual prescriptions.

Well, the detective thought otherwise, and time would show whether his suspicions were right or not.

As Blake was about to step into the street, a tall man with a light moustache came up the steps.

"Hello, Bradley!" said Blake, as he stopped and held out his hand.

"Why, good-morning Mr. Blake," said Inspector Bradley. "Fancy seeing you here. Professional call?"

"I've just called with Miss Valentine," said Blake shortly.

The inspector gave a knowing wink at Blake.

"You're generally on somebody's track when I run up against you," he laughed. "Having a holiday today, I suppose?"

"No," said Blake. "I'm still living up to my reputation."

The inspector hesitated for a moment or two.

"Why," he said at length, "you don't think there is anything underhand about this Grant affair, do you?"

"Then where is Mr. Grant?" asked Blake quietly.

Inspector Bradley eyed Blake queerly.

"Is that a joke, Mr. Blake?" he asked. "Mr. Grant, as you know, is here now."

"You are sure of that, Bradley?"

Inspector Bradley came closer to the detective.

"Look here, Mr. Blake," he said confidently. "I have a great opinion of your cleverness, as you know, that's why I don't want to see you make a fool of yourself. Take my tip, there's nothing doing in this business. We've got the matter in hand; it's simply a case of loss of memory. So I shouldn't waste my time if I were you. You just leave it to me."

Inwardly Blake was bursting with laughter, but outwardly his face was grave and serious.

"And you are quite sure, Bradley, that Mr. Grant is upstairs?" he reiterated.

The inspector was getting a little bit huffed.

"I don't know what you're driving at, Mr. Blake," he said, "but you seem to be on the wrong track this time. Of course it's Mr. Grant, who else could it be? Why, he was found by one of my own men walking about in the street. He's got all his private papers and letters in his pockets to prove his identity. There isn't the slightest doubt about it; just a case of loss of memory, that's all. Don't see at all what you're making a fuss about."

"Well, perhaps you will by-and-by," laughed Blake.

Just then Miss Valentine came down the stairs, and nodding to Inspector Bradley, the detective helped the actress into the car, and they drove off.

Chapter 8
A Startling Discovery

I SAY, guv'nor, you've been staring at that blotting pad for the last half-hour. It's getting on my nerves. I know you've got something big on, you might tell a chap."

Tinker was right. Sexton Blake had been sitting with his head resting on his elbow for the last half an hour or more, silently staring at the blotting-pad—at least that is how it appeared to Tinker.

Presently Blake looked up.

"As a matter of fact, Tinker, my boy, you're wrong," he said. "I'm not staring at the blotting-pad."

Tinker looked rather incredulously at his master.

He was used to his little peculiarities, and his lengthy experience with the great detective, as his assistant, had taught him to enter into his master's moods and preoccupations without questioning his motives.

Yet he was evidently puzzled at the detective's enigmatic reply.

"Well guv'nor," he said bluntly. "I've made a mistake, I suppose. But I'm dashed if I can make it out."

"Come here, Tinker!" ordered Blake peremptorily.

Tinker came over to the detective's desk and leant over his shoulder.

"Do you see what I'm looking at now, Tinker?" asked Blake.

Tinker gave a sniff of surprise.

"Why," he said, "they're two bits of finger-nails. Most likely they're mine, I was cutting them just now."

"They're not yours, Tinker," said Blake quietly.

"Then whose are they?" asked Tinker.

"Well, as a matter of fact, Tinker, I brought them away with me this morning. Mr. Grant was good enough to make me a present of them."

Blake glanced up slyly into his young assistant's face. Tinker's expression of incredulity was so comic that Blake burst out into a hearty laughter.

"But fancy a chap making you a present of his finger-nail chippings," said Tinker. "Why, he must be loopy."

Blake put on a serious expression.

"I was only kidding you, Tinker," he said. "He didn't give them to me, I picked them up off the carpet, when he wasn't looking."

"But what for, guv'nor? Don't see what use they can be."

Blake did not reply for some minutes. Tinker waited expectantly. When Blake paused thoughtfully like that, he generally had something important to say.

"Look here, Tinker," said the detective at length. "You don't know everything, and this happens to be one of the things you've got to learn. Do you know, I could find out quite a number of things about you merely from a tiny piece of your finger-nail? I could find out what your habits were, where you've been, and what you've been up to during the last few days."

"Don't cotton you, guv'nor," said Tinker in bewilderment.

"Well, you just listen, Tinker. Stored under your finger-nails is a certain amount of matter. It makes no difference how much you wash them, you never wash it all away. An expert puts your piece of finger nail under a high-powered microscope, and is able to analyse exactly what this matter consists of. He's got you cold—he knows all about you. You can't get away from it, your finger-nails betray you."

Tinker took a deep breath.

"You're a marvel, guv'nor," he said admiringly. "If that ain't just a knockout, why, it beats me stiff. And what about those finger-nails there? What are you going to do with them?"

"I'm going straight away now to Professor Bailey, he'll do the job for me. I'll tell you all about it later on."

Blake carefully put the pieces of finger-nail into his case, and, getting up, put on his hat and coat.

"Sha'n't be long, Tinker," he said, and went out.

The detective took the tube to Hampstead, and about half an hour later was shown into the laboratory of Professor Bailey, at the School of Modern Science.

"Hello, Mr. Blake. How are you?" said the professor pleasantly, looking up from his retort stand at which he was busily engaged. "Long time since you paid me a visit."

Blake shook the professor warmly by the hand.

"I know that, professor," he said, "but perhaps it's just as well I don't come more often, for I've generally got some work for you."

"Fire away," said the professor. "Always delighted to assist in any way I can."

The detective felt in his pocket and drew out his card case. Then taking out the pieces of finger-nail, he laid them on the bench.

"I want you to make an analysis of these finger-nails," he said, "and tell me everything you can about them."

"Certainly, Mr. Blake. I'll start straight away. I'll send you along the analysis in about three hours time, if you like."

"Thanks very much, professor," said Blake. "That will do splendidly, if it is not troubling you too much."

"Not in the least, Mr. Blake. It's quite a pleasure, I assure you."

After one or two other remarks the detective left the professor's laboratory and wended his way back to his rooms. About four o'clock that afternoon Tinker came in to Blake with an envelope in his hands.

"Messenger just brought this, guv'nor," he said. "Any answer?"

"No," said Blake. "I don't want him."

Blake hurriedly cut the envelope with his paper knife, and drew out a thin sheet of paper. With a look of intense interest on his face he read the contents.

"Ah!" he said, suddenly looking up. "I thought so."

"Thought what, guv'nor?" asked Tinker, who had been watching his master curiously.

Blake swung round in his chair. It was clear that he had come to some startling conclusion. Tinker, seeing that something important had happened, waited impatiently for enlightenment.

"Tinker," said Blake quietly, "that chap is an impostor."

"What chap?" asked Tinker in surprise.

"Why, the man who is supposed to be 'Granite' Grant, and whom they say is suffering from loss of memory," said the detective.

Tinker looked astonished.

"How do you know that, guv'nor?" he asked.

"Just listen," said Blake. He took up the sheet of paper, and read out the following: "I have made a minute microscopic examination of the finger-nails, and have come to the following conclusion. The nails evidently belong to a man who has been working for some time on board ship. The deposits seem to indicate that he was a steward, and was in the habit of wearing a white linen hat and cotton overalls.

"For the last few days, however, he seems to have been living in some house—there are various reasons for assuming this, which I will state more clearly when I have finished my tests. I have discovered fibres of a grey flannel material, and also fibres of red plush commonly used for upholstering purposes. There were also traces of a peculiar aromatic soap. I am still engaged on the tests."

Blake finished reading, and looked keenly at his young assistant.

"You see, Tinker," he said, "there is no doubt that the man is an impostor. I thought as much, but I couldn't prove it. What do you think of that?"

Tinker was too dumbfounded to reply. He had had many occasions to feel amazed at the detective's ingenuity before, but that he should find out all this merely from two pieces of finger-nail was quite beyond his understanding. But the detective was plainly very pleased with his discoveries.

"We're getting a move on now, Tinker," he said. "We know to some extent what we're up against. We've got our work cut out, but we'll come out on top, you bet."

"You bet we will," said Tinker confidently. "But why don't you go and have that bloke arrested straight away, guv'nor?"

Blake gave a superior sort of smile.

"No," replied Blake. "We've got to find 'Granite' Grant first. If we went and kicked up a shindy about this we should give the show away."

"Well, what's the next move, guv'nor?" asked Tinker.

"We must get on the track of 'Granite' Grant, that's our next job. And I don't mind telling you, Tinker, that it's a mighty stiff proposition. But we shall do it, I have no doubt of that."

"Well, I'm with you, guv'nor," cried Tinker excitedly. "This job's about just getting interesting."

Chapter 9
The Soho Murder

IT was late that same night. For three solid hours the rain had been pouring down and drenching the streets of London. Most people had long since taken refuge in their own homes, and comfortably seated in front of their warm firesides, sat and listened, with a feeling of thankfulness, to the wind that moaned outside and the rain that beat in heavy gusts against their window panes.

In one of the sinister foreign little cafés in a particularly disreputable part of Soho, two men sat drinking.

It was nearly closing time, and they had evidently consumed more liquor than was good for them. Yet neither moved from the table.

One of these men was a heavy jowled, ugly-looking customer with prominent teeth. The reader will quickly recognise him as the ruffian, Bill Dykes. The other man was his friend and fellow student in crime, Joe Crick.

It was evident that they were in the midst of a violent quarrel. Both men were drunk, and both were in a particularly villainous mood. Crick had just finished speaking, his face was flushed and there was an evil glitter in his eyes.

With a string of foul oaths Dykes turned on his companion in vice, and, hitting the table with his fist so that it shook on its rickety legs, shouted in a loud drunken voice:

"You go to blazes, Crick! I tell you the swag's mine. I've done all the work, and I've earned it. You've got a hundred, and I'm hanged if you'll touch another penny."

Dykes tapped his breast pocket significantly.

"It's in there, d'yer see?" he bragged. "And that's where it's going to stop. Get me?"

For a second Crick contemplated hurling himself at the throat of his companion, but deeming discretion the better part of valour, he contented himself with an ugly leer.

"Yes, I get yer all right," he said, and his small, ferret-like eyes glittered with suppressed rage. "Going to swing it on me, are you? So that's yer game. Well, just listen to me! No man can't say Joe Crick lets it be put acrost him. I'll get even with you one of these days, s'help me if I don't!"

Dykes shook his fist contemptuously in Joe Crick's face.

"Don't come any of the heavy stuff with me," he muttered threateningly. "You've got your share, and I've got mine. And I'll see that I keep it."

It looked as if the two ruffians would come to blows; but at that moment the barman came round to the door, and called in a sharp voice:

"Now, gents, time's up! Out you go!"

The two men staggered to their feet, and mumbling dire threats at each other, reeled out into the street.

The wind blew in angry spurts round the corner of the building, flinging gusts of rain in their faces. It was pitch dark, the streets were deserted; not a soul was in sight.

The forms of the two men loomed vaguely in the black mist and rain as they reeled along the swimming pavements, swaying drunkenly from one side to the other.

Neither man spoke now; both seemed too intent on getting back to the dosshouse, where they could get under shelter for the night.

Presently they entered a narrow passage between two blocks of buildings. There was no room for them to walk abreast, and Dykes strode on a couple of paces ahead.

A sudden thought flashed through Crick's besotted brain. In front was the man he hated, the man who had roughly jeered at him a moment or two before, who had hurled violent threats at him and heaped curses on his head.

In his pocket were the four hundred pounds[4] in notes; by rights, some of it belonged to him, for had they not taken equal risks in the removal of Granite Grant?

Crick pulled himself together and glanced furtively over his shoulder. All was dark

---

[4] £400 in 1920 is worth about £23,000.00 in 2023

and silent; this narrow passage was just the spot to commit any dark deed. On such a night as this it was extremely unlikely that anyone would come this way.

The thought of those four hundred pounds in crisp notes lying in his companion's pockets acted like a magnet on Crick's drunken mind.

He cast another quick glance behind him, then, stealthily creeping closer to the unsuspecting man in front, he suddenly sprang on him and dealt him a blow on the head with his clenched fist.

Before Dykes could recover from the surprise of this sudden attack Crick's expert fingers had thrust themselves into the breast pocket of his coat.

A second later Crick had turned, and was disappearing back along the passage with the bundle of notes grasped in his fingers.

But the blow had only momentarily stunned Dykes; his skull was too thick for anything but a sledge-hammer to make any impression on it.

He recovered his balance with an effort, and with a muttered imprecation swung round and raced blindly back along the passage in the direction Crick had taken.

With the start he had had, and aided by the darkness, Crick would doubtless have made good his escape, had not he made the mistake of turning to the right instead of the left when he came to the bend in the passage.

Then he suddenly found his path barred by a row of iron railings, and as he turned to retrace his steps Dykes sprang at him out of the darkness with an angry snarl.

The two men rolled over and over in the mud, clutching wildly at each other's clothes, and pouring forth a stream of foul, invective.

For a time neither got the mastery; their cursings had ceased now, both knew it was a life and death struggle. In that dark alley a grim tragedy was being enacted, while the rain beat remorselessly down and wetted them to the bone.

The sound of their low, panting breaths was lost in the stillness of the night, and the two vague forms writhed and twisted and struggled for supremacy.

But presently Dykes' weight began to tell; he managed to get Crick beneath him, and with his knee planted in his stomach and his hands clutching his throat in a vice-like grip, he began to crash the head of the prostrate man against the stonework in demoniacal frenzy.

For some moments he remained there, kneeling on his adversary and throttling the life out of him. Then he felt Crick's body grow limp and unresisting, and releasing his strangle-hold, Dykes rose slowly to his feet.

The bundle of notes was lying at his feet; Dykes stooped hastily and thrust them into his pocket. He was covered with mud from head to foot, his clothes were torn to shreds, and his hands and face were covered with blood.

Dykes looked about for his cap; he found it lying in a puddle of water, and picking it up, wrung the water out of it. Then he glanced down at the still form of the other man.

He could see the pallid, white face and the glazed eyes staring up at him. With a sudden shiver Dykes began to back fearfully towards the entrance of the passage. Suddenly he turned on his heels, and with an inarticulate cry fled like a madman from the spot.

Chapter 10
The Plot Deepens

ARLY edishun. 'Orrible tragedy in Soho. Body found in Soho Alley."

The warm rays of the midday sun were slanting through the trees as Sexton Blake strode thoughtfully along the Embankment. He had been spending the morning in making one or two inquiries concerning the events of the preceding day, and was hurrying in the direction of the Strand to have a hasty lunch when the cries of the newsboys attracted his attention.

He stopped one of the lads as he came rushing by, and buying a paper, thrust it into his pocket. Then, turning to the right up Savoy Street, he entered the famous restaurant.

For some while Blake sat idly watching the number of well-dressed people that passed in and out of the luncheon-room.

Frequently somebody or other would recognise the famous detective and would exchange a cheery greeting; but for the most part he remained unnoticed, sitting at a corner table, which he had carefully chosen to avoid being seen. Blake did not go out of his way to court publicity.

Presently two men entered the dining-room, and after looking around for a vacant table, came and sat down near Sexton Blake.

So used was the detective to sizing people up that it had become almost a second nature with him.

Consequently he found himself critically examining the two strangers and idly wondering who they were.

One of them was a tall, well-bred looking man, dressed very fashionably, but with an air of quiet distinction about him.

The other man had his back towards the detective, but he appeared to be somewhat shorter in build, with a closely cropped black beard and bristly moustache.

Both men were slightly foreign in appearance.

For a time neither spoke. Then the waiter came up, and the tall man ordered lunch.

Directly the waiter had departed on his errand the shorter of the two men leaned across the table and began talking excitedly to the other in low tones.

The other nodded his head several times, then felt in his pocket and, taking out a newspaper, spread it open on the table.

For a few moments he remained silently reading some item of news, then looking up at his companion, he shook his head vigorously, and handed him the paper across the table.

The two men seemed so interested in this particular piece of news that Blake's curiosity was aroused.

He craned his neck to see if he could get a glimpse of the paragraph which had caused all the excitement, but the table was too far off.

Then he recollected that he had bought a paper just a little while before on the Embankment, and feeling in his pocket dragged it forth.

He glanced over at the other table. The two men were studying the front page.

Blake ran his eye over the headlines; the account of the Soho murder caught his eye.

"Early this morning," the article read, "the body of a man was found in an alley in Soho. The head was terribly mutilated and battered, and it is clear that he had been the victim of a murderous attack. Death appeared to be due to strangulation. The only clue, so far, to the identity of the stranger is a piece of paper found in one of his pockets bearing the name of 'J. Crick.' The motive of the crime is not clear."

A description of the man followed, and it went on to say that the police were making inquiries, and that anyone able to give information concerning the dead man should communicate at once with the authorities.

Blake glanced up again at the two men sitting opposite. They were still talking together in excited whispers. Presently the tall man, who was facing Blake, turned his head slightly and cast a swift glance at the detective.

Blake immediately began to turn over his paper with an unconcerned look, yet he felt sure that as the stranger's eyes had rested on him he had given way to a half-concealed start of recognition.

Without appearing to do so the detective carefully scrutinised the man out of the corner of his eye. He saw him lean across the table to his companion and mutter something in a low voice.

The other man appeared to listen with intense interest; then he very deliberately dropped his napkin on the floor, and as he stooped down to pick it up, he casually glanced round and stared full at Blake.

Then he muttered something to his companion, and nodded his head several times.

As Blake was wondering what possible interest these two strangers could have in himself, the tall man called a passing waiter, and after chatting to him for a moment or two, paid his bill.

A few minutes later both men rose from the table and left the dining-room without further incident.

By this time Blake had also finished his lunch. He beckoned to the waiter and asked for his bill.

"By the way, waiter," he said, slipping a half-crown into the man's hand, "do you know who those two gentlemen were who were sitting at the table over there?"

"The two gents who have just left, sir?"

"Yes," said Blake.

"Well, to tell you the truth, sir, I don't," said the waiter. "But it's rather funny you should ask me that, because the tall gent also asked me if you were Mr. Blake."

"He did?" echoed Blake, somewhat taken back. "And what did you say?"

"Well, of course, sir, I said you were Mr. Sexton Blake, right enough."

"And you've never seen them before?"

"Not to my knowledge, sir."

Blake finished his cigarette and a few moments later left the restaurant.

As he made his way in the direction of Baker Street the detective could not help puzzling over the incident that had just taken place in the dining-room of the famous hotel.

He was rather inclined, for some reason or other, to attach more importance to it than it seemed to warrant.

Why had the distinguished-looking stranger given that involuntary start when he first set eyes on Blake? And why had he asked the waiter for his name?

However, he dismissed the matter from his mind at last. After all, many more people than Blake knew by sight were familiar with the features of the great detective.

No doubt the stranger had recognised him from a photograph, and had sought the waiter's confirmation merely out of idle curiosity. The matter was not worth troubling about.

The detective found Tinker at Baker Street impatiently waiting his return. He greeted his master hurriedly as he entered the room.

"I say, guv'nor," he said, "Professor Bailey has been ringing you up. Something important to tell you. Says he'll send a message along."

"How long ago was that?" asked Blake.

"Oh, about two hours," said Tinker. "The messenger should be here by this time."

"Well, perhaps he won't be long now," said the detective, and was soon busied in attending to a mass of correspondence.

In about half-an-hour a double knock sounded at the street door, and Tinker hurried from the room. He returned almost immediately, and handed his master a small blue envelope. Blake took it quickly and tore it open. It was from Professor Bailey, and was scribbled on a half-sheet of paper in the professor's well-known hand.

"Dear Mr. Blake," it read. "Just to tell you. I was called in at the post-mortem on the body of the man found at Soho this morning. Fingernail analysis revealed red plush fibres and traces of that peculiar aromatic soap. Thought it would interest you in view of the analysis I undertook for you yesterday. May be a pure coincidence, of course; so don't attach too much importance to it. However, thought I would just let you know. Good-bye.—"BAILEY."

"Phew!" muttered Blake, and carefully read the message through again. What amazing fact had he stumbled on? What was the meaning of this new turn of events? What connection could this tragedy at Soho have with the mystery of Granite Grant? Or was it simply a case of coincidence, as Professor Bailey suggested it might be?

These questions, and many more besides, passed swiftly through the detective's active mind. The incident in the restaurant, which had been half forgotten, came back to him now with renewed significance.

Why had those two strange men been so interested in the account of the crime? And why had they stared so curiously at the detective, and even gone to the length of asking the waiter if he were really Mr. Blake?

Presently the detective gave a dry sort of smile. After all, wasn't he rather making a mountain out of a mole-hill? Wasn't it rather natural that this Soho murder should attract attention? And then, recognising the famous detective sitting nearby, the men would of course associate him with the mystery. Yes, that would be quite a natural explanation of the incident. But there still remained the professor's startling discovery with regard to the fingernails. He had yet to account for that.

For a long while the detective sat and puzzled over these extraordinary events; in some inexplicable manner they were all connected together, he felt sure.

Yet he could not fathom the mystery. Truly, the task which he had undertaken was becoming more involved every day.

Suddenly Blake's face cleared a little; he looked up quickly.

"I say, Tinker," he said, "I want you to do a job for me."

"Right oh, guv'nor!" said Tinker. "I'm on it."

"It's not very exciting, I'm afraid," said Blake, "but it's rather important. I want you to go straight over to Professor Bailey at Hampstead, and ask him to give you a piece of cloth from the clothes of the man whose body was found at Soho this morning. Do you understand?"

"I've got you, guv'nor," said Tinker.

"Right! Off you go. I'll get on the phone to the professor at once, and tell him you're coming."

Tinker seized his hat, and departed on his errand without further discussion.

About half an hour after he had gone the telephone bell on Blake's desk suddenly started ringing. The detective took off the receiver, and put it to his ear.

"Hallo!" he said.

A woman's voice sounded from the other end.

"Hallo. Mr. Blake! Is that you? This is Miss Valentine speaking. I want you to have dinner with me tonight at Dalgrety's. Will you come?"

"Delighted!" said Blake.

"That is awfully good of you, Mr. Blake," said Miss Valentine. "I shall expect you there at seven o'clock sharp. I've got to be at the Jollity at eight-thirty."

"Right oh!" said the detective. "I shall be there."

"Thank you. Good-bye!"

"Good-bye!" said Blake.

Chapter 11
A Strange Meeting

THE gorgeous dining-room of Dalgretty's was ablaze with light. Ladies dressed in beautiful clothes and bedecked with glittering jewels, and men in evening-dress, with their wide expanse of shirt front, sat about at the snow-white tables, and laughed and chatted gaily over their glasses of sparkling wine.

As Sexton Blake strode down the thick-carpeted aisle between the tables the strains of the band came floating to his ears to the soft, dreamy tune of a waltz.

The great detective glanced around with a growing sense of appreciation; for a while he forgot the brooding mysteries in which he lived. It was good to throw off one's anxieties sometimes; and tonight he felt like entering into the spirit of the gay and happy scene.

He was to dine with the beautiful and famous actress, Miss Laura Valentine. It was an honour that was not vouchsafed to many men, and tonight he was sure to be the object of many envious eyes.

He stood still in the centre of the room, and glanced about him. The actress had said that she would book a table under the clock. She should be here by now.

His eye roved rapidly up and down the room. Yes; there she was, beckoning to him. Certainly, she looked very charming. He was a lucky man, thought Blake, who was to win her for a wife.

As the detective wended his way towards her, he noticed that the table was set for three. So there was to be a third person. He wondered who it might be; perhaps some theatrical friend of the actress.

The actress rose with a smile as he came up, and greeted him with outstretched hand. Blake bowed gallantly, and held her chair for her while she seated herself again; then took the chair on her right.

Yes, thought Blake, as he glanced at her admiringly, she was certainly very beautiful.

He could see that from time to time men nudged their companions and whispered together, and cast admiring glances in her direction.

They certainly seemed to envy him his luck. Yet his keen glance also noted the dark rings that edged the young woman's eyes, and the troubled look that shadowed her face every now and then.

Blake knew the cause of that. He knew of the secret grief that lay brooding at the back of her mind, no matter how she attempted to hide it.

However, tonight they would spend a pleasant hour or so together. He would not refer to her trouble unless she herself mentioned it.

She rested her dainty fingers lightly on his arm.

"I did not tell you, Mr. Blake," she said, "I am expecting a friend of mine to dinner, a Baron Rodanoff, I met him some years ago, when I was touring in Russia. It was before the war. Strangely enough, I came across him today. He used to be in the diplomatic service. But he is very eager to make your acquaintance; that is why I asked him to come along."

"I shall be very charmed to meet any friend of yours," said Blake.

"That's very nice of you, Mr. Blake," said the actress, smiling. "And now, just to talk shop for a moment; I promise not to do so any more this evening. Mr. Grant—you know who I mean—they have taken him to a nursing-home at Bournemouth."

The detective nodded his head.

"Yes," he said; "I am keeping in touch with events. You may rely on me."

The actress was about to reply, but checked herself, and glanced expectantly over Blake's shoulder.

"Here is the Baron!" she said.

The man was approaching them from behind, so that the detective did not have a chance of seeing his face before he had reached the table.

"Ah, Baron, you have arrived," said the actress gaily, as she rose to meet him. "May I introduce Mr. Sexton Blake—Baron Rodanoff!"

The detective rose to his feet, and turned toward the stranger. For one instant a thrill of incredible astonishment shot through him; the next moment the two men were gravely bowing to each other.

They ceremoniously took their seats. Blake's face was imperturbable and cold, not the vestige of an expression crossed it to indicate his tumultuous feelings.

Yet in that first moment of meeting he had recognised in this Baron Rodanoff the man he had seen at the Savoy earlier on in the day—the same man who had stared at him with such curiosity and had asked the waiter if he were really Mr. Blake.

Why had he expressed the wish to meet him? Who was he? What was he doing here? Was he involved in the mystery that surrounded the fate of Granite Grant?

Did he know anything of the murder that had taken place the night before in that dark passage in Soho? And how much did Miss Valentine know of his history?

Blake was sure that it was very little. She had met him, she said, in Russia before the war. Just a passing acquaintance, evidently, to whom she had been introduced at some function or other.

After all, the actress had a world-wide reputation, and she must meet innumerable people in whom she had not the slightest interest, and for whom she entertained no feelings of friendship.

All these thoughts crowded swiftly through the detective's mind in the space of a few seconds. At that moment the waiter came up, and he found himself glancing down the menu.

"Will you take 'hors d'oeuvre,' Miss Valentine?" he asked.

The actress nodded her head, and continued chatting intimately with the Baron.

"Let me see! How many years ago was it when we met at Petrograd—or St. Petersburg, as it then was?" she asked gaily.

"It was six years, mademoiselle," he laughed. "Just think! Only six short years, and the Great War has come and gone. Is it not incredible?"

He turned suddenly to Sexton Blake.

"Mr. Blake," he said, "I am greatly honoured to dine with you. I have heard much of your extraordinary career in the detection of crime; your reputation is world-wide. It is indeed a pleasure."

Blake's keen grey eyes were fixed searchingly on the Baron's smiling face. Blake was wondering what were his motives.

Was he playing some deep game? Or had he come along out of mere curiosity to meet the famous detective?

Blake determined to sound him at the first opportunity that presented itself.

For the next half-hour nothing of importance occurred. The detective was thoroughly enjoying his dinner, and the good wine and the splendid music had the effect of making him feel friendly disposed towards his companion. After all, the man was jolly good company.

Blake could see also that the actress had succeeded in throwing off that strained, anxious expression which had overshadowed her face in the early part of the evening.

He was rather glad of this. Whatever were the real intentions of the man who sat facing Blake, she, at any rate, was quite innocent of any deception. He felt sure of that.

Suddenly the detective leaned towards the Baron. He looked him full in the face.

"Baron Rodanoff," he said, "I have just recollected we have met before. In the Savoy today at lunch-time you sat at a table near mine, and seemed very much interested in the Soho crime."

It was a cute shot, and the suddenness and unexpectedness of the challenge quite took the Baron off his guard. He started violently, and recovered himself with an effort.

For the space of a minute or two, the two men glared across the table at each other. Neither spoke. It was a conflict of wills, and both men were strong-willed and resolute.

But Baron Rodanoff's eyes wavered; Blake could see that he was fighting hard to conceal his embarrassment. At last he spoke.

"Really, Mr. Blake," he said, "you surprise me. Fancy my being so near to you without my knowing it!"

For the moment there was an awkward silence. The Baron looked uneasy; those steel grey eyes of Blake seemed to be boring holes in him. What was the meaning of that slight smile of mockery that played over the detective's thin lips? Baron Rodanoff felt strangely uncomfortable, but he tried to pass the incident off with a forced laugh, and turned to the actress.

But Blake knew that he had deliberately lied; for had he not asked the waiter if he were Mr. Blake? More than that, Blake felt sure that Baron Rodanoff also knew that the detective suspected him.

When the Baron turned to him again there was a sinister glint in his eyes, as if he recognised that between them was proceeding a struggle of wills.

"Mr. Blake," he said. "Now that you have referred to this mysterious murder in Soho, I should like to know what your opinion is as to the motive of the crime."

The detective's lip curled slightly, but he answered without a moment's hesitation.

"I think," he said very deliberately, "that the motive was robbery. But behind it there is something bigger at stake. If I am not greatly mistaken, the crime is connected in some strange way with diplomatic intrigue. It remains to be seen whether I am right or wrong."

This time the Baron was plainly disconcerted. He could not forbear a start of surprise, and his fingers plucked nervously at the table-cloth.

It was merely a chance shot on Blake's part. He had no evidence on which to base his startling theory, excepting the deductions to which his own cleverness had led him. But he noted the Baron's embarrassment with secret satisfaction.

Presently Baron Rodanoff spoke again.

"I think, Mr. Blake," he said, "you are rather melodramatic. The crime is just a simple case of robbery, nothing else. At any rate, if there is a deeper motive behind it, as you suggest, then I am sure it will not be discovered until the information is too late to be of any use. I am willing to stake a hundred pounds[5] on that."

The detective leaned suddenly forward.

"Done!" he said quietly. "I accept your challenge, Baron Rodanoff."

Baron Rodanoff pushed his chair back with a jerk. He had never expected Blake's prompt reply. He immediately regretted his rash statement.

But it was too late now to withdraw it; the only thing left was to put as bold a face on it as possible. He gave a queer little laugh, but his eyes were blazing fiercely.

"Good, Mr. Blake!" he said. And he put out his hand. "It is a bet!"

The detective gravely shook hands with the Baron, as if the difference between them was just a simple matter of opinion.

But he knew all the time that he had embarked on a grim struggle that the man whose hand he grasped was connected in some inexplicable way with the mystery that confronted him, and that his anxiety to meet him tonight had been merely due to his desire to find out how much he knew.

Well, Blake had nothing to fear. He did not underestimate the qualities of the man with whom he was matched, but he had no doubt of his own abilities.

Certainly, there was a hundred pounds at stake, but he had pulled through before, and he would pull through this time.

He glanced at the glowing face of the actress; she had been following the conversation with intense interest. Well, it was worthwhile solving this mystery merely for the sake of earning her gratitude.

Presently, the Baron got up, and, apologising, bade them good-night and strode from the room.

Soon after, Miss Valentine rose to go. Blake saw her to her car, and, as he was bidding her good-night, asked her how much she knew of the Baron.

"Not very much, I am afraid, Mr. Blake," she said. "He used to move in very good Russian society, and I think he is very wealthy."

"Do you know where he is staying?" asked Blake.

"Yes, Mr. Blake. At the Imperial Club. He is a member."

"Thank you!" said Blake, "Goodnight!" And raised his hat.

Chapter 12
A Night Journey

WHEN Baron Rodanoff left Dalgretty's that evening, he made his way straight to the Imperial Club, where, later on, Dulac joined him in the smoke-room. There, over several whiskies-and-sodas, they conversed for a long time in low, earnest tones.

---

[5] £100 in 1920 is worth about £5,700.00 in 2023

"I tell you, Dulac," the Baron was saying, "that man Blake must be carefully watched. He is amazingly clever. How much he knows I cannot guess, but that he suspects us is very evident."

A look of fear came into Dulac's face. He twisted his fingers together nervously.

"But what do you propose to do, Baron?" he asked presently.

"We must get Grant out of London, Dulac. And that at once. Even then it will not be safe, but we shall have time to think. We must get him down to that house at Denesford. That will be the best place; nobody is likely to stumble on that. We must have the car along tonight at about twelve, and get the job done."

"But supposing he puts up a fight?" asked Dulac.

"No fear of that, Dulac," said the Baron. "We'll drug him; he won't cause any trouble then."

The two men smoked on in silence for a while. Then Baron Rodanoff spoke again.

"You have not found out where that fool Dykes is hiding, I suppose, Dulac?" he asked.

"No," said Dulac. "I have made a number of inquiries, but he seems to have disappeared entirely."

The Baron cursed below his breath.

"The fool!" he said savagely. "Why did they want to quarrel? Pity they didn't kill each other. But while he remains at large it's unsafe, Dulac. He may be arrested at any moment, and give the whole show away. He must be found at all costs."

Dulac made no answer. Presently, Baron Rodanoff took out his watch and glanced at the time.

"We had better go now, Dulac," he said. "Will you phone Denvers and ask him to bring the car round at once?"

Dulac immediately got up and left the smoke-room. After a few minutes, he returned again.

"Denvers is on his way now, Baron," he said.

Baron Rodanoff got up from his seat, and together they went out into the large vestibule. They waited a few moments, until the big limousine drew up in front of the door of the club, when they both got in.

Just as the car glided away from the pavement, a man crept out of the shadows, and, with a quick spring, grabbed hold of the rear-board and clung on.

The car sped swiftly down the road and crossed Vauxhall Bridge, and ten minutes later pulled up in front of the house in Kennington.

The man on the back sprang clear, and crept off into the shadow of the houses. As he passed under the light of the street-lamp, an observer would have recognised the clean-cut features of Sexton Blake.

The two men got out of the car, which moved off again. They entered the gate of a house and passed up the steps, and a moment later the door closed behind them.

Sexton Blake walked slowly past the house and noted the number. Then he turned and strode quickly away.

Half an hour or so later the big limousine came purring softly down the mews at the back of the mansion and drew up close to the wall. The yard door swung silently open and three men came out.

The man in the middle seemed to stumble and hang heavily on the arms of the other two. They dragged him inside and closed the door. The car gave a jerk forward, sped up the mews, and was quickly swallowed up in the night.

Scarcely had the car disappeared from sight when a man crept stealthily along the mews, keeping carefully in the shadow of the walls. He was a thick-set individual, in a heavy greatcoat. His cap was pulled down over his eyes so that his face was almost concealed.

Of evil and sinister appearance, this man crept along like a hunted animal. Every moment he cast nervous, frightened glances over his shoulders, as if he expected someone to spring at him out of the darkness.

It seemed as if this strange man were fleeing from justice and the vengeance of mankind. And so he was, for he was none other than big Bill Dykes, the man who was wanted for the Soho murder.

Reaching the yard door of the house, Dykes gently tried the handle. The door was locked. He glanced furtively up and down the mews, then, with a sudden leap, scaled the wall, and dropped softly on the other side.

He stood still a moment, breathing hard and listening intently. Then, evidently somewhat reassured, he stole noiselessly across the yard into the shadow of the house.

The place was in darkness, and the back door was securely fastened. Dykes leant his weight against it, but it would not budge an inch. He took a pace back, and stood for a moment wondering what to do. Then he noticed a little window in the wing of the house that jutted out on the right.

He padded quickly across to it, and reached up; his fingers just touched the windowsill. Drawing his huge body up with ease by means of his powerful arms, Dykes rested a moment on the ledge, and listened again.

No sound reached his ears; he put his elbow against the glass, and pressed.

Suddenly it gave way with a loud crack, and a shower of splintered glass, shivered on the ground.

The beads of perspiration stood out for a moment on Dykes' forehead; he gritted his teeth savagely, and, putting his arm through the broken pane, undid the catch.

The next moment he had squeezed himself through.

Dykes stole silently up the stairs and entered the billiard-room. He did not dare to switch on the light, but struck a match from a box which he took from his pocket. In the feeble, spluttering light the evil features of Bill Dykes showed up like a ghostly apparition.

The room was empty; Dykes strode across to the bedroom and pushed open the door. That was empty also. For a moment Dykes stood there blinking, uncertain what to do; then he let fall a savage oath.

"Flown!" he muttered. "They've hooked it!"

Suddenly he caught sight of the brandy-bottle, standing on the table. With a snarl of satisfaction he caught it up and took a big pull of the fiery liquid.

The drink seemed to give him fresh courage; he glanced round the room again, and laughed mockingly.

"Done a bunk!" he snarled. "Well, I'll find 'em. Trust old Bill Dykes. I've got them taped; they won't diddle me!"

He took another pull at the bottle, then crept out of the room and down the stairs.

A few moments later the sinister figure of Bill Dykes slunk down the mews and was quickly lost in the labyrinths of London.

Chapter 13
Pedro on the Scent

TINKER had long returned from Hampstead when Blake got back that night. He was wondering rather at the detective's absence, for he knew nothing of the dinner at Dalgretty's. He was, therefore, somewhat relieved when he heard the familiar footsteps of his master on the stairs.

"Well, Tinker," said Blake, "have you done the needful?"

"I should say so, guv'nor!" said Tinker, producing from his pocket a bright red handkerchief, and unfolding it. Here's the piece of cloth. Professor Bailey cut it from the dead man's clothes himself."

"Good!" said Blake, gingerly taking the dirty piece of rag from his assistant's fingers, "'Tain't over-clean, is it, Tinker?"

"I say, guv'nor, I've got something else!" said Tinker mysteriously.

"What is it?" asked Blake quickly.

"A photograph of the fingerprints on the man's throat. I saw it on the professor's desk, and asked him for it."

"Capital!" said Blake. "That's one to you, Tinker."

Tinker carefully unwrapped the freshly taken print, and laid it on Blake's desk. The detective rested his chin on his hand, and began poring over it.

To the average man the small photograph with the strange markings on it would have conveyed nothing; he would not even have recognised what it was supposed to represent.

But to the great detective it conveyed quite a number of things; he read it as easily as if it were an open book.

For a long time Blake sat engrossed in studying the photograph, turning it this way and that way, and scrutinising it through a powerful magnifying glass.

At last he glanced at his assistant with a look of unconcealed satisfaction.

"Tinker," he said quietly, "the man who murdered this fellow Crick has a finger missing—the little finger on the left hand."

Tinker stared at his master with an air of doubt.

"Why, how do you know that?" he asked.

"Just look at this photograph, Tinker," said Blake. "Do you see those five marks there? Well, they correspond to the fingers and thumb of the right hand."

Tinker stared down at the photograph.

"I suppose you're right, as usual, guv'nor," he said, only half-convinced; "but I'm hanged if I would have known it."

"Now, just look at these marks here; you'll see them better through the glass. There, do you see? How many can you count?"

"Why, guv'nor," said Tinker, after a moment or two, "there certainly seems to be only four comparing them with the other side. But I shouldn't have noticed it if you hadn't pointed it out."

Blake laughed softly.

"It's as clear as a pike-staff to me, Tinker," he said. "I've studied too many of these photographs in my time to be mistaken over a thing like that. The man who killed Crick, Tinker, had three fingers only on his left hand; the fourth finger was missing."

Tinker scratched his head in puzzlement.

"Well, it just beats me, guv'nor," he murmured, "how you seem to tumble on these things."

The detective did not speak for some moments; he seemed to be considering some weighty problem.

Suddenly he turned to his young assistant.

"Get Pedro, Tinker," he demanded shortly. "We're going on the warpath."

Tinker's eyes sparkled with excitement.

"That's the stuff, guv'nor!" he cried delightedly. "I don't know what the game is, but I'm with you."

He turned to leave the room. Blake, with a gesture of his hand, stopped him.

"Just a minute, Tinker," he said. "You are quite right; you ought to know everything. Just sit down a moment, and I'll tell you the story."

Tinker sat down by Blake's desk and listened intently while the detective told him of the events that had taken place that evening.

"So you see, Tinker," Blake finished up, "we are involved in one of the most amazing mysteries we've ever stumbled across. I want to make sure now that my deductions are correct, and that there is some connection between the Soho murder and the mystery of Granite Grant."

Five minutes later Sexton Blake, Tinker, and Pedro left the house. The bloodhound was in a state of great excitement, and tugged frantically at the lead, pulling Tinker along at the double.

"Steady on, Pedro, old fellow!" said Blake. "Save your wind; you may want it before the night's out."

The great hound looked up at the sound of his master's voice, and gave a little yelp of delight. The intelligent brute seemed to understand Blake's meaning, for he went more soberly after that.

They strode on in silence for some time, both men's thoughts being occupied with the mystery that confronted them.

Very few people were abroad; they only passed about two, and they glanced rather curiously at the detective and his young assistant; then, seeing Pedro straining on the lead, moved quickly on one side until they had passed.

About half an hour's sharp walk brought them to Vauxhall Bridge, and, after crossing it, Blake quickly left the main road and plunged into some side-turnings. Presently he caught hold of Tinker's arm.

"This is the street, Tinker," he whispered. "The house is down there on the right. Stay here with Pedro, and if I'm not back in ten minutes, come and look for me."

"Right, guv'nor!" said Tinker, as he watched his master stride swiftly down the street.

It seemed to Tinker as if he had been waiting there quite half an hour, although his watch told him it was only five minutes, when he saw Blake's familiar form appear out of the darkness.

"The house is in absolute darkness, Tinker," said Blake. "I don't believe anybody is there. But I discovered a mews at the back, and climbed over the wall, and undid the gate. Come on! We'll see what Pedro makes of it."

Very cautiously Tinker, with Pedro pulling hard on the lead, followed the detective along the street, until they came to the entrance of the mews.

At the third gate on the left Blake paused and gently turned the handle. The door swung back easily, and, motioning Tinker to follow him, the detective stole across the yard.

In the shadow of the house Blake took a small aluminium box from his pocket, and, removing the lid, took out the piece of cloth which Tinker had brought back from his visit to Professor Bailey.

"Here, Pedro!" he muttered, holding the piece of cloth out for the dog to scent. "Good dog, Pedro! Have it, boy!"

The bloodhound buried his nose in the rag, growling low and quivering with excitement. Then Blake took the cloth away.

"Now, boy!" he said. "After it!"

Pedro cast a swift glance of inquiry at his master, wagged his tail as if he were pleased, then lifted his great nose and sniffed suspiciously at the air. Then his head went down, and he pattered noiselessly to and fro for a few moments, with his nose to the ground.

Presently he stopped dead, sniffing the ground, and growling to himself; then he gave a little yelp of satisfaction and ran across the yard, sniffing the ground all the while.

Blake drew in his breath.

"By Jove, Tinker!" he said. "He's picked up the scent. I was right, then. Baron Rodanoff is in some way connected with the Soho murder. That poor fellow, Crick, must have been here within the last day or two. Very likely he left here on the very same night that he met his death."

Blake stopped suddenly as Pedro came slowly towards them. The dog was well on the scent now and was engrossed in his work; he came close to the wall and followed the trail along by the house. Then he stopped suddenly in the shadow, growling savagely and pawing at the back door.

"Ah!" said Blake, hurrying to the spot. "So Crick must have entered the house by this door. We must get inside somehow, Tinker, even if it happens to be occupied."

The detective tried the door, but it was locked from the inside. He took a pace back to look up at the windows, and his feet crunched loudly on something lying on the ground. He stooped down and felt in the darkness.

"Broken glass!" he said shortly; then took another look at the wall to the right.

"See!" he said. "There is a small window there. Somebody has made their way in there tonight. Just give me a hoist up, Tinker."

The next moment Blake had scrambled through the window.

"I'll open the door in a moment, Tinker," he whispered, and dropped inside.

In a few moments the bolts were shot back, and the door gently opened.

"This way, Tinker," said the detective. "Hold on to Pedro, and see where he goes."

The dog sniffed at the floor, and moved forward in the darkness. Blake took out an electric torch, and shot a thin beam of light ahead.

A few yards to the right was a broad staircase, towards which Pedro was making, with Blake and Tinker following hard behind.

They climbed the stairs, and Pedro led them along the passage to a door on the first floor, where he stopped and sniffed.

Blake tried the handle: it turned easily, and the door swung back.

The room was in darkness. Feeling for the electric switch, Blake flooded the place with light.

The room was vacant; the furniture appeared new, as if it had not been there long. In the centre stood a full-size billiard-table.

The detective began casting swift glances around.

Pedro had been slowly nosing about the room. Presently he came to the door on the other side, and, after one or two sniffs, he pushed it open and disappeared inside.

Blake and Tinker quickly followed him. This room was also in darkness, but Blake switched on the light and gazed curiously around.

Over in the corner stood a bed; it was flattened and disordered, as if someone had recently been lying upon it.

"Tinker," said Blake suddenly, "do you notice those chairs? They are upholstered in red plush."

Tinker looked puzzled for a moment.

"I've got you, guv'nor!" he muttered suddenly. "What Professor Bailey said about the finger-nails!"

"Just so," said Blake. "It may be merely a coincidence, of course, but it seems strange."

Then an idea suddenly occurred to him. He strode over to the washstand, and, lifting the lid of the soap-box, took out a piece of soap. Blake took one smell at it, and uttered an exclamation of surprise.

"Tinker," he cried excitedly, "just smell this!"

Tinker took the piece of soap and did as he was told.

"What a funny smell it's got, guv'nor!" he said. "But it's jolly nice, all the same."

The detective did not speak for some moments; he seemed to be deep in thought.

"Do you know, Tinker," he said at length, "that is the very aromatic soap which Professor Bailey found, not only on the nails of that poor chap, Crick, but also on the nails of the man who is posing as Granite Grant?"

Tinker could only look astonished, and wait for Blake to continue.

"Yes," said the detective, "there are the red-plush chairs, and here is the soap. Taken separately, neither is very strong evidence; but together they prove one thing, and that is, that the man now occupying Granite Grant's position and this fellow, Joe Crick, must have both at some, time been in this room."

The detective then began an exhaustive search of the two rooms, but, after a long and minute examination, he was unable to discover anything else of importance. Pedro had now given up the scent, and had stretched himself on the carpet.

Blake and Tinker then made a search of the whole house, but nothing came to light of any value in the solution of the mystery. With the exception of the two rooms on the first floor, the remainder of the house was quite unfurnished.

Blake at length decided to give up the hunt for that night.

"We must keep a close watch on this place," he said, as they were going down the stairs. So far, I am rather at a loss for an explanation of the whole strange business. No doubt these men will return here in a day or two, so I think I'd better lock the back door and climb through the window again; we don't want them to know we've been here in their absence."

Tinker and Pedro passed out into the yard, and, having bolted the door. Blake proceeded to hoist himself through the window. Just as he was balancing himself in the frame, however, he was struck with a sudden thought.

He took out his pocket-torch and carefully scrutinised the woodwork. A moment later he gave a quick cry of amazement.

"Tinker," he whispered hoarsely, "what do you think? There are two sets of finger-prints plainly discernable on the window-sill here, and the little finger of the left hand is missing. The Soho murderer must have broken this window and climbed through here. And it must have happened within the last hour or two."

Chapter 14
Tinker on the Watch

FOR three solid hours Tinker had kept a furtive watch on the house in Kennington. Many people had passed up and down the road, and quite a good number had been in and out of the mews, but not a soul had entered that particular house, and nothing had occurred to arouse Tinker's suspicions.

Tinker was feeling a trifle "fed up"; it was a cold November day, and a biting wind was blowing round the corner, which seemed to penetrate the very marrow of his bones.

Tinker was just deciding to "hook it" and get something warm to drink, when he chanced to glance down the road again. A man was approaching from the other end; something in his appearance and gait seemed to attract Tinker's attention.

"Might as well see where he goes!" muttered Tinker. "Looks as if he'd got the breeze up over something."

Tinker crept back to his corner, from where he could obtain a good view of the house without being seen himself.

As the man approached, Tinker noticed that his cap was pulled down over his eyes, and the collar of his coat was turned up, so that he could see little of his face.

Tinker watched the stranger curiously as he slowly passed the house and stared up at the windows. Then Tinker saw him stop, and, after giving a rapid glance up and down the road, turn and slowly pass the house again.

Tinker's interest was now thoroughly aroused. Craning his neck forward, he watched the man repeat his performance several times, each time casting that swift glance up at the windows.

"Now what's his game, I wonder," muttered Tinker, "does he expect something to happen? Hello, he's coming this way!"

Tinker drew himself back behind the corner, preparing to look as unconcerned as possible, should the man come along and notice him.

Not hearing the approaching footsteps after waiting a few moments, Tinker took another peep round, the corner.

The stranger was nowhere in sight.

"He must have gone down the mews," muttered Tinker, and ran swiftly across the road to the entrance.

He was right. The stranger had paused outside the third gate, and, after giving a swift glance around, he made a spring on to the wall, and the next moment had dropped to the other side.

Now, greatly excited and eager to see what the stranger would do, Tinker ran quickly to the gate and peered through the keyhole. He was just in time to observe the man's legs disappear through the broken window.

For a moment Tinker was undecided whether he should scale the wall and chance his luck in meeting the stranger, or stay where he was. He determined, however, to stay where he was for a time and see if anything happened.

For five minutes or more Tinker remained with his eye glued to the keyhole. Then he saw the stranger's head poke through the window again, as he scrambled out of the small opening.

Without stopping, he strode straight across the yard towards the door through which Tinker was peeping. Tinker beat a hurried, retreat up the mews.

He was just in time, for, hardly had he concealed himself, when the man dropped lightly over the wall, and, after looking up and down the mews, strode swiftly away, muttering angrily to himself.

Tinker quickly made up his mind. At all costs he must keep him in sight and see where he was going; there was something very fishy about this man's movements. Tinker felt he was well on the way to making an important discovery, and it was too good an opportunity to miss.

For ten minutes or more Tinker dogged the footsteps of the stranger, keeping well behind him, but never losing sight of his quarry.

Presently they came to Vauxhall Bridge, and Tinker began to close up until he was barely a dozen yards or so behind. Then something startling happened.

They were just about half-way across the bridge, when a taxi, which was speeding towards them from the direction of Victoria, suddenly pulled up abruptly.

Tinker saw a man poke his head out of the window and gesticulate wildly to the driver. The cab immediately skidded round in the road, and came to a stop alongside the man Tinker had been following.

The stranger gave a start of surprise, and made as if to run away; but the occupant of the cab flung open the door and grabbed him by the shoulder.

For a few seconds the two seemed to be having a fierce argument over something, then the other man pulled the stranger roughly into the taxi, gave some order to the driver, and slammed the door.

The car swung round again, and sped off in the direction of south-east London.

The whole incident had happened so quickly that it was over before Tinker had had time to grasp properly what was going on. As the cab went by, however, he caught a brief glimpse of a bearded face peering out of the window.

Tinker gave a swift glance at the back of the cab and made a mental note of the number.

For a moment he was minded to follow, but there was no spare taxi in sight. After watching the cab until it disappeared in the distance, Tinker turned and hurried in the direction of Baker Street.

Chapter 15
A Fresh Clue

"WELL, Tinker, any news?" asked Sexton Blake, as his young assistant came hurriedly into the room.

"Yes, guv'nor!" said Tinker, somewhat out of breath from his hurried walk. "A queer-looking cove got into the house a short time ago through the same little window that we used last night."

"Ah!" said the detective, immediately interested. "Sit down, Tinker, and tell me all about it."

Tinker sat down and told his master exactly what had happened, right up to the incident of the taxi on Vauxhall Bridge.

"What sort of chap was the man you saw in the taxi?" asked Blake, when Tinker had finished.

Tinker described the bearded stranger as nearly as he could from the brief glimpse he had had of him as the cab passed by.

"Umph!" said Blake, after listening carefully to Tinker's description. "Seems as if it might be that chap who lunched with Baron Rodanoff in the Savoy yesterday."

The detective asked his assistant one or two more questions, then he got up from his chair and put on his hat.

"I sha'n' be long, Tinker," he said. "I'm just going round to Scotland Yard to find out the owner of that taxi. Good job you took the number; this may lead to something important."

It did not take Blake long to reach Scotland Yard; there he quickly found out the owner of the taxi, whose garage was in the Waterloo Road.

He determined to make inquiries straight away, and hurried off. Just as he was leaving the building, however, he ran into Inspector Bradley.

"Hello, Mr. Blake!" said the inspector patronisingly. "How do you find things?"

"Oh, with my hands, you know, inspector!" said Blake curtly, somewhat resenting the other's manner.

Inspector Bradley's face went a trifle red.

"I'm referring to that affair of Granite Grant, Mr. Blake," he said rather huffily.

"Oh, yes!" said Blake." "Any news?"

"No, but I thought you might have some, though, Mr. Blake," the Inspector answered, with a trace of sarcasm. "I suppose you've dropped all your strange theories about it?"

"Not at all," said Blake cheerfully. "I'm still hot on the scent."

Inspector Bradley gave a superior sort of smile.

"Well, Mr. Blake," he said, "I hope you're not wasting your time. But, I must hurry off; I'm on something big this time."

"Pleased to hear it!" said Blake. "What case is that, if I may be so bold as to ask?"

"It's the Soho murder, you know!" said Bradley confidentially.

"Really? Well, that's funny, Inspector Bradley. I happen to be on the same job myself. Quite unofficially, of course!"

The inspector cast a curious look at the detective, as if he thought this was another of Sexton Blake's little jokes.

"But I don't understand you, Mr. Blake," he said. "Just now you told me you were still following up this Grant affair."

"So I am," said Blake. "As a matter of fact, Bradley, I've thought of some more startling theories since I saw you last; my latest is that the Grant affair and this Soho murder are very intimately connected!"

For the moment it looked as if Inspector Bradley could not restrain his anger; but he controlled himself with an effort and burst out into a forced laugh.

"You're pulling my leg, Mr. Blake," he said. "I've got this Soho business well in hand, and we'll have an arrest shortly."

"Splendid!" said Blake, "and so we will. But I'm afraid you won't do the arresting."

Inspector Bradley stared at Blake with undisguised annoyance.

"Well," he said, tartly, "we shall see about that. But I've got some important work to do, and must get on. You'll find you've backed a loser this time, though."

And, with this parting shot, the inspector turned on his heel and strode off in a rage. Blake laughed softly to himself.

"Poor old Bradley!" he said. "But he's really quite a good sort, when you know him."

The detective continued his way towards the Waterloo Road, and eventually arrived at the garage.

The taxi had not yet returned, however, and the only driver who happened to be in told Blake that that particular cab was plying for hire at Charing Cross Station.

The detective immediately jumped on a passing bus and made his way thither.

But although Blake examined every cab outside the station, the one with the required number was not there. He waited about for some time, and looked at every taxi that entered the station, but without success.

He therefore went and had some lunch at a restaurant near by, and came back again in about an hour's time.

Then, after hanging about for nearly six hours, his patience was rewarded. A taxi came towards him looking very dusty, as if it had been on a long journey, and when Blake glanced at the back he found it carried the number he was looking for.

Blake met the driver as he climbed out of the seat.

"Just a moment, driver," he said. "This morning you were passing over Vauxhall Bridge with a fare when you suddenly stopped and picked up another man and then went off again."

"That's so, boss!" agreed the driver. "Just come back from that journey; had a fifty mile run or more."

"I should like to know where you took them," said Blake, slipping a coin into the man's hand; "I happen to know the gentlemen."

The driver regarded Blake thoughtfully for a moment.

"Right, boss!" he said at last. "No reason that I know of why I should keep it a secret. I picked the gent up here this morning; he asked me to drive him to Kennington. Then he stopped me on Vauxhall Bridge and picked up the other cove. He evidently changed his mind then, and promised me twenty quid if I'd take them down to Denesford— about a fifty-mile run."

"Thanks!" said Blake. "And did you stop at a house there?"

"No, I didn't," said the man. "They asked me to drop them just outside the village, which I did. Wasn't no concern of mine. They paid me; that was quite good enough for me."

"Quite so!" said Blake. "That's all right. Thanks very much. Good-day!"

The detective went straight back to his rooms in Baker Street. He found Tinker still there waiting for his return and told him what he had learnt.

"Tinker," he said, "we must get a bustle on. Just find out where that place Denesford happens to be; I think it's down the river somewhere. I'll pack a few necessary things. We will try to catch the next train."

Chapter 16
Free!

WHEN Granite Grant left the house in Kennington late the previous night in company with the Baron and Dulac he was to all outward signs dead to the world. Dulac had previously seen to that by putting a powerful drug in his coffee.

Granite Grant, however, was a man of considerable resource and cuteness. Something in Dulac's manner had aroused his suspicions; he had made a pretence of drinking the coffee, and while Dulac's back was turned he had deftly emptied the contents of the cup underneath the counterpane of the bed.

Grant then set himself to watch Dulac's movements. He saw him leave the room, and heard him conversing in low tones with the Baron in the next room. Presently the door was gently pushed ajar, and Dulac glanced furtively at Grant, who was lying on the bed.

Granite Grant closed his eyes, and pretended he was asleep. He did not have to wait long. Presently he heard footsteps softly approaching him, and Dulac leant over him for a moment or two.

"He's off all right," he whispered to the baron. "That's wonderful stuff for sending them to sleep."

"Good!" muttered Baron Rodanoff. "Well, the car's outside; we'll get him into it straight away."

They took the shackles off Grant's wrists and ankles, and, supporting him between them, took him downstairs and out to the car that was waiting in the mews.

The door shut behind them, and the car moved off into the night, with Grant's apparently unconscious form half reclining on the seat between the Baron and Dulac.

An hour or more fled by. The car rushed steadily on through the silent night, its powerful engines throbbing with a low rhythmic note as mile after mile flashed by.

Lying with his eyes closed, Grant eagerly drank in every word which the two men on either side of him were saying.

Little they thought that this silent, slumbering man between them was fully awake and alert, and was closely following every word that was uttered.

So completely had Grant hoodwinked them that not a suspicion crossed their minds that he was not drugged and could not possibly come round until some hours had elapsed.

If they had had the slightest doubt on this point they would not have left him unfettered, but would have put the shackles back on his hands and feet.

But Granite Grant was waiting his chance. Presently it would come, and he would make one supreme bid for liberty. He had no idea where he was or where they were taking him. He dared not stir, nor open his eyes to glance out of the window, for fear of betraying his condition.

Several times he prepared to make that great spring, to fling open the door and jump out. Yet he held back; he must make no mistake this time; he must take his jailors completely by surprise. They were both heavily armed, he knew, and he must not give them the opportunity of using their weapons on him.

Another half an hour went by. Grant was feeling rather cramped in his legs; he could not endure the pain much longer. Should he make his dash for liberty now?

And at that moment the car slowed up at a sharp bend in the road.

"Now or never!" thought Grant.

With a quick movement he shot out his arms and encircled the heads of the men on either side, then, with all his amazing strength, he swung them together.

The two heads met with a tremendous impact; the next moment Granite Grant had sprung to his feet, unfastened the door, and leapt out.

It was some minutes before either of the two men recovered their senses; the whole thing had been so sudden and unexpected, and their heads had crashed together with such force, that they lay sprawling on the door of the car, absolutely dazed and stunned.

They laid thus for two or three moments, then, as the baron's wits slowly returned to him, he clutched wildly at the seat and staggered to his feet.

"Denvers!" he shouted, banging with his fist on the window behind the driver's seat. "Stop, stop!"

Then, as the brakes were put on and the car came to a standstill, he gripped Dulac's collar and dragged him to his feet.

"Dulac!" he shouted savagely, "pull yourself together, man! Quick, the fellow's escaped."

Dulac quickly came to a realisation of the peril that faced them.

"What shall we do?" he asked, trembling violently, and rubbing his bruised and aching head.

"Turn back, Denvers!" shouted Baron Rodanoff, now thoroughly roused to his danger. "Turn back—quickly, and don't go too fast! Search that side of the road, Dulac! I'll keep my eyes open on this side."

The car backed round in the road and started off in the other direction. The baron and Dulac gazed anxiously at the hedges on either side, as they came within the circle of the great head-lights. But no sign of Granite Grant was forthcoming.

After they had proceeded thus for about two hundred yards the baron ordered Denvers to stop.

"Dulac," he said excitedly, "this is about the spot where he made a jump for it. You search the fields on that side; I'll see if I can find him this way. If you come across him, don't hesitate; shoot him in the leg. But, remember, he's quite safe; he's got no weapons. Get him at all costs, though, even if you have to kill him."

The two men commenced their difficult search on either side of the road, breaking through the hedges into the fields, and watching the ground for any stray footmarks of their escaped prisoner.

But the search proved fruitless. Grant had completely vanished. After about a quarter of an hour the baron met Dulac again by the car.

His face was white and stern, and his hands were also bleeding from contact with the sharp prickles and barbed wire. Altogether he was considerably shaken.

The two men discussed the situation for a time. It was evident that Dulac was all for throwing up the sponge and making good their escape. But Baron Rodanoff was loth to admit himself beaten.

"There is just one chance left, Dulac," he said. "Grant will doubtless try to make his way to London. He can't get a train for some hours yet, and the chances are that he will start walking. We may come across him on the road. And, if not, he is certain to be in London too early to see anybody. Remember, this is not a case for the civil police; he will fight us through the Secret Service. And before he goes to Whitehall he'll want to make himself presentable, so he'll make for his rooms at Chelsea. That is our one chance; we may catch him yet."

He caught hold of Dulac's arm and dragged him back into the car.

"Denvers," he said, "drive back—straight to London! Not too quickly, and keep your eyes open all the while."

Chapter 17
Recaptured

BARON RODANOFF proved fairly correct in his calculations, as will be seen. After "Granite" Grant had made his daring leap for liberty he picked himself up from the roadside and climbed quickly through the hedge. He had sustained only a slight shaking from his spring through the open door, for the car was at that moment slowing down round the bend. After pausing a moment, therefore, to regain his breath, he ran as swiftly as he could across a ploughed field.

Just as he reached the other side he saw the headlights of the car turning down the road. He watched it pull up, and saw the two men jump out and begin their search, and laughed softly to himself; it was like looking for a pin in a haystack, he was free again, and he would want some catching this time.

Then he fancied he heard heavy footsteps coming towards him across the field. It was too dark to discern much; and he could not tell if both or only one of the men were approaching.

If he could have been certain that there was only one he would have boldly faced his assailant, in spite of the fact that he knew they were both heavily armed while he was without a weapon of any sort.

But he prized his newly won freedom too highly to take the risk of falling into the hands of his would-be captors again, so he hurried as fast as he could along the hedge, and, finding a path that led through an orchard, broke into a swift run.

For five minutes or more he kept on, then, judging that by this time he had effectively thrown off his pursuers, he came to a stop, and began to think over his position.

He had no very clear idea as to where he was; judging by the time they had been on the road, he estimated that he must be some thirty miles from London. He had no watch, and he could only roughly guess that it was now about three in the morning.

Well, there was no chance of getting a train yet awhile, and, moreover, he had no money. He would try to get on the main road to London and begin walking; very likely in an hour or two the market-carts would be taking their produce to town, and he could then get a lift.

Presently the path he was following led him out into a road. It was not the main road, but no doubt he would come upon that lower down. After walking for ten minutes he came upon some cross-roads, in the middle of which stood a white sign-post.

It was too dark to read the directions on it from where he stood, so he clambered up the post and peered closely at the pointing-hand. He had been fairly right in his estimation—it was twenty-eight miles to London.

With a light heart, "Granite" Grant commenced his long tramp: in any case, he would be in London in the morning, even if he had to walk the whole way; he would go straight to Whitehall and acquaint Sir Vrymer Fane with what had happened. Then the tables would be turned on his unscrupulous foes; he would certainly get the laugh of Baron Rodanoff.

But he was not worrying much about his enemies; after all, it was all a great game; and, as far as the civilian law was concerned, it afforded him no protection, for his work was carried on outside that.

He thought of the great task which Sir Vrymer Fane had placed in his hands; the fact that he had been singled out to undertake the mission was a great honour and trust. Well, he would not fail them; there was time yet.

He had been walking quickly now for nearly an hour. He was beginning to feel rather tired and hungry; he had had nothing to eat from the evening of the day before, and he had undergone a considerable strain since.

Suddenly the crunching of wheels on the gritty road sounded some distance behind him. He drew back into the hedge, and waited. Soon a waggon loaded with sacks of potatoes, and drawn by two heavy horses, hove in view.

This will do, thought Grant. He crouched down in the hedge and waited until the waggon had passed by, then he ran swiftly to the rear and clambered up.

The driver was nodding sleepily, and was quite unaware of the fact that he had picked up a passenger. Grant decided it was better not to make his presence known.

He wedged himself in between two sacks and made himself as comfortable as possible. No doubt the waggon was going to London: at any rate, he would keep where he was until it turned off the road.

But the events of the night had told on Grant; he found himself dozing off to sleep, and several times pulled himself together with an effort. At last, however, the tiredness got the better, of him, and he fell into a sound slumber.

It seemed to Grant that he had only just fallen off to sleep when he was aroused by someone roughly pulling at his leg. He opened his eyes sleepily.

"What's the matter?" he asked.

"Come on, now. Off yer git!" said a loud, surly voice.

Suddenly Grant was wide awake. He scrambled out of the sacks and slid to the ground. The driver was standing eyeing him suspiciously.

"What's yer little game?" he asked, glaring at Grant's unshaven and unkempt face.

"Just had a lift!" said Grant, fumbling in his pocket from force of habit for the money that wasn't there. He looked at the sulky driver with a humorous expression on his face.

"Sorry," he said; "I'm stony!"

"You just git on out of it," said the driver mistrustfully. "Met your sort before. Go on—out you git!"

Grant strode away without further remark. He could not help smiling grimly at the man's ill-temper; he evidently took Grant for a common loafer.

What a strange-looking object he must appear. At any rate, there was some comfort in knowing that no one would recognise in this disreputable fellow the famous and well-bred Secret Service agent.

When he had fallen asleep it had been pitch dark, but it was now broad daylight. With a start of surprise Grant suddenly realised that he was in Covent Garden.

This was a stroke of luck; he felt quite kindly disposed towards his surly friend, the waggon-driver. Just then he heard a church clock strike the hour of seven.

He stood still a moment, thinking what his next move would be. It was too early yet to see Sir Vrymer Fane; besides, he could hardly go to Whitehall in his present condition.

Then he thought of his flat in Chelsea. Yes, he would go there. He could get all he wanted then; and although he had no key, Mrs. Smith, his housekeeper, would let him in; she was used to his returning suddenly at all manner of queer times.

He made his way up the Strand; at Trafalgar Square he stopped at a coffee-stall and had something to eat and a cup of tea. He felt perfectly fit after that, and, humming a tune to himself, he directed his steps to Chelsea.

When he arrived at Number 12 he found the maid outside cleaning the brass knocker.

Instead of walking up the steps Grant strode straight past the house; he suddenly felt strangely conscious of his dirty appearance.

He wished he could get to his rooms without being seen, so that he could have a chance of making himself appear presentable.

He turned round and strolled towards the house again.

"Well, here goes!" he muttered, and pushed open the gate.

As he did so, the maid suddenly stopped her cleaning and disappeared inside to get a duster, or some such thing.

In a flash Grant had sprung up the flight of steps and along the hall, and, creeping silently up the carpeted stairs, entered his rooms.

As he gently closed his door he heard the maid pattering across the hall to the front door again. He laughed silently to himself as if it were a great joke, and started on his toilet.

But "Granite" Grant's return had not been as secret as he had supposed. Outside in the street two men stood and exchanged a few quick words; then one of them hurried away, while the other took up his position a short distance off, where he could keep Number 12 under observation without attracting attention.

"Granite" Grant's first move was to have a change of clothes. He went to the chest of drawers in his bedroom and took out a suit of blue serge, which he quietly got into.

He looked at himself in the mirror: he could hardly refrain from laughing; certainly he looked a disreputable object.

He had a wash and clipped his beard, which had grown straggly during the last few days. After that he began to look more like his old self.

The ormolu clock on the mantelpiece was still tinkling merrily; it was now a quarter past eight. There was just time to get some breakfast and still be at Whitehall at nine. Then, as he was leaving the room, he caught sight of the telephone.

For a moment or two he stood with a thoughtful expression on his face; then went over to the instrument and placed the receiver to his ear.

"Gerrard 004!" he said.

"Hallo!" he began, after waiting a few minutes. "Is Miss Valentine there?"

The maid answered him. Miss Valentine was not up yet, she said.

"Will you tell her it is important?" he said.

"What name, sir?"

"Mr. James Grant."

For some moments Grant held on; then suddenly his heart gave a quick bound as he heard the familiar voice of the woman he loved.

"Hallo, yes!" she said half-doubtfully.

"Laura—is that Laura? This is Jimmy."

He heard the woman at the other end give a start of surprise, then the sound of the receiver dropping with a crash to the table came along the wires.

"Hallo!" he shouted wildly. "What is the matter? Laura, Laura, what on earth has happened?"

After a few anxious moments "Granite" Grant heard his sweetheart's voice again.

"Hallo, Jimmy," she said, "is that really you? But I know it is. I recognised your voice immediately. It was that which gave me such a turn."

"My dear Laura," said Grant, "I am so sorry to have alarmed you. But, you see, I don't know exactly what has happened while I've been away."

"But where have you been, Jimmy? What has happened to you? Where are you now?"

"Why, dear," laughed Grant, "how can I answer so many questions all at once? I am at my flat at Chelsea now; I have just, returned. I've got a very exciting story to tell you; but it must wait until I see you. I am just off to Whitehall to see Sir Vrymer Fane. I will ring you up again later on, and take you out to lunch."

"But, Jimmy, I don't understand."

"You will, dear, directly I get you in my arms again," laughed Grant. "But I must ring off now, sweetheart. You will not be going out until I ring up again, will you?"

"No, Jimmy dear! But I am frightfully impatient to see you and know everything that has happened. It is all so strange."

"Well, that won't be very long, sweetheart!" said Grant.

"Mind it's not, Jimmy! Good-bye."

"Good-bye, dear!"

Granite Grant replaced the receiver and glanced at the clock. It was just 8.30. There was no time to have breakfast now; he would go straight to Whitehall.

He seized his hat and strode down the stairs. Mrs. Smith and the maid were evidently down in the basement; well, he could not stop now; he opened the street door and let himself out.

A taxi was coming slowly down the road; as it drew level with Grant it slowed down.

"Taxi, sir?" said the driver.

"Yes!" said Grant, opening the door and jumping in. "Take me to Whitehall Court as fast as you like!"

The cab jerked forward and sped off. "Granite" Grant leant back in his seat with a feeling of great content; soon he would have a private audience with Sir Vrymer Fane and recount his experiences.

Then he would wash his hands of the whole affair; Baron Rodanoff and his companions would not bother him any more; he had more important business to attend to.

He thought of the beautiful actress whom he would soon clasp again in his arms; how happy he was to know that his safety meant so much to her.

Suddenly he glanced out of the window. The streets through which they were passing seemed unfamiliar; the buildings were close on either side. It was a narrow, dirty, little turning. He leant forward and tapped on the glass angrily.

"Hi!" where on earth are you going?" he shouted.

The driver looked round and slowed up. And at that moment the doors on either side were flung open, two men leapt in and closed the doors behind them. The driver accelerated, and the car shot quickly forward.

There was a brief struggle; the butt of a revolver descended on Grant's forehead, and he remembered no more.

Baron Rodanoff wiped the perspiration from his forehead.

"My word, Dulac," he said, "that was a close thing, Well, he won't escape again, if I know it.

Presently the taxi entered a garage and drew up alongside the Baron's limousine, into which they dragged Grant's unconscious form. Denvers, who had been driving the taxi, immediately started up the engine.

"Dulac," said the Baron, "you know what to do. Get hold of that fellow Dykes at all costs. You leave Grant to me. He won't escape a second time."

The limousine, with its blinds drawn down, moved out of the garage, leaving Dulac behind. It was later on in the morning, as has already been stated, that Dulac saw Dykes on Vauxhall Bridge.

Chapter 18
"The Grim House"

ON the evening of that same day Sexton Blake and Tinker, with Pedro on the lead, got out of a train that stopped at Sunford Junction."

"How far is Denesford?" asked Blake of the only porter on the platform.

"Denesford, sir?" asked the porter, casting an anxious look at Pedro; "well, it's about six miles from here."

"Six miles?" said Blake; "why, isn't there another station nearer than this?"

"No, sir; this is the nearest. As a matter of fact, Denesford only consists of about a half-dozen cottages and a pub."

"Oh!" said Blake; "well, I suppose we shall have to walk, then?"

"Well!" said the porter, "old Bloggs over there has got a trap. I dare say he'll take you, if you ask nicely."

"Right, thanks!" said Blake. They crossed the road to the little harness shop, on the door of which was the name, "T. M. Bloggs."

Old Bloggs was quite willing to run them down to Denesford for a ten-shilling note, to which Blake agreed, and soon they were jogging along in the dog-cart through the pretty country lanes of Kent.

"What kind of place is Denesford?" asked Blake of old Bloggs presently.

"It's only a one-eyed sort of show, sir; don't know much about it. There's a pub there called the Chequers Inn. Not many people go there, though. You see, it's rather out of the way."

They jogged on in silence for the rest of the journey. The road was very uneven and hilly, and was evidently very little used by motorists. Frequently rabbits shot out of the hedge, and, hearing the sound of the cart, scurried away to cover again.

After about three-quarters of an hour's ride old Bloggs suddenly pulled up.

"Where shall I drop you, sir?" he asked. "This is Denesford."

"But I can't see any houses," said Blake, in surprise.

"Well, they're scattered about, rather," said old Bloggs. "That's one of them over there between the trees; there are several more down by the shore. The Chequers Inn is round the corner here."

"Well, drop us there!" said Blake.

As they rounded the bend in the road the inn hove in view. It was a low-lying little building, and had an air of snugness and comfort about it.

Evidently, from the cultivated look of the fields at the back, the innkeeper made most of his living from the soil.

The trap pulled up outside the inn, and Blake and Tinker dismounted.

Blake paid old Bloggs his money.

"By the way," he said, "there may be some letters re-addressed to me 'Care of Sunford Junction Post Office'; you might enquire there, and if any arrive bring them along to me here."

"What name, sir?"

"Mr. Sexton Blake!"

Old Bloggs gazed at the detective with awe.

"So you be the famous detective?" he said, with great respect. "Right-ho, sir; I'll bring your letters along all right."

Blake gave a dry smile.

"Good-night!" he said, and turned to the inn. A warm glow showed through the red blinds at the window; the place looked cosy and inviting.

"Not a bad little show, is it, Tinker, to spend the night in?" said Blake.

"I should say so," said Tinker. Just about my mark; sort of country holiday. I should just like to sit in front of the fire in a snug little bar-parlour, and forget for a time that there was such a place as London."

The detective laughed at his young assistant's enthusiasm.

"But we've come down here to work, Tinker!" he said. "However, just wait here while I explore things; we don't want to create a sensation by all trooping in at once; they'll think there's a raid on, or something."

The detective opened the door and strode into the bar.

About half a dozen yokels were sitting round the old-fashioned grate, sipping beer out of a pewter pot, which they passed from hand to hand.

A chorus of "Good-evening, sur's!" greeted Blake's entry.

"Good-evening, gentlemen!" said Blake pleasantly, as he made his way towards the innkeeper, who was standing behind the bar.

"Good-evening, sur!" said the innkeeper respectfully, eyeing his visitor with some surprise.

"Have you a spare room?" asked Blake, lowering his voice so as not to be overheard by the other customers; "my friend and I want to be put up here for a day or two."

The innkeeper scratched his head dubiously.

"Doan know about that, sur——" he began. But Blake would not take a denial.

"Look here," he said, "we've got to stay here tonight." He pushed a note into the man's hand. "You shall be well paid."

The innkeeper crushed the note in his hand and put it in his pocket.

"That's all right, sur," he said; "come this way."

Ten minutes later Blake and Tinker were seated at the table in the cosy little bar-parlour, doing justice to a huge shepherd's pie and a bowl of steaming potatoes, which their host had prepared for them.

Pedro was safely stowed away in a stable with plenty of hay, and was getting busy with a mutton bone.

"This is a bit of orlright, ain't it guv'nor?" said Tinker, already feeling the pleasant effects of the good beer and substantial food. "I could do this for duration."

"You wait until we get going, Tinker," said Blake. "You seem to forget that we're not down here for a rest-cure."

"All right, guv'nor," said Tinker, "I ain't forgetting. But it all seems so peaceful here that it's difficult to think about criminals and things of that sort."

Tinker wiped his mouth with a sigh of satisfaction, and got up to go and sit by the fire.

As he passed the door that led into the bar he happened to glance above the frosted glass window. Immediately he gave a gasp of surprise and ducked his head.

"What's the matter, Tinker?" asked Blake sharply.

"S'hush!" whispered Tinker, coming closer; "there's a chap standing by the bar having a drink; it's the same chap who climbed into the house at Kennington this morning, and who got into the taxi on Vauxhall Bridge!"

The detective tip-toed to the door and peeped above it. Presently he came back to where Tinker was standing.

"Tinker!" he said impressively, "that man has only three fingers on his left hand; the fourth finger is missing. It is the man who murdered Joe Crick in Soho, unless I am greatly mistaken."

Tinker gave a low whistle.

"Well, what are you going to do, guv'nor?" he asked.

"Follow him, Tinker!" said the detective; "very likely we shall get some clue as to the whereabouts of Granite' Grant."

At that moment they heard the bar door shut to. Blake took a hasty glance into the next compartment.

"Come on, Tinker," he said, "out of the back door. We must find out where he's going."

Without making any noise, Blake unfastened the yard door, and, followed closely by his young assistant, crept out into the yard.

A low hedge separated them from a lane leading down on the right of the inn. As they got outside the figure of a man vanished swiftly round the corner.

It did not take Blake and Tinker long to vault that hedge; the next moment they were dogging the footsteps of the stranger as he strode quickly down the winding, narrow lane.

For about ten minutes they crept on in silence: the lane was soft and muddy and their feet made no sound. It was now getting dark, and it was very difficult to keep sight of the man in front; presently they lost him altogether.

Blake and Tinker crept stealthily forward, hiding in the shadow of the hedge as much as possible. Then they came upon a gate on the right of the lane, which led to a path across the fields.

"This must have been the way he went," whispered Blake. "Come on, Tinker! Mind how you go!"

They climbed the gate and hurried across the field. Soon the dark form of the stranger loomed up again in front, and they went more slowly.

They must have been walking thus for nearly twenty minutes, when presently there loomed up against the skyline a great, gaunt-looking house.

The place seemed silent and deserted, no lights shone in any of the windows, an air of profound, gloom hung over the whole place. From just beyond came the low murmur of the sea breaking on the shore.

Blake and Tinker were now standing among some tall fir-trees; the man they had been following had strode straight towards the house, and had disappeared in the shadow of the walls.

"So that's where he's hiding!" muttered Blake. "Well, we're hot on the scent now, Tinker, my boy! I wonder whom this place belongs to? It stands in its own grounds, and they're pretty extensive, too! Look, they reach for miles, and cover all this wood to the right. There's the sea just over there, too; you can hear it."

"Look, guv'nor!" said Tinker suddenly. "There's a light in that room; it wasn't there a moment ago."

"You're right, Tinker," said Blake; "someone's pulling down the blind, too."

They watched in silence for some time.

Blake was thinking out his plans. Presently he turned to Tinker.

"Tinker," he said, "I'm going back to the inn. I want to find out whom this place belongs to, and also to fetch Pedro along. You had better wait here for an hour or so until I come back. I'll give the signal when I do. If I don't return in an hour you might come on to the inn."

"Right you are, guv'nor!" said Tinker.

The detective made his way as quickly as possible back to the inn. He felt very pleased with the turn of events; that this man was the murderer of Joe Crick he had not the slightest doubt; for the moment he was not concerned very much whether he was arrested or not; that could wait.

But its bearing on the mystery of Granite Grant's fate was the chief thing: the two were closely connected, he knew; and by solving one he felt sure he could discover the other.

As he came out of the lane that ran by the inn he noticed with some surprise that the dog-cart was standing outside. Old Bloggs came out of the bar just as he was entering the door.

"Just looking for you, sir!" he said. "Here's a telegram. Found it at the post office when I got back. Came directly after you left."

"Thanks!" said the detective, taking the envelope and tearing it open.

He stood staring at the message with a puzzled look on his face. It ran thus:

"COME AT ONCE, PLEASE. IMPORTANT. LAURA VALENTINE."

Greatly perplexed, Blake read the message through several times before he quite realised its import. What did it mean? Why did the actress wish to see him so urgently? What startling development had taken place?

For a moment the detective was perplexed what to do. It was evident that something extraordinary had occurred to cause her to wire him. No doubt she had rung him up and obtained his address from the housekeeper.

Blake glanced at the message again; yes, he must see her, at all costs. Perhaps something had happened to throw an important light on the mystery on which he was engaged. He turned suddenly to old Bloggs.

"What time is the next train to London?" he asked.

Old Bloggs turned out his watch and stared at it for a few moments.

"There's one in about three-quarters of an hour," he said.

"Can you get me there in time?"

"I'll try, sir, if you start at once."

"Good!" said the detective. "I'll be with you in one minute."

He ran into the bar-parlour, tore a leaf from his note-book, and scribbled a few lines to Tinker, which he put in an envelope.

"When my friend comes back," he said to the innkeeper, "please give him that. I shall be back in the morning."

Without waiting for the innkeeper to reply, Blake hastened outside and climbed into the dog-cart.

Chapter 19
Blake's Bewilderment

IT was nearly a quarter past ten that night when Sexton Blake stepped out of the train at London Bridge. He was determined to see Miss Valentine that same night, and ascertain what had caused her to wire him so urgently.

As she was engaged at the Jollity Theatre Blake resolved to go there straight away, in the hopes of catching her just before she left.

If he missed her there he could go on to her flat without having wasted much time. The detective, therefore, jumped into a taxi and drove off.

He got to the Jollity Theatre just as the performance was over, and the people were flocking out, and, making his way to the stage-door, sent up his card.

He did not have to wait long; in a few moments the porter reappeared, and conducted the detective to Miss Valentine's dressing-room.

The famous actress showed signs of great relief at seeing Blake; she motioned him into a chair, and, closing the door, began speaking in very agitated tones.

"Mr. Blake, I cannot tell you how relieved I am to see you. I rang you up this morning, and found out from your housekeeper where I might wire you. I hope you did not mind."

"Not in the least, I assure you," said the detective earnestly. "I only received your message about three hours or so ago, and immediately caught the next train to London. Now pray do not distress yourself. What has happened? You can rely upon me."

"Thank you, Mr. Blake," she said gratefully. "I cannot tell you how much I appreciate your help; if it were not for that I think I should break down altogether. Early this morning, Mr. Blake, my maid came into my room and said, with some excitement, that Mr. Grant wanted me on the 'phone.

"I was in bed at the time, but, not being quite sure what she meant by 'Mr. Grant,' I slipped on my dressing-gown and went to the telephone. Mr. Blake, you may think me mad, but I assure you that it was Jimmy—that is, Mr. Grant—who spoke to me. I recognised his voice immediately."

Blake gazed at the actress with some astonishment, not quite realising her meaning.

"Mr. Grant!" he repeated. "Do you mean that he rang you up from Bournemouth?"

"No, no, no!" cried the actress, half hysterically. "That is not Mr. Grant—that is, he is not my fiancé. But this morning I spoke to Jimmy. I know it was he; I will swear to it!"

The actress sank back into her chair, overcome by her feelings.

For a moment Blake was still puzzled; then he suddenly saw her meaning.

"You are sure of this?" he said, in a low, intense voice. "You are quite certain that you are not making a mistake?"

The actress recovered herself with an effort. She turned to the detective, and answered him in a calm, clear voice.

"Mr. Blake, there is no mistake, believe me! This morning I was speaking to Mr. Grant on the telephone—the real Mr. Grant. But listen: I have not told you all yet. He said he was speaking from his flat in Chelsea; he had just returned, and knew nothing of what had been happening while he was away. He said he had a very exciting story to tell me."

The detective listened in wrapt attention; his face was very grave, but it betrayed none of the utter astonishment which he felt.

"This is most extraordinary!" he muttered. "But where is he now? What has happened since?"

"I have not finished yet, Mr. Blake," said the actress. "Mr. Grant said he was just off to see Sir Vrymer Fane; he said it was absolutely necessary to see him at once. He promised most faithfully to meet me later on in the morning; he said he would ring me up again and take me out to lunch."

"Well?" queried the detective.

"I waited for him all the morning, Mr. Blake. You can imagine the state I was in. But I heard nothing more. At last I could stand the suspense no longer; I went round to Whitehall to make inquiries. Nothing was known. I saw Inspector Bradley at Scotland Yard; he was very polite, but I knew all the time that he thought I was simply suffering from a severe attack of nerves; I could see that he discredited my story. I even insisted on seeing Sir Vrymer Fane. He listened to me with great astonishment, and promised to give me every assistance; but Mr. Grant had had no interview with him that morning. He was somewhat bewildered."

The detective sat in a brown study after the actress had ceased speaking. This new and sudden turn of events had completely upset his theories; the mystery of "Granite" Grant remained as much a mystery as ever.

If this had been the real "Granite" Grant, who had spoken to the actress that very morning, then where was he now? Why had he not kept his appointment? Where had he been?

But had it really been "Granite" Grant? Perhaps Bradley was right after all; this was merely a case of nerves. Miss Valentine was suffering from a delusion. The events of the last few days had preyed upon her mind.

Blake took a keen glance at the actress; very likely she had fancied that the voice was that of her lover. After all, it was not always easy to recognise a person's voice over the telephone, even when one knows it so well.

The someone who had rung her up had been playing a joke on her—a very cruel sort of joke.

As if she divined his thoughts, the actress turned quickly to the detective.

"You are thinking, Mr. Blake," she said, "that I have possibly made a mistake. That is natural; and we all make mistakes at times. But there can be no mistake here. You must remember that my maid answered the telephone at first; she knows Mr. Grant's voice well, for she has often answered him before, and she swears now that it was his voice."

"That is certainly a very strong point," admitted the detective.

He puckered his brows again and thought deeply.

"Have you been to Mr. Grant's flat at Chelsea?" he asked presently.

"Yes, I have, Mr. Blake. I spoke to Mrs. Smith, the housekeeper, on the telephone. Then I went over and saw her; but she knows absolutely nothing. It seems strange; but then he may have been speaking from some other place."

"But why should he say he was at Chelsea, then?" asked Blake.

"I cannot say, Mr. Blake."

The detective took out his watch.

"It is a quarter to eleven," he said. "I must go over to Chelsea. Is it too late tonight?"

"No, Mr. Blake. The housekeeper may have gone to bed; but I have a key."

"Well, I will go there immediately, if I may borrow your key?"

"Certainly you may," said the actress; "but I will come with you."

Blake was about to remonstrate, but Miss Valentine shook her head decidedly.

"No," she said, "I shall not be able to sleep until I know what you think. I may as well come; and my car is outside."

Chapter 20
Whose Footprints?

SEXTON BLAKE and the actress left the theatre together. The car was already waiting outside, and it did not take them very long to get to Chelsea. The housekeeper was just bolting the door of Number 12 when they climbed the steps.

"Just in time!" said Blake, turning to the actress. "You see, your key wouldn't have been much use; we should have had to wake them up."

"We are sorry to trouble you, Mrs. Smith," said the actress, "but this gentleman is Mr. Blake, the detective. He wishes to look at Mr. Grant's rooms. We will not keep you long."

"Quite welcome, Miss Valentine," said the housekeeper, looking at Mr. Blake with great respect.

Mrs. Smith was quite mystified by the events that had taken place in her house during the last few days, but, as it was none of her business, she did not attempt to offer any remarks.

Blake followed the actress upstairs, and entered the suite of rooms which belonged to Granite Grant.

For ten minutes or more he made a minute examination of the furniture and windows for any marks, that might indicate that the rooms had been entered recently.

Miss Valentine stood by and watched his methods with keen interest.

Presently the detective pushed open the door leading to the bedroom, and went inside.

"Miss Valentine," he said suddenly, pointing to a grey flannel suit of clothes that was lying on a chair in the corner, "do you know whose clothes they are?"

The actress stared at the coat and trousers for some moments.

"I have never seen them before," she said, turning to the detective. "I am sure they do not belong to Jimmy."

She picked up the coat, and looked inside for the name of the maker; there was no name at all.

"Why," she said, "all Jimmy's clothes have the name of his tailors inside. Look!"

She went to the wardrobe and pulled open the bottom drawer. Blake was standing by her side.

"Aren't those things rather disordered?" he asked, staring at the apparel in the drawer. "It looks as if someone had hastily taken some things out; and quite recently, too."

"That does seem so, Mr. Blake," said the actress; "but look at this coat. See, here is the tailor's name quite clearly."

But Blake did not heed what she was saying; he was staring at a pair of muddy boots that were beneath the chair, and had at first escaped his notice. He stooped and picked them up, and stood looking at them critically.

"Do you recognise these boots?" he asked.

"No, that I do not," said Miss Valentine; "they are much too heavy for Jimmy. And, besides, there are iron studs in the soles. Look! He would never wear such things."

The actress was right. Embedded in each sole were six iron studs. How came these muddy boots to be there? wondered Blake. To whom did they belong? Then there was this suit of flannels; that was rather a mystery.

Suddenly he remembered that the fingernail analysis had revealed traces of the fibres of a grey flannel suit; that might simply be a coincidence, of course; but——

Blake strode to the door.

"Mrs. Smith!" he called.

"Yes, sir!" answered the housekeeper, as she came running up the stairs.

"Do you know how these boots and this suit of clothes came here?" asked Blake, pointing to the chair.

The housekeeper stared curiously at the garments.

"No, sir," she said. "I don't recognise them."

"When did you last tidy up this room?" asked Blake.

"Yesterday, sir. I haven't been in since, as the rooms are unoccupied."

"And do you remember seeing these things there then?"

"That I don't, sir. I should have folded them up and put them away if I had done so."

Blake picked up the coat.

"You don't mind me feeling in the pockets and seeing if there is anything there, do you?" he asked the actress.

"Not at all, Mr. Blake. Do just as you please."

But, although he searched every pocket Blake could find no clue as to the identity of the owner; all the pockets were empty.

After continuing his search for some time longer, the detective turned to Mrs. Smith.

"I think that will be sufficient for tonight," he said. "I shall very likely call again in the morning. Will you please see that these rooms are kept locked."

They went downstairs together; but, as the detective was crossing the hall, he suddenly stopped; and, stooping to the floor, took out his pocket torch.

A moment or so later he rose to his feet with a thoughtful look on his face, and turned to the housekeeper.

"When was this linoleum last cleaned, Mrs. Smith?" he asked.

For a moment the housekeeper was taken back.

"Why, whatever makes you ask, sir?" she said, with an attempt at dignity. "It is washed every morning regularly."

The detective gave a low chuckle.

"I wasn't casting aspersions on your cleanliness, Mrs. Smith," he said; "I'm sure it does you much credit. Now did you wash this linoleum this morning?"

"The maid did; yes, of course!"

"Ah!" muttered Blake. "Now we are getting on. Where is the maid? Can I speak to her?"

Mrs. Smith disappeared for a moment, and returned directly with the maid, who seemed only too pleased to join in the excitement.

"I want you to tell me," said Blake, "what time it was when you washed this floor this morning. Now, think carefully before you answer me!"

But the maid answered without the slightest hesitation.

"It was between a quarter and half past seven, sir," she said.

The detective seemed to be working out some mathematical calculation. Presently he spoke again.

"After you had washed this floor, what was the next thing you did?" he asked. "Now, try and remember!"

But the maid needed no prompting; evidently she performed the same tasks each day in precisely the same rotation.

"I went and cleaned the street-door knocker, sir."

The detective pointed an admonishing finger at the young woman.

"Ah!" he said very deliberately. "And you left the street-door open and went away for a few minutes; now, didn't you?"

The maid was about to give an emphatic denial. Suddenly she coloured up with an air of confusion.

"Yes," she said, "I remember now! I ran downstairs for a duster, sir."

Blake turned to the actress with a look of triumph on his face.

"It is quite clear, Miss Valentine," he said. "During these few minutes this morning, when this door was left open, someone entered this hall and strode across there to the stairs. And the man, whoever he was, was wearing the boots with the six iron studs in the soles."

"But how do you know, Mr. Blake?"

For answer the detective strode over to the mat in front of the door: from there he took four strides, the fourth landing him on the mat in front of the stairs.

He turned to Miss Valentine.

"You see," he said, "that my feet touched the linoleum three times in crossing from mat to mat: but I have made no marks on the floor. Yet if you look closely at those three spots where my feet touched you will observe a footprint in each of the places; it is very faint, but the six iron studs in the soles are unmistakable. Look!"

All three of the women bent down while the detective pointed out the faint footprints by the aid of his torch.

"Now," he continued, "these foot-marks must have been made while the linoleum was still wet, otherwise they would have made no impression. It is evident, therefore, that they were made this morning somewhere about half-past seven; and the stranger entered this hall during those few minutes when this door was open and the maid was downstairs."

There was a brief silence while his audience stood astonished at the detective's clever reasoning and startling deductions. Then Mrs. Smith spoke:

"Now I come to think of it, sir," she said, "I remember hearing the street door being shut to about eight-thirty. I wondered at the time who had gone out."

"Ah!" said Blake. "Then that was very likely when this man left the house; he had been upstairs for an hour."

But the maid, who had been standing by with her mouth open while Blake expounded his theory, now broke in excitedly:

"But the mats weren't down when I washed the floor," she said; "I always take them up; so how could he have stood on them?"

The detective could hardly repress a smile at this amusing outburst. He strode to the door, pulled away the mat and took a swift glance at the linoleum. Then he did the same to the mat by the stairs.

"That strengthens my case," he said; "there is a footprint beneath both these mats."

After making a few more observations, Blake and the actress left the house.

"Mr. Blake," she said, "I think you are simply wonderful. I cannot understand how you think of all these things; and yet they appear so simple when you explain them."

Blake gave vent to his familiar low chuckle:

"I cannot understand how you sing as you do, Miss Valentine," he said; "and yet when I listen to you it seems so simple."

The beautiful actress blushed a little at the gallant compliment of the great detective.

"Of course, you will let me drive you to your chambers!" she said. "It is not the slightest bit out of my way."

"If you will be good enough to excuse me, Miss Valentine," said Blake, "I should prefer to walk. I want to do some hard thinking; and walking is conducive to thought."

"Certainly, if you prefer it, Mr. Blake. But I am so glad that you do not think I have imagined what took place this morning, like the others do at Scotland Yard."

"I think we have rather proved that Mr. Grant came here this morning," said Blake, "and that he spoke to you on the 'phone. But, as yet, that fact takes us no further; in fact, it rather complicates matters. However, you leave it to me, Miss Valentine, and do not distress yourself more than you can help. I am sure it will all come right in the end."

"You are very kind, Mr. Blake," said the actress simply, giving the detective her hand.

"Good-night!" said Blake, closing the door. "I will keep you informed of what is happening."

He watched the car glide off into the darkness, then turned on his heel and strode off.

Chapter 21
"A Further Discovery"

WHEN Sexton Blake declined Miss Valentine's kind offer to drive him to Baker Street the reason he gave for his refusal was quite correct. As he said, he wanted to do some hard thinking, and he could think better while he was walking.

As he made his way slowly up Sloane Street towards Knightsbridge, a veritable fusillade of questions shot through his brain.

What on earth did it all mean? Why had "Granite" Grant thus so suddenly returned to his rooms, and then disappeared again? Had it really been he who had made this unexpected visit, or was it some other man?

But who else could it be; and what could be his motive in ringing up the actress and giving her that strange message?

The detective could find no reasonable answer to these numerous questions. He began again to turn the whole series of queer happenings over in his mind.

Who was this Baron Rodanoff? Why was he here? Was he interested in frustrating those secret diplomatic negotiations that were concerned with the tangled internal affairs of Russia, and of which Sir Vrymer Fane had hinted in that first interview?

If that were so, then he could understand his anxiety to get "Granite" Grant out of the way. But it seemed that "Granite" Grant was at large.

That brought him back again to the identity of the man who had entered the Chelsea flat. What was the meaning of that grey flannel suit of clothes?

Professor Bailey had found grey flannel fibres on the finger-nails of the man who was posing as "Granite" Grant, and who was now at Bournemouth. That he had not left Bournemouth Blake was sure, for he was having his movements watched.

Of course, this flannel suit might be simply coincidence; but then there was also the evidence of the red plush chairs and the aromatic soap.

Finally there was this mysterious Soho murder—but it was all too confusing.

For a time Blake strode along in silence. The thoughts still crowded through his mind; but as fast as he arrived at a solution of the problem some other aspect of the case would arise and present fresh difficulties.

Whose boots were they which had been left in the flat? Why—— Blake suddenly came to a standstill. Yes, there was one other thing he would do that night which might throw more light on these mysteries. Yes, he would do it at once.

He turned about and began striding rapidly in the other direction. Presently a taxi came gliding towards him; he stepped into the road and held up his hand. The driver put on the brakes and pulled up beside him.

"To Kennington, please!" said Blake.

"What part, sir?"

"I'll tell you when we get there," said Blake as he got in and shut the door.

The detective stopped the cab in the Upper Kennington Lane, and after paying his fare, continued his way on foot.

He found the house in darkness, as he had expected. For some reason or other he did not expect anyone to be there tonight; he had an idea that the house had now ceased to play an important part in the drama on which he was engaged.

However, he did not care much if anyone was there, it would not take him long to accomplish the object of his visit.

The detective crept silently up the mews and scaled the wall. He dropped on the soft ground without making any noise; but he was careful not to land at the entrance to the yard-door; he did not wish to disturb the soft earth there.

Then he took out his torch and began a careful examination of the soil.

He soon found what he was looking for; there, clearly discernible on the soft ground in front of the door, was the impression of three pairs of boots, and those in the centre bore the marks of six iron studs.

The footprints had been trampled on since, but he was able to trace them back across the yard right to the door of the house.

But Blake had not quite finished yet; there was something peculiar about these middle footprints; they seemed to be disturbed, as if they had been lengthened in some way, and the toes appeared to have stuck in the soil at every two or three paces.

For some time the detective studied these marks, critically comparing them with those on either side. What was the cause of this strange elongation? How had it occurred?

Perhaps the man who had worn these boots was a cripple and had to be supported by the two men on either side.

Suddenly Blake pursed his lips, and those two deep lines of thought showed on his forehead. He knew now. The man who had worn these studded boots was not a cripple; no, he had been drugged, or in some way rendered unconscious.

That would explain those curious footmarks. He had been forcibly taken across the yard, supported on either side by the two men whose footprints also showed so clearly.

That this was the correct explanation, Blake had not the slightest doubt; it was the most feasible.

No doubt this strange man had occupied that bed-room in the interior of the house; he had been kept a prisoner there, and then he had been taken away.

But the footprints must have been made before the detective and Tinker had paid their visit to the house last night, for the occupants had vanished when they arrived.

Yet Baron Radanoff had been here an hour or so before, for Blake had seen him enter with his companion.

The man wearing the studded boots must have been taken away then immediately before Blake arrived; and he had paid a visit to Chelsea only that morning.

If he were being held a prisoner by force, then he must have made his escape during the night. But where was he now? It seemed as if he must still be in London. Then what had Denesford to do with the mystery?

The detective suddenly remembered that he had left his young assistant down at Denesford. He must get down there tomorrow and hear what had happened; but he must see Sir Vrymer first.

However, the man with three fingers on his left hand—the man whom, he felt sure, had killed Joe Crick—was down at Denesford; that was a point worth remembering.

That started Blake wondering again what the Soho crime had to do with the disappearance of "Granite" Grant. But he gave it up for that night and began retracing his steps.

After all, the clue of the studded boots was a very important one; just one other link in the chain of events, and everything might be explained. But Blake had yet to discover that missing link.

***

Sexton Blake had been closeted with Sir Vrymer Fane for close on an hour. The great statesman was weighed down with anxiety; deep lines of care marked his face.

The two men had discussed the same problem again and again, going over every little detail together. Now they sat silent and engrossed, both full of harassing doubts and conflictions.

At last the statesman rose from his chair.

"What you tell me, Mr. Blake," he said, "only confirms my first impression; and yet I am helpless. The doctors maintain that the man will suddenly recover; they insist that it is simply a case of loss of memory. And while we are waiting, this Russian problem is swiftly moving to a crisis."

He paused for a moment to wet his lips, and continued:

"There is one man who could save the situation. If we could rush him out there within the next week, or ten days at the most, then the difficulty would be solved. That man, Mr. Blake, is James Grant—"Granite" Grant, as he is called."

A fighting look came into the detective's cold grey eyes; he rose suddenly to his feet and put out his hand impulsively.

"'Granite' Grant shall be found," he said quietly, "and within a week!"

The next moment the detective had gone.

Chapter 22
"The Night Horror"

FOR some time after Blake had left him, to return to the inn, Tinker remained standing silently in the grounds of the grim-looking house at Denesford.

A strange stillness seemed to have stolen over the place; there was not the sound of the slightest movement or the rustle of the trees. The sky had clouded over and the night was inky black.

In front loomed the vague dark outline of the house, rising gaunt and ghostly out of the darkness that spread around.

The light still shone through the red blind of the room on the second floor. Otherwise the whole place was shrouded in darkness.

Tinker was beginning to feel a trifle chilly; he had left the inn so hurriedly that he had not had time to bring his overcoat; he wished he had it now.

He did not much relish an hour's wait in this lonely spot; it was much nicer in front of the fire in the cosy little bar-parlour of the inn.

Tinker glanced again at the lighted window. It seemed rather to fascinate him; he wondered what was going on behind it.

Who was in the room? Was it the strange man whom they had followed from the inn to this lonely spot? Who did the place belong to, anyhow? Surely there must be other people in this great house beside him!

Sexton Blake had said that this man was the author of the Soho crime. Then what was he doing down here? Tinker could make neither head nor tail of it.

But his master knew what he was doing. What Blake said was good enough for him. Blake was always right. Well, Tinker wished he would hurry up and come back; this place was getting on his nerves.

While these thoughts had been surging through his mind, Tinker had been unconsciously creeping nearer and nearer to the house.

He pulled up suddenly, to find that he was almost within thirty yards of the building.

He was now out in the open without any cover of any sort. At all events he must not stand there, at any moment someone might come out of the house and discover his presence.

He was about to turn back and make for the cover of the trees again, when he noticed a privet hedge a little to his right and about ten yards ahead.

Tinker glanced at the window again. Yes, he must get closer. That window certainly seemed to exercise some powerful attraction over him.

Without further thought he bent his body to the double and ran swiftly forward. His feet made no noise on the springy turf; he reached the hedge and hid behind it.

From his position now Tinker could get a near view of the house without running any danger of being seen. He stuck his head above the hedge and peered over.

Another light had now appeared. It shone through a window in the basement. It seemed to be made of heavy opaque glass, and a number of thick iron bars crossed it on the outside. From the sill projected a row of spikes.

What was happening in there? thought Tinker. If he could only get a peep inside! His curiosity almost made him forget the biting cold.

But Blake would be back soon, he must listen for that peculiar bird-like whistle of his. Then they might get a move on.

Suddenly Tinker gave a start and almost stopped breathing. For a time he remained listening intently. Had his ears deceived him? What was that strange cry he had heard; or had it only been his fancy?

He listened again, feeling his heart throbbing painfully at the bottom of his throat.

"Pah!" he muttered at length. "You're getting windy, Tinker, my boy! Pull yourself together."

But the place was getting on his nerves. He glanced anxiously over his shoulder. If Blake would only hurry up!

Then suddenly he heard it again; this time distinctly. It came from the room on the basement, a strange, snarling cry—angry, menacing, full of horror.

For a moment Tinker remained petrified with fear. He had his full share of grit, and could stand up in a fair fight with a man twice his own weight and take his gruelling without a murmur.

But this was different. That ghastly, inhuman cry seemed fairly to freeze the very marrow in his bones.

He remained where he was, incapable of moving, and gazing with wild terrified eyes at the room from which the sound came.

Suddenly that fearful snarl rang out again, and with it came the sounds of commotion, something crashed to the floor like a table being overturned, then across the frosted window came the shadow of a man.

For one instant only did Tinker see it; the shadow of a man with his arm upraised as if he were striking at something. Then followed the lash, lash of a heavy whip falling on some body.

Again a shadow crossed the window, a monstrous, ungainly shape, and swiftly disappeared, and those same savage snarls rang out. Then, with a crash, the light went out, and all was darkness.

Scarcely daring to breathe, Tinker stood as if turned to stone, unable to stir a limb through sheer cold fright. The sweat stood out on his forehead in icy beads, and a cold hand seemed to clutch at his spine.

Suddenly there was a smashing of glass, and the weird ghastly cries grew louder, mingled with the hoarse shouts of men.

Following immediately after came a strange panting noise and the crumbling of brickwork, then the sound of a body falling to the ground as if the iron-barred grating in front of the window had been wrenched from the frame.

Quite unable to move, Tinker stood behind the privet hedge trying to pierce the darkness in front. Something was bounding towards him, some great uncouth thing.

What was it? What could this frightful thing be with such superhuman strength? It was almost on him now, yet Tinker did not attempt to stir.

The next moment the thing had fled past and went bounding towards the trees. But its terrible snarls still rang in Tinker's ears. Then several other figures came racing from the house, shouting to each other in short excited tones. They shot by Tinker also, and made for the trees.

Directly after a shot rang out, then another, and after an interval four or five in quick succession.

Gradually the noise subsided in the distance and all was deathly silence once more.

For nearly ten minutes Tinker stood there listening. He wanted to fly, to run away from this night of horror, but his limbs seemed to have turned to stone; he did not seem capable of moving them.

But he heard no more. The house remained dark and silent, no noise came from it now; the men who had rushed so madly after the strange thing that had escaped from the room had not returned.

Perhaps they were still hunting it! At any rate, he could hear no more cries or sounds of firing. By this time they might be miles away.

With an effort Tinker crept from his hiding-place. He must return to the inn, and find Blake. Perhaps he would meet him on the way, he should be back here by now; that is, if he intended coming back.

That was the direction over there through the trees, the path across the fields was just the other side. Once he was there he could easily find his way back.

He stole across the open. How weak his legs seemed, he could scarcely drag himself along. But he must get through this wood, and as quickly as possible.

Tinker was by this time among the trees, it was so dark that he had to grope his way with his hands. Where was the path? It must be close at hand now, perhaps within a few yards. He paused a moment and peered around, then pushed on again.

Suddenly he tripped over something lying on the grass, and put out his hands to save himself. What was this soft warm thing that was beneath him?

Then he gave a gasp, and drew back dismayed. It was the body of a man; he could just make out the vague white smudge of the upturned face.

The dreadful fear came over Tinker again; he stood rooted to the spot, gazing in horror at the dark indistinct form.

The terrible thought came to him that this silent man might be his beloved master, Blake; perhaps he had been shot as he was coming back through the wood.

Then the sharp snap of the branch of a tree sounded a dozen yards away.

Horror-struck, Tinker stood straining his ears and trying to pierce the gloom in the direction of the sound. What was that? Something was moving, some big monstrous shape creeping stealthily towards him.

Tinker tried to open his mouth to shout, but his tongue clove to the roof; for a moment he seemed as if he would drop dead with fright; then, turning on his heel, he rushed like a madman through the wood.

The thing was following him, he could hear its soft padded feet close behind; it was gaining on him.

He tried to shake it off, dodging behind trees, falling in holes, tearing his clothes on prickly plants and sharp wire, and bruising his hands in his mad flight.

But the thing was getting nearer and nearer; it was almost on him now; he could feel its hot, panting breath fanning his cheek. A second more and its great hairy arms would be reaching out to grasp him.

Then Tinker suddenly felt the ground give way beneath his feet. He flung up his arms, gave one piercing shriek, and shot down.

Down he went, down, down into a black, bottomless pit. He flung out his arms and clutched frantically at the sides, gripping at pieces of tree roots and projecting stones to save himself from the dizzy fall into inky blackness below.

His hands were torn and bleeding, and his body bruised and battered as it was flung from side to side. Yet he still went down and down.

Then his feet struck a projecting side of the pit; he swung violently round, clutched wildly in the darkness, and held on momentarily to the root of a tree.

It broke beneath his weight, and he went down again. But only a few feet this time, for immediately after he pulled up with a shattering jerk.

Tinker lay at the bottom of the pit unconscious and bleeding, with a deathly pallor on his thin, drawn face.

Chapter 23
Where is Tinker?

IT was about three in the afternoon of the same day that he had had his second interview with Sir Vrymer Fane, when Sexton Blake climbed down from old Bloggs's dog-cart and strode into the bar of the Chequers Inn.

The inn-keeper hurried out of the back kitchen and met the detective, with a relieved expression on his unintelligent face.

"Wondered what had happened to you, sir!" he said. "Couldn't quite make it out."

Blake glanced at him curiously.

"Why," he said, "my assistant is here, I suppose! He told you I was called away on business, didn't he? Where is he now?"

The inn-keeper looked puzzled.

"The young gent?" he queried, not seeming quite sure of the detective's meaning.

"What do you mean?" asked Blake sharply. "There were only two of us. My friend who stayed here last night!"

The inn-keeper gaped at Blake in astonishment.

"But he didn't," he stammered; "he's never been here at all; I haven't set eyes on him since yesterday evening, when you both went out together."

It was Blake's turn to look astonished. For the moment he still thought some mistake was being made.

"Do you mean to tell me," he said at last, "that Tinker didn't sleep here last night, didn't even come back after I left?"

Suddenly Blake thought of the letter he had written to his young assistant, explaining his absence.

"How about the letter I wrote?" he added quickly. "Has he had that?"

"I tell you, sir," said the man solemnly, "that I haven't seen the young gent since yesterday evening; I haven't set eyes on him since. He never came back here, to the best of my knowledge. Your letter is lying on the table now, waiting for him."

For the moment Blake was stunned by this piece of news. So unexpected had it been, and so unaccountable was Tinker's absence, that even now he was loth to believe that the inn-keeper was speaking the truth.

He strode into the bar-parlour and glanced round the room, half-expecting to see Tinker there. But there was the letter on the table, unopened, just as he had left it. What on earth had happened to Tinker? Why had he not come back?

A shade of anxiety crossed the detective's face. He was not in the habit of showing sentiment; he had too great a control over his emotions to give way to that sort of thing.

But beneath his impassive exterior beat a warm heart and a kindly nature, and for his friends the great detective held an affection that was as strong as it was unostentatious.

And Tinker, although only his assistant, had, by his happy disposition and the many perils they had faced together, endeared himself to Blake himself more than he cared to admit.

And Tinker had now disappeared! Blake felt a tightening sensation in his throat. Nothing else mattered for the moment; he must find Tinker—dead or alive.

Something seemed to suggest to him that his young assistant had met foul play. At the thought of that Blake's hands clenched, and a cold glitter came into his grey eyes.

If it were so, somebody would pay the price. Nothing should stand in the way of his vengeance. Let any man hurt a hair of Tinker's head, and Blake would be after his body—and quick, too!

Suddenly a familiar sound smote on Blake's ears; it was the muffled baying of a great hound. He turned on the inn-keeper, who had been standing by silently watching him.

"Where's my dog—where's Pedro?" he asked sternly.

The man glanced nervously at Blake.

"He's in the stable, sir. We dare not go near him; he seems so ferocious."

"Do you mean to say that you have given him nothing to eat?" Blake asked, and his face grew suddenly white and dangerous.

"But I dare not go near him, sir," said the inn-keeper, backing towards the door.

With a swift movement the detective swept him aside.

"Pah!" he said contemptuously, and strode quickly out into the yard.

The baying of the bloodhound sounded louder now; the sagacious animal scented the approach of his beloved master, and began whimpering and pawing at the side of the stable.

Striding over to the shed, Blake shot back the bolts and flung open the door. With one great spring Pedro landed out in the open, and began dancing and leaping up at his master with deep throaty yelps of joy.

"Poor old chap!" said the detective, caressing the animal and stroking his great head. "Poor old dog! Nothing to eat, nothing to drink. Come on, old fellow, we'll soon find you something."

He returned to the inn with Pedro gamboling around his legs. In a dish on the kitchen-table lay part of a leg of mutton. Blake caught it up and flung it on the floor.

"There you are old chap!" he said. "Just get busy, and get outside that."

The inn-keeper stood at the door and began to remonstrate.

"Here, Pedro!" said Blake. "After his body, boy!"

The bloodhound dropped the mutton-bone from his jaws, and, raising his great head, very deliberately stole towards the inn-keeper.

With a cry of fear, the man turned on his heels and fled from the room.

Blake burst into a roar of laughter.

"Good dog, Pedro!" he said; "that put the breeze up him. Get on with your dinner, old chap!"

Pedro needed no second invitation. His great jaws closed on the mutton-bone like steel traps, while his tail wagged to and fro in sheer contentment.

Blake found the inn-keeper hiding behind the bar and shaking with terror.

"Come out of there!" he said; "he won't hurt you. Here you are; go and buy another mutton bone."

So saying, the detective pushed a note into the man's hand.

"And now," said Blake, when the inn keeper had somewhat recovered from his fright, "I want to talk to you. There is a big stone house standing all alone in its own grounds about two miles from here, near the shore. Do you know anything about it?"

"Ah! You mean the haunted house, sir," said the inn-keeper, sinking his voice.

"The haunted house!" repeated Blake. "What on earth do you mean?"

"Yes, sir! That is the house. It is supposed to be haunted. Nobody ever goes near it. Many years ago a murder was committed in the woods. For some time after it was empty; then it was bought by a foreign gentleman. But strange noises have been heard there at night-time."

"Ah!" said Blake, deeply interested. "And who is this foreign gentleman who owns it now?"

"Can't say, sir! He is very seldom seen; comes down in a car. As a matter of fact, nobody is particularly anxious to make his acquaintance; those things are best left alone."

"Rubbish, my good man!" said Blake contemptuously. "There are no such things as ghosts. What exactly do you mean?"

"Why, sir, I have told you. Strange noises have been heard, not only in the house, but even in the woods. Inhuman noises; they make one's blood run cold."

As if even the recollection had the same effect, the inn-keeper's teeth chattered, and he gave a quick shiver.

"And that is all you know?" asked the detective.

"That's about all, sir. As I say, those things are best left alone."

Blake eyed him narrowly for a moment. Was he speaking the truth, or was he deliberately lying? But he seemed a simple kind of fellow, and not the sort to be involved in any cunningly laid schemes.

Blake came to the conclusion that as far as he believed he was speaking the truth; he honestly thought the house was haunted, and would not go near it at any price.

The detective scoffed at the idea of ghosts, only simple, superstitious folk took any notice of such things. But there was certainly some mystery surrounding this house, and he felt sure that it was connected in some way with Tinker's absence.

He must find out what had caused the place to earn its present evil reputation; he must discover to whom it belonged, and why the stranger with the missing finger had made his way there the previous night.

The detective called Pedro. The dog came bounding in to his master joyfully, licking his great chops with evident relish.

"Where's Tinker, Pedro?" said Blake.

The great hound pricked up his ears, darted an intelligent look at his master, and ran round the room, sniffing the floor. Then he came back to Blake again, and stood looking at him inquiringly.

"Well, where is he, Pedro?" said Blake again.

The animal began to whimper softly, and after running round the room again, sat down on his haunches in front of his master, and gazed up at him dejectedly.

Blake took from his hip-pocket a shiny little automatic pistol and fingered it lovingly. Then he replaced it.

"Come on, Pedro!" he said. "We're going to find Tinker."

Pedro gave a yelp of delight. He seemed to understand every word his master said. Together they passed out of the inn door.

Chapter 24
The Dene-Hole

BLAKE, with Pedro at his heels, strode quickly down the lane that skirted the right of the inn. It did not take him long to reach the gate in the hedge, and vaulting over it, he began trudging across the fields by the same path that he had taken the previous night.

He kept a sharp look-out on the newly ploughed ground on each side for footmarks that might indicate which way Tinker had gone; but nothing attracted his attention.

After nearly half an hour's walk, the gaunt outline of the house hove in view. Blake went more cautiously now; he did not know who might be on the look-out for trespassers, or whom he might meet in the vicinity of the house, and he did not wish his presence to be discovered.

Presently Blake found himself among the fir trees where he and Tinker stood the night before. The trees were crowded so closely together that very little light penetrated to the ground below, which was thickly strewn with leaves, in which their feet sunk without making any noise.

Through the rising trunks the broad, sweeping lawn ran down to the house, and Blake had an uninterrupted view without running any danger of being observed.

He stood gazing intently for some minutes at the forbidding-looking building. What was this mystery that surrounded it? he wondered. Who occupied the place? Was there any truth in those stories of strange noises being heard in its vicinity? And where was Tinker? Was he somewhere inside, or——

Blake's face grew hard. Yes, he must find Tinker; that was his first task; everything could wait until that had been accomplished. He began to take a rapid stock of his surroundings. Where exactly had he left Tinker the night before? There was no chance of discovering any footmarks; the thick carpet of leaves effectually prevented that.

It must have been about here, thought Blake, after carefully measuring his steps. This is where they must have stood, on the verge of the wood, and between these two great trees.

Would Pedro be able to pick up the scent from here? Nearly twenty-four hours had passed by—it seemed more like a week to Blake. It was rather a severe test for Pedro. Would he succeed?

Blake looked hasty round for the bloodhound. He could not see him immediately. He called him softly by his name. Through the trees there echoed to Blake's ears the sound of a low, savage growl.

The detective stood listening for a moment.

"Pedro!" he called again, and began threading his way through the trees in the direction of the sound.

Suddenly he came upon the animal a dozen yards or so away.

Blake stood still, silently watching him. Something was the matter with Pedro; along the ridge of his back the hair was bristling in a straight line, his ears were held back, and his tail drooped peculiarly between his hind legs.

He was sniffing at the ground around a big fir tree, and all the time the great hound kept up that deep, angry growl.

Half fascinated, Blake did not attempt to interrupt him. Nothing was there as far as he could see, only the great gnarled roots of the tree projecting about the carpet of dead leaves.

Presently the bloodhound began to steal stealthily away from the spot with his nose to the ground as if he were on the scent.

Blake watched him pause for a moment, undecided; then he went on again, and drew nearer and nearer the edge of the wood.

The animal was now on the fringe of the trees at the spot where Blake judged he had left Tinker standing last night. The dog thrust out his nose towards the wide, sweeping lawn which led down to the house, and sniffed the air suspiciously.

Again the detective called him.

"Pedro, Pedro!" he said softly.

But the faithful animal failed to answer to his master's call.

Blake began to creep quietly towards the spot, but at that moment the dog sank his head again and stole stealthily out into the open.

Greatly puzzled, he watched him as he went across the level stretch of grass. The animal moved in little spurts, running forward a few paces with his belly close to the ground, then pausing and nosing the air with his ears held back.

Nearer and nearer he approached to the house. Was he making for it? Was this Tinker's scent he had picked up, and was Tinker in the grim stone building?

Blake's hand went to his hip-pocket reassuringly. He would let the hound get a little nearer; he must make sure that it was the house that Pedro was heading for, then Blake would follow him up.

But it was Pedro's strange manner that was puzzling Blake. He had never seen the dog like this before. That he was uneasy he could see. There was something here which the dog could not understand, something that made those bristles stand up on his back and his tail hang straight down.

Was Pedro half afraid? But no! Pedro was too stout-hearted for that. Yet the dog was plainly greatly disturbed.

The animal was not within thirty yards of the house, and still he crept furtively nearer. Then suddenly he turned sharply to the right and ran towards the privet-hedge that skirted the right wing of the building.

For some moments Pedro nosed close up to the hedge, then he turned about, and, with his head held low, came creeping back across the lawn towards where the detective was standing.

Blake was by now utterly mystified. That the animal was on Tinker's scent he had no doubt; his quick mind immediately grasped the fact that after he had left him, Tinker had stolen across the lawn to the privet-hedge in order to get a closer view of the House.

That was all straightforward. And he could also understand the bloodhound retracing his steps, for it was evident that after satisfying his curiosity Tinker would return to his former position among the trees.

But what puzzled Blake was Pedro's strange behaviour. What other factor was present to account for that? There was something uncanny here.

He suddenly thought of the inn-keeper's words about the strange noises that had been heard near the house. What was this mystery? Was the place really haunted?

The dog knew something. There was some presence here that filled him with deadly anger, something—— If Pedro could only speak!

Blake pulled himself together. This wouldn't do; he was getting morbid. The mystery of the place was getting a hold on his iron nerves. He shook himself savagely and gave a dry little chuckle.

"Pah!" he muttered, "you're dreaming, Blake, my boy! You've got the wind up!"

He chuckled again, and the old familiar, resolute look came back into his face.

He glanced round again for Pedro. The dog was back again at the roots of the big tree, sniffing at the ground. What was it that was attracting the animal's attention?

The detective made his way towards him, and, kneeling down at the base of the tree, carefully scrutinised the spot.

Something had laid here; some body had pressed down the leaves. An ordinary person would not have noticed anything wrong, but to Blake's expert eyes it was plain.

Some pressure had caused that slight flattening of the leaves, and by the shape of it Blake judged that it was caused by the body of a man.

Yes, there was no doubt about it, for just where the damp earth protruded round the roots there was a slight depression as if, in falling, the man's arm and elbow had hit the soft earth first.

Who had laid there? the detective wondered. Had it been Tinker? And, if so, who had removed his body? Blake was just rising to his feet, when a piece of metal just showing above the leaves caught his eye.

He hastily dragged it forth and held it up, gazing at it with a frown on his face.

It was a cigarette-case made of solid silver. But that was not the point that was troubling Blake; he was wondering where he had seen it before, for it seemed familiar.

Then suddenly he knew. This cigarette-case belonged to Baron Rodanoff. He remembered now; he had offered Blake a cigarette that night the three of them had dined together at Dalgretty's.

There was no mistaking it; he would have recognised that peculiar design and workmanship anywhere.

Blake tried to think clearly. So Baron Rodanoff had been here, and Tinker also! What had happened? Whose body was it that had laid on the ground? Was it Tinker, or was it the baron? Had they fought together? And, if so——

Again the thought of foul play came to Blake's mind. He could not conceal his anxiety. He must get on the track of Tinker's body immediately. The great hound was still nosing among the leaves. Blake caught hold of him by the scruff of the neck.

"Pedro!" he whispered hoarsely. "Tinker! Where's Tinker? Good boy, find him then!"

The bloodhound lifted up his head to his master; his eyes were blazing madly, and the froth dripped from his red jaws. But that one look had been almost human. Blake knew that he understood.

Something was worrying the animal that Blake could not fathom. But he would find Tinker; he was sure of that.

He slipped the cigarette-case in his pocket and rose to his feet. The bloodhound had picked up another trail this time; he was moving off into the heart of the wood.

Keeping close behind, the detective followed him as he threaded his way in and out of the trees. The trail wound about in a perfect maze, and as he went along Blake's quick eyes noted the broken twigs and trampled ferns that strewed the path.

Several strong branches even that had been torn off lay dotted about. Who could possibly have done that? Something possessed of incredible strength. What could it have been?

The trees grew thicker and thicker; it was almost as dark as night. Blake had a difficulty in keeping up with the hound. Where he was leading him he could not guess.

But he trusted Pedro; the dog was on the scent—Blake knew that much. And sooner or later he would bring him to Tinker—dead or alive.

For ten minutes or more Blake forced his way through the wood; he could still see Pedro some yards ahead nosing the ground intently.

Presently, in front there appeared a small clearing, thickly overgrown with ferns and mosses; and suddenly he saw the bloodhound leap back a couple of paces, and stand growling fiercely, with his nose stuck forward.

Then very cautiously Pedro crept forward, and came to a standstill, with his body quivering.

A second or so later Blake pulled himself up with a start. At his very feet yawned a black, unfathomable pit.

He had not halted a second too soon—he was on the very brink of it; already the soft earth was crumbling beneath his feet.

So this was the explanation of Tinker's disappearance. He had been hurled down this frightful chasm; Blake had not the slightest doubt about that. Pedro's unerring sense of smell had led him right.

Blake knew all about these pits; this was one of the famous Dene holes that abound in that part of the country; they were dug many centuries ago by the Druids. They led into subterranean caverns, where they used to perform their pagan religious rites.

The detective stood trying to pierce the black opening beneath his feet; at the bottom of this pit, perhaps a hundred or more feet below, Tinker was lying crushed and bleeding.

At the thought of it the cold sweat stood out on Blake's forehead. He forgot that other strange presence that had been with them ever since they entered the wood, and which had caused that smouldering anger of Pedro. His young assistant was lying down there, crushed to death; he must get at him at all costs.

He looked around wildly for some means of descent. If he only had a rope! But there was nothing handy—nothing he could use. Yet he must get a rope from somewhere. The only thing to do was to hasten back to the inn. He could get one there, he knew. Blake turned to Pedro.

"Good dog!" he said. "Good dog, Pedro! Guard Tinker!"

The bloodhound growled deeply, and sank down with his great paws hanging over the brink of the chasm. Blake turned and sped through the wood back to the inn.

Chapter 25
Lost Underground

IT was many hours after Tinker had fallen down the Dene hole that consciousness began slowly to return to his numbed and bruised body. That last frantic clutch at the tree-root had saved him; it had checked his fall. All through that night he lay at the bottom of the pit, senseless and bleeding, but with no bones broken.

For a time he lay perfectly still, winking up at the chasm above him. He could not quite make out what had happened to him, or where he was.

Above him seemed to reach an enormous darkness, in the centre of which was a tiny circle of pale blue light. He idly watched it, not puzzling very much. Was he looking through the big end of a gigantic telescope?

It was all so peculiar. What was that tiny blue patch? Was that a star that had suddenly appeared on the edge? He watched it, and presently it disappeared again. But it had looked like a star.

Then that patch must be the sky; and it was night. Tinker did not know that, from a deep pit or coal-mine the stars can be seen in the daytime. It was now broad daylight.

Suddenly memories began to rush back into Tinker's mind. The recollection of that last awful drop down into this unfathomable black pit came back to him with renewed force. He could feel himself falling again; the dreadful sensation was almost unbearable.

Then he remembered with a shiver that frantic race through the wood, with that strange, fearful thing padding behind him. What was it? What could it have been? Had it also toppled over the brink of the chasm?

At the thought of that, a thrill of fear went through Tinker's body; perhaps it was lying beside him now, all crushed and mangled!

A feeling of sickness came over him; he tried to raise himself to glance around, but sank back with a groan.

His limbs were stiff and cold; he could not move them, the pain was so intense.

But he must raise himself; it was no use lying there. He tried again, gently moving his arms. He could hear the joints crack as he worked them to and fro; but he gritted his teeth and stuck it.

They were getting a little easier now; but the effort was torture.

However, he must not give way; he would keep on with his task. Presently the blood began to circulate through his numbed body.

The pain was excruciating; seemed to be shooting daggers through his body. He was bruised all over; every bone in his body seemed to be out of joint.

After a time his limbs moved more freely; he began gently rubbing himself from the waist downwards. He tried to raise himself again; this time he succeeded.

Sitting up, and supporting himself on his arms, he looked fearfully around. It was pitch dark: nothing could be seen but that tiny blue patch far above.

Then Tinker remembered the torch which he always carried in his pocket. He felt for it, and dragged it forth.

That was a stroke of luck; but perhaps it was smashed. It would be strange if it wasn't, after that frightful drop from above.

He pressed the button; a thin beam of light shot forth. He flashed it around, and stared into the darkness. He could see very little; the light seemed so feeble in that impalpable blackness. But there was no sign of that mangled shape that he so much dreaded. That was a great relief.

The walls of the pit seemed to rise up sheer on all sides; they seemed to be made of a dirty-white, chalky substance. But what was that black smudge just over there? Was it the entrance to a tunnel?

Tinker slowly and painfully rose to his feet. He felt as weak as a rat; he could scarcely drag his legs along.

Yes, it was a tunnel! It seemed to branch away right into the bowels of the earth. He flashed the torch over the walls; it was roughly circular, and was composed of that same chalky substance.

He came back again, and stared up at that luminous blue patch. How could he get out? Was it possible to scale those steep walls?

He glanced around for some foothold; but the cavern opened out like a great funnel, with the pit above him as the spout. He could not even find a means of getting to the mouth of the pit.

But he must do something; it was no use standing there. He might remain where he was for ever, and nobody would discover him. He must do something quickly, for already the pangs of hunger were getting unbearable.

He thought of the tunnel again. Where did it lead? It must lead somewhere. But it might be merely a blind alley. However, there was no harm in investigating it; very likely it would lead to the surface somewhere; or, at any rate, to another pit that was easier to climb than this one.

Tinker made his way again to the dark mouth of the tunnel, and began to proceed very cautiously along it, flashing his torch over the uneven floor on which he was treading. The air was intensely cold, and smelt rank and musty. He wondered how long ago it could be since somebody had made his way along this labyrinth; perhaps centuries had passed since then.

For some time Tinker proceeded thus. Often he stumbled, and just saved himself from falling; sometimes he put his foot in holes full of water, that seemed to percolate from the roof, and drew back shivering.

The tunnel wound in and out like a maze. He passed a number of smaller openings on each side; no doubt they were little tunnels, branching off from this main one.

But there seemed to be no ending to this labyrinth. Tinker stopped from time to time to peer ahead: if he could only see a patch of light suddenly appear in that awful darkness, how welcome it would be!

But no such patch of light appeared to buoy up Tinker's hopes; the darkness was as black as pitch.

He had been walking now for over half an hour; the sameness of the place was oppressive. This was no good, he thought, suddenly coming to a standstill. There did not seem to be any way out in this direction.

He had better turn and retrace his steps; perhaps, after all, there was some way of scaling that steep pit. At any rate, he must try again; that seemed the only hope.

Tinker began to retrace his steps. This was easy, he thought. The tunnel wound about a good deal, but he had only to follow the path he had come and it must bring him back to the pit's mouth.

He plodded on. His steps were getting rather erratic now; he had been walking for some time, and had had nothing to eat since yesterday evening, and the hardships he had undergone since were beginning to tell on him.

It was also intensely cold and damp, and the air was stagnant. The feeling of sickness was coming over Tinker again.

Would he never get to the end of this tunnel? Surely he should be getting near the pit's mouth by this time. Yet no patch of light hove in view to show where the exit was.

Ah! Here was a sudden bend; no doubt he would find the pit just round here. He sped on with renewed hope, only to find, on rounding the bend, that same all-pervading darkness in front.

Presently the tunnel swerved again, and Tinker hurried hopefully forward. But still no feeble light ahead met his straining eyes.

Then Tinker seemed to see pit-mouths staring out at him from all sides, and he rushed madly towards them, only to be brought up with a crash against the hard, solid walls.

Suddenly Tinker came to a dead stop. At that awful moment the actual truth flashed across his mind that he had somehow taken the wrong turning, and wandered off into one of the branch tunnels.

Once realising this, he did not stop to question if it were correct or not; he simply turned and sped off in the opposite direction.

A little way on the right he saw one of those black, yawning mouths. He would go down here, this might be the way. Yes, no doubt this was where he had made his mistake in the first place.

For another ten minutes Tinker stumbled frantically on; sometimes the roof of the cavern came so low that his head crashed against the hard surface, and he had to crouch down. At another time he floundered down two or three steps, rudely cut in the chalk, which he hadn't noticed.

Then Tinker's legs failed him; he could not go any further. He leant against the damp wall, exhausted, panting for breath; and he knew then that he was lost—lost in this frightful labyrinth, where no living thing ever dared to penetrate.

Then, to add to his horror, the feeble light of the torch slowly faded away into the impalpable blackness of night.

So this was the end: he was to die here alone! Perhaps his body would never be found; in fact, it would be rather impossible to discover him at all. To the outside world he would have disappeared, leaving behind no trace of the awful fate that had befallen him.

What would his beloved master think when he never returned? Would he search for him? But where would he look?—where could he look? He would never be able to find him; and, if he ever did, Tinker's eyes would have long closed on his short, eventful existence.

He would never see Sexton Blake any more! And, at the thought of this, Tinker could no longer contain himself. He raised his voice, and from his parched throat a wild, despairing cry rang out through those subterranean vaults.

It seemed to Tinker as if that one dreadful cry of his had wakened a thousand devils. The tunnels seemed alive with piercing voices, which echoed up and down until they gradually subsided once more into deathly silence. He remained listening fearfully while the echoes gradually ceased. The stillness now seemed all the more oppressive. Had they really been merely the echoes of his own voice?

He strained his ears painfully. Was that his fancy, or did he hear something moving away there in the darkness?

No! This time he heard it distinctly, those soft, stealthy, padding steps coming towards him; he heard that half-human snarl again.

Cold, clammy beads of sweat dripped into Tinker's eyes. What was it? What could this thing be? Then suddenly he knew; it was the horror he had encountered in the woods the night before! This ghastly thing was coming towards him, softly padding down that silent corridor.

Tinker did not try to move; he was transfixed. He opened his mouth, and tried to shout the name of his beloved master; but his voice only sounded in a hoarse, gurgling whisper:

"Blake! Blake!"

Then he felt that he was raving mad; he laughed a hysterical, croaking gurgle, and sank to the ground.

For a brief moment his fevered brain mocked him with the sound of Blake's voice echoing some distance along the corridor.

Then he remembered no more.

Chapter 26
Too Late?

IT did not take Blake long to find his way back to the inn after leaving Pedro on guard at the mouth of the Dene hole. He had never run so fast before. The thought of his young assistant lying there at the bottom of the pit, crushed and bleeding, added wings to his feet. He covered the ground in record time.

The innkeeper saw him coming down the lane, and immediately beat a hasty retreat into the bar parlour.

"Hi!" shouted the detective breathlessly, as he got to the door of the inn. "Come here! Get me a rope! Don't stand there gaping; get a move on! Quick, or Pedro will be after your body!"

The man wanted no further persuasion; he could not see Pedro anywhere about; but the threat was enough.

He did not understand why this strange, masterful man wanted a rope so badly; but it was best to humour him; he seemed a dangerous character.

The innkeeper backed nervously towards the yard-door.

"There is a rope in the stable, sir!" he said.

Blake vaulted over the bar and rushed after him.

"Here!" he said, grasping the innkeeper by the arm. "I'll get it. You go and get some food—cheese, bread, biscuits anything! Do it up in a small parcel—and quick!"

He gave the man a push that sent him flying into the kitchen. If anyone had asked the detective at that moment why he wanted food, he would have been at a loss for an answer.

Yet he really wanted it for Tinker, for at the back of his mind was the vague, notion that Tinker could not possibly be dead. But he did not stop to think; striding to the stable, he flung open the door.

A coil of stout rope was hanging from a nail on the wall; Blake caught hold of it and turned it over; altogether there were about fifty yards.

"This is the stuff!" thought Blake.

He glanced towards the kitchen; the man was busily slicing up a piece of beef.

"Get a move on!" shouted the detective, by way of encouragement.

Then, pulling the end of the rope free, he began to tie knots along it at distances of about a yard.

In about five minutes he had completed the task, and, picking up the coil, he flung it over his shoulder and returned to the kitchen. The innkeeper was just tying the string to the brown paper parcel.

"Good!" said Blake. "That will do!"

He snatched up the parcel, and, without a word, rushed out of the house. The innkeeper gazed after him in astonishment; then he shook his head and tapped his forehead significantly.

"Mad!" he muttered, with an air of conviction. "Quite mad!"

It took Blake even less time to get back to the Dene hole than it had taken him to get to the inn; the way was getting familiar now, and he knew the most direct path.

He found Pedro where he had left him a short time before, on guard at the brink of the chasm. The animal wagged his tail by way of recognition.

Blake picked up a piece of clinker lying near by, and tied it securely to the end of the rope. Then he dropped it over the side and began paying out the rope. What a great depth the pit must be! He began to wonder if the rope would be long enough. There was not much left now; would it hold out? Then presently the rope began to sag, and he knew that the clinker had touched the bottom.

Blake glanced round. About half a dozen yards away was a stout fir-tree; he backed towards it, letting the rope run through his fingers as he moved away from the pit.

He had just sufficient for his purpose. Flinging the end of the rope round the trunk of the tree, he tied it securely, then leant his weight against it. Yes, that would do; it would hold him all right.

Tying the parcel round his neck, Blake took one more glance around, then lowered himself over the chasm.

"You stay here, Pedro," he said. "Good old fellow!"

Pedro, who had been anxiously watching his master, sank down on his belly, and with his nose between his paws, began to snivel.

"Good dog, Pedro!" said Blake again, and began his descent into the pit.

He found his task quite easy; the knots in the rope gave him a good grip, and prevented his hands from slipping.

Down he went, lower and lower! The mouth of the pit gradually became smaller and smaller, until presently it was merely a faint, luminous patch above.

He was just wondering if he would ever reach the bottom, when suddenly he felt his feet touch the solid earth.

He glanced about apprehensively. How dark it was! He could see nothing but blackness. He flashed his torch around. Where was Tinker? There was no sign of him.

But something had fallen down here quite recently, that was certain. There was a sprinkling of debris on the bottom that had been displaced from the sides.

Blake stooped down and examined the ground; it was composed of a chalky substance, and footmarks did not easily show on it. But here was something. This was a piece of soft earth that had fallen from above, and someone had trodden on it, for it was flattened out to the shape of a sole of a boot.

Was this Tinker's footprint? It looked about his size, and it must have been made quite recently. Then where was Tinker?

He stared about him again. Ah, what was this? A tunnel running into the earth. Had Tinker gone along there? With the aid of his torch, the detective crept cautiously a little way down the opening.

He paused a moment, and shouted, "Tinker! Tinker!" and waited until the echoes had died down. He listened intently. But no Tinker answered.

What should he do? Had Tinker lost himself down here in this loathsome place? Blake knew all about these caves; sometimes they reached for miles underground.

He remembered once visiting the Chislehurst Caves; there were miles and miles of tunnels there that had never been explored. Perhaps this one was even a prolongation of those.

But it was too dangerous to penetrate any further into this noisome labyrinth. What should he do? Suddenly Blake thought of Pedro. That would be the thing! Pedro might pick up Tinker's scent, and lead him straight to him. He would get Pedro.

Blake hurried back to the pit-mouth, and began to scale the rope. It was harder work going up than coming down, but the knots gave him a good hold.

Presently he emerged again at the surface, puffing somewhat from his efforts, and with the skin chafed from his knuckles, but otherwise unhurt.

He took a deep breath, and filled his lungs with the fresh air. How gloriously pure it seemed up here after the fetid atmosphere below. However, there was work to be done!

"You're going down there, Pedro," said Blake, pointing to the gaping pit.

The dog wagged his tail excitedly, as much as to say:

"I knew you'd want me. I'm ready!"

Blake began hauling up the rope until the clinker appeared again. Then he undid it, and taking a scarfpin from his pocket, made a sling for Pedro. Fixing it securely round the animal's belly, he lowered him down the pit.

Presently the rope sagged, then followed a series of jerks. The detective smiled to himself; Pedro was already trying to get free to follow up the scent.

Blake let himself down again, and a few minutes later touched bottom. Pedro was struggling furiously to get loose. He undid the fastening; but he did not let the dog go; he tied his handkerchief to his collar, and held him back.

"Now, Pedro!" he said, "where's Tinker? After him, boy!"

The dog growled excitedly, and began pulling Blake towards the entrance to the tunnel.

"Pedro's on his track," thought Blake. He felt a pleasant thrill of excitement; the hope of soon finding Tinker spurred him on.

Tinker was alive, he felt sure. In some marvellous way he had escaped being smashed to pulp after that dizzy fall from up above.

Of course, he might be very much hurt: but the fact that he had been able to walk proved that he was not dead; otherwise Blake would have found his poor mangled body lying at the bottom of the pit.

What a frightful place this was; so black was it that the light from his torch only intensified the darkness about him; he could not see where he was going. But Pedro knew; he trusted Pedro implicitly.

It seemed to Blake as if he were in a maze; he passed quite a number of small tunnels that branched off on the left and right. Several times it seemed that he was going over the same ground again.

Twice Pedro had deliberately turned about, and, with his nose on the ground, had gone back again.

They still continued on, traversing the dark, silent corridors. They had been underground for nearly an hour now; Blake was beginning to feel anxious, yet Pedro still led on as if he were quite certain of himself.

Then suddenly the detective's head came in contact with the roof; he gave a sharp exclamation, and went more carefully, bending his body until the roof rose again.

Suddenly Pedro stopped dead still.

Blake flashed the light on him; the dog was standing tense and quivering, with his nose thrust forward and the hair along his back bristling in the same strange way as it had done an hour or so ago in the wood.

Then he gave vent to that low, ominous growl, and began to move stealthily forward. Wondering what had so disturbed the animal, Blake crept after him, holding tightly to the handkerchief that was tied to his collar. Suddenly through those gloomy corridors a ghastly cry rang out.

Blake stood stock still, petrified, his ears straining painfully as the dreadful cry echoed up and down the tunnel.

The next moment the handkerchief slipped from his grasp; Pedro had sprung away into the darkness with a fierce, savage snarl.

"Tinker! Tinker!" shouted Blake madly, blundering forward with his torch flashing on the ground in front. "Tinker, where are you!"

At that instant the cavern was filled with a frightful din. A fierce struggle was going on in the darkness somewhere in front; there were ghastly snarling screams, and a rushing to and fro, as if Pedro were being dragged over the hard surface of the tunnel.

But above the awful din rose always that deep, throaty baying of the great bloodhound, as he fought that grim, unseen death-struggle in the black abysmal caverns of the labyrinth.

Pedro had at last come to grips with that strange, invisible foe that he had been relentlessly following through the wood.

But Blake had no ears for this gruesome struggle; at that moment, he had stumbled across a body lying close to the cavern wall, and flashing his torch on it, stood staring down at the white, upturned face of his young assistant.

Chapter 27
"Imprisoned"

FOR a moment Blake could not move; as he stood staring into Tinker's upturned face a great lump came into his throat. Had he arrived just too late? Was Tinker dead? Had he tracked him right through these dark winding tunnels but to find that Tinker had passed beyond mortal aid?

Suddenly Blake knelt down beside the still form, and, placing his hand over Tinker's heart, remained thus, scarcely daring to breathe.

Presently a great look of joy came into his face. Tinker still lived; Blake's sensitive hands had felt that tell-tale flutter of the heart which told that life was not yet extinct.

It would be a fight to bring him round. Tinker was in a bad way. But while there was life there was hope; he must work like a Trojan.

Propping Tinker's head on his knee, Blake took a brandy flask from his pocket and forced some of the fiery liquid between Tinker's closely clenched teeth.

Then he began rubbing and slapping his cold, stiff hands and legs, and working them about, in an endeavour to restore the circulation.

Five or ten minutes went by; Blake worked unceasingly; every second told; he must not stop; he was dragging Tinker back from the grave.

From away down the tunnel that echoing noise of that grim, savage struggle still came to his ears: above those demoniacal screams sounded always the ferocious baying of the great dog.

A sickening thought shot through Blake; had Pedro at last met his match? Was this strange thing with which he was fighting for dear life too much for the gallant animal?

Very likely he was fighting grimly there, and listening in vain for the familiar footsteps of his master to turn the tide of battle.

Well, Pedro must fight it out alone; Blake could not lend a hand. Tinker required all his aid; and until Tinker was safe the brave dog must fend for himself. But Blake felt a great surge of pity for his beloved dumb friend.

He glanced at Tinker's white face again. Was that a flicker of the eyelids—just a faint movement of the white, upturned pupils? Yes! There it was again—quite unmistakable this time.

Hastily Blake dragged out the flask again, and poured a few more drops of brandy between his teeth.

A moment later Tinker's eyes quivered and opened, and he gazed wonderingly at the detective. Then he spluttered feebly, and tried to sit up.

Blake sank against the wall, breathing heavily; at last Tinker was safe. But the effort had exhausted Blake; he leant limply against the wall, and rested in sheer fatigue.

And from the end of the tunnel came the low sobbing of the great bloodhound, but those other sounds had ceased; all was now quiet.

Presently Tinker spoke; his voice came in a hoarse whisper.

"Is that you, guv'nor?" he asked.

Blake put his hand reassuringly on his young assistant's arm.

"Yes, Tinker," he said; "it's me, right enough."

For some moments neither spoke. Blake began wiping the sweat from his forehead with his handkerchief; then he took a pull at the flask, and felt stronger.

"How are you feeling, Tinker?" he asked. "Can you stand up yet? Let me help you!"

He put his hands under Tinker's arms and pulled him to his feet. Tinker leant gasping against the wall of the cavern.

"How did you get here, guv'nor?" he asked slowly. "Can't think straight yet."

Blake chuckled drily.

"Don't try to think yet, Tinker, my boy!" he said. "You'll be all right in a few minutes."

The sobbing moan of the bloodhound still sounded in the distance. Tinker heard it, too, and a shiver of fear shot through his body.

Suddenly he remembered that grim shape that had haunted the passage. Blake's quick eyes noted Tinker's sudden fear.

"That's all right now, Tinker," he said reassuringly. "Don't worry; that's Pedro making that noise."

"Pedro?" repeated Tinker.

"Yes! I'm afraid he wants some assistance. Just wait here a moment while I go along to him."

"Don't leave me here, guv'nor!" whispered Tinker nervously. "I'm all right; I'll come along with you."

He tried to move, but he would have fallen if Blake's hand had not been there.

"Just hold on to me, Tinker," he said. "That's the style; now we're moving."

Half-supporting his young assistant, Blake moved forward in the direction from whence the sound proceeded. Presently he heard Pedro a few yards ahead in the darkness.

"Lean against the wall, Tinker," he said; "that's right. Now for Pedro."

He stepped cautiously forward, flashing his torch around. In the feeble circle of light a strange scene met Blake's eyes.

Lying on the cold floor of the cavern was the monstrous, hairy form of a great baboon, and sprawled across it was the body of Pedro.

Blake took a step nearer, and gazed repugnantly at the uncouth creature. It was dead now, dead as a door-nail; yet as he looked at its gigantic limbs and its huge size the detective suddenly understood what a fearful odds the brave dog had been up against.

But what was the matter with Pedro? The dog was still sobbing softly, but he did not attempt to move.

Blake knelt down and looked more closely at him; the great bloodhound's teeth were buried deeply in the creature's throat.

So that was how Pedro had won his great fight; he had taken that awful strangle-grip on the creature's throat from the commencement. And once he took that grip Pedro never let go.

Blake began to have some idea now of the fury of that struggle.

Driven to frenzy by the dog's remorseless grip, the creature had tried every possible means to fling him off, rushing madly to and fro in this silent tunnel, and beating the bloodhound's body against the hard walls and ground.

Yet Pedro's grip had never slackened; he had won against fearful odds by sheer tenacity.

"Pedro!" whispered Blake coaxingly. "Good dog, Pedro! Leave go, boy!"

But the dog took no notice of his master. Blake caught hold of his collar and gently pulled him away.

The bloodhound rolled over on his side, with his tongue hanging out, absolutely exhausted and "beat to the wide."

As Blake looked at the faithful animal tears of gratitude came into his eyes. Pedro had again turned up trumps; Blake knew that he had fought that grim fight for his beloved master and Tinker.

He stooped over the animal and felt his bruised body. Fortunately, no limbs seemed to be broken; but poor Pedro had "been through the mill," and his coat was ripped and torn and covered with blood.

Very gently Blake lifted the great dog in his arms and stumbled back to where he had left Tinker.

"Tinker," he whispered, "Pedro has had rather a rough house; I shall have to carry him for a time. Let's get away from this spot. Can you manage to hold on to me?"

"I can manage all right now, guv'nor," said Tinker; "but I'm mighty hungry and thirsty."

"I've got some grub, Tinker," said Blake; "and we can find some water along here. But let's get away from this place first."

They made their way slowly down the tunnel until they came into a wider one, and there Blake stopped where some water trickled down the sides of the wall, and put Pedro down.

"Get busy on these sandwiches, Tinker," said Blake, handing him the parcel; "and you'll find this water quite clean. There's a pool on the ground here, and it's well filtered through the chalk."

The detective soaked his handkerchief in the water, and began to bathe Pedro's bruised body. The animal was slowly recovering from his exhaustion, and licked his master's hands in gratitude.

At last the dog took a long drink of the refreshing water, and started to lick his wounds.

"You'll do," said Blake. "Gallant old veteran!"

He turned to Tinker, who was munching stolidly in the darkness as if he had never eaten before.

"Don't eat them all, Tinker!" he laughed; "save a little for Pedro; I expect he's hungry."

"Right you are, guv'nor!" said Tinker, and Blake noted with a feeling of satisfaction that the words sounded more like Tinker's old self; "I ain't eating them all. But, by gum, I've never been so hungry in my life!"

"And never so frightened, Tinker!" said Blake slyly.

"But, guv'nor——" began Tinker.

"Nuff said, Tinker!" interrupted Blake: "don't let's talk now. We'll get out of this frightful dark hole first, and talk after. The place is driving me crazy."

"It would," said Tinker, "if you'd spent all night and half the day here. But how did you manage to get down the hole, guv'nor?"

"By a rope, of course, Tinker. That's why I'm in a hurry to get back; it'll be good to breathe the fresh air once more. Ready?"

"Yes!" said Tinker.

"Right! Pedro, good dog! Which way, Pedro?"

Poor Pedro was still in rather a shaky condition; but he was a game animal, and knew what was required of him.

Blake did not have to hold him back this time, however; Pedro was too tired other than to patter on silently just in front of Blake and Tinker.

So they wended their way back through the maze of those dark, tortuous passages. Neither of them spoke much; Blake's one desire was to get out in the open once more; the labyrinth filled him with a sense of nausea.

When, on rounding a bend, he at last saw that faint patch of light ahead he could hardly repress a sigh of relief and thankfulness.

A few minutes later the three of them stumbled into the circle of light cast by the yawning mouth of the pit.

For one incredible moment Blake gazed up at that great circular shaft; then he rubbed his eyes and looked again.

Yes, he was right. The rope had gone! Somebody had hauled it up from the top. They were imprisoned in this appalling subterranean chasm.

Chapter 28
The Baron's Triumph

IT is necessary here to pause a moment and return to the doings of Baron Rodanoff and his felonious associates.

When Dulac suddenly recognised Bill Dykes on Vauxhall Bridge he was on his way to the house in Kennington, from which Dykes was just returning.

That finding of Dykes had lifted a great deal of anxiety from his mind; while Dykes was at large their plans were in danger.

At any moment he might be arrested for the Soho murder, and then "the fat would be in the fire" with a vengeance, for he would no doubt not hesitate a moment to split on his companions.

Dulac had little difficulty in persuading the ruffian to accompany him to Denesford.

He would be safe there for a time; at any rate, he would run less chance of discovery there than he did in London.

Besides, Dulac only wanted secrecy for another ten days or so, and after that he did not care what happened, as far as Dykes was concerned.

So eager was he to get Dykes safely away, that he did not hesitate to hire the taxi to take them all the way to Denesford; expense was nothing when it meant security.

A certain feeling of cautiousness, however, made him dismiss the cab before they reached the house, and the two continued their way on foot.

Dulac learned that Baron Rodanoff had arrived safely with Granite Grant some hours previously, and he went immediately to impart the news of Dykes' recovery.

The Baron could not conceal his satisfaction at this piece of news.

"Everything is going swimmingly now, Dulac," he said. "I don't think that fellow Blake, with all his cuteness, will be able to stumble on this spot. I must confess that I had misgivings last night; I even quietly warned Reval, at the club, to be prepared for the plot to fall through. He had made all arrangements for us to get across to the Continent at a moment's notice. Now we have only to keep this fellow Grant concealed here for another ten days, and the Foreign Office will be effectively snookered. What a state Sir Vrymer Fane must be in!"

Baron Rodanoff rubbed his hands together with great satisfaction, and smoked his cigar in silence for a time.

"Where have you put Grant?" asked Dulac presently.

"He is locked in the next room," said the Baron.

"Is it safe?" asked Dulac. "You know what a tough customer he is."

"I know that," said Baron Rodanoff. "I have put Denvers in there with him. We have tied him up well, and Denvers is armed. You see, there is no better place."

Dulac thought for a moment or two. Suddenly he looked up.

"How about putting him in that room downstairs where you keep that baboon?" he suggested. "The window is securely barred, and the floor is stone-flagged. There is not the slightest chance of his getting out of there."

"That's certainly a good idea," said Baron Rodanoff thoughtfully; "but where shall we put the monkey?"

"Lock it in one of the empty rooms for the time," said Dulac. "Old Mason has got it well under his control. It feeds out of his hand."

Baron Rodanoff got up out of his chair.

"I think that is a good plan," he said. "Let's go and see old Mason; we'll ask him what he thinks. And I should like to see the brute; I haven't seen it for years."

They found Mason downstairs in the company of Bill Dykes. Mason was the Baron's old valet; he had followed his master about all over the globe, and had been mixed up in many of his numerous escapades.

On one of these, in the Congo a few years before, they had come across the baboon. The animal was then a young, agile, little creature, and had caused them considerable amusement.

The baron had brought it to this country and placed it in the house at Denesford in charge of Mason, who was now getting too old to follow his master's fortunes.

The baboon, however, was no longer a plaything; it had grown to a gigantic size, and Mason was the only person who could manage it. The strange noises which the creature made were responsible for the house getting the reputation of being haunted.

This latter fact rather pleased the baron; it gave the house a seclusion which fell in with his plans.

Mason rose unsteadily to his feet as Baron Rodanoff entered. He led such a solitary life down at this lonely spot that even the company of a ruffian like Bill Dykes was a good excuse to celebrate the occasion, and they had been drinking together heavily.

"Mason," said Baron Rodanoff, "I want to put the monkey in one of the spare rooms upstairs for a few days. Is he quite docile?"

"Well," said Mason, scratching his head, "he is and he isn't. I can generally manage him all right; but sometimes he gets hasty fits of rage. He's mighty strong, and I sometimes wonder what would happen if he started throwing his weight about."

"Let's have a look at him," said the baron; "I haven't seen him for a long while; the brute must have grown considerably."

"He's a handful, I can tell you!" said Mason, taking down a heavy whip and leading the way.

The three of them, with Dykes following behind, went down a flight of steps, and paused outside a heavily barred door, in which was a small iron grating.

A hurricane lamp was burning outside in the passage, and the light shining through the grating fell on a heap of straw, in one corner of which was reclining the great baboon.

The animal seemed quite docile and contented, and sat blinking up at its visitors without attempting to stir.

"By Jove!" muttered Baron Rodanoff, "what a size the brute has grown. I shouldn't have thought it possible. Aren't you afraid to enter, Mason?"

Mason, who was somewhat intoxicated, appeared to take this remark of his master as a sort of challenge.

"Afraid?" he laughed scornfully; "not me! Why, the animal feeds out of my hand! You just watch!"

He shot back the bolts, took down the hurricane lamp, and entered the chamber.

For a few moments the creature took no notice of his presence, but sat there unconcerned, blinking cunningly at his keeper.

This had the effect of throwing Mason off his guard; out of sheer bravado he went up to the animal and prodded it with his whip.

"Get up, Bojo!" he said. "Come, show yourself, my boy. There's some gentlemen to see you."

The great baboon rose clumsily to his feet and tried to move his ungainly body out of reach of his tormentor. Mason laughed drunkenly.

"Come on, my pet!" he cried. "Don't be shy!"

He turned to the baron, who was standing at the open door.

"He ain't used to company, sir," he said, "but you see, he's quite tame."

But Baron Rodanoff was evidently not so sure of this.

"You just be careful, Mason," he said, with a note of warning in his voice. "I don't like the look of the brute."

At the sound of his voice the creature seemed suddenly to become aware of the open door and the three strangers who clustered around.

A crafty look crept into his wicked little eyes; he began to snarl menacingly at Mason.

"Look out, Mason!" cried the baron sharply. "Come out, man!"

But Mason only laughed disdainfully.

"He's all right," he said, "it's only his playful little ways."

But suddenly the creature made a dive for the door. In a moment Mason had intercepted it.

"Back, back!" he cried, threateningly brandishing the heavy whip.

The baboon paused a moment, snarling fiercely and darting swift little glances between his keeper and the half-open door. Then it began to advance menacingly on Mason.

Mason raised his whip and cut at the animal fiercely. With a sharp cry of pain the baboon flung himself on his tormentor. Mason leapt aside with a hoarse shout and rained more blows on the animal.

Now thoroughly aroused, the baboon rushed wildly towards the door at which the three men were standing.

The baron, in his haste to get out of the way of the infuriated brute, jumped inside and overturned the table on which the lamp was standing. It fell to the floor with a crash, and the room was immediately plunged in darkness.

There followed a few minutes of frightful pandemonium in which the creature, driven mad with fury, flung its huge body about in the darkness. Then it crashed against the window, which shivered to splinters.

With superhuman strength it grasped the iron bars and wrenched them from the plaster. The next moment it had climbed through the opening and was speeding across the park.

The baron and his companions, now thoroughly alarmed, followed after as soon as they could collect their senses.

"Shoot the brute!" shouted Baron Rodanoff. "Don't let it escape."

All four of them raced madly across the level stretch of lawn in close pursuit of the animal. When among the trees, the baron, who was in front, suddenly came upon the beast.

The baboon turned on his pursuer with a snarl of fury, and grasping him in his enormous arms, flung him to the ground as if he were an infant. Then, hearing his enemies close behind, the animal quickly swarmed up a tree.

After searching for an hour or more they at last decided to give up the hunt until the morning.

The absence of the baron caused Dulac some uneasiness, but he reassured himself by thinking that he had already returned to the house.

However, when he arrived, Dulac found that Baron Rodanoff had not returned, and full of misgivings, Dulac and his companions set forth again to scour the woods.

Fortunately, Dulac stumbled across his master's body immediately he entered the trees. For the moment he thought that Baron Rodanoff had met with a violent death, but, finding that he was only stunned, they carried him back to the house, where, after a little stimulant, he revived, not much the worse for his experience.

Chapter 29
The Baron's Message to Blake

THE escape of the baboon caused Baron Rodanoff considerable anxiety. The next day he sent out his men in different directions to see if they could discover any news of the animal. But without avail; the baboon had absolutely disappeared; not a scrap of information could be obtained as to its whereabouts. Later on in the afternoon Baron Rodanoff met Dulac again, who had just returned from a fruitless search in the surrounding countryside.

The baron carried his hand in a sling, having had it badly sprained the night before when he met the creature in the wood. He was not in a very pleasant frame of mind.

"You have not been able to discover anything of the brute, I suppose, Dulac?" he asked darkly.

"No, baron; nothing at all. The thing seems to have been completely swallowed up. I cannot make it out."

The baron maintained a surly silence for a time; he was greatly vexed that Mason's foolhardiness should have so endangered his plans when, as he thought, they were working smoothly and were well on the way to a successful ending.

"The trouble is, Dulac," he said presently, "that the brute is bound to make its appearance somewhere sooner or later. Then the papers will make a nine days' wonder of it, and we shall have all manner of people meddling and nosing about down here."

"And in the meantime, is it safe to keep Grant here?" asked Dulac. "Hadn't we better remove him to some other place?"

"I was just thinking of that same question myself, Dulac. Perhaps we had better wait a little while and see what happens. It may be that we shall be able to recover the baboon without making much fuss."

Dulac was about to offer a further remark when he heard the sound of heavy footsteps hurrying along the passage towards them.

Both men sat listening intently while the footsteps approached, and the next moment Bill Dykes burst into the room.

Dykes gazed from one man to the other with a comical look of fright on his ugly face. He had evidently been running fast, for he was breathing hard, and was unable to speak for a moment. In his hand he held a tangle of rope, which he had hastily wound into a bundle.

"What the devil is the matter with you?" growled the baron angrily. "Have you seen a ghost, man?"

"The baboon!" muttered Dykes hoarsely, when he had somewhat recovered his breath. "It must be down that big hole in the woods."

The baron and Dulac stared at Dykes in astonishment.

"What are you talking about?" said the former at length. "Have you suddenly gone crazy?"

"But this rope was hanging over the side," said Dykes, as if that fact placed the matter beyond the slightest doubt. "There is a big hole in the woods, and——"

"He means the Dene hole, baron," said Dulac quietly.

"Ah, yes!" said Baron Rodanoff, becoming interested. "A very nasty spot to step into in the dark. But what does the man mean? Come on, don't stand there like a fool!"

"I'm just a-telling yer," said Dykes surlily, "the baboon must have got down that hole. I found this rope tied to a tree, and hanging over the side."

The baron got up from his chair and took the rope from Dykes's hand. He examined it curiously; evidently there was something in this after all.

But Dykes's story of the baboon climbing down the hole only amused him. Dykes was a simple fellow, and to his childish mind the rope seemed to explain the fact of the animal's disappearance.

But Baron Rodanoff was not so easily taken in.

"Do you mean to tell me," he said contemptuously, "that the monkey tied this rope to the tree and let himself down? Why, it's even knotted! You don't expect a monkey could do that, do you?"

Dykes looked disconcerted somewhat at this aspect of the case. Not having any further explanation to offer, he said nothing.

"However," continued Baron Rodanoff, "somebody must have done it. You did quite right in removing the rope. We must find out first of all who's down there. It is certainly most extraordinary. We will go and have a look at the spot."

The three men left the house and made their way to the centre of the wood, where they came across the pit in the clearing of the trees.

"The rope was tied to that tree and slung over the side, was it?" said Rodanoff, standing on the brink and gazing down the yawning chasm. "So the party concerned must be down there now. Well, whoever they are, I hope they're enjoying themselves."

The baron chuckled to himself over his joke, and stared curiously around. Presently his eye caught sight of the footmarks which were plainly imprinted in the soft earth around the rim of the pit.

"Seems as if quite a number of people had been interested in this historic spot of late," he said. "I wonder what's down there; I always thought it was half full of water."

He stared at the ground again.

"What do you make of these footprints, Dulac?" he asked presently. "Don't they seem like the feet of a dog?"

Dulac and Dykes both stooped down and examined the ground.

"You are quite right, baron," said Dulac, looking up. "They seem to belong to a big dog, too. Then there are several pairs of boot-marks, as if two or three persons had been here."

A look of fear suddenly crept into Dykes's harsh features; he glanced furtively from one man to the other.

"Perhaps it's Sexton Blake and his bloodhound!" he said.

Baron Rodanoff looked up quickly.

"What's that?" he asked sharply. "Sexton Blake? Why, it's impossible——"

But Baron Rodanoff was plainly perturbed by this unexpected turn of events. He stood silent for a moment with a frown on his face. Then he turned to Dulac.

"Run down to the village," he said, "and see if you can discover anything. Something must be known there of this. But be very cautious; if Blake has been there he may have men hiding close by. Be as quick as you can, we will wait for you here."

Without a word Dulac hurried off to make inquiries. Baron Rodanoff, with a dark scowl on his face sat down near the pit to await his return:

In less than an hour Dulac was back again, breathless and panting.

"Last night," he gasped, "two men and a bloodhound came to the Chequers Inn. The innkeeper is an old fool, but he thinks the elder man's name was Blake. They were both away all night. A few hours ago the elder man returned to the inn and borrowed a rope and went off immediately with the dog."

Dykes's evil face had gone ashy white; he was trembling violently and had to steady himself against a tree.

"That's Blake right enough," he muttered. "Blake, Tinker, and Pedro. They've tracked us down."

Baron Rodanoff swore below his breath.

"Well," he said savagely, "Sexton Blake's bitten off more than he can chew this time. He's down this hole, and down he'll stop."

"That's the stuff," muttered Dykes, with an evil grin. "Starve the hounds to death. Serve 'em right!"

The baron turned on him fiercely.

"You shut your mouth," he said. "I'm not thinking of your precious skin now. Sexton Blake is a clever fellow, and I rather respect him. But this time I've got him beat to a frazzle. He's going to stop down that hole for the next week, but I'm not going to let my guests go hungry, I'll drop him his dinner—he won't starve. But he's safe there, and there he'll stop until he can't do any more harm to my plans."

He laughed to himself again and rubbed his hands in great satisfaction. But Bill Dykes only glowered at him ominously; this sudden generosity of the baron did not please him at all, but he was too cowardly to offer any objection, and, determined to bide his time.

A sudden idea occurred to the baron, he smiled with great glee, and felt in his pocket.

Drawing out an envelope, he scribbled away for a few moments, still smiling blandly, then picking up a pebble, he placed it inside the envelope and dropped the missive over the pit.

Chapter 30
"An Exit"

FOR a while Sexton Blake was too appalled by this dreadful catastrophe to think clearly. The hope of soon being able to escape from this frightful hole, and of once again breathing the fresh air, had buoyed up his spirits all through that trying time when they were stumbling, through the winding maze of the dark and loathsome tunnels.

It had never occurred to him that his enemies would stumble across his whereabouts, and by removing the rope cut off his only means of egress.

As a matter of fact, so intent had he been on rescuing Tinker that he had quite forgotten the real object of his visit to this lonely spot.

Yet that some persons knew of his arrival at Denesford, and his subsequent movements, was quite evident.

They had followed him to this spot in the woods and waited until he and Pedro had disappeared down the chasm, then they had deliberately removed the rope, thus condemning him to a fearful lingering death.

The detective and his young assistant stared at each other with grim, careworn faces; even Pedro seemed to realise the tragic fate that had overtaken them, and stood listless and dejected with his tail between his legs.

But Sexton Blake was not the man to throw up the sponge without a struggle. Presently he pulled himself together, and a fighting look came into his eyes. He put his hand gently but firmly on his young assistant's shoulder.

"Tinker," he said quietly, "we're up against it, old chap. They've bottled us up nicely, whoever they are. They're mighty clever, I admit, but we're not dead yet, Tinker. We've got to think this out."

The quiet, reassuring tones of his master had the effect of a tonic on Tinker, even Pedro began to throw off his listless manner and take an interest in his surroundings.

"I'm not worrying, guv'nor," he said stoutly. "We've been in worse holes than this before now, and we're still alive and kicking."

Blake smiled at Tinker's remark.

"Not in a strictly literal sense, Tinker," he said. "This is the worst hole I've struck, I think. But you mean right, we've certainly been in some tight corners, so we won't despair."

As he finished speaking he caught sight of something white lying a few yards away. He stooped down and picked it up, and gazed at it curiously.

It was an envelope with a pebble inside of it, and written on it was a message scrawled in pencil.

"To Mr. Blake, with Baron Rodanoff's compliments," it read,—"Sorry I am compelled to offer you such rude hospitality, but it was your own choice. However, it will only be for one week, so please make yourself at home and as comfortable as possible. I think I shall have to trouble you for that hundred pounds after all. Meals will be served at the usual time."

Blake read this message through with an air of surprise. Then he handed it to Tinker with a chuckle of appreciation.

"Baron Rodanoff is always the perfect gentleman," he said quietly, "but he hasn't got the hundred pounds yet. That's still to be decided."

"But what does he mean, guv'nor," asked Tinker, "by saying that meals will be served at the usual times?"

"That's only one of his little jokes, I suppose," muttered Blake.

He gritted his teeth, and continued:

"You see, he mentions a week there. I've made up my mind, to discover Grant in a week; I've promised Sir Vrymer as much. Somehow it must be done, otherwise it will be useless."

But Tinker was still thinking over that phrase about the meals.

"If the baron can keep us out of the way for a week, then," he said, "there is no object in his starving us. Perhaps he really means to drop us something to eat."

"Perhaps he does!" admitted the detective. "That remains to be seen!"

But Tinker was quite right.

A few minutes later they glanced up to the mouth of the pit and saw a basket being lowered on a piece of cord.

Presently it came within reach, Tinker caught hold of it eagerly and opened the lid. Inside was a pot of tea, two cups, and quite a good feed.

"There you are, guv'nor," said Tinker joyfully, "tea has arrived. By Jove, I'm half beginning to like this Baron Rodanoff; he certainly believes in playing the game."

The string was jerked several times from the top. Tinker hastily removed the contents and the basket was hauled up again.

Stuck in the lid of the teapot was a piece of paper bearing the words: "dinner at seven."

It did not take Tinker long to have the food spread out in front of him. The steaming cups of tea refreshed them immensely, and, Pedro also had his share.

Then they made a hearty meal and felt better than they had done for some hours.

"It'll be mighty cold down here tonight, guv'nor," said Tinker; "I wish the baron would chuck us down some blankets."

But Blake did not answer, he was turning something over in his mind. Presently he spoke.

"Tinker, how on earth did that animal get down in that tunnel? It couldn't have fallen down this pit."

"Not likely, guv'nor!" said Tinker. "I hadn't thought of that before."

Blake thought again for some moments.

"Well," he said at length, "if it didn't come down this way there must be another entrance to the tunnels somewhere."

Tinker suddenly became very interested.

"You're right there, guv'nor," he said, "of course there must."

"And we've got to find it, Tinker. That's just our job. Somehow that ape got down below here, and if it could do that, then we can surely get out by the same way."

"But we'll get lost directly, we get into those beastly tunnels again," said Tinker with a shiver.

"We should, I admit that, Tinker. But how about Pedro? You're forgetting him. He doesn't make mistakes; and if we could once get him on the scent of the ape he would be bound to smell his way to the exit."

Blake looked doubtfully at the bloodhound.

"Poor old chap!" he said. "He's had a bad mauling, I doubt if he's got the strength to walk far."

But Tinker was now thoroughly excited.

"It's worth trying, guv'nor," he said. "After all, we shall never be able to stick this for a week, it's too awful to think about. We might as well have a shot at escaping, and the sooner the better."

"I'm determined on that already," said the detective quietly, "but I think we'd better wait until they send us the next meal. If we don't take the stuff out of the basket their suspicions will be aroused. We can start directly after that; it doesn't matter whether it's night or day, it's all one down in this benighted place."

Blake took out his watch; it was now six o'clock.

"We've just got an hour, Tinker, until they chuck us down some more grub. We'll wait about till then, and push off directly after."

That hour seemed an interminable time to Blake and Tinker, but it passed at last. Punctually at seven o'clock the basket was lowered into the pit, and Blake found quite a good spread prepared for them.

Instead of releasing the basket, however, Blake asked Tinker to hold it while he scribbled a hasty note on a piece of paper.

"With Sexton Blake's compliments," he wrote. "Baron Rodanoff's hospitality would be better appreciated if he would be kind enough to provide his guests with blankets."

"That will allay their suspicions," he said to Tinker. "The baron will think that we are quite resigned to our fate, and are making ourselves snug for the night. Besides, we may want them!"

They ate some of the food while they were waiting, then, about a quarter of an hour later, several blankets tied to a string were lowered into the pit. Blake undid the string, and it was pulled up again.

"Now," said the detective, "if we can't get out, at any rate we've got something to keep us warm for the night. Are you ready, Tinker? Off we go!"

They plunged into the tunnel again, with Pedro following the previous scent. Poor Pedro was tired out, and did not want any holding back this time; but the brave dog kept on gamely all the same.

They had not gone more than a hundred yards when the sudden noise of an explosion shook the cavern, then followed the sound of falling, earth and debris.

Blake and Tinker stood still with blanched faces until the sounds ceased.

"The fiends!" muttered Blake savagely. "They've blown in the mouth of the pit. We were only just in time, Tinker. Come on!"

They followed Pedro through the maze of tunnels through which they had passed before. They were compelled to go very slowly, for Blake's torch was giving out, and it only threw a dim; red light ahead.

Eventually, however, they approached the spot where Pedro put up such a splendid fight a few hours since.

The dog was still suspicious of his old foe, and moved very stealthily, with his hair bristling, as he made his way towards the body of the brute lying in the cold and silent corridor. Tinker could not repress a shiver of fear and repugnance.

"Now," said Blake, "I wonder if Pedro will pick up the scent?"

He stooped down and patted the animal.

"Good old fellow!" he said. "Which way now; Pedro?"

But the dog did not seem to answer to his master this time; the poor animal was plainly dead beat.

"Come on, old chap!" said, Blake coaxingly. "Nose him out!"

He gently pulled the dog towards the dead body of the baboon. Pedro resisted violently. He clearly disliked and mistrusted his vanquished foe. The detective then moved further up the corridor.

"On it, boy!" he said sharply. "On the scent, Pedro!"

Pedro cast an appealing look at his master, then sniffed listlessly at the floor. He pattered on a little way, and then began smelling again.

This time he did not lift his head, but continued his way silently up the tunnel, with his nose to the ground.

"I believe he's picked it up," whispered Blake. "Poor old chap! It's a shame to overwork him. But it must be done."

They held on in silence for a time.

Pedro was evidently following on the scent, although he did not betray his usual excitement. It was clear that he was not leading them in and out of these winding tunnels on a wild-goose chase.

Suddenly Blake stopped still, listening intently.

"Did you hear that noise?" he asked Tinker.

Both stood straining their ears. In the distance came the low, muffled beat of the waves on the long line of shore.

"The sea!" said Blake. "Come on, Tinker; we're almost free."

They went on again. Sometimes the noise of the breakers sounded loud, and sometimes far away. At times they lost it altogether. Blake knew that they must be pursuing an erratic path, owing to the wandering of the ape in the labyrinth. But it was best to trust to Pedro; sooner or later the scent must lead them to the exit.

Suddenly, on rounding a bend in the tunnel, the boom of the waves rose to a crescendo; the seashore was close at hand.

Hurrying forward, Blake and Tinker rounded another bend, and gave a gasp of great relief and joy. In front of them was a great gap of luminous blue light, from whence a glorious current of pure sea air swept inward.

They drew in their breaths and filled their lungs with a sigh of satisfaction. It was like wine after the foetid atmosphere in which they had been imprisoned for so many hours.

They climbed up the steep slopes towards the opening, and a few moments later were standing at the entrance to the cave. Before them stretched the sea, with its long line of foam-flecked billows breaking on the shore, and above reached the great dark dome of the sky, ablaze with innumerable stars.

They were free—once more!

Chapter 31
Whitehall Again

IT was noon next day when Blake and Tinker with Pedro, arrived at London Bridge. Before leaving Denesford, however, the detective had hung about the house where the baron was hiding, and had actually succeeded in getting a glimpse of Grant through the blind of one of the rooms and for this reason he had caught an early train to town.

They drove straight to Baker Street, where there were several things that required attention. Blake's first care was for Pedro. The dog had been badly mauled in his great fight in the tunnel, and there were two or three very nasty wounds.

After bathing them in warm water, Blake rubbed in salve, and Pedro quickly fell asleep.

While they were having a hasty lunch, Blake, who was reading the morning paper, caught sight of a paragraph that interested him. After reading it through again, he looked up.

"Just listen to this, Tinker!" he said, and commenced reading the following: "'We understand that an arrest has been made in connection with the murder of Joe Crick at Soho. The man will be formally charged at Bow Street this afternoon.'"

"Now what do you think of that, Tinker?" asked Blake. "I wonder if it's Bradley's doing. But what evidence can he possibly have? Whatever it is, I'm afraid he'll find he's making a fool of himself."

The detective finished his lunch at length, and, going over to the telephone, put the receiver to his ear.

"Hello!" he said. "Gerrard 004, please!"

He waited a moment, then began again.

"Hello! Is that you, Miss Valentine? This is Sexton Blake."

"How are you, Mr. Blake?" asked the actress.

"I'm quite well, thanks. I'm going to ask you to do a strange thing, Miss Valentine."

"And what is that, Mr. Blake?"

"I want you to ask me to dine with you again tonight at Dalgretty's, and to bring Baron Rodanoff along, too."

"Why, Mr. Blake," laughed the actress, "of course I will. I should like it immensely. But you mystify me altogether."

"I will explain everything when I see you, Miss Valentine."

"Then you have news—good news?" asked the actress eagerly.

"Yes, but you shall know all in good time. In the meantime, do not worry; everything is going well."

"But I am so impatient, Mr. Blake. What time shall you be at Dalgretty's?"

"At six-thirty sharp. Do not ask the Baron to come along until seven o'clock; it will enable us to have half an hour's quiet talk."

"Very good, Mr. Blake!"

"One other thing, Miss Valentine! Do not tell Baron Rodanoff that I shall be dining with you; I do not wish him to know. You understand?"

"Yes, yes! And yet I am more mystified than ever now, Mr. Blake."

The detective chuckled softly.

"Well, don't forget-six-thirty, sharp! Good-bye!"

Ten minutes later Blake was on his way to Whitehall Court. He did not have to wait there very long; in a few minutes he was shown up to Sir Vrymer Fane.

The statesman looked at the detective anxiously.

"Well, Mr. Blake," he said, "any news?"

"Yes, Sir Vrymer," said Blake quietly. "I believe that the last time I saw you here I promised to discover the whereabouts of Mr. Grant within a week?"

"Well, Mr. Blake; and you are finding the task hopeless?"

"On the contrary, sir, I have redeemed my promise long before that time has elapsed!"

Sir Vrymer Fane rose from his chair. His hand was trembling, but he made an effort at composure.

"Do you mean to say, Mr. Blake," he asked, "that you know where he is?"

He eyed the detective gravely for a moment, and went on:

"You are not joking, Mr. Blake? Remember, this is a very serious matter!"

"I am not joking, Sir Vrymer," said the detective calmly. "I said that I have discovered the whereabouts of Mr. Grant; but I have not rescued him."

"Ah! Then he has been abducted? And this other man is an impostor?"

"Quite so, Sir Vrymer!"

"And what do you advise, Mr. Blake? Is it possible to effect his release?"

"That is precisely why I have come to see you, sir. I propose to bring him along to you here tonight. It will be very late; more probably somewhere between two and three in the morning."

"Mr. Blake, if you can do that I will willingly stay here all night. But are you prepared to promise that?"

"Without the least hesitation, Sir Vrymer—but with one condition."

"And that is, Mr. Blake?" asked the statesman eagerly.

"That you lend me a fast car, and six reliable men."

"You shall have that, Mr. Blake; you shall have my own touring car. I will see to it myself."

He put out his hand to touch the bell, but the detective stayed him.

"One moment, Sir Vrymer!" he said. "I want the car outside Dalgretty's at a quarter past seven this evening."

"It shall be there, Mr. Blake. I promise you that."

"Thank you, sir! Then that is all."

"But, Mr. Blake, I do not know what your plans are; I am trusting you implicitly. If Mr. Grant is here by tomorrow we may rush him off immediately and save the situation. But, remember, there must be no fuss. I am in the dark absolutely as to what you know; but have you any idea as to who was responsible for Mr. Grant's abduction?"

"Yes, Sir Vrymer; a certain Baron Rodanoff!"

"Baron Rodanoff? Ah, I did not think of him! Yes, of course! Before the war he was closely connected with Central European politics. That accounts for much. Again let me impress upon you, Mr. Blake, the urgency of secrecy. In the affairs of diplomacy we play a big game, but it is played behind the scenes. We want nothing of this to appear in the Press: any publicity would be detrimental to our interests. When you have rescued Mr. Grant you will have rendered us a remarkable service. It is not desirable to take any proceedings against Baron Rodanoff and his accomplices. You understand that?"

"Precisely, Sir Vrymer. But, unfortunately, it may not be so easy to keep the matter entirely out of the Press."

"Why, Mr. Blake?"

"Because, sir, this man Joe Crick, who was murdered at Soho, was, I am convinced, concerned with the abduction of Mr. Grant. If my theories are correct, the man who killed him was also involved in the conspiracy. Furthermore, they were both employed by Baron Rodanoff. This afternoon a man is to be charged at Bow Street with being implicated in the crime. I do not know what the evidence will be; but I do know that he cannot be the guilty party. It seems, therefore, that the whole business must be dragged into court sooner or later."

Sir Vrymer, Fane was plainly disconcerted at this piece of information.

"You see, Mr. Blake," he said, "these things are quite apart from the ordinary course of justice. In the realm of international affairs we work without any regard to the common law of the land. Cannot something be done to smooth the matter over and prevent it from being discussed in the courts?"

The detective pondered deeply for some time; at length he looked up.

"If you will leave it to me, Sir Vrymer," he said, "it is possible that I may see some way out of the difficulty."

"Willingly, Mr. Blake! I will leave you to act as you think best."

"Thank you, sir. Then you will see that the car is outside Dalgretty's at seven-fifteen?"

"You may rely on that, Mr. Blake. And I shall remain here throughout the night until you come along or send me a message."

"I shall be along, Sir Vrymer; never fear!"

The statesman shook hands with Sexton Blake and saw him to the door, then he returned to his chair and sat thinking deeply.

Chapter 32
Bradley Disturbed

AFTER his interview with Sir Vrymer Fane at Whitehall, Sexton Blake drove straight to Bow Street. He wanted, if he could, to quash the charge against this other man before it came on for hearing; in that event, when the real murderer was brought to book, as he hoped he soon would be, the detective would not be dragged in to give evidence that would only result in Granite Grant's name being mentioned; then the whole affair would be dragged into the papers.

In the waiting-room at Bow Street Blake came across Inspector Bradley.

"You here, Bradley?" said Blake. "Then it is you who are making this charge in connection with the Soho affair?"

"Quite so, Mr. Blake," said Bradley. "I effected the arrest myself."

He looked pugnaciously at the detective, but Blake could see that he wasn't quite so sure of himself, as he pretended to be. He must have a talk with the man, and try to get him to listen to reason.

"Look here, Bradley," he said, "I'm deadly serious now; I don't want you to do anything stupid. After all, we're old friends. Now, what evidence can you possibly have to base a charge on? Just think! It won't do your reputation any good if you make a bloomer."

"I'm not making any bloomers this time," said Bradley stubbornly. "I'll tell you my evidence, Mr. Blake, if you like."

"Fire away, then!"

"Well, it didn't come out in the papers at the time of the inquest, but fifty quid in five-pound notes was found in one of Joe Crick's pockets, when he was picked up. I immediately sent a private inquiry round to the banks to find out if any notes with concurrent numbers had been changed recently. Well, it appears that a chap living quite near the scene of the crime changed two fivers with concurrent numbers on that same day that the body was discovered.

To cut a long story short, I had him searched, and there were another forty pounds in fivers in his pocket, and the numbers followed those which were found on Crick. He straightway confessed to stealing them from the pockets of the dead man; but he swears that the man was dead long before he arrived on the scene. But that don't wash with me; I've heard those tales before!"

"So you don't believe his story?" asked Blake.

The inspector shook his head dubiously.

"No, I don't!" he said obstinately. "It sounds rather fishy."

"It certainly does at first," agreed Blake. "But why didn't he take the other fifty? Why should he leave them in the dead man's pocket?"

"Didn't know they were there, I suppose," said Bradley.

"Precisely!" said Blake. "But if he committed the crime from motives of robbery, as you seem to suggest, then he would certainly have known they were there; at any rate, he would have made sure. That chap seems to me to be speaking the truth; no doubt he yielded to a sudden impulse. Seeing the notes sticking out of Crick's pocket, he grabbed them without stopping to think, and made off."

"There's a lot in what you say, Mr. Blake," agreed the inspector, scratching his head.

"Right!" said Blake. "Now about the fingerprints on the dead man's throat?"

"Oh, they're no use at all as evidence," said Bradley. "The experts say they're too indistinct to prove anything."

"I grant you that," said Blake, "that is, as far as the actual impressions of the fingers are concerned. But there's something they show which you can't get away from, Bradley."

"What's that?" sked Bradley quickly.

"The man who killed Joe Crick had only three fingers on his left hand; the fourth finger was missing."

"What?" exclaimed Inspector Bradley. "Only three fingers on his left hand? How on earth do you know that?"

Blake drew a portfolio from his pocket and took out the photograph of the fingermarks.

"If you look at that closely through a glass, you'll see what I mean, Bradley," he said. "In fact, you can see it without a glass. Look! Do you see those five marks there? Well, they correspond to the thumb and fingers of the right hand."

"Quite so!" agreed Bradley.

"Right! Now on this side you will see the marks made by the thumb and fingers of the left hand. You see, there are only four marks the thumb and three fingers."

"There certainly seems to be something in what you say," said the inspector, looking rather shaken, after gazing at the photograph; "but you can't call that very conclusive evidence."

"Don't you believe it, Bradley; that's conclusive enough. Now I'll tell you one other thing: I've seen the man who made those impressions on Joe Crick's throat, and I know the little finger of his left hand is missing; I've actually made certain of that with my own eyes."

"You have, Mr. Blake?"

"That I have! Now look here, Bradley, be a sensible chap! I'm not out for doing myself a good turn: don't think that. I actually know where this fellow's hiding; in fact, I'm going to have him arrested tonight."

Bradley did not know now whether he was on his head or his feet; Blake had got him thoroughly bewildered. He could only gaze at the detective in astonishment.

"Yes," continued Blake. "I am going to put some more evidence in your possession, Bradley. Joe Crick and this other fellow were in the Peacock Café on that very night Crick was killed. I found out all this from the barman there. They were both dead drunk, and were quarrelling violently over money matters; the barman heard Crick, threaten this other fellow that he would 'get even with him some day.' No doubt there was a bit of a fight outside, and Crick got the worst of it. That fact ought to save this other chap's neck. You're following what I'm telling you, Bradley?"

"Every word, Mr. Blake."

"Well, do you know why I'm telling you all this?"

"Don't quite see the point," said Bradley.

"I'll tell you, Bradley. If you like I'll put the whole matter in your hands; you can come along with me tonight and make the arrest, and you can take all the credit for it."

"Well, that's sporty of you, Mr. Blake, I must say. But I don't like taking the bread out of your mouth."

"Not at all, Bradley! You will be obliging me. I'm far too busy to fiddle about with this Soho affair; I shall be glad if you will take it out of my hands. I'm about to solve something far more important than that—the mysterious case of Mr. James Grant."

"What?" said Bradley, "you're still on that? But you're not sticking to the same old theories?"

"Oh, yes, I am, Bradley. And before many hours have elapsed I shall have proved them correct. But about this Soho business do you agree to come in?"

"Well, if it's like that, Mr. Blake, I certainly do. Thanks very much; it's very good of you. But you haven't told me everything yet?"

"Listen, then. A car will be outside Dalgretty's at seven-fifteen sharp this evening; we shall push off immediately. If you will be there, I'll tell you what is happening as we go along."

"I'll be there right enough, Mr. Blake!"

"Very good, then. You'd better not make it later than seven. Now, how about this other charge—what are you going to do about it?"

"You leave that to me, Mr. Blake. I'll settle that."

"Put it there, Bradley!" said Blake.

The two men shook hands, and Blake immediately left the inspector and departed for Baker Street, very well pleased at his afternoon's work.

He found Tinker at home and having tea by himself.

"Tinker," he said, "would you like to come down to Denesford tonight and see this job through?"

"That's me, guv'nor, every time!" said Tinker.

"Very well, then! A car will be outside Dalgretty's at seven-fifteen. You come along there and jump right in. Don't be late because I sha'n't wait for you."

"I sha'n't be late, guv'nor," said Tinker.

An hour later Blake left Baker Street to keep his appointment with the actress.

Chapter 33
Rodanoff Has a Shock

AS Sexton Blake strode again up the aisle of Dalgretty's sumptuous dining-room he could not help contrasting his present position with that of a few days ago, when he had last dined with the actress at this self-same restaurant.

Then he had seemed nowhere near a solution of the mystery with which he was grappling; all the issues had seemed confused and unrelated.

Certainly he had never for one moment doubted his ability to pull through with the task, which Sir Vrymer Fane had assigned to him under such strange circumstances.

Yet that he should now, after the lapse of a few short days, be on the eve of releasing the famous King's Spy and 'delivering the goods,' as it were, to Sir Vrymer Fane, seemed too good to be true.

The detective entertained not the slightest doubt that in a few short hours at the most he would be bringing Granite Grant back to London, safe and sound.

The touring car was already outside, and Bradley and Tinker and the six men were inside waiting.

Blake had delayed attempting the rescue for the simple reason that he wished to involve Baron Rodanoff in a great anti-climax.

Baron Rodanoff was no ordinary criminal, who could be tracked down and punished by the usual methods.

In his way he was just as courageous and resolute as was Granite Grant, for the two men played the same big game in the secret and hidden undercurrent of European politics.

Sir Vrymer Fane had expressly stated that he wished no publicity to be given to the drama in which Blake had played such an important part.

It must remain for ever but one more of those secret intrigues of those who pull the strings of international affairs.

For these reasons Blake had taken it upon himself to administer a bitter pill to the proud and haughty baron; it was a little personal triumph that he could not bring himself to forego.

He had felt a sneaking admiration for the baron until that last treacherous act of his in blowing in the mouth of the tunnel.

Blake did not know that the baron was not responsible for that; he could only regard it as a very dirty trick.

However, it made his position all the stronger. The baron would have the surprise of his life when he met Blake presently, for he must think that the detective and his assistant were lying at the bottom of the pit, buried beneath the mass of debris.

These were the thoughts that were surging through Blake's mind as he wended his way towards the table at which the actress was already sitting awaiting him.

"Ah, Mr. Blake!" she said. "I am dreadfully anxious to know what you have to tell me. Your 'phone message simply set me furiously thinking; but I am all at sixes and sevens. Please satisfy my curiosity."

"I certainly will, my dear young lady!" said the detective, sitting down beside her. "But, first of all, how long have we to talk before Baron Rodanoff arrives?"

"He promised to be here at seven, Mr. Blake."

"Well, we have just twenty minutes, so I will fire away. The most important thing which I have to tell you is that I have discovered the whereabouts of Mr. James Grant."

The actress caught her breath.

"Mr. Blake," she said, in a low voice, "is that really true?"

"Yes, it is really true. In fact, I promise to bring him to London within a few hours or, at any rate, early tomorrow morning."

"It all seems like a dream," said Miss Valentine, clasping her hands. "My mind is too confused to frame any questions. But then I shall see him soon—very soon now? And he is quite well? But where is he? What is the meaning of it all?"

The detective laughed softly.

"I am going to let Mr. Grant have the opportunity of answering all those questions when you meet him," he said. "I am sure he will be able to answer them much better than I can. But you know that his work is very important, and that he lives behind the screen, as it were, of the ordinary, everyday affairs of life. It was because of this fact, and also that he had undertaken a very delicate diplomatic mission, that led to his abduction."

"Then he has been abducted?"

"Yes, and is being forcibly detained. But I am off to secure his release directly I have seen Baron Rodanoff."

"But what has Baron Rodanoff to do with it?" asked the actress, in surprise.

Blake gave a dry laugh.

"Don't you remember our bet, Miss Valentine, on the last occasion we dined together here?"

"Yes, but that was to do with the Soho affair!"

"Precisely."

"Then you have won, and Baron Rodanoff owes you one hundred pounds?"[6]

"He will do very soon; unless I have made a great mistake," said Blake.

The actress was about to reply, when, happening to glance across the room, she saw Baron Rodanoff approaching.

"Here comes the baron!" she whispered.

Baron Rodanoff came across the carpeted floor with an air of preoccupation on his handsome face.

The detective's back was turned towards him, and he did not trouble to look closely at this third member of the party.

He was frowning heavily, as if some incident had caused him irritation and annoyance.

As a matter of fact the cause of this look of annoyance was a telegram, which at that moment was crushed in the pocket of his dinner-jacket.

He had received it earlier on in the afternoon from Dulac, informing him that the side of the pit had caved in during the night.

"So that was the end of Sexton Blake," thought Baron Rodanoff. "Well, it was rather a pity, but it couldn't be helped."

He rather respected the famous detective, as well as feared him. Sexton Blake was certainly a man to be reckoned with and worthy of his steel.

---

[6] £100 in 1920 is worth about £5,700.00 in 2023

Moreover, he had come very near wrecking the baron's carefully laid plans.

However, it was no use worrying over that now. The baron felt a tinge of regret at the thought of that brilliant intellect lying there at the bottom of the cold pit, with several tons of earth above him.

Yet, in a sense, it helped his plans; he was playing a safe game now, and a few more days would see it brought to a successful issue.

As long as Sexton Blake was alive there was always an element of danger present— even when he had got him safely bottled up in the pit. You never could tell what Blake was up to next; he was always springing surprises. But now——

Baron Rodanoff shrugged his shoulders, and, dismissing the subject from his mind, bowed to the actress.

"You have met this gentleman before, Baron Rodanoff," said Miss Valentine, as Blake rose to his feet.

Baron Rodanoff turned affably to the detective with a bland smile of welcome.

The next instant his face went livid and then turned grey; he swayed violently, and clutched at the back of the chair for support. Then, with a superhuman effort, he had recovered his usual sang-froid.

"I beg your pardon," he said, turning politely to the actress; "just a sudden twinge of my old complaint. I hope I have not alarmed you."

"Let us help you to a chair!" said Miss Valentine, greatly distressed at what she thought was a sudden attack of illness. "I am so very sorry. Perhaps you will take a little wine?"

"Yes, I will take a little wine, thanks," said the Baron, sitting down rather heavily; "but it is nothing, I assure you. Pray, do not distress yourself. I am quite well now."

He turned to the detective and stared him straight in the eyes. He was quite composed now, although the pallor still hung about his face. Blake could not but admire that iron self-discipline which had enabled him to carry the thing off so well.

"It is just these little attacks, Mr. Blake," he said, "that remind one that one is getting old. You, doubtless, are immune from such trifling ailments of the flesh?"

Blake's lips curled ironically.

"Well, you certainly did your best last night to make me immune from all earthly troubles," he said quietly.

Baron Rodanoff regarded Blake with a puzzled expression for a moment. Then he leant across the table and spoke in a low voice.

"I do not quite understand that last remark of yours, Mr. Blake," he said. "Do you refer to the caving in of the pit-mouth?"

"Exactly," said the detective.

"Then, Mr. Blake, believe me when I say that as far as I am concerned it was a pure accident. I knew nothing about it until an hour or so ago, when I received a message from one of my men."

Blake looked searchingly into the face of his vis-à-vis, as if he were probing into his mind. Then that last infamous act was not sanctioned by the baron; he was not responsible for that.

Either it was a pure accident, as he suggested, or else one of his men had taken the responsibility on himself to make sure that Blake and Tinker should never come out of the pit alive.

But it had been no accident, for he had plainly heard the explosion. Then it must have been the ruffian who had committed the Soho crime; Dykes was the one most likely to benefit by Blake's death.

Well, at any rate, his hours were numbered; Bradley would, soon have him under arrest.

"I am glad, Baron Rodanoff," he said drily, "that you have cleared yourself of that outrage. It was certainly a breach of the hospitality which you so generously extended to me and my assistant."

The Baron was about to reply when Miss Valentine, who had been following the conversation with the utmost astonishment, interrupted.

"Whatever are you two whispering about?" she asked. "Really, you seem both to have been involved in some mysterious intrigue."

"As a matter of fact, Miss Valentine," remarked Blake, with a laugh, "I was about to remind Baron Rodanoff of the bet we made on the last occasion which he dined here. I think, baron, that in a very short time now you will be owing me one hundred pounds."

Baron Rodanoff shot a look of keen inquiry at the detective; he had an uncomfortable feeling that Blake was playing with him as a cat plays with the mouse.

He had now recovered from the first shock of surprise that he had felt at meeting him here in Dalgretty's, of all places, when he believed he was lying dead at the bottom of the Dene hole. How he had escaped that fate was a mystery he would solve later.

But the important question now was how much did this calm, dispassionate man know of his schemes? What was to be his next move?

Was he really only concerned with this Soho crime, or did he know that Granite Grant was a prisoner at the house at Denesford? Baron Rodanoff was not sure of himself at all.

"What exactly do you mean by that, Mr. Blake?" he asked. "How should I owe you a hundred pounds?"

"But you surely have not forgotten our little bet with regard to the Soho murder, baron?" said the detective sarcastically.

"Not at all, Mr. Blake! I remember it perfectly well. I think your opinion was that the crime was connected in some way with diplomatic affairs."

"Precisely, Baron Rodanoff!"

"While I maintained that it was a simple case of robbery?"

"Yes!"

The baron hesitated, and seemed disinclined to continue. But Blake would not let him escape.

"Go on!" he said quietly.

"I further maintained that if you were right in your theory, and there was a deeper motive behind the crime, it would not be discovered until the information was too late to be of any use. I think I was willing to stake a hundred pounds on that."

"You were not only willing, Baron, but I accepted it as a bet."

"Yes, Mr. Blake, I do not deny it. But I do not see your argument; you have yet to prove your case."

The detective took out his watch; it was just seven-thirty. He got up from his seat.

"You will excuse me, Miss Valentine," he asked; then, turning to the baron, added:

"I am just off now, Baron Rodanoff, to prove my case, and I shall prove it beyond question or argument. We may yet meet again. Good-night!" and without another word Sexton Blake left the dining-room.

Baron Rodanoff bit his lip, and gazed after the retreating figure of the great detective with a mingled look of anger and bafflement on his face. What did he mean, he wondered, by that last strange remark? How much did he know? And where was he off to now? Was he going to Denesford? He turned to the actress:

"Perhaps you will excuse me, too, Miss Valentine." he said; "I also have an appointment."

He bowed low, and hurried after Sexton Blake.

Chapter 34
The Last Card

OUTSIDE Dalgretty's Blake found Sir Vrymer Fane's touring-car, with the engine already ticking over, ready to start at a moment's notice. The men were all in plain clothes, and Blake recognised most of them. They were all used to working silently and swiftly in the inner affairs of the Secret Service, and could be relied upon in an emergency.

He had already given the driver instructions where to go, and the car jerked forward directly the door had closed behind him. His dramatic meeting with Baron Rodanoff had given Blake a sense of keen satisfaction.

He had certainly bested him so far in this exciting struggle against time; and in a few hours now he hoped to be able to wash his hands of the trust that he had voluntarily taken upon his shoulders.

The detective leant back against the upholstered seat, and, closing his eyes, began reviewing the events of the evening.

He wondered what the Baron was thinking now; he laughed softly to himself at the thought of his mortification.

Did he guess, Blake wondered, where he was off to when he so suddenly left the dining-room of Dalgretty's?

Well, it did not matter much if he did; he would be unable to interfere with his plans. If he wired to Denesford it would not get there until the morning, and the whole affair would be over by then.

There was nothing that he could possibly do to circumvent Blake's schemes; the detective had worked the thing out too well for that. Well, Baron Rodanoff would have another surprise in the morning.

They were now speeding along the hilly roads of Kent. It was a fine, crisp night, and the powerful touring-car was running smoothly and silently, taking the hills without the slightest effort.

They sped on and on until at last they drew near to Denesford.

They had now passed Sunford Junction, and were running along the road that led down to the beach. Some ten minutes later Blake told the driver to slow up, and they slowly approached the house without showing any lights.

When they were within a few hundred yards Blake stopped the car altogether, and, leaving the driver in charge, cautiously made his way towards the house, with the others following close behind.

Near the great iron gate, which stood at the entrance of the drive, the detective told Bradley to wait behind with the men while he and Tinker made a closer investigation.

The front of the house was in darkness, save for that one window on the second floor where a glimmer of light still showed though the slat of the blind.

"I don't think they've had any warning," whispered Blake.

"It doesn't seem like it, guv'nor, does it?" said Tinker. "How about getting in through that window in the basement where the ape wrenched away the bars? I don't suppose they've boarded it up."

"That's a good idea, Tinker. Let's go round and explore first."

They crept round to the rear of the building, where the level stretch of grass reached to the wood. In one of the windows on the second floor was another light.

"Be careful!" whispered Blake; "someone may be on the watch."

Stealing noiselessly along in the shadow of the wall, they came upon the window through which the baboon had made its escape two nights ago. The iron grating was still lying on the ground in front of the window, and nothing had been done to close up the opening.

Blake and Tinker quickly climbed through into the chamber, and the detective flashed his torch around.

The floor was covered with straw; in one corner was lying the smashed lamp, with the overturned table, just as it had happened two nights ago.

"Let's try the door," said Blake; "but I expect it's locked."

He turned the handle, but, as he surmised, it was locked from the outside.

"Won't take me long to pick that, Tinker," he said. "Go and fetch Bradley and the men, and I'll have it open when you get back. Be very careful not to arouse anybody in the house."

Tinker stole through the window again, and departed on his errand. When he returned with Bradley and the others a little later Blake had already picked the lock.

"Now," whispered the detective, "follow me, and keep your weapons handy!"

He gently pushed open the door and looked out into the passage; all was in darkness. Closely followed by the others, Blake tiptoed along the corridor, flashing his torch in front of him.

Presently they came to a flight of stone steps, and after climbing up them, they found themselves in another corridor.

Suddenly the sound of voices raised in argument smote upon Blake's ears. A little further along the corridor a streak of light crept out from beneath a door.

Blake uttered a low warning, crept forward a dozen paces, grasped the handle and flung it open.

Two men, who were sitting at the table playing cards, sprang to their feet, with exclamations of frightened surprise, to find themselves staring at Blake's wicked little automatic.

"Put your hands up!" he ordered.

One of the men immediately complied, but the other seemed petrified with fear, he stood staring at the detective with a blanched look on his face, as if he had seen a ghost.

It was Bill Dykes. As Blake looked at his terror-stricken face he knew who it was who had blown in the mouth of the Dene hole.

"That's your man, Bradley!" he said.

Inspector Bradley went up to Dykes and clapped a pair of gyves on his wrists before he could recover from his fright and surprise.

"I arrest you on a charge of having murdered Joe Crick at Soho last Monday," he said. "Anything you say will be used as evidence against you!"

But Bill Dykes was incapable of saying anything; he could only gaze at Sexton Blake with his eyes staring out of his head.

"One of you stay with Bradley," said Blake; "the rest follow me."

They went on up another flight of stairs, and were just going along the second-floor corridor, when the door opened at the further end, and Dulac came out.

He stood chock still at seeing Blake and his companions advancing towards him, quite overcome with amazement.

"Hands up!" shouted Blake, rushing at him.

But before he could get near enough Dulac had turned and sprang back into his room. Blake grasped the handle just as the key was turned in the lock from the inside.

"Doesn't matter about him," he said. "Our man's in the front of the house. This way!"

They hurried to the left, and raced down the passage to a door on the right. Blake tried the handle; it was locked. He tapped gently on the door.

"Who's there?" asked a voice, and footsteps approached from the inside.

"Who's there?" asked the voice again.

There was no reply.

Blake heard the key turn in the lock; then, with a quick twist, he turned the handle and flung his weight against the door. The door shot open, sending Denvers sprawling to the floor.

"Just see to him!" said Blake to one of his men, and turned to the man who sat in the further corner of the room, and who had calmly closed the book he had been reading as if nothing had happened to get excited over.

"I am pleased to meet you, Mr. Grant."

"By Jove! Mr. Blake!" said the other, rising to his feet with some difficulty. "I should like to shake your hand, if you will be good enough to remove these bangles."

Chapter 35
Congratulations

IN the early hours of the morning, while London was wrapt in slumber, three men met together in a room in Whitehall Court; they were Sir Vrymer Fane, Granite Grant, and Sexton Blake.

There were tears in the great statesman's eyes, which he tried vainly to control, as he kept shaking hands alternately with Grant and the detective. For a while he was speechless with emotion.

"It seems incredible," he muttered, finding his voice at last. "You have, indeed, rendered us a service which can never be repaid, Mr. Blake. I congratulate you, and myself also on seeking your advice. It was a step which has been fully justified, I am thankful to say."

The great detective seemed rather embarrassed by this expression of gratitude and acknowledgment of his cleverness and wonderful capacities.

Calm and self-possessed as he was in the many crises that came to him in the "ups and downs" of his profession, yet when it was a question of thanking him for his services, his simple modesty would not allow him to admit any merit in his own enterprise.

"Believe me, Sir Vrymer," he said hurriedly, "there are no thanks due to me at all. It is all in my day's work. Pray do not let us mention it!"

Sir Vrymer Fane laughed sympathetically.

"I understand, Mr. Blake," he said, "perfectly! We will not refer to the matter again. But you will allow me to assure you that you will always command our respect and esteem."

"I, too, Mr. Blake," said Granite Grant, who had been standing attentively by, "wish to echo the sentiments expressed by Sir Vrymer Fane. Perhaps there are no thanks necessary between you and me; and you know my feelings too well. But you and I both have very much in common; we both work silently and relentlessly off the beaten tracks of society. Perhaps the only difference is that I specialise more than you do. However, you will understand me when I say that I am honoured to shake your hand."

The two men, so different in many respects, and yet so alike—both fearless and resolute, both strong in mind and body, and whose professions brought both in constant contact with that strange current in human affairs that flows beyond the pale—silently shook hands and vowed eternal friendship.

Although neither registered his vow in words, yet it is probable that those two strong characters understood each other at that moment with a sympathy that is denied us lesser mortals.

"And now, Mr. Grant, to get to business!" said Sir Vrymer Fane. "How are you feeling? Is it absolutely necessary that you have a rest? I know you want it; but if you could possibly start right away! I have arranged everything———"

He glanced anxiously at the tall figure of his subordinate.

"You know," he added, "that the matter is serious—deadly serious!"

"I am ready, sir, now!" said Grant, "but——"

He hesitated, as if slightly embarrassed. His chief looked puzzled for a moment, then his face cleared.

"Ah!" he said, with a knowing smile. "I was forgetting. How stupid of me."

He turned to the detective.

"You have told this lady what has happened?" he asked.

But Blake did not reply; he was listening intently. Yes, that was the sound of a car pulling up outside; then Tinker had carried out his instructions. He turned to Sir Vrymer with a guilty look.

"I think, sir," he said, "that this is Miss Valentine; she is just coming up the stairs."

Sir Vrymer gave a startled exclamation.

"Good gracious!" he said. "How forgetful I am! I must run upstairs at once. Pardon me!"

And, slipping his arm through that of Sexton Blake, he hurriedly left the room, dragging the detective with him.

A moment later the beautiful actress, flushed and bright-eyed, entered the room, and, with a little cry of joy, was folded in the strong arms of her lover.

***

"I think Bradley carried that through quite well, Tinker!"

Blake and Tinker were having breakfast in their rooms some time later, and the detective had just been reading the account of the trial of Bill Dykes for the murder of Joe Crick at Soho.

"You mean he didn't drag us into the business, guv'nor?" said Tinker. "Well, considering that it was you who gave him his opportunity, Bradley ought to be jolly well grateful."

"Oh, that's nothing to do with the matter," said Blake airily. "I'm glad enough to be out of the whole business. That's the only thing about my profession that I dislike—being dragged into court. Dykes has gotten years, I see. I think the evidence of the barman at the Peacock Café rather went in his favour. At any rate, it saved his neck. The jury took the view that Crick was killed during a violent quarrel, and that he had previously threatened Dykes. They regard that as a mitigating circumstance."

"Mitigating fiddlesticks!" growled his young assistant contemptuously. "It's not his fault that we are not lying stark and stiff at the bottom of that beastly hole now. The jury didn't take that into consideration."

"Well, naturally! They didn't know about that, Tinker!"

They went on reading in silence for some time.

"By the way, guv'nor!" said Tinker presently. "What's happened to that cove who pretended he was Granite Grant? Didn't he get it in the neck?"

"No! He was only a cat's-paw, Tinker. We found out all about him from Professor Bailey's finger-nail analysis; made inquiries at the docks, and found he had been missing from his vessel for about a week. Remarkable likeness to Granite Grant, though. The baron happened to come across on that same vessel—that's how he met him. But the fellow is an inveterate drug fiend; he's in a home for mental deficients at the present moment."

"Let us hope he stops there!" said Tinker unsympathetically. "But how about Baron Rodanoff? Any news of him?"

"Yes, Tinker, rather good news! As a matter of fact, he's on the Continent now; but he sent me this."

Tinker took the slip of paper with a look of wonderment.

"Why," he said, "it's a cheque for one hundred pounds. What does it say here: With Baron Rodanoff's compliments! Now what the blazes does that mean?"

"Well, we had a little bet together, Tinker, and I happened to win. You see, Baron Rodanoff's not a bad sort. He's honourable enough to pay his debts, at any rate. I hope I meet him again some day."

"I hope so, too," agreed Tinker, "if he chucks away a hundred quids like that."

Chapter 36
Conclusion

TWO months had elapsed since the events recorded in the last chapter. Those two months had been so full of fresh incident in Blake's strenuous career that already the case of the King's Spy seemed distant and half forgotten.

Yet as the great detective strode down the carpeted aisle of Dalgretty's once more, the whole record of that short eventful week crowded back into his mind as fresh as if it had only just taken place.

The recollection of those two former occasions when he had dined at the famous restaurant came back to him very vividly at that moment.

The first occasion had been when the actress had introduced him to Baron Rodanoff. He remembered how surprised he had been then, and how baffling had seemed the task on which he had just embarked.

Then, on the second occasion, the same three had met again. Blake had held the trump card then. It was a bitter pill which he had forced the baron to swallow.

He smiled to himself at the recollection. Well, Baron Rodanoff had lost. But he had some good points about him: he had "paid up and kept smiling."

Then there had been that meeting with——

"Whatever are you frowning about, Mr. Blake?"

The detective looked up with a start, and gave vent to his familiar dry sort of laugh.

"I must confess, Mrs. Grant," he said, smiling, "that you certainly caught me dreaming that time."

He turned to the tall, bronzed man who was sitting next to the actress and shook him cordially by the hand, and sat down.

"Congratulations," he said, "to both of you! I could not get along to your wedding, but I am sure that you have forgiven me that. However, this is better still, for it is one of the rare occasions where three is jolly good company. You will admit that that is indeed a rare occasion?"

Granite Grant leaned across the table to his guest.

"Believe me, Mr. Blake," he said earnestly, "and I think my wife will also agree with me—your company can never be other than welcome, no matter what the number may be."

"That is very nice of you to say so," said the detective simply, "I am quite ready to accept that—all the more so since I desire nothing better."

The strains of the orchestra floated down to them at that moment; it was playing that same soothing waltz that Blake had heard on that first evening.

The actress noticed his look of appreciation.

"Ah!" she said. "I see you also remember it. Much water has flowed under the bridge since we last heard that, Mr. Blake!"

"You are right, Mrs. Grant!" he said seriously; "yet everything has come out straight, you see!"

"Thanks to you!"

The detective waved his hand airily.

"Thanks rather to you, I think!" he said.

He turned to Granite Grant.

"I read in the papers a short while ago of the settlement of that Russian difficulty," he said. "Of course, none of the inner history of the crisis was mentioned, but I knew it was your doing. You were only just in time!"

A flicker of amusement passed over Grant's tanned face.

"That is the nature of my profession, Mr. Blake," he said, "to be just in time!"

They were silent for a while, all three seeming a little preoccupied.

The soft, voluptuous music of the orchestra rose and fell to the rhythm of the waltz, now swelling out into a deep volume of sound that flooded the great dining-room, then sinking down to a soft murmuring sigh.

Blake glanced appreciatively round at the other people who were dining there. They were the usual crowd, well-dressed, wealthy, and important-looking, the frequenters of polite society.

How very much the same everything seemed! It was precisely as he had seen it on that evening over two months ago, and on the occasion a few days later.

Nothing had changed; nothing even had seemed to have happened in the interval. If he came back in twenty years' time the scene would be the same, thought Blake.

And yet his life was full of change. There was no sameness about that.

That mysterious undercurrent in human affairs in which he groped his way swept him relentlessly onward from one exciting adventure to another. No; there was no standing still as far as he was concerned. Nor was there with Granite Grant.

Blake glanced up at him.

"They have given you a holiday—eh?" he asked. "Yet not for long, I suppose!"

Grant looked at the beautiful woman who was sitting at his side, and who was now his wife. A look of great tenderness crept into his strong face.

"I think it will be a long holiday this time, Mr. Blake," he said quietly, "a very long holiday!"

"You are thinking of settling down?" queried Blake.

"Yes! My life has been one of strenuous endeavour in the service of my country, and now I long for quietness. Perhaps some day—but I do not know!"

The actress laid her hand on that of her husband.

"And I, too, Mr. Blake!" she said shyly. "I, too, am thinking of settling down."

"You?" said the detective in surprise.

"Yes! And you must come to my farewell performance next week."

Blake glanced from one to the other. Then he gave that familiar boyish laugh.

"Well," he said, "everybody seems to be settling down except me. But here's the very best!"

All three of them raised their glasses and silently drank the toast.

Stirring, Long, Complete Tales
SEXTON BLAKE v. HIS GREATEST FOES

"Some of the most
daring criminals
I have known, have
been the pleasantest
and most gentlemanly
fellows you could
wish to meet."

~Sexton Blake,
The Secret Report, 1913

An excellent place to
start for readers new
to Sexton Blake.

*Introducing
all the Famous
Characters :—*

Ivor Carlac
Prof. Kew
Prince Wu Ling
The Scorpion
Leon Kestrel
The Bat
The Maitlands
Waldo the Wonder-Man
Monsieur Zenith

Now on Sale

YVONNE'S VENGEANCE: THE EPIC SERIES

GREAT NEW SERIES—YVONNE v. SEXTON BLAKE.

40,000-WORD YVONNE YARN.

YVONNE v. SEXTON BLAKE!

Our FINEST Yvonne Story

The Paper that is Sexton Blake's OWN.   40,000-word Yarn of Yvonne v. Sexton Blake

Sexton Blake—Airman!

Sexton Blake Disappears!

Yvonne's Last Revenge!

READ ALL 8 TALES IN THE TEED FILES #1

Telling how a curious call for help came to Sexton Blake. Introducing "Granite" Grant, the Secret-Service Man. By the Author of "The Case of the King's Spy," etc., etc.

Cunning, Furtive and Utterly Ruthless
PROFESSOR FRANCIS KEW
CARLAC THE MASTER CRIMINAL
Read about their exploits in
The Kew Files and The Carlac Files
ROH PRESS

Four new volumes of the SEXTON BLAKE LIBRARY are issued on the first Friday in every month. Please give your newsagent a standing order for them.

The Case of the Strange Wireless Message.

A Tale of Sexton Blake, Tinker, and Pedro, Introducing "Granite" Grant, the King's Spy.

The Prologue

AND so, Grant, you're going back to the old life again! I thought that would happen sooner or later. You're not the sort to settle down and take life easy; you're cut out for big things."

James Grant, the King's Spy, the man who moved so mysteriously among the most exclusive circles of society, who understood the great game of diplomatic intrigues as no other man understood it, and whose iron nerves and cool daring had won him the nickname "Granite" nodded pleasantly to his companion's remark and then glanced swiftly across the lounge of the West End hotel.

His companion was no less famous than himself, for he was none other than Sexton Blake, the renowned and celebrated detective. In outward respects the two men were curiously dissimilar; for while the detective presented to the eye a well-knit and wiry figure, with a somewhat lean and ascetic face, the secret service agent, on the other hand, was a big-boned man of undoubted physical strength, with a bronzed and angular face, which always wore a look of grim determination.

But although outwardly they were so unlike each other, yet in many other ways they had much in common.

Both men's work brought them into constant contact with forces that were quite outside the knowledge of the average law-abiding citizen; both men were only too well acquainted with the seamy side of human nature, for it was against the cunning and duplicity of their fellow men that they were compelled to measure their wits.

Both men were strong, resolute, and daring, and attached very little value to their own lives in the execution of their duties; and, like all strong men, each had a large circle of friends and as large a circle of enemies.

But there was this difference between them; the one used his faculties in ferreting out international intrigues, while the other directed all the energies of his resourceful brain to tracking down the criminal. In spite of this fact, however, there were occasions when they both found themselves striving to reach the same goal; it happened sometimes that crime and diplomacy were inseparably interwoven.

The secret service man was still gazing intently across the lounge; his eyes had narrowed down to two small slits, and there was a tense expression on his face. Sexton Blake glanced idly at the mirror facing him.

A lady had just entered the room; she was dressed very elegantly, and the costly sable fur that she was wearing had slipped from her shoulders and revealed the low-cut bodice of her evening dress.

As she pulled off the glove from her hand the detective's quick eyes noticed that her fingers sparkled with valuable gems.

A gentleman had risen from his seat at her approach and had bowed an acknowledgment. She nodded her head in quick response, and made her way towards him. They both sat down at an adjoining table, and began to converse in low, earnest tones.

Presently she raised her veil, and gave a petulant toss of her head, and Blake caught a brief glimpse of her face.

She appeared to be very young and innocent, and although Blake was not much given to sentiment he had to admit that she was one of the most strikingly beautiful women he had seen.

"I suppose we're both cut out for the big things, Blake."

The detective glanced swiftly at his companion. "Granite" Grant's face had softened somewhat; there was a flicker of amusement in his eyes.

"Handy things sometimes—the mirror, Blake, for seeing without being seen!" he said dryly.

The detective chuckled appreciatively.

"Well," he laughed, "apparently I'm not the only person who's susceptible to feminine charms. Who's the lady, may I ask?"

"Granite" Grant did not move a muscle; he stared steadily into his companion's face and deliberately ignored the question.

"Strange I should meet you tonight, Blake," he said. "Very likely it will be some time before we meet again."

For an instant Blake felt a momentary surge of resentment. But it was stifled ere it was formed. He understood this blunt man who sat facing him; it was his way of shelving an inconvenient question—deliberately to ignore it. After all, whoever the lady might be, it was none of his business. And it was evident that if "Granite" Grant knew her it did not serve his purpose at that moment to disclose her identity.

"Then you are going abroad, Grant?"

"Perhaps!"

"You're not in a very communicative mood."

The King's Spy chuckled softly.

"We're neither of us blabbers, Blake," he said. "It doesn't pay us to be."

"You're right there, Grant!" laughed the detective. "But it's confoundedly awkward when you want to have a quiet chat about nothing in particular. Seems to me the only safe topic is the weather."

"And it's not always safe to talk about that, Blake."

They were silent for a time; presently the detective spoke again.

"You said something about the British Museum a short time, ago," he said. "I had forgotten that."

"I spent several hours there today, Blake—that's all!"

"Looking at the mummies?"

"No; in the reading-room."

"Very studious sort of place, Grant! Do you often go there?"

The Secret Service agent did not answer; his gaze had travelled across the room again; a moment later he rose abruptly to his feet.

"I must be going, Blake," he said. "Good-bye!"

"Well, good-bye, Grant. Take care of yourself."

Blake glanced at the mirror.

The young woman in the sable wrap had risen to her feet; she seemed to be having a dispute with her companion. Then, with an angry gesture, she turned away and sped swiftly towards the door. The man remained where he was, puffing contentedly at a cigar, and with a supercilious smile playing about the corners of his mouth.

"Granite" Grant was also making his way across the lounge. Suddenly Blake saw him hesitate, and then begin to retrace his steps. A moment later he felt his hand resting on his shoulder.

"Blake," he said quietly, "we don' talk too much about our affairs—you and I, but I think we understand each other. You once did me a good turn, and I do not forget that. I might want your assistance again some day. You're about the only man I care to trust. If you ever receive the message 'KO' you'll know that it comes from me, and that I'm in a tight corner. It's easy to remember—it's the opposite to 'OK.' Got me?"

"I've got you, Grant!"

The next moment the King's Spy was gone.

For some time the detective smoked on in silence. He was fast friends with this big-boned service man; he admired him immensely. As he had said, "Granite" Grant was cut out for big things. He had not known him for long; once before the detective had been able to render him a service, and the Secret Service man had never forgotten it.

He wondered what was the present job on which he was engaged. Granite Grant usually wore a closely cropped Vandyke beard, today he was clean shaven. Blake would have passed him by without recognising him had not the other stopped him.

Was there any significance in that trifling detail, or was it simply a sudden whim or fancy?

Then, again, who was that beautiful woman in the sable wrap? Did Grant know her? And had he followed her out of the lounge, or was that merely a coincidence?

Perhaps in the lounge of this swagger hotel this evening had been enacted one more scene in that invisible drama of diplomatic intrigue and cunning in which "Granite" Grant played such a leading part.

He pondered over the matter for some minutes, then dismissed it from his mind. After all, it was none of his business; he had his own affairs to attend to, and they employed all his time and energies. He finished his coffee and strode from the lounge.

Yet if Blake had known then of the web of intrigue in which he was to be involved through that chance meeting that day with the King's Spy, and of the thrilling adventures which he and his young assistant were to meet with, he might not have dismissed the subject so lightly.

But three months were to pass before he was to be reminded again of those last strange words of "Granite "Grant.

The End of the Prologue

Chapter 1
The Mysterious Wireless Message

A RATHER youthful figure was strolling slowly up Baker Street. He was dressed in the blue uniform of a wireless operator of the mercantile marine, and from the idle way that he stared about him it was evident that he was in no great hurry to get anywhere, and that he found something novel and entertaining in being in London again after a somewhat lengthy voyage.

Presently he came to a halt in front of a certain house, glanced up at the number rather doubtfully, then, as if suddenly making up his mind, pushed open the gate and strode up the steps. The housekeeper opened the door in answer to his summons; he exchanged a few words with her, and disappeared inside.

"There's a naval Johnnie wants to see you, guv'nor!"

Sexton Blake glanced up momentarily from his correspondence file.

"What's he want, Tinker?" he asked with a slight trace of irritation in his voice.

"Got some message for you, guv'nor," said his assistant. "Won't say what it's about."

"Ah, well, show him in!"

Tinker left the room, to return a moment later, followed by the youth in the blue uniform and the gold lace. He seemed to be rather disconcerted at being in the presence of the great detective, and played nervously with the shiny-peaked cap which he held in his hand.

"Well, my lad, and what can I do for you?" asked Blake kindly.

The youth seemed to suddenly lose his shyness, he showed his white teeth in a broad grin, and, striding up to the table, flung down his hat.

"Are you Mr. Sexton Blake, the detective?" he asked breezily.

"Yes, that happens to be me," said the detective, somewhat amused.

The youth felt in one of his pockets, and evidently not finding what he wanted there, went through each in turn.

"Had the wind up about seeing you at first, sir!" he muttered.

"Thought I would eat you, I suppose!" said Blake. "What on earth are you turning your pockets out for? Got something to sell?"

"Had a piece of paper, sir. Dash it! Here it is, though."

The youth dragged from his vest pocket a piece of crumpled paper, which he proceeded to smooth out. Then, without a word, he handed it to the detective.

With a look of interest on his face Blake took the missive and laid it on his desk in front of him. Across it was pencilled in capital letters the following message:

"CQ CQ CQ Blake London BM OC G2437 KO KO KO."

The detective stared at the message for some time with contracted brows. At length he looked up.

"What is this?" he asked quietly.

"A wireless message, sir!"

"And where did you get it from?"

"Picked it up on the Marconi ship-set, sir—one night when we were about five days out from Panama."

"How long ago was that?"

"About three weeks ago now, sir."

Blake stared down at the strange message again. This was certainly rather extraordinary. What could it mean? Was it really intended for him, and if so, who had sent it?

"What made you bring it to me?" he asked presently.

"I was a bit curious, sir. It's got 'Blake London' on it, so I just thought I'd bring it along to you directly we got to port. It's a bit rummy—that's why I thought it might be intended for you."

"I see!" said Blake, with a dry smile. "I've evidently got a reputation for dealing with rummy things, as you call them."

"You bet your life, sir," said the wireless man, with great conviction.

"I suppose I ought to be rather flattered by that," muttered the detective. "By the way, who are you?"

"I'm Jones, sir—Charlie Jones, of the steamship *Wildfly*. One of the boats of the Green Star Line, trading between Liverpool and Valparaiso, I'm the wireless operator."

"And you picked up this wireless message yourself?"

"I did, sir. Happened to be amusing myself at the time. This came through on a different wave-length."

"A different wave-length! What do you mean by that? Different from what?"

"Different from that used on board ship, sir. Ships generally work on three hundred metres; this came through on about two thousand metres, I should think."

"I think I understand what you're getting at," said Blake. "You mean to say that this message wasn't sent out by a ship?"

"That's it, sir."

"Then who was it sent out by?"

"Haven't the vaguest notion, sir."

"The deuce you haven't!" muttered Blake. "And what do you make of it?"

"Not much, sir! It seems to be in code. Thought you might understand it."

"I'm dashed if I do, Jones!" rejoined the detective, and stared at the message again.

"What does CQ mean? Do you know?" he asked presently.

"Yes, sir! That's easy! 'CQ' is a call to all stations."

"A call to all stations!" echoed Blake, "You mean to say that this message wasn't sent out to a particular station? It was sent out for any station to pick up?"

"You've got it first time, sir! The Johnnie who sent that out did so on the chance that someone would pick it up and forward it on to its destination."

"And that's all you can understand of it?" asked Blake.

"That's about all, sir. Thought the 'Blake, London' might refer to you; but I'm blowed if I can make head or tail of the rest. As the 'KO' was repeated three times, I thought at first that that was the code call of the station, but there isn't a station with 'KO' as the call signal."

"How do you know there's not?"

"Looked it up, sir, in the handbook of radio-telegraph stations. No station there with 'KO' as the code-call."

But Blake wasn't listening. A startling thought had shot through his mind. Suddenly he had remembered that last occasion on which he had seen "Granite" Grant, the King's Spy. It was over three months ago now; he had had dinner with him at the Karlton. He was trying to recollect the last words he had uttered; they seemed to have slipped his memory.

He closed his eyes and creased his forehead in an endeavour to remember. Then, suddenly, they came rushing back to his mind:

"If you ever receive the message KO, you'll know I'm in a tight corner. It's easy to remember—it's the opposite to OK. Got me?"

He could hear the deep, quiet tones of the Secret Service man now uttering those words as he laid his hand on Blake's shoulder. He had not thought much of them at the time; he had been thinking of other things, and till now he had never had occasion to remember them. But they had stuck in his memory, all the same, to be recalled in this mysterious fashion.

Was this simply a coincidence? Was it mere chance that this secret wireless message should contain those three "KO's"? After all, such a combination of letters was not uncommon. There might be quite a number of meanings to it other than that which the Secret Service man meant it to convey.

The detective read the message through again. There were those two words, "Blake, London." Surely that could not be a coincidence as well? In conjunction with those other two letters his own name was so startlingly significant that it was impossible to dismiss it as simply a chance combination of words.

Was it possible that "Granite" Grant had sent that message, or caused it to be sent? And had he done so in the hope that some ship fitted with wireless would pick it up and forward it on to the detective? If that were the case, then he had not been wrong in his surmises, for the message had certainly got into the detective's hands.

But if this message had come from "Granite" Grant, then it must contain something which he particularly wished the detective to know. Blake stared at the piece of paper in bewilderment. Somewhere in that peculiar combination of letters and figures was contained a message—some vital piece of information that "Granite" Grant was trying to get through to him. He must decipher this message at all costs. Its meaning could not be very obscure; Grant would have worded it so that the detective would have little difficulty in deciphering it.

Blake picked up a pencil and began copying out the letters on a sheet of paper. He had no doubt now that this message was intended for him, and for him alone. The strangeness of the thing gripped him; no similar case had ever come within his experience. He had not the slightest notion as to the whereabouts of the King's Spy. For all he knew to the contrary he might be in Timbuctoo; he had not seen him nor heard of him for over three months now.

Yet from some unknown place "Granite" Grant had been able to send out that wireless message for aid; it had been picked up in the Atlantic Ocean by the operator of the *Wildfly*, and had reached the detective safely from all those thousands of miles away. Certainly it was the most amazing thing Blake had ever stumbled across.

For some time Blake worked away in silence. Then, suddenly, he threw down his pencil and glanced up at the wireless man. His face betrayed no emotion, and there was nothing to show that he had discovered anything of any importance. But Tinker had been furtively watching him all the time, and he could read his master's face like a book. While Blake was speaking he could hardly restrain his excitement; if he were not mistaken his master would have something astounding to tell him in a few minutes.

"Jones," said the detective quietly, "you did quite right in bringing this message to me. I congratulate you on your smartness. I can promise you that it won't be overlooked. How long are you staying in London?"

"Seven days, sir," said the wireless man, flushing with pleasure at the great detective's words of praise.

"Then, Jones, you might leave me your address. Very likely I shall want to communicate with you during the next day or so."

"Certainly, sir! Here it is—24, Truebridge Road, S.W."

"Thank you, Jones. Well, good-bye. You shall hear from me in any case before you sail."

Looking very proud of himself, Charlie Jones shook hands with the detective, and swaggered out of the room. He spent the afternoon in boasting to an admiring circle of friends of how he had had a chat with Sexton Blake, the famous detective, and had even shaken hands with the great man.

Chapter 2
Tragedy at the Library

AS the door closed behind Charlie Jones, Tinker turned swiftly to his master.
"You've got something big on, guv'nor," he said. "I can see it in your face."
"I've certainly discovered something rather interesting, Tinker," rejoined Blake.

"Of course, I may be mistaken, but if I've deciphered this message correctly, then you and I are going to get busy shortly."

Tinker was staring curiously at the jumbled scrawl of letters:

"Do you mean to say that you know what it means, guv'nor?" he asked.

"I think I do, Tinker. At any rate, I'm going to put my theory to the test in a few minutes. Now, just listen carefully while I explain things to you."

He smoothed out the piece of paper and began again.

"You see those letters 'CQ,' Tinker? Well, you heard what that wireless chap said about those; that's a code call to all stations, so we won't trouble about that just now. Next comes my name, followed by the word 'London.' That also doesn't want any explaining. But after that comes three groups, followed by the letters KO three times. Got me so far?"

"Yes, I see that, guv'nor."

"Right!" continued Blake. "Well, when I saw Granite Grant over three months ago now, the last words he said to me were these: 'If you ever receive the message KO you'll know that I'm in a tight corner.' That's rather significant—don't you think, Tinker?"

"Seems rather rummy, I must admit, guv'nor," said Tinker. "And you think Granite Grant sent this wireless message in the hopes that it would reach you?"

"You've got it, Tinker!"

"But what does it mean, guv'nor?" cried Tinker, in bewilderment. "How can it be a message? Can't see any sense in it."

Blake chuckled softly to himself.

"I'm coming to that, Tinker," he said. "Now, it's quite evident that if this message contains any information it must be wrapt up in those three remaining groups: BM OC G2437. That's obvious, isn't it?"

Tinker nodded his head in approval of this bit of reasoning.

"Well," continued the detective, "it's also pretty evident that since 'Granite' Grant— that's taking for granted the fact that he sent the message—since Granite expected me to read this code he wouldn't make it very hard to decipher. It must refer to something that's pretty obvious and straightforward. Follow me there, Tinker?"

Again Tinker nodded his head.

"To proceed, then," said Blake. "The first conclusion one would jump at is that this code message refers to something that happened on the last occasion we met. That happens also to be the right conclusion. On the day I met Granite Grant at the Karlton he mentioned to me the fact that he had just spent some hours in the reading-room of the British Museum. See what I'm driving at, Tinker?"

"You mean, guv'nor, that the BM in this message refers to the British Museum Library?"

"Precisely, Tinker! Now, the next two letters in the message are OC, and in the library of the British Museum are an 'Inner' and an 'Outer Circle.' Is that clear?"

"The 'OC' stands for the 'Outer Circle,' guv'nor?" exclaimed Tinker, now in a state of great excitement.

"That's right, my lad! And to cut a long story short, the "G2437" means the volume number 2437 which stands in the G row of the 'Outer Circle.' Any complaints?"

Tinker evidently had no complaints; at least, if he had he didn't think it worthwhile, mentioning them. He simply stared at his master in silence, and waited for him to proceed.

"It amounts to this, then, Tinker. 'Granite' Grant's evidently in a fix somewhere, although where he is I haven't the vaguest notion. But for some reason or other he wants me to go to the reading-room of the British Museum and look at that book number 2437, which stands on the G row of the outer circle. And I'm going there straight away, Tinker, so you'd better look slippy if you want to come along too."

Tinker wanted no second invitation. He was going to see this thing through. He was filled with a vague sense of mystery; perhaps this volume would contain some startling piece of information. He was certainly very curious to see it. This was a most extraordinary turn of events; nothing like this had ever happened within his knowledge. It did not take him long to get into his hat and coat, and together the two left the house and made their way to Bloomsbury.

An impressive silence brooded beneath the great dome of the British Museum Library; it is this strange stillness that first strikes one on entering the swing doors of the reading-room.

Dotted about at the black, shiny tables were the usual number of frequenters of the library—men and women of all sorts and conditions; journalists, doctors, students, with the usual sprinkling of Anglo-Indians, and all were poring industriously over some musty old volume or treatise on the subject in which they were interested. Some even were authors themselves, who had come to seek information regarding some matter or other which had floored them.

Dusk was beginning to fall as Blake and his assistant pushed open the swing doors. The mellow light from the big dome overhead fell directly on the centre of the great hall, and left the wide, sweeping outer circle in vague, shadowy, half-tones.

For a moment Blake stood irresolute, glancing swiftly around the great building, then he turned to the left an began to move slowly along the "outer circle" with his eyes fixed on the closely packed shelves of books that lined the walls from top to bottom.

Presently he came to a halt, and ran his finger swiftly along the volumes in row "G."

"Number 2436," he muttered, "number 2438!"

With an exclamation of annoyance the detective turned to his assistant.

"Why, No. 2437 seems to be missing, Tinker!" he said.

He stared again at the space where volume No. 2437 should have been, as if to convince himself that he had not made a mistake. But he was quite right—the volume in question had certainly been taken out.

Blake felt his pulses quicken. It was strange that while all the other books were there this particular volume should be missing. Of course, there was no reason why some other frequenter of the library should not have taken the volume out for his own purposes; the books were there for anyone to read.

Yet something told Blake that this was no mere coincidence; he could see that these particular books were very little used. In the normal course of events it was a hundred chances to one that some other reader should have chosen to look at this book at this precise moment.

Feeling a little nonplussed, Blake stood glancing casually around. Suddenly he noticed two eyes glaring at him from behind a bookshelf a little to his left. Somewhat perturbed, the detective stared at the stranger inquiringly, sensing that something was wrong.

The two eyes never shifted from Blake's face. They watched him furtively, and in the fixed gaze was something so fearful and terrifying that, involuntarily, the detective moved towards him. Then the stranger abruptly turned away, and moved swiftly down the room.

For a brief moment Blake's brain was in a turmoil. Where had he seen that face before? Something about it was familiar; he was certain that some time or other he had met the man. There was that little oblique scar over the right eye. Where on earth——

Then, suddenly, he had it—the whole scene came rushing vividly back to his mind. He had seen this man in the Karlton on the very day he had dined with Granite Grant; he was the companion of that mysterious and beautiful woman whom the King's Spy had followed from the lounge.

Blake gripped his assistant by the arm.

"That man!" he whispered hoarsely. "He's just going out of the door. Follow him, Tinker! Quick!"

Without a word, Tinker sped swiftly down the room, and vanished through the swing-doors.

The detective went round to the back of the shelf where the stranger had been standing. Another man was seated at a desk close by, and sprawled in a peculiar fashion across the table. His left arm was resting on an open volume.

A sudden suspicion flashed across Blake's mind. He put his hand on the man's shoulder, and gently shook him. The man lurched forward heavily, and slid to the floor. He was dead!

For a moment Blake was too surprised to move. Then he reached out his hand to the book, and, turning over the cover, took a swift glance at the number. It was the missing volume; for on the binding, in gilt letters, was the number 2,437. Turning down the corner of the page at which it was open, Blake closed the book and placed it on the table again, then beckoned to a passing attendant.

"This gentleman has suddenly expired," he said. "You had better get a doctor, although I'm afraid it's quite useless."

"Why, bless my soul!" exclaimed the man. "How unfortunate! Just one moment, sir!"

He sped swiftly across the library, and returned a moment later with two of the officials.

"Had a fit, sir?" said one of them to Blake.

"Very likely!" said the detective. "At any rate, you'd better see what the doctor says."

The man nodded his head, and together they picked up the dead man and moved slowly away down the library.

A number of the other readers had now hurried to the spot, and stood gazing curiously at the detective. But their interest quickly subsided, and, after making various exclamations, they returned one by one to their seats again.

A few minutes later the attendant came up to Blake.

"May I have your name and address, sir?" he asked. "It is possible that you may be wanted at the inquest."

"Certainly," said the detective, and handed him his card.

The man stared at the name, and then shot a quick glance at the detective.

"Thank you, sir!" he said, with a tone of great respect. "I hope you won't be bothered unnecessarily. "But it doesn't rest with me; of course."

"I understand that," said Blake, and, turning to the desk, sat down in the chair, and began to scrutinise the volume.

The book was a rather old edition, and its leaves were very faded. But, in spite of that fact, it had evidently been very little used, for it bore none of the usual marks that are to be found on a much read book.

The fact that interested Blake, however, was that it happened to be the records of an expedition which had been sent out some years before to make a survey of the Caribbean Sea. This appeared to be rather a significant fact, and he could not help associating it with the mysterious wireless message which had been picked up by the operator of the *Wildfly* some weeks before.

What secret did this book contain? Why had Granite Grant sent him that message urging him to go and look up this particular book? Did he expect him to read through the whole of these thousand pages?

Blake began quickly to turn the pages over, glancing casually at each one in turn. Very likely Grant had written some message on one of them, some note that would indicate roughly where he was and the nature of the task on which he was engaged. At all events, he was bound to something that would attract his attention, Grant must have had some strong reason for asking him to look at this book.

He turned to the inside cover again, and glanced down the index. Then suddenly he noticed an item against which a cross had been put in pencil. At the side, in small type, was printed:

"Map......page 465."

With feverish haste, Blake began to turn over the leaves of the book.

"Four-six-three," he read, "four-six-four——"

He stopped suddenly, with a look of deep perplexity. Page 465 was missing: It had been torn out, and the ragged edge still stuck out of the binding. The corner of page 466 was turned down; it was the place at which the book had been open when Blake had discovered the dead man lying across the desk.

What was the meaning of this amazing happening? Had that map contained the key to some strange mystery in which Granite Grant was involved? And, if so, what were these other two men doing in the library with this selfsame book?

Then there was the mystery of this dead man that had to be explained. Blake felt sure now that he had not died from natural causes. Some grim tragedy had taken place that afternoon in the library. This man had met his death by foul means, and the solution of this baffling mystery was contained in that map which had been torn from this volume.

Blake suddenly closed the book, and, getting up from his chair, strode over to the wall, and replaced it on the shelf. He must find out the identity of this dead man; that would very likely give him some clue to the mystery. He was bound to have some letter or card on him that would show who he was, or, at any rate, where he had come from.

He met the attendant at the door.

"Where have they taken the gentleman who expired a short while ago?" he asked.

"Just outside, in the little room on the left, sir! The doctor has just arrived, and a man from Scotland Yard. This way, sir!"

They stepped out into the corridor, and entered a room on the left. The doctor was stooping over the prostrate man, with the stethoscope to his ear, listening for the faintest flutter that would show that life was not yet extinct. The two library officials and a police inspector were standing by, watching him closely.

At Blake's entry, the inspector looked up, and, recognising the detective, came silently towards him.

"Hallo, Blake!" he whispered. "Rummy affair this, don't you think?"

Blake nodded his head.

"It is, rather," he said. "He's quite dead, isn't he?"

"Dead as a door-nail!" muttered the inspector.

"Found anything on him to show who he is, Brown?" asked Blake.

"No, not a thing. Been through his pockets, too. Found this in his waistcoat. Looks like a telegram, but I'm blowed if I can make head or tail of it!"

Blake took the slip of paper, with a puzzled expression on his face. The inspector was right; it was a telegram. But the top half had been torn off. The message, however, was still intact, and it was written in pencil, in the usual distinct post-office hand.

"Victory ball tonight wear red rosette.—Julie."

Wondering what it could mean, Blake read the strange message through again. There was nothing to be got from those few words, nothing at all that gave the slightest clue as to the identity of this stranger, who had died under such peculiar circumstances.

It seemed to Blake that this man had deliberately avoided carrying anything in his pocket by which he could be known. He had even torn this telegram across, so that the name of the addressee and the office of origin should not be discovered. What could possibly be his reason for such a strange procedure? Why had he gone to such lengths to make sure that no one should know who he was? Was it because the work he was engaged on was of such a secret nature that he did not dare to risk discovery?

Blake was still staring at the message. Suddenly it occurred to him that this telegram might serve some useful purpose, after all. It no doubt referred to the Victory ball that was to be held that night at the Hermon Hall. He had read about it in the papers only that morning. The dancers were to wear masks, and many society folk had signified their intention of being present.

That might be the reason for wearing the red rosette: it would serve as a means of identification. Julie, whoever the lady was, would evidently he there, and she was expecting to meet this man, for some reason or other. She had telegraphed him to that effect. It was certainly a clever idea. If they were being watched, as he supposed they were, then they could not have chosen a better plan for eluding the vigilance of their pursuers, for no one would recognise them at a masked ball.

The detective quickly made up his mind. He would go to the Hermon Hall that night, with a mask on his face and wearing a red rosette. Then he would see what happened; he would leave the rest to chance.

The doctor had finished his examination by now, and Inspector Brown had been carefully scrutinising the clothes of the dead man again.

"I say, Blake!" he said, looking up. "I think he must be a Frenchman. At any rate, all his clothes seem to bear the mark of a Paris shop."

The detective nodded his head.

"That may prove useful," he said. "You may find out who he is from that. However, I must leave you now. You might let me know if you discover anything fresh."

"Right-ho, Blake!" said Inspector Brown. "See you again soon. I expect you'll be wanted at the inquest."

"I dare say I will!" muttered Blake.

Chapter 3
Tinker's Chase

AFTER Tinker had made his hasty exit from the reading-room of the British Museum, he hurried, as fast as he could, along the corridor that led to the entrance. He caught a momentary glimpse of his quarry as he vanished through the outer doors, and a few seconds later was running down the flight of stone steps that led into the courtyard.

The man he was pursuing turned to the right directly he passed through the massive iron gates, and Tinker had no difficulty in keeping him well in sight. At the corner of Oxford Street he saw him pause and wait for a 'bus. This gave Tinker time to catch him up, and immediately he boarded the vehicle Tinker also clambered on behind, and followed him up to the top deck.

The stranger seemed quite unconscious of the fact that he was being shadowed, and would have had a nasty shock if he had known that the youthful person sitting behind him was intently watching his every movement.

The 'bus continued its way up Oxford Street until it came to the corner of Edgware Road, when the stranger suddenly jumped up from his seat and got off. Tinker followed suit, and kept close behind him, as he strode in the direction of Maida Vale.

Presently he turned into a side-street, continued for about a hundred yards, then vanished inside one of the buildings on the left. A moment later Tinker was standing outside, staring up at the name over the doorway.

For some time he stood there, with a frown on his face, wondering exactly what he should do. Blake's hurried instructions had been that he should follow this man. He had had no time to be more explicit. And, having tracked him to this hotel, Tinker was wondering whether he should hasten back and inform Blake of this fact, or hang about outside for a time, on the chance of discovering something more about the stranger.

He quickly made up his mind, however. He would wait about here for a bit, and see if he could pick up some further information. He commenced striding up and down the street, with a frown on his face, turning over in his mind a number of schemes to help him out of his difficulty.

Over half an hour must have gone by like this, and still Tinker was no nearer a solution of his problem. Then a commissionaire came out of the hotel, and blew a whistle, and a few minutes later a taxi drew up outside. Immediately after, two men came hastening down the steps and made their way to the cab.

Tinker immediately recognised one of them as the stranger he had been pursuing. He hurried along the pavement, and was just in time to overhear what the driver said.

"Charing Cross, sir? Right!"

As Tinker reached the corner of the street the taxi swept past him and turned in the direction of Marble Arch. He glanced anxiously about him; there was no other cab in sight. For a moment he hesitated, then clambered on a passing 'bus that was going southwards.

Before he reached Charing Cross, Tinker had boarded quite a number of 'buses; but he made the journey in record time, and felt sure that the taxi that came out of the station as he entered was the one he had tried to follow.

He darted through the booking-office into the station, and cast a hasty glance round. There was the usual crowd of people waiting about outside the platforms, but at first he could not see the two men for whom he was searching.

Then he observed that they had separated, and were both strolling up and down as if unconscious of each other's presence. Not a little curious as to their motives, and feeling convinced that something interesting would happen before very long, Tinker took up his position by the luggage office, and waited patiently for their next move.

An hour went by, and still nothing happened to attract Tinker's attention. The men were still walking to and fro, but he noticed that now they cast anxious looks at the clock every now and then, as if they were expecting someone.

Tinker was becoming somewhat restive under his forced inactivity when a train came steaming into one of the platforms, and as if by design the two men walked towards the barrier and took up their positions on either side. Tinker noted the fact that they stood well back, as if they were rather anxious not to be observed.

A number of people who had come up by the train were now streaming past the ticket-collector, and the two men were eyeing them searchingly. Presently Tinker saw one of them nod significantly to the other, and they both turned and walked away. They seemed to be following a lady who had come off the train, and who was walking beside the porter who carried her portmanteau.

Following them out into the station-yard, Tinker saw the lady get into a taxi and drive off. The two men immediately hailed another cab, and, pointing significantly to the one that had just left, clambered inside and were whisked away.

By this time Tinker was getting somewhat excited and curious. He glanced round swiftly; a man was just getting out of a taxi that had drawn up alongside the kerb. He ran quickly to the driver.

"That taxi just going out of the gate!" he said quickly. "Double fare if you follow it!" And jumped in.

The cab shot forward; evidently Tinker's driver was after that double fare. As they sped round Trafalgar Square, Tinker noted with a gleam of satisfaction that the other car was only just in front. His driver was keeping close behind; he had understood Tinker perfectly.

They sped up Knightbridge and continued in a westerly direction for some time. Then, soon after passing Hammersmith High Street, the car in front slowed up, one of the men jumped out, and the car shot forward again. Tinker was just wondering what to do when he noticed a third car, which had just turned round in the road and was coming towards him. It occurred to him immediately that this was the taxi the unknown lady had taken, and that she must have just got out.

Deciding on the instant, he signalled his driver to stop, paid his fare, and began retracing his steps. The man who had got out of the taxi was standing in front of a block of flats, gazing up at them rather curiously. As Tinker approached he suddenly turned on his heel, strode across the road, and entered a little shop which bore the sign, "Afternoon teas served here."

It did not take Tinker long to put two and two together. The strange woman, whoever she was, must have entered this block of flats, and the man who, for some reason or other, was spying on her movements, had gone across to the tea-shop in order to watch the building opposite in comfort and without being seen.

Having once embarked on this wild-goose chase, Tinker was not going to give up now. He did not quite relish paying a double taxi fare without getting something in return. He crossed the road and boldly entered the shop, and, sitting down at a little marble-topped table, ordered some tea.

Presently he glanced around cautiously. His suspicions had been quite correct. The stranger was sitting at a table near the door, and was staring attentively across the road at the block of buildings on the opposite side, as if he were expecting someone to come out.

It seemed an interminable time to Tinker before anything else happened. He had consumed three teas, and was just thinking of ordering another when the stranger suddenly rose from his seat, paid his bill, and left the shop.

When Tinker got outside he saw the man just vanishing across the road. It was dark by this time, but the road was well lighted, so that he had little difficulty in keeping his quarry in view. He crept up close behind the man, and dogged his footsteps for fifty yards or so. Then it suddenly dawned on him that the stranger was also following someone a little way in front.

He could not see very distinctly—it was too dark for that—but he had no doubt who this third person was. It was the lady they had followed from Charing Cross, and who must have entered the block of flats opposite the tea-shop.

A minute or so later he saw her halt by the kerb and hold up her hand to a taxi that was approaching. Ignoring the man he had been shadowing, Tinker hurried forward and managed to overhear the instructions she gave to the driver.

"To the Hermon Hall, please!" she said.

As she stepped into the cab Tinker caught sight of a dainty foot shod in gold brocade, and the glistening of silk beneath her opera cloak. The next moment the cab was gone.

The other man had lost no time. Somehow he managed to get hold of another cab, and already he was following the first taxi in close pursuit.

Tinker stood biting his nails in perplexity. He was getting rather tired of chasing people; there seemed no end to the business. Where was the Hermon Hall, at any rate? He had certainly heard of it before, but he could not quite place it. Should he get back to Baker Street now, and see if Blake could make anything of this wild-goose chase? Or should he make one more effort to unravel the mystery?

Then he suddenly decided that he would go on to the Hermon Hall and see what was doing there.

Chapter 4
The Masked Ball

WHEN Blake got back to Baker Street, Tinker had not yet arrived. He was not surprised at that, for he did not expect his young assistant to be back for an hour or more yet. He glanced through the evening paper which he had bought as he came along, and soon found what he was looking for. There was nearly half a column of chatty talk on the Victory ball; in fact, the affair at the Hermon Hall that night seemed to be the chief topic of the press.

But Blake was not interested enough to know what time the doors would be open, and he found that in the first three lines. The dance was booked to commence at eight o'clock. He looked at his watch; it was a quarter to six. He had a good two hours yet, and Tinker was sure to be back before then. But, at all events, he must be there exactly at eight o'clock; it would give him an opportunity to have a look round.

He went to the drawer and took out his dress-suit. It was rather creased, for he had not worn it for some time. He hung it carefully over the back of the chair, and then prepared to have a shave and a general wash and brush up.

It was five minutes past seven when Blake again glanced at the clock. He gave a start of surprise, and began to get busy. In thinking over the queer events of the day he had not noticed that the time was slipping by. Where on earth could Tinker have got to? He had been gone over four hours now; he should be back by this time, surely!

Blake got into his white, starched shirt and proceeded to put on his evening clothes. The black garments suited him admirably, and showed up his clean, well-knit figure to advantage. Coming along, he had stopped at a shop in Oxford Street and bought a black mask and red rosette. He put them carefully into the pocket of his swallow-tail coat, and then glanced anxiously at the clock again.

What possibly could have happened to Tinker? Why in the name of goodness didn't he turn up? He determined to wait another five minutes, and if he had not returned by that time to go without him.

The five minutes passed by, and still no Tinker appeared. With an impatient exclamation, Blake picked up a pencil and scribbled a few lines on a sheet of paper.

Then, with another glance at himself in the mirror, he left the room. He hailed a passing taxi a few yards along the street, and was soon being whisked rapidly towards the scene of the dance.

He got to the Hermon Hall at a minute past eight. A blaze of light shone from the open doors, and the people were already flocking in. As the cab started away from the kerb, Blake adjusted his mask. He did not want to be recognised under any circumstances tonight, and he was taking no chances. But he did not put the rosette in his button-hole; he decided to keep that in his pocket for a little while.

The beautiful, spacious ballroom was already the scene of great bustle and activity. The orchestra had struck up to the tune of a lively fox-trot, and across the highly polished floor a number of masked couples were gliding.

The detective stood near the door and watched the people as they entered. He did not expect the fair Julie, whoever she was, would be here yet, and he wanted to take stock of her before he made his presence known.

He was surprised to observe how difficult it was to recognise a face beneath the mask. Although only a part of the face was concealed and the nose and mouth were quite free, yet the disguise was absolutely complete.

For nearly a quarter of an hour Blake watched by the door. Yet nothing happened to arouse his suspicions. Very few people entered now; the hall was crowded, and the excitement tense.

The whirling couples threaded in and out of each other with merry jest and laughter; everybody was doing something, everybody was excited and happy, while fair ladies and tall, immaculate gentlemen stared through the eyelet holes in their masks and wondered vaguely who their partners might be.

And above the medley of noise and the scraping of hundreds of feet sounded the lively strains of the jazz band as the performers worked away at their instruments with fiery zest and zeal.

As the detective gazed on the wonderful scene, the romance and the glamour began to fascinate him. Ten years seemed to drop from his shoulders; he felt himself a youth again, with his blood tingling in his veins with excitement.

Flinging caution to the wind, he felt in the pocket of his tailed coat, and pulling out the red rosette, stuck it in his button-hole.

Then he stepped on to the polished floor, and, clasping a lady round the waist, who chanced to cross his path, was soon whirling rapidly in and out of the excited throng.

Blake was enjoying himself immensely. He was a good dancer, although he very seldom found time to indulge in such pleasures now, and his partner was no less proficient. As he gazed down at her masked face he wondered what she was like.

But he did not betray any curiosity. There was no time to do anything or say anything; the mad strains of the music seemed to force one to keep on dancing, one's legs kept up that rhythmic movement without any conscious effort.

Then, with a wild crescendo, the band abruptly ceased. As if by magic, the whirling couples suddenly stopped in their mad revel, the floor began quickly to clear, and Blake found himself alone with his fair partner.

"Thank you!" said Blake, bowing politely. "I enjoyed that immensely. I hope you will pardon my rudeness in catching hold of you so unceremoniously."

The lady laughed gaily.

"I am very glad you did," she said. "I wouldn't have missed it for anything!"

"Well, it's very nice of you to say that," rejoined the detective; "and as everyone seems to be making their way to the refreshment bar, I think, we will go, too."

He offered the lady his arm, and together they walked across the hall.

Blake had forgotten altogether the reason why he had come to the dance. He was enjoying himself so much that he did not give a thought to the mystery that he had come here to unravel.

He had forgotten even the existence of the red rosette, which he still wore in his buttonhole. He was feeling young tonight, and he meant to make the most of the occasion.

As they were entering the refreshment-room a little man darted suddenly in front of Blake and nearly upset him. The detective glared round angrily, and then gave a grim chuckle.

"Look at that funny little man who nearly tripped me up just now!" he said to his partner. "He seems to have got into someone else's dress-suit!"

The lady turned her head and glanced over her shoulder.

"Yes," she said, with a merry laugh, "it certainly seems rather too big for him. But he seems to know you. He's staring this way."

Blake turned round and had another look. She was right; the little man was standing by the door, gazing in his direction. He could see two ferrety-looking eyes twinkling behind the black mask with an expression of curiosity.

"Hope he'll know me next time!" muttered Blake; and, dismissing the incident from his mind, began to push his way towards the bar.

He procured some refreshments for his partner, and stood chatting with her for a few minutes. Then the band started up again, and everybody made a rush for the ball-room.

"I must leave you," said the lady hurriedly. "I'm engaged for this dance."

"Perhaps I shall have the pleasure of another?" asked the detective, as she left his side.

"Later on!" she cried, hastening from the room.

Blake finished his drink, and glanced swiftly around. The little man in the ill-fitting clothes was leaning against the bar, sipping a lemonade, but Blake could see that he was furtively watching him all the time. With a sense of irritation Blake walked slowly towards the door.

He was wondering if the fellow's interest proceeded from mere idle curiosity or whether he was deliberately spying on him. At any rate, he would keep a sharp look-out to see if he were being followed.

Feeling somewhat puzzled, the detective stepped out into the ball-room. The dance was now in full swing; the room was crowded with joyous couples, who swayed to and fro to the rhythm of the music.

He hesitated a moment at the door, gazing appreciatively at the gay and brilliant scene. Suddenly he felt a soft hand clasp his arm, and a low, musical voice spoke in French.

"It is you, Monsieur Jacques?"

He swung round quickly, and stared down into the masked face that was tilted up to his own. The stranger was dressed in shimmering gold, and even her dainty feet were shod in slippers of old gold brocade. The light glistened on her fair, wavy hair, which was encircled by a velvet band of black ribbon, and sparkled with precious gems.

The black mask cut strikingly across her oval face, and seemed to accentuate the delicate fairness of her complexion. And in the low-cut bodice of her evening was pinned one solitary red dress rosette.

Blake took all these details in at a glance. He was thinking furiously; the reason of his presence here tonight had flashed back to his mind. This must be the mysterious Julie who had sent that telegram to the strange man who had died so suddenly in the library earlier on in the day. He must have been the "Monsieur Jacques" to whom she had just alluded, and she was mistaking Blake for him.

He did not wonder at that. He was about the same height and of the same build as the dead man, and the mask hid his features. Besides, he was wearing the red rosette. It did not take Blake an instant to come to a decision. He would keep up the deception— for a time, at any rate. He looked down into his fair partner's face.

"You managed to get here, then, Julie?" he said.

She nodded quickly, and began talking rapidly in French. The detective understood French very well, and was quite a fluent speaker, but in her excitement the woman spoke so quickly that he could not follow her in the confusion that was going on around.

"Julie," he whispered, "speak in English; it may arouse suspicion."

It was a cute shot, and worthy of Blake's resourceful brain. The woman gave a quick glance around.

"You are cautious, monsieur," she said in English; "but you are always right."

"And so you had no difficulty in getting here?" said Blake, cunningly feeling his way.

"Yes, Monsieur Jacques, it was very difficult. I only landed at Dover a few moments before I sent the telegram. You got that?"

Blake nodded an affirmative.

"Yes," he said. "That is why I am here."

The woman cast an eager look across the ball-room. Her fascinated gaze rested long-ingly on the whirling couples that glided over the polished floor. The seductive strains of the band proved too much for her.

"Come, monsieur!" she said, putting a white, rounded arm on Blake's shoulder. "We will talk afterwards."

Nothing loth, Blake's strong arm went round her slender waist, and for the second time that night he lost himself in the magic and excitement of the dance.

His partner was exquisite; she seemed to interpret his every step and movement. They glided down the polished floor, swaying gently, and circling gracefully in and out of the thronging figures that moved around them like the colours of a kaleidoscope.

The thrall of the dance had caught Blake in its toils; he had entered into the spirit of the thing now. The spell seemed also to have gripped his partner; a flush of excitement had mounted to her forehead, delicately fading away into the roots of her hair. Behind the mask her eyes were sparkling as brilliantly as the gems that glittered in her hair.

A great desire came over Blake to tear the mask from her face; but he resisted it with an effort. He would have given everything at that moment, however, to have seen her face. His curiosity was getting the better of him.

His mind went back to that last meeting with "Granite" Grant at the Karlton. Was this the beautiful woman he had seen there in the lounge—the woman whom Grant had followed from the room?

He could see that she was tremendously attractive and fascinating. Even his cold, rea-soning nature felt the glamour of her presence; a more emotional man might have lost his head altogether under such circumstances.

They danced on in silence for a time. The woman did not seem to want to speak, and it required all Blake's attention to pilot her in and out of the crowd of dancers.

There was an air of unreality about the scene. The moving figures appeared to be mere puppets driven on by some ceaseless energy. The enchantment of the place took a strong hold on Blake's fancy.

Then, abruptly, the music stopped, the floor began to clear, and he found himself left behind with his unknown companion.

With a quaint little gesture she clasped her hands together and turned to him.

"But it was wonderful, monsieur!" she said. "I had forgotten everything!"

"And so had I!" rejoined Blake.

Her joy was infectious; she was as happy as a child. Blake looked down at her admir-ingly, and again that strong impulse came over him to tear the mask from her face so that he might catch but one glimpse of her features.

But he restrained his curiosity. He could not be guilty of such an unchivalrous action. Common decency and politeness made him bound to respect her incognito.

Suddenly her attitude changed; the smile faded from her lips, and an alert expression came into her eyes. She caught hold of his arm.

"Come, monsieur," she said. "Let us find some place where we may not be interrupted. There is work to do!"

"We will go into the winter garden, mademoiselle," said the detective. "We shall not be interrupted there."

With her hand resting lightly on his arm, they went out into the corridor and made their way towards the great glass conservatory at the far end.

As they left the ballroom the band was just striking up again, and a number of couples came hurrying towards them to take part in the next dance.

Blake was bracing himself to face what was to follow. In the next few minutes he would have to face some awkward questions; it would require all his wits to answer them without arousing the woman's suspicions too soon.

Later on he might let her into the secret of his identity; that depended entirely on circumstances. But first of all he must find out what this mystery was in which she and "Granite" Grant and the two strange men at the library all seemed in some fashion to be involved.

By this time they had reached the winter garden. A few scattered fairy lamps shone between the thick foliage of plants and shrubberies; but there were only sufficient of them to cast a subdued light around. The air was heavy with the perfume of exotic flowers and strange, fragrant mosses.

"We will sit here, Mademoiselle Julie," said Blake, motioning her to a seat that was half-hidden in a giant cluster of fern fronds. The woman sat down and turned to him swiftly.

"And you have the map, Monsieur Jacques?" she asked, in a low whisper.

"Yes," said Blake, "I have the map."

The woman clasped her hands together with a sigh of satisfaction.

"I am so glad!" she said. "I thought it would be too late."

"Why?" asked Blake quietly.

"They were following me—the others. I saw The Leopard in Paris. I think he suspects."

"The Leopard!" repeated Blake, in a puzzled tone.

"Yes, yes, monsieur! You know whom I mean. But it does not matter now. You have the map. That is well. Where is it, Monsieur Jacques?"

Blake hesitated a moment. He had no doubt as to what she was referring. The map in question was the very one that had been torn from the book that day in the reading-room of the British Museum; of that there could not be the slightest doubt. She had come across from France that day, and had arranged to meet Monsieur Jacques here in order to get possession of this map. Now she was asking him for it. Somehow he must put her off; he must try to get her to talk.

"The map is safe, mademoiselle," he said evasively.

"Then where is it?" she demanded impatiently.

"It is locked up in my room, Mademoiselle Julie."

"You have left it at the hotel, monsieur? At the Cosmopolitan? But it is foolish———"

She shrugged her shoulders with a gesture of annoyance. Feeling he was treading on insecure ground Blake began again cautiously.

"You are too impatient, mademoiselle," he said. "It is safe there."

Suddenly she turned on him apprehensively: a sudden suspicion seemed to have flashed across her mind. With a quick movement she thrust out her hand and wrenched the mask from his face.

For a moment she stared at him in bewilderment; then, like a tigress she sprang to her feet with her eyes blazing in anger.

"*Polisson!*" she cried hoarsely. "It is a lie; it is not Monsieur Jacques. You have deceived me—*perfide!*"

She stamped her little feet in a paroxysm of rage, then, with a swish of her silk skirts, fled from the room.

With an exclamation of dismay Blake sprang to his feet and darted after her. As he broke impetuously through the screen of ferns he collided violently with a dark form that had made a frantic effort to get out of his way.

He clutched wildly at the rockery to save himself from falling, then glared angrily at the intruder.

It was the little man in the ill-fitting dress-suit. He was standing rubbing his knees and breathing quickly.

"What the deuce are you doing here?" growled Blake, advancing on him threateningly.

The little man recoiled before the fury of Blake's wrath.

"Hold hard, guv'nor!" he said entreatingly.

Blake took a step forward, and, grasping him by the collar, whipped off his mask. The next instant he sprang back in surprise.

"Tinker!" he gasped with open-mouthed astonishment.

Chapter 5
An Unknown Burglar

IT would be difficult to say which was the most surprised at this dramatic meeting—Sexton Blake or his young assistant. After Blake's involuntary exclamation neither spoke for several seconds; they stood staring at one another in speechless amazement.

Then, presently, the detective recovered somewhat from his first shock of surprise, and the humour of the situation suddenly dawned upon him. He looked down at Tinker's grotesque figure and then burst out laughing; he laughed so heartily that the tears rolled down his cheeks.

With a look of deep perplexity on his face Tinker stared at his master as if he thought he had suddenly taken leave of his senses.

"What's the joke, guv'nor?" he asked guilelessly, after waiting for Blake's merriment to subside.

Tinker's face bore such a ludicrous expression that Blake exploded again. He held on to the rockery with both hands, and shook so violently that he dislodged one of the bricks, which dropped down on Tinker's toe and made him jump away with a sharp yelp of pain.

"Why, you! You're the joke, Tinker!" gasped Blake between his spasms of mirth.

A look of intense indignation swept over Tinker's face. He glared resentfully at his master, and tried to assume a dignified attitude.

"Me!" he exclaimed, in a high-pitched voice. "But I don't quite cotton you, guv'nor. Didn't know there was anything wrong with me."

"But there is," declared Blake, wiping his eyes on his handkerchief. "You're a sort of misfit, Tinker."

"A misfit, guv'nor! What d'you mean? I'm quite all right."

"But you're not, Tinker! You're all wrong. You look just like a scarecrow. But where on earth did you get them, Tinker?" asked Blake, rather more kindly, seeing Tinker's obvious discomfiture.

"I hired them, guv'nor, from a shop. I had no time to go home and change. The chap said they fitted like a glove."

Blake's mouth twitched suspiciously, but he controlled his feelings and became immediately grave and serious.

"Ah, well, Tinker!" he said soothingly. "However, let's hear the news! What made you come to this place? And how about the chap you followed from the British Museum?"

"That's just why I came here, guv'nor! I chased him along Oxford Street till we got to Edgware Road; then he suddenly disappeared inside a hotel."

"What hotel?" asked Blake quickly.

"The Cos—— Blow it, guv'nor, I've forgotten the name, and I felt sure I should remember it, too."

"The Cosmopolitan, Tinker?"

"That's it, guv'nor—the Cosmopolitan!"

"I see!" muttered Blake, significantly. "Go on, Tinker!"

Tinker proceeded to give his master a lucid account of the successive happenings that had led up to his discovery by Blake in the winter garden in this dramatic fashion.

"You see, guv'nor," he explained, "I hadn't the slightest notion that it was you. I recognised the lady by her gold-coloured shoes, and when I saw her go up to you I made sure that it was this Johnnie who had been following her."

"I understand, Tinker. And so you are not really certain that this other fellow was at the dance. You didn't see him enter?"

"No, I didn't, guv'nor. You see, I got here rather late. But I guessed he'd come on. The last I saw of him was when he got in the taxi at Kensington."

"Was he the man you followed from the British Museum?"

"Yes, the very same man, guv'nor."

"Then no doubt this other fellow was his accomplice. And having pointed the lady out to him at Charing Cross he left him to watch her movements, for some reason or other."

"That's so, guv'nor."

"I wonder if that other fellow is at the dance, Tinker? And what the deuce was his game?"

"You've got me beat there, guv'nor," Tinker rejoined. "I'm dashed if I can make daylight out of the business."

The detective looked thoughtful for a few moments.

"Well, it's no use staying here, Tinker," he said at last. "Let's get back to Baker Street. I must do some hard thinking. Besides, it's getting rather late now. How about those togs you've got on? Have you got your other clothes here?"

"Yes, they're in the cloak-room, guv'nor. I'll just slip along and change them."

"Yes. Be quick. I'm coming that way, too."

As they were making their way towards the corridor the detective suddenly stopped and stood listening intently.

"Did you hear anything, Tinker?" he whispered.

"No, guv'nor! Can't say that I did."

"Thought I heard somebody moving behind those ferns over there."

He listened again, and then added:

"However, I suppose it was merely my fancy. Come on."

The dance was in full swing as they crossed the hall, and the excitement was at its height. Blake, however, took no notice of what was going on around him. For him the dance had lost its fascination; pleasure had given way to duty, and he was absorbed in seeking some explanation of the strange happenings that had taken place that day.

He waited while his assistant had changed into his every-day clothes, then both of them stepped out into the street.

"It's a beautiful night, Tinker," said Blake. "What do you say to walking home. In any case, it's rather late to get a taxi."

"I'm game, guv'nor."

"This way, then."

They began walking briskly in the direction of Baker Street. The air was crisp and invigorating, and the pavements rang hard and clear to the sound of their feet. They strode on in silence, each pondering over the strange events of the day. There were very few people abroad; the hour was late; the theatregoers had long since returned to their homes.

Presently the detective glanced down at his assistant.

"Can't help having an idea that we are being followed, Tinker," he said in a casual tone of voice.

"What makes you think that, guv'nor?" asked Tinker, somewhat startled.

Blake made no reply, but kept up the same pace for about a dozen yards. Suddenly he caught hold of Tinker's arm and dragged him to a standstill.

"Listen," he muttered.

Far away up the street came the regular tramp of approaching footsteps. Then abruptly they ceased and all was silence.

"Let's walk on again, Tinker," said Blake.

They continued their way along the road for about a hundred yards, then suddenly stopped again. As before, the sound of echoing footsteps came from a little distance behind, and then as abruptly ceased again.

Blake gave an impatient shrug of his shoulders.

"Come on, Tinker," he said. "It doesn't really matter; perhaps it's only a coincidence after all. At any rate, we'll be on our guard against any possible surprise."

But nothing further occurred to occasion them any alarm. If they were being followed their pursuer, whoever he was, took good care not to come near enough to reveal himself, and about twenty minutes later they turned into Baker Street and entered their house.

"Well, Tinker," said the detective, "I'm just about dog tired, so I'm going to flop straight into bed. I'll think about things in the morning; my brain's not clear enough to work properly at the present moment."

"Same here, guv'nor," said Tinker. "I bet it doesn't take me long to get down to it. Good night!"

"Good-night, Tinker!"

***

Two hours or more must have passed before Blake again awoke, although it seemed to him that he had only just laid his head on the pillow. He sat up with a start, listening intently.

He was vaguely aware that something had happened to cause this sudden awakening, but for the moment he could not gather his wits together sufficiently to understand what it was.

Then immediately he heard it again—the deep, furious growling of Pedro, and it seemed to come from the floor beneath. In an instant Blake had sprang out of bed, snatched up his electric torch and the small automatic which always stood on the table at his side, and was hastening downstairs.

The door of his consulting-room was open, a cold current of air was blowing through, and from the darkness ahead came that deep, sullen growl of Pedro.

A thin beam of light from the torch swept across the room, and Blake gave an exclamation of amazement as his eyes rested on the litter of papers that lay about the floor. The drawers of his desk had been forced open and the contents flung all over the place.

"Pedro!" he called. "Good fellow! What is it?" And flashed the light on the great bloodhound.

The dog was crouching down beneath the window, growling furiously and shaking something in his massive jaws.

Blake caught hold of the animal by the scruff of the neck and dragged from his mouth a piece of cloth. He stared down at it in surprise. It was a piece of striped material like that commonly used for trousering, and the edges were all ragged and frayed as if it had been violently torn apart.

As the detective was still staring at this object Tinker came hurrying into the room.

"What's the matter, guv'nor?" he asked in a startled voice.

Blake gave a dry chuckle.

"We seem to have had visitors tonight, Tinker," he said. "Pedro evidently came in to pay his respects, but they wouldn't wait to discuss matters with him. The fellow left his card, though—here it is."

Blake held out the piece of cloth for Tinker to inspect.

"Well I'm blowed!" muttered Tinker. "Pedro must have taken a mouthful out of the chap's trousers. But how did he get away?"

Blake pointed to the window.

"Easy," he said. "But I bet he had a fright when Pedro made a grab at his anatomy. If he hadn't slammed the window behind him Pedro would have been through in a jiffy."

"But Pedro was shut in the back room, guv'nor. Wonder the fellow waited for him to get through; he must have heard him growling."

"Trust old Pedro for that!" said Blake. "He doesn't growl when he's after somebody's body—he's far too cunning for that."

Tinker cast a look at the litter of papers.

"What on earth does it mean?" he asked. "Does this fellow think we keep money locked up in your desk?"

"No!" said Blake decisively. "This is no ordinary thief, Tinker. As I thought, we were being followed here tonight from the Hermon Hall. That fellow suspects that we've got something else in our possession. What it is I don't exactly know at the present moment, but he certainly wasn't after our money."

Blake carefully put the piece of cloth away in a tin box, and then proceeded to collect the papers that were lying on the floor.

"Come on, Tinker!" he said presently. "It's no use worrying about the matter tonight. Let's get back to bed and finish our sleep. We'll leave Pedro here to keep guard; we're not likely to be disturbed again."

After another look round, the detective and his assistant went back to bed.

Chapter 6
Venner, the "Leopard"

IN the early hours of the morning, not long after Blake and his young assistant had dozed off to sleep again after their rude and sudden awakening, a man crept up the steps of the Cosmopolitan Hotel, just off the Edgware Road, and angrily shook the handle of the door.

A few moments later the door was opened by the night-porter, who gazed at the intruder with sleepy eyes, and, evidently recognising him as stopping there, stepped aside and allowed him to pass.

With a brief nod to, the porter, the man strode across the foyer and ascended the winding staircase. A few moments later he disappeared inside a room on the first floor corridor.

At his entry, a man, who was striding up and down in front of the fire that still smouldered in the grate, paused abruptly and then came towards him.

"Well, any luck, Venner?" he asked anxiously.

The man addressed as Venner gave vent to a stifled oath and flung his hat savagely on the bed.

There was something peculiar and sinister about this man; over his right eye was a little oblique scar, and his face was spotted with red blotches.

It was partly owing to this latter characteristic that he had been given the name of The Leopard, and partly because of the low cunning and craft with which he carried out his plans.

For years The Leopard had been mixed up in all manner of shady enterprises on the Continent. He had lived in every capital of Europe, and was in the habit of appearing and disappearing in the most startling manner.

Outwardly, he was just plain Mr. Venner, a gentleman of independent means, and an Englishman when in England, a German when in Germany, an American when in the United States, and so on. Only the Secret Service knew him for what he was—an Austrian of mixed birth who sold himself to the highest bidder provided the work required of him was unscrupulous enough and held out hopes of a big reward. And it was in Secret Service circles that he had gained the name of The Leopard.

The Leopard turned to his companion with an angry frown on his face.

"Look!" he said, and thrust out his leg. "That was a near thing, Von Rosenburg!"

The other man stared curiously at the trouser leg. Just below the calf there was a great rent where a piece of the cloth had been torn away.

"How on earth did that happen?" Rosenburg asked.

"A great brute of a dog!" said The Leopard. "The beast suddenly leapt at me. Lucky thing I left the window open for an emergency. I was only just in time—an instant more and the brute would have had me."

Von Rosenburg gave an impatient exclamation.

"But tell me what happened, Venner!" he said quickly. "How about the map—did you recover it?"

"No, I didn't!" rapped out The Leopard. "To tell you the truth, I can't quite get the hang of things. Julie seems to be playing some double game, but at the moment she has got me beaten."

"What do you mean, Venner? Where did she go when I left you?"

"To the Hermon Hall—I followed her there."

She went to the Victory ball?"

"Yes. I lost a little time in getting into some clothes and obtaining a mask, but I recognised her directly I got inside. She looked very gorgeous."

"She always does," muttered Von Rosenburg, and a peculiar gleam shone in his eyes. "But what happened after that, Venner?"

"She met some man. It had evidently been prearranged, for they both wore red rosettes."

"But that is very remarkable, Venner. Who could it possibly have been? Surely we could not have been misinformed! She was expecting to meet Jacques, and Jacques——"

Von Rosenburg shrugged his shoulders significantly, and left the sentence unfinished.

"Precisely!" said The Leopard. "But I have not finished yet. They danced together, and then went out into the winter garden. I followed them there. I had to be very careful, for there was another fellow who seemed mighty interested in them as well."

"But this is more mysterious than ever, Venner. Who could this fellow have been?"

"A moment, Von Rosenburg! I hid behind some ferns and waited. Julie and the other man sat down on a seat and began talking earnestly. I could not hear what they said, I was too far away; but I distinctly heard the word 'map' mentioned several times. Suddenly Julie sprang to her feet. She seemed to be in a great rage about something; apparently her companion refused to give up the map."

Von Rosenburg's face flushed to the colour of beetroot; in his excitement the veins stood out on his forehead.

"What!" he exclaimed. "You think this man had the map! But who is he? And how could he possibly have obtained it?"

"Wait, Von Rosenburg, until you've heard the rest. I heard Julie talking in angry, excited tones, then she suddenly turned on her heel and sped from the place. Her companion jumped to his feet and made as if to follow her; but the next moment he had collided with this other fellow, who seemed to be on the same game as myself."

"He was spying on them, Venner?"

"Yes, so it seemed. I could not follow what happened then, I was afraid of being discovered; but the strange part about it is that they both went off together as if they were the best of friends. They seemed to treat the whole thing as a joke, for the big fellow was roaring with laughter."

"But who were they, Venner? Haven't you the slightest idea?"

The Leopard gave a low, nervous chuckle.

"Yes," he said quietly; "I have. The big fellow was the very man whom I met in the British Museum today, and who gave me such a nasty shock. He was Sexton Blake, the world-famous English detective, and the younger fellow was Tinker, his assistant."

Von Rosenburg started back, and a pasty look spread over his face.

"Sexton Blake!" he gasped. "A thousand devils, Venner! But what the deuce had he got to do with the business?"

"Quite a lot, it seems," said The Leopard, scowling savagely. "He's about one of the cutest fellows we're ever likely to come up against. It's rather unfortunate for us that he happens to have a finger in the pie."

"But are you sure he has a finger in the pie, Venner?"

The Leopard cast a contemptuous look at his companion.

"Sure!" he said. "But it's quite evident. I watched Jacques tear the map from the book and saw him conceal it. And then——"

"And then you killed him," said Von Rosenburg quietly. "It was a clumsy job, Venner; but go on."

The Leopard's face had gone as white as a sheet; there was a scared look in his eyes.

"Yes, I killed him," he said hoarsely. "But I did not bungle it, Von Rosenburg. It was our only chance. If this meddlesome detective had not turned up I should have had the map, and we could have been away by now."

"But you haven't got the map, Venner, so it's no good supposing anything. Where is it now that's the vital question?"

"Listen, Von Rosenburg! Somehow Sexton Blake is mixed up in this business. He came to the British Museum today for the express purpose of getting that map; there is no doubt about that. When he found out that someone had been there first, he would naturally have Jacques thoroughly searched; then he would be certain to discover it. Isn't that perfectly clear?"

The other man nodded his head in agreement.

"Very well, then," continued The Leopard. "That is why, I followed him to Baker Street tonight. If it wasn't for that brute of a dog, I might have been successful in my search. But there's no doubt that it's still in his possession; he wouldn't have time to make use of it yet. And we've still got a chance to get hold of it."

Von Rosenburg stroked his chin thoughtfully.

"Do you think he can be bought, Venner?" he asked presently.

"Every man has his price, Von Rosenburg!"

"You are right, Venner. Then try him—offer him ten thousand.[7] It is a big price, but it's worth it."

"Very good, Von Rosenburg, it shall be done. And if that doesn't fetch him, well——"

The two men exchanged significant glances.

"It will be the worse for him," muttered Von Rosenburg fiercely.

Chapter 7
Ten Thousand Pounds

IT was with an extremely thoughtful look on his face that Sexton Blake, sat at his desk staring abstractedly in front of him. It was the morning following the events related in the last chapter, and the great detective had been puzzling over them for the last hour or more now without having been able to arrive at any definite conclusions.

Of one thing, however, he was certain. And that was that by some strange chance he had been suddenly plunged into the net of Secret Service intrigue and cunning, and that even if he so wished he could not extricate himself now—he must go through with it.

Already unknown forces were arrayed against him; during the night his room had been broken into and his drawers ransacked. His enemies, whoever they might be, had not

---

[7] £10,000 in 1920 is worth about £570,000.00 in 2023

wasted any time; it was clear they suspected him, and that they would stick at nothing to achieve their ends.

But why had they broken into his room? What were they searching for? There was only one conclusion to be drawn from that—they were looking for this map, and they evidently suspected that it might be in his possession.

The man who had broken in last night must have been an accomplice of the mysterious Julie. He had led her to believe that he had the map, and no doubt she had set this man to follow him immediately after her dramatic flight from the Hermon Hall.

Who was Julie? he wondered. How did she come to be mixed up in this dangerous game of duplicity and cunning? He had not seen her face, but he felt sure that she was the same young woman he had seen that day at the Karlton.

She was very beautiful and fascinating; it seemed absurd to associate her with violent deeds and shady intrigues. He remembered how angry she had been with him; she had stamped her little foot in her rage and called him all manner of hard names.

The recollection brought a flicker of amusement into the detective's stern face.

Then he thought of the man who had died so mysteriously in the reading-room of the British Museum. That was another side to the problem. Who could he have been? What was his business? Julie had known him. She had called him Monsieur Jacques; it was she who had sent him that telegram.

How had this man died? From what cause had he met death so suddenly? There was a paragraph in the morning paper about it. Although the cause of death was not stated, there was a vague hint that it might be heart failure, or some other quite natural cause.

The police seemed to be more concerned in discovering who he might be. The paper stated that the body was lying in the mortuary, awaiting identification.

Blake determined that he would go there very shortly. Since yesterday afternoon something might have been discovered which would throw some light on the mystery.

He did not believe that the man had died from heart failure. There was more in it than that. Something seemed to suggest to him that he had met with foul play.

Then, again, what was that other man doing in the library—the man with the little oblique scar above the right eye? He remembered the startled expression that had come into his face when he met those of the detective, and how he had rushed madly from the reading-room.

Then there was Tinker's extraordinary account of what had happened afterwards when he had followed him out of the Museum. What could possibly———"

"Gent wants to see you rather particularly, guv'nor."

The detective looked up at his assistant, with a start.

"What's his name, Tinker?" he asked.

"Don't know, guv'nor. I haven't seen him yet. Mrs. B. opened the door to him. Shall I go and ask?"

"No; tell her to show him in."

A moment later the door opened again, and a man stepped inside. The detective cast a swift glance at his visitor, and a thrill of amazement shot through him.

He had recognised him instantly. Over the right eye was that little familiar oblique scar. It was the man whom he had first seen at the Karlton, over three months ago, and who had been in the reading-room of the British Museum on the previous day.

He glanced across at Tinker. His assistant had also come to the same conclusion. He was staring at the stranger, with mingled surprise and incredulity.

Blake's steel-grey eyes narrowed somewhat as he turned towards his visitor. The imperturbable look had not once left his face; he was still outwardly calm and self-possessed.

"Good-morning!" he said, in cold, even tones. "Will you please take a seat?"

The Leopard—for it was none other than he—took a step towards the detective, but did not take the proffered chair.

"I believe I have the honour of speaking to Mr. Sexton Blake?" he said politely.

The detective inclined his head.

"That is my name," he said. "And yours?"

The Leopard ignored the question, and looked at Tinker suspiciously.

"I have come about a highly confidential and private matter, Mr. Blake," he said, and again glanced at Tinker significantly.

The man's meaning was not lost on Blake. He answered curtly and abruptly.

"My assistant is in my confidence," he said coldly. "His presence need not disturb you."

"But this is extremely confidential, Mr. Blake," persisted the other man. "If it is all the same to you, I would rather we were alone."

For a moment Blake hesitated. Tinker fully shared all his secrets, and he was rather loth to turn him out of the room.

However, it did not matter very much one way or the other; he could easily tell him what had transpired afterwards.

"As you wish!" he said, and gave a brief nod to Tinker.

"And now, sir," continued Blake, when they were alone, "perhaps you will be good enough to tell me your name?"

"It is of no consequence, Mr. Blake," said The Leopard hurriedly. "If you like, you may call me Mr. Smith."

"Very well. Mr. Smith. Then I take it that your business is more important than your name."

"Just so, Mr. Blake——"

The man hesitated and seemed at a loss how to continue.

The detective sat back in his chair, and eyed him searchingly.

"Pray proceed," he said quietly. "My time is valuable, and strictly limited."

"Then I will get to the point immediately, Mr. Blake. I believe you have something in your possession which, strictly speaking, is not your property."

"That is quite possible, Mr. Smith."

"You do not commit yourself, Mr. Blake."

"You are not very explicit, Mr. Smith."

"Then I will explain myself," said The Leopard. "The thing to which I allude was taken from the reading-room of the British Museum yesterday afternoon. Is that plain, Mr. Blake?"

"Quite," said the detective.

"And it is in your possession?"

Behind Blake's impassive features a swift process of reasoning was going on in his mind.

He had no doubt as to what the stranger was alluding to. It was the map that had been torn from the book on the previous day. Evidently, then, this man had not been able to get hold of it, as he had supposed, and, for some reason or other, he suspected that Blake had it in his possession.

Well, he would let him think so. He would lead him on, and see if he would throw any fresh light on this strange mystery with which he was grappling.

"I should say that was very probable, Mr. Smith," he said.

The Leopard came nearer to the detective. There was a strange glitter in his eyes.

"Then you have the map, Mr. Blake?" he said, in a hoarse whisper.

"Well, Mr. Smith! And if I have?"

The man moistened his lips, and carefully chose his words.

"Mr. Blake," he said, "I do not know what your motives are, or how it is that you should be concerned in this little affair. Possibly that was a pure accident as far as you are concerned. If it were, then you will be guided by me, and have nothing further to do with what cannot possibly concern you. But that is a matter for your own good sense and judgment. In the meantime, it is very necessary that you should hand that map over to my keeping."

"Indeed, Mr. Smith! You seem to attach considerable importance to this map."

"I do, Mr. Blake!"

"For what reasons, Mr. Smith?"

The Leopard gave a little shrug of the shoulders.

"For purely sentimental reasons, Mr. Blake," he replied vaguely.

"And supposing I do not agree to give you the map?"

"I am hoping you will not be so ill-advised, Mr. Blake. I am here to make you a very substantial offer, which I do not think you would be so foolish to refuse."

"What is your offer?"

"Five thousand pounds,[8] Mr. Blake!"

The detective looked thoughtful for a moment. He was beginning to realise now the great value which this man placed on the page that had been stolen from the reading-room.

Even if the map were in Blake's possession, he would not have parted with it for ten times the amount; not being in his possession, it was useless to argue.

"No," he said; "I cannot accept your offer, Mr. Smith."

---

[8] £5,000 in 1920 is worth about £286,000.00 in 2023

The Leopard stifled an angry exclamation, and his brows clouded.

"It is not enough, Mr. Blake?" he said. "Very well, then, we will make it ten thousand. Ten thousand pounds! It is a lot of money, Mr. Blake!"

"It is!" admitted the detective.

"And you accept?" asked the other man eagerly.

Blake felt in the inside of his coat, and, drawing forth his pocket-book, carelessly turned it over in his hands several times. It was his way of playing with his visitor, of leading him on. Then he replaced the case, and leant back in his chair.

"No!" he said decisively. "I cannot accept your offer, Mr. Smith. I have to wish you good-day!"

A livid expression came into The Leopard's face. He gazed across at the detective with the light of fierce hatred in his eyes. Then he suddenly dragged his hand from his pocket, and the next instant Sexton Blake found himself looking down the barrel of a wicked little automatic.

"That pocket-book!" he hissed. "Quick! Or it'll be the worse for you!"

A faint smile played about the corner of the detective's mouth. It did not matter much whether he had the pocketbook or not; he would not find what he wanted inside.

Blake fumbled in his pocket, and slowly drew out the wallet. He was about to hand it to his adversary, when something drastic happened.

The door of the room shot open, as if it had received a blow from a battering ram, and, with a roar of fury, the body of the great bloodhound came hurtling through the air.

The Leopard gave a yell of terror, and turned to flee, but Pedro was too quick for him. The next instant the great dog had sprang at his throat, and borne him, crashing, to the floor.

Blake was on his feet in a second.

"Pedro!" he thundered. "Down—down, boy, I say!"

At the sound of his master's voice, the dog lifted his great head, and, growling savagely, slunk away from the prostrate man. But he still watched him furtively, as if he only wanted the slightest nod from his master to hurl himself at his enemy's throat again.

More frightened than hurt, The Leopard climbed to his feet, and retreated to the further end of the room. Blake eyed the man narrowly. A sudden thought had swept across his mind.

"My dog seems to have taken an affection to you," he said sarcastically. "That is rather strange—seems to have met you before."

He pulled open the drawer of his desk, and took out the piece of cloth that he had found Pedro worrying the night before.

"Here, Pedro!" he said, flinging it on the floor in front of the animal. "Whose is this? Have it, boy!"

The hair along the dog's back bristled with rage. He gave a low growl of fury, and stole towards the shaking man, with his great fangs showing.

Blake gave a low chuckle of understanding.

"All right, old chap!" he said, coaxingly. "Let him alone! He's nearly dead with fright as it is."

He cast a contemptuous glance in the direction of the trembling man.

"So it was you," he said, "who broke into this room early this morning, and ransacked my drawers! Your interest in my affairs does me too much honour, Mr. Smith. Please get out of my sight, as quickly as possible, before I have you arrested as an ordinary thief and housebreaker."

The Leopard stood glowering at the detective, with a look of baffled rage on his face.

"This will be a bad morning's work for you, Mr. Blake," he hissed.

"Pedro!" said Blake meaningly.

The bloodhound gave his master a quick look of understanding, and crouched down on his belly.

But The Leopard did not wait for Pedro to spring. He cast one startled glance at the animal, then, with a cry of fear, turned on his heels, and fled from the room.

Chapter 8
An Unexpected Attack

FOR some time after his strange visitor had fled from the room Blake stood silently considering this new, and altogether unexpected turn of events. Tinker had rushed to the door directly after Pedro had broken loose, and had been an eye-witness of what had occurred. He watched his master curiously, not venturing to disturb him in his present contemplative mood.

A number of questions were passing through the detective's mind, but the answers seemed to contradict one another. It was one of those rare occasions in which he found it impossible to piece together the known facts of the situation, and so obtain some workable theory of what was going on behind the scenes.

He was certain of one thing, and that was that this map that had been stolen from the British Museum contained some clue as to the present whereabouts of Granite Grant. Of that there could no doubt.

But where was the map? How had it disappeared? And why had this strange Mr. Smith placed such an enormous value on it, and gone to such extremes to get hold of it?

Then there was Julie! Who in the name of goodness was Julie? And what part did she play in this mysterious drama?

A sudden realisation came to the detective of the tremendous task that he had involuntarily taken upon his shoulders. All unwittingly, he had been called upon to solve something that was bigger and more important than his usual professional work of tracking down the criminal.

He had been drawn into the web of international intrigue, and the fate of Granite Grant—and even his own fate—was but a small matter when placed against the interests of his country.

It was this thought that decided Blake. He would go and see Sir Vrymer Fane, the head of the Secret Service. He would be sure to know what the mission was that Granite Grant had undertaken, and very possibly he might see things clearer then.

He did not doubt that Sir Vrymer Fane would grant him an interview. Once before the great statesman had honoured him by seeking his advice, and he had paid a great compliment to the detective's cleverness and ingenuity. This time Blake would seek Sir Vrymer's advice, and he would be guided by what he might disclose.

But there were one or two other things which demanded his attention first. There was the strange death of the unknown man at the British Museum yesterday to be accounted for.

The body was lying at the mortuary awaiting identification. He would go along there and see if anything else had transpired.

Then there was the inquest to be held; he would know then if his suspicions were correct—whether or not the man had met with foul play.

Blake suddenly dropped his mood of reflection, and turned briskly to his assistant.

"That was the man you followed from the reading-room yesterday, Tinker, wasn't it?" he asked.

"That's him, guv'nor."

"You'll be interested to know, Tinker, that I've just missed making my fortune. Our friend came to offer me ten thousand pounds in exchange for the map."

Tinker drew in his breath with a gasp.

"You're not kidding, guv'nor, are you?"

"No; honest truth, Tinker!"

"Then it's a great pity you couldn't close with the bargain, guv'nor!"

"It's a pity I haven't the map, Tinker. But if I had I wouldn't have parted with it for ten times that amount. If this fellow is willing to give me that for it, you can imagine what it would be worth to the British Foreign Office."

"But what's it all about, guv'nor? Why should a piece of paper be worth a fortune?"

"Ask me another, Tinker. Frankly, I don't know at the present moment. But it's pretty evident that that map contains some very important information, and that "Granite" Grant, as usual, has managed to get in first. The fellow who's just gone out must be in the pay of some other country. He's a wily sort of rogue, and we shall have to keep our eyes skinned. He's not thrown up the sponge yet by any means—you mark my words!"

"But why didn't you have the fellow arrested, guv'nor, for breaking into here last night?"

"It's not advisable, Tinker. He's no ordinary criminal, and if we put him in quod it would lead to some pretty awkward questions that I'm not prepared to answer. Besides, the Secret Service people would only regard us as a pair of meddlesome fools."

"Well, what's the next move, guv'nor?"

"I'm going round to the mortuary now, Tinker, to see if anything else has been discovered about the man who died at the British Museum yesterday. You might wait here until I return; I may have something to tell you."

"Right you are, guv'nor!" said Tinker.

It was about half an hour later where Blake arrived at the mortuary. As he strode down the dark corridor towards the room where the body was lying, he suddenly collided with a man who was hurrying in the opposite direction.

"Beg your pardon!" muttered the other, as he made to resume his way.

But Blake caught hold of his arm.

"Is that you, Brown?" he asked, looking into his face.

Inspector Brown gave a little start of recognition.

"Why, yes, Mr. Blake!" he said. "How are you? I wasn't expecting to meet you!"

"Nor I you, Brown. I've just come along to see if anyone has identified the body. Anything fresh come to light?"

"No, nothing to speak of. There's one old chap in there now who seems mighty interested in the corpse; but I think it's merely a case of idle curiosity with him."

"Then there're no new facts at all, Brown?"

"No, nothing much, Mr. Blake."

Blake looked searchingly at the inspector. Something in the man's tone aroused his suspicions; he felt that he was keeping something back.

"Are you quite sure, Brown," he asked, "that you've discovered nothing else?"

Blake's keen eyes seemed to pierce through the inspector, and the latter began to shuffle uneasily. Suddenly the vague suspicion in the detective's mind that he was concealing something grew stronger. With his usual quick wit and cleverness he followed up his line of reasoning.

"You have found a map, Brown!" he said quietly.

It was a cute shot on Blake's part. He had relied on his extraordinary intuition and his faculty of reading a man's thoughts, and once again he was right. Inspector Brown stared at the detective in astonishment, and it was evident that he was completely taken by surprise.

"Why, I'm blowed!" he stammered. "But what a chap you are, Blake, for finding out things!"

"Then you did find a map, Brown?" asked the detective.

Although he tried to put the question casually, it was with the utmost difficulty that Blake could restrain his eagerness.

"Yes, I did, Mr. Blake. But it just beats me how you managed to find that out. I found it stuck in the man's boot. A piece of the leather was cut out, and the map folded up and stuck inside. I wouldn't have noticed it if I hadn't seen the corner sticking out."

"And have you got it got it with you, Brown?"

The inspector's hand went swiftly to the breast-pocket of his coat.

"You bet I have, Mr. Blake!" he said. "It's in there, and there it's going to stop!"

"Can I have a look at it?" asked Blake quietly.

Inspector Brown took a step back: an obstinate look had crept into his face. He stared at the detective suspiciously, then slowly winked his eye.

"Nothing doing, Mr. Blake!" he said.

Blake struggled hard to keep his temper. Inspector Brown's intelligence was of the heavy, stodgy type. He had made a discovery, and he was going to keep it to himself. In his desire to claim all the credit for himself he was becoming cautious to the extent of stupidity.

But, somehow, Blake must get hold of that map; his anxiety was increasing every moment. He knew the invisible forces by which they were surrounded; his enemies would stick at nothing to achieve their ends. If they once knew that Brown had the map in his pocket his life wouldn't be worth a moment's purchase.

"Look here, Brown," he said coaxingly, "I'm merely asking you to let me look at this map. Surely there's no harm in that?"

But Brown still shook his head obstinately.

"Sorry, Mr. Blake," he said. "But this happens to be my job, and I'm not sharing it with anyone."

"But I'm not asking you to share it with me, Brown. I simply want to look at that map. Great Scott, man, you don't know what you're up against. This is no ordinary sort of crime; there's more in it than meets the eye, I tell you——"

The detective stopped abruptly as a footstep sounded behind. An old man, leaning heavily on a thick stick, and with a white, straggly beard, was slowly passing down the corridor.

"Didn't recognise him, I suppose?" called out the inspector.

The old man shook his head, and continued his way without pausing.

"I tell you, Brown," continued Blake, "that this is a bigger job than you suppose. It's absolutely urgent that I should see that map."

But the earnestness of Blake's words had the opposite effect to what he intended. Inspector Brown was so impressed that he began to think that he was on a very good thing. Already visions of a rapid promotion flitted before his eyes. He was more determined than ever not to let anyone else have a share in the credit.

"What business is it of yours, Mr. Blake?" he asked angrily. "This is my job, and my job it's going to remain! I know what I'm up to, and I don't want you to interfere. I tell you once and for all that you're not going to look at the map!"

Blake saw that it was useless to argue further with the man; he only became more obstinate every moment. He must think of some other method of gaining possession of the map.

That he would get hold of it he was determined, even if he had to employ underhand means; but he must think the matter over first.

"Very well, Brown," he said quietly. "If you won't listen to reason, then it's useless to discuss the matter further. But I warn you that you're up against a tough proposition. You'll find out that you've bitten off more than you can chew."

"Well, that's my business, Mr. Blake. I know what I'm about, don't you worry. However, we're wasting time here; I must be going. Good-day!"

The Scotland Yard man turned on his heel and strode away down the corridor, leaving Blake full of grave fears and full of anxieties.

For a moment the detective was at a loss what to do. He hesitated in silent perplexity, then slowly followed the Scotland Yard man down the corridor.

Some instinct told him that it would be wise to keep the inspector in sight; something might happen at any moment, and then the map might be lost beyond recovery.

When he reached the entrance to the mortuary, Blake saw Inspector Brown just crossing the road about a hundred yards or so to the right.

Still intent on keeping him in sight, he began to walk in the same direction. And then, with a suddenness that absolutely took the inspector by surprise, the very thing happened that Blake had feared.

A bent, old man with a thick stick seemed suddenly to appear from nowhere. He abruptly cut across the inspector's path, and in avoiding him the latter slipped and grasped hold of the railings to save himself.

At that moment two other men jostled into him; there was a brief scuffle, and Inspector Brown went staggering back with a blow on the chin.

An instant later three men had sprung into a taxi, that had appeared as if by magic, and were being whisked rapidly away into the distance.

The whole thing happened so quickly that it was over by the time Blake had raced to the spot. Inspector Brown stood on the pavement, stupidly rubbing his chin and staring about him in a dazed fashion.

One or two passers-by were eyeing him curiously; but the attack had been so sudden that none of them realised what had occurred.

Blake grasped the inspector by the arm, and shook him savagely.

"The map, man!" he gasped. "Have you still got it? Pull yourself together!"

Inspector Brown's hand shot to his breast-pocket, then he gave a quick exclamation of dismay.

"By gosh!" he muttered in amazement. "It's gone, Blake!"

"Of course it has, Brown!" said the detective quietly. "That's exactly what I expected!"

The Scotland Yard man glared about him in bewilderment.

"Who the deuce were they?" he asked. "I simply didn't get a chance. They were on me before I knew what was up."

"One of them was the old man who passed us in the mortuary, Brown. He seemed mighty agile all of a sudden! Well, I warned you, but you wouldn't listen to me; you've only yourself to blame. This is the worse day's work you've ever done, Brown!"

A troubled look came into the inspector's face; it was plain that he had received a nasty jar.

"Can't be helped now, Mr. Blake," he said apologetically. "We all make mistakes. There's no need for you to make a song about it."

"Pshaw!" muttered the detective. And, turning on his heel, strode off in the other direction.

Chapter 9
Blake Sees Sir Vrymer

YOU are asking me a very peculiar question, Mr. Blake, and were it not for the fact that I have a very high opinion of your capabilities, I should not for an instant entertain the idea of discussing the matter with you."

Sir Vrymer Fane, the head of the Secret Service, looked across at his visitor with a faint air of puzzlement and doubt. The Minister had but just returned from attending some Court function, and on his breast there still glittered the insignia of the many high orders and honours that had been bestowed upon him.

Sexton Blake met the statesman's gaze with calm assurance.

"I am quite aware, sir," he answered, "that my question is somewhat peculiar. But I would remind you that once before I was able to render you a slight service which you were pleased to regard somewhat highly. It is possible that my services may again stand you in good stead; therefore I am asking you to give me some information of Mr. James Grant."

"Yes, yes," said Sir Vrymer Fane quickly. "I do not forget that, Mr. Blake. On that occasion you rendered us a signal service. I will give you the information you ask; but impress upon you the need for absolute secrecy; what I tell you is for you alone, and you must on no account disclose my confidence. Is that clear?"

"Quite clear, Sir Vrymer."

"Very well, then. I last saw Mr. Grant over three months ago now; I have not seen him nor heard from him since. You will understand that his duties compel him to work silently and secretly. We commission him to undertake some particularly difficult task, and, having once left this office, we know him no more; he is lost to us until he suddenly reappears again to notify us of his success or to explain his failure. It is possible, Mr. Blake, that he may never come back—we do not know."

"I think he will, Sir Vrymer!" said Blake quietly.

The Minister shot a swift glance at his companion.

"Why do you say that, Mr. Blake?" he asked quickly.

"Because, although you have not heard from Granite Grant for over three months, Sir Vrymer, he has communicated with me as recently as a few weeks ago."

Sir Vrymer Fane sprang to his feet in his excitement. It was evident that this piece of information had greatly agitated him. He gazed at the detective in astonishment, while his fingers played nervously with his badge of office that hung suspended from his neck.

"Communicated with you, Mr. Blake!" he said incredulously. "But it is impossible!"

"It is not impossible, sir; it is an actual fact. Three or four weeks ago an artless message was picked up by a ship in the vicinity of the West Indies; the addressee was simply 'Blake, London.' But it was sufficient to ensure its getting into my hands. I discovered that the text contained a code signal that was known only to myself and Granite Grant. It will be sufficient for my purpose, sir, if I say that, at the time of sending that message, Mr. Grant was in urgent need of assistance."

The Minister had recovered his composure by this time. He sat down in his chair again, but he did not attempt to conceal the importance that he attached to Blake's startling disclosure.

For a few seconds he did not speak, but sat staring in front of him with a troubled expression on his face.

"Mr. Blake," he said at length, "I will not attempt to deny the surprise you have occasioned me; I have never been so astonished in my life. But you have somewhat altered the aspect of affairs; instead of seeking information from me, I am going to give it to you willingly; it may be that your courage and skill can again be used in the service of your country."

"I am entirely at your service, sir," said the detective.

"Very good, then, Mr. Blake. Listen carefully. In 1918, at the time of the German offensive on the Western front, the Intelligence Department learnt that at certain vessel, named the *Spitzbergen*, which had put to sea a few days previously, and was making for a German port, had on board a million and a half of bullion."

The Minister paused a moment, and Blake took the opportunity of asking a question.

"Where did the vessel sail from, sir?"

"From Central America, Mr. Blake. However, let me proceed. Instructions were immediately issued to our Naval Squadron in the Atlantic to intercept her at all costs. But several weeks elapsed, and nothing was heard of her. Then one day she was wrecked in a storm on the coast of Haiti."

"Do you mean to say, Sir Vrymer, that the ship disappeared for several weeks, and that the British Navy had not the slightest notion where she could have got to during that time?"

"That is exactly what I do mean, Mr. Blake. But that is not the chief point. She was sighted very soon after she ran aground; then the startling discovery was made that her priceless cargo had vanished; the million and a half of bullion had completely disappeared, and nothing of any value remained."

"But it may have gone to the bottom in the wreck, sir?"

"No, Mr. Blake: the ship did not break up until several days had elapsed."

"But how about the crew, sir? What explanation did the captain give?"

"The crew perished, Mr. Blake. They tried to reach the shore in the boat, but it was swamped. Strangely enough, only ten bodies out of a crew of twenty-two were washed up on the shore; the others were never recovered."

"But what theory do you suggest to account for the missing bullion, sir?"

"We thought at the time, Mr. Blake, that, seeing it was impossible to dodge our warships, the captain of the *Spitzbergen* had thrown his cargo overboard rather than run the risk of its falling into enemy hands. We discovered that those were the instructions given him prior to sailing."

"But is it not possible, Sir Vrymer, that during those weeks that the vessel was missing she had entered another port and discharged her valuable cargo there?"

"That is possible, but distinctly improbable, Mr. Blake. There is no port in the world where a million and a half of bullion could be unloaded without the fact eventually leaking out. Besides, we have made very searching inquiries, and are certain that that is not the explanation."

"Then you incline to the theory that the bullion is at this moment lying at the bottom of the sea?"

"No, Mr. Blake. While the war lasted we were unable to follow up our inquiries; other matters of a more urgent nature demanded all our attention. A few months ago, however, we became aware of the movements of certain Continental agents, who were being carefully watched by our Secret Service, and we came to the conclusion that the bullion was concealed somewhere, and that an attempt was being made to secure it on the part of a foreign Power."

"You think, then, that during the time she was missing the *Spitzbergen* had touched some unknown spot and there hidden its cargo before putting out to sea again?"

"Precisely, Mr. Blake! Information reached us through certain channels that all the crew had not perished when the boat was swamped, but that one survivor had managed to reach Haiti. We even heard that he was now in this country. But we were unable to trace him; our efforts in that direction were fruitless."

"Then if this bullion is still in existence, the secret of its hiding-place must be in this man's possession, Sir Vrymer?"

"If he is only an ordinary seaman, Mr. Blake, he may not know the actual position of the spot where the bullion was unloaded, but he would certainly be able to provide very useful information."

For a moment the two men lapsed into silence. Then the Minister spoke again.

"One other thing, Mr. Blake," he said. "We have recently come to the conclusion that the reason why the *Spitzbergen* went ashore was because of the fact that she was short-handed. We believe that some of the crew had been left behind to take care of this bullion."

"And what was the nature of Granite Grant's mission, sir?"

"To discover the whereabouts of this bullion, Mr. Blake; he had *carte blanche* to follow up his inquiries as he wished. It was an exceedingly difficult and hazardous mission, and for that reason it was entrusted to Mr. Grant. If any man could bring it to a successful conclusion he could, and we have unlimited confidence in his abilities. But I am only too well aware of the unscrupulous forces that he would have to come up against."

"And may I ask what was the last news you had of Granite Grant, sir?"

"Certainly, Mr. Blake. I understood that he had booked a passage on a ship bound for the West Indies; he did not tell me this himself, but you will understand that I have other means of obtaining information. Since that time I have received not the slightest indication of his whereabouts."

The Minister lapsed into silence again, and Blake did not make any attempt at further conversation for some time. He was pondering deeply over what Sir Vrymer Fane had said, and slowly, but surely, the whole tangled web of mystery in which he was involved was becoming clear and precise.

The things that had baffled him before, and had seemed so contradictory, were now fitting their several niches, and suggested a simple explanation to the whole amazing problem.

He glanced up presently, with a look of keen satisfaction on his face.

"Now that you have been good enough to furnish me with these details, Sir Vrymer," he said, "I think it is in my power to fill up the gaps in the story."

"Really, Mr. Blake. Then pray let me know what you think."

"In the first place, sir, I think it is pretty evident that the vessel unloaded and concealed the bullion on one of the many uncharted islands in the Caribbean Sea."

"What makes you think that, Mr. Blake?"

"Yesterday, Sir Vrymer, a map was stolen from the reading-room of the British Museum. I have reason to believe that it was stolen by one of those Continental spies of whom you spoke a short while ago."

"But what was it a map of, Mr. Blake?"

"Unfortunately, I have never seen it, Sir Vrymer. But I have very strong reasons for supposing that it was a map of the West Indies and Central America, and that it contained a chart of the Caribbean Sea, giving the position of the island in which the bullion has been hidden.

"Great Scott, Mr. Blake! But how did you discover all this?" asked the Minister, his eyes sparkling with excitement.

"By putting several other facts that have come to my knowledge to the story you have just told me, sir. It was just over three months ago when I last saw Granite Grant, and he must have sailed for the West Indies immediately after. That very day he had spent several hours in the reading-room of the British Museum, and yesterday I received a wireless message which I am positive he either sent out himself of caused to be sent out."

"The message was in code, Mr. Blake?"

"Yes; but after a little thought I managed to decipher it. I was instructed to go to the reading-room of the British Museum and take down a certain volume. I did so; but I was just too late. Quite a number of people seem to have taken an interest in that particular book, and the map was missing."

"This is extraordinary, Mr. Blake. And what do you suppose the map contained?"

"I think that this unknown island is clearly marked there, and that it happens to be the only map in existence on which the island is charted."

"Really, Mr. Blake, you astonish me! And where could Mr. Grant be to have sent out that message?"

"I should think that, somehow, he has managed to reach this island, and that he is still on it at the present moment. Unless——"

The Minister noticed Blake's significant pause, and took him up sharply.

"Unless what, Mr. Blake?" he asked.

"You forget," said Blake seriously, "that a certain number of the crew could not be accounted for. If they were left behind to take care of the bullion, they will be anxiously awaiting their countrymen to effect their rescue. Now that the war is over they will be expecting the relief ship, not knowing that the *Spitzbergen* was wrecked and their presence on the island still a secret. But if they find out who Granite Grant really is, they're not likely to give him much of a welcome."

"But how could Mr. Grant send out this wireless message, Mr. Blake?"

"The *Spitzbergen* would be equipped with wireless, sir. No doubt she left it behind at the island, thinking it would come in handy. And it certainly has—although not in the way expected by the captain of the *Spitzbergen*."

"That is exactly what must have happened, Mr. Blake; and it explains why no wireless calls for assistance were received from the vessel when she ran ashore on the coast of Haiti."

Sir Vrymer Fane rose to his feet. His face had grown very grave and anxious, and he seemed to be greatly perturbed by what the detective had said.

"I will not try to disguise the seriousness of our position, Mr. Blake," he said. "You say the map has been stolen. It is very obvious who is responsible for that. The fact we have to face is this: If that million and a half of bullion finds its way into the coffers of the Central Powers it will upset all our calculations; it will lead to a very grave financial crisis in Throgmorton Street, which may have very far-reaching effects. Somehow, Mr. Blake, that must be prevented—at all costs, we must not let that happen."

He ceased speaking, and looked at the detective as if seeking his advice.

"The only way to prevent that from happening, Sir Vrymer, is to gain possession of the map," said Blake.

"And do you think you could undertake to do that, Mr. Blake?" asked the Minister quickly.

"I can at least try, sir."

Sir Vrymer Fane grasped the detective by the hand, and wrung it with some emotion.

"Thank you, Mr. Blake," he said, "I know I cannot leave the matter in more skilful hands. Please keep me closely informed of what is happening, and remember that un-limited funds are at your disposal, should you require them."

It was with an extremely thoughtful look on his face that the detective made his way down the broad, carpeted staircase and stepped out into Whitehall Court.

It was dark outside, for it was getting late now. Blake had had a very strenuous day; every moment had been fully occupied, and he had barely found time to get anything to eat.

That afternoon he had attended the inquest on the unknown man who had died in the reading-room of the British Museum. The evidence had been very unsatisfactory, and the jury completely mystified. The coroner had ordered a post-mortem.

Blake had taken the opportunity to have a few words in private with the doctor who had first examined the body and had declared life to be extinct. His suspicions of foul play had been confirmed. A tiny puncture had been discovered on the dead man's neck, evidently caused by the injection of a syringe.

Until the post-mortem took place nothing definite could be stated, but Blake was of the opinion that the man had been killed by one of those bizarre and deadly poisons like curarine, the active principle of arrow poison. Very likely an alkaloid obtained from woorari had been used.

As he strode towards Trafalgar Square the cries of the newsboys attracted his attention. He could not quite catch what they were saying, but presently he stopped abruptly, and stood staring at a placard. In bold, heavy type were the words:

"MYSTERIOUS SHOOTING TRAGEDY AT KENSINGTON FLAT."

Feeling strangely curious to know more of the occurrence, Blake bought a paper and opened it under the light of a street-lamp. At first he could not find what he was searching for, then the stop-press column caught his eye.

"TRAGEDY AT KENSINGTON FLAT.

"A man of foreign appearance was found shot this evening in a flat off Kensington High Street. Although several papers were found on the deceased, the police are still somewhat puzzled as to his identity. The motive of the crime is not apparent. Fuller details are expected to follow."

Blake thoughtfully folded up the paper and continued his way to Baker Street.

A number of thoughts were speeding across his mind; the reference to the flat at Kensington High Street had reminded him of the mysterious and beautiful Mademoiselle Julie. Who could she possibly be? he wondered. And what part was she playing in this strange drama of intrigue?

Events had moved so rapidly since yesterday that he had the utmost difficulty in keeping all the threads of this extraordinary case in his grasp.

In filling in the gaps from the information supplied by Sir Vrymer Fane he had forgotten to find a place for Julie. Her presence seemed rather unaccountable, and he had still to reckon with her.

Perhaps it was she who was responsible for the successful attack on Inspector Brown that morning! If so, then she must have the map in her possession, and it was up to him to track her down.

But who had shot this unknown foreigner at Kensington?

Blake could not throw off the feeling that this latest tragedy was in some way connected with the mystery that was occupying his attention.

But if that were the case, what part had Julie played in the crime? Was she in some way responsible for this man's death?

Blake remembered then how beautiful and charming she was. It seemed impossible that she should be capable of such deeds of violence; such a thought seemed revolting, and opposed to all his natural instincts and respect for the other sex. But who, in the name of reason, could this woman be?

The detective was still puzzling over these things when he entered his rooms in Baker Street.

Chapter 10
The Telephone Call

THE white-bearded old man who had been at the mortuary earlier on in the day, and who had passed Inspector Brown and the detective in the corridor, was none other than "The Leopard."

After his somewhat hurried exit from Blake's room in Baker Street he had met his friend Von Rosenburg, and another accomplice, who had been anxiously waiting to hear the results of the interview.

They had had a hasty consultation together and discussed the matter in all its aspects. Von Rosenburg rather doubted that the map was in the detective's possession; he was a firm believer in the proverb that "every man has his price," and not being troubled with any scruples of conscience himself, he could not understand the detective refusing the offer of ten thousand pounds. The only logical conclusion seemed to him to be the fact that Blake did not have the map to sell.

The Leopard" would not see his friend's point of view at first, and argued the matter rather heatedly; but at length Von Rosenburg overcame his objections, and it was decided that one of them should pay a visit to the mortuary and try to discover any further information.

The "Leopard," who was rather good at disguising himself—and, indeed, was more often disguised than not—was chosen to undertake this task; and thus it was that he entered the room where the body was lying just before Inspector Brown left.

It did not take the "Leopard" long to discover who the inspector was, and by a few cunning and skilful questions he soon had the Scotland Yard man talking freely about himself.

He went so far as to boast to his questioner of the important discovery he had made, but when pressed to be more explicit he suddenly became very reticent, and soon after left the room.

But the "Leopard" had heard quite enough to arouse his suspicions. He followed the inspector from the room, and crept after him as he made his way down the darkened corridor.

When the Scotland Yard man had suddenly collided with Sexton Blake he was a few yards behind, and quite near enough to overhear most of the conversation that ensued.

The references to the map confirmed the "Leopard's" suspicions; he immediately decided to get outside and see Von Rosenburg before the inspector left the building.

His confederates were waiting for him across the road, and listened to the "Leopard's" account of what had happened. They determined there and then to make a supreme effort to get possession of the map. The success which attended their plans is already known.

About a quarter of an hour after the sudden assault on Inspector Brown a taxi drew up in front of the Cosmopolitan Hotel, and Von Rosenburg and his companion got out. They went up the winding staircase together and disappeared inside the room on the first-floor corridor.

The "Leopard" carefully locked the door behind him, and turned to his companion with a flush of triumph.

"It seems too good to be true, Von Rosenburg," he said in suppressed tones. "What a stroke of luck!"

Von Rosenburg was no less excited than his companion. He felt in his pocket with trembling fingers, and drew out the folded piece of paper, to obtain which they had taken such great risks.

"By Jove, Venner!" he muttered. "We certainly made a scoop there. I can hardly believe it now."

He smoothed out the map on the table, and stood staring down at it with an enigmatic smile on his face.

"There's the spot," he said, pointing with his finger. "Someone had put a cross against it. Now who could that have been, I wonder?"

The "Leopard" stared down at the mark, and his brows contracted thoughtfully.

"Is there any news of Granite Grant?" he asked quickly.

"Nothing whatever, Venner! Our men have completely lost trace of him."

"I saw him in London about three months ago, Von Rosenburg. We had information that the English Foreign Office had placed the matter in his hands. I discovered that he had been seen in the company of one of the crew of the *Spitzbergen*. But from that day we have not been able to trace either of them."

"Do you think he found this map, Venner, and placed this mark against the island?"

"It is quite possible, Von Rosenburg. Granite Grant is the brains of the British Secret Service, and I respect him as much as I hate him. He does not know what fear means, and he has never yet admitted himself to be beaten."

"A grave look came into Von Rosenburg's face; he stood silently biting his lip for some moments. Presently his face cleared.

"It does not matter," he said. "We are sure that nothing has leaked out yet; the Foreign Office is still in the dark. Was Julie also in London on the occasion you have just mentioned?"

The "Leopard" darted a look of suspicion at his companion, and his face darkened.

"Yes," he said, "she was! I should be very careful of her, Von Rosenburg; she is crafty and cunning, and, being a woman—and also very pretty—makes her all the more dangerous."

Von Rosenburg chuckled softly to himself.

"You are not very gallant, Venner," he said. "She is a very charming little person, and amuses me immensely. I think you are rather jealous because she spurns your advances. However, I will be cautious, Venner; I am not in the habit of allowing my pleasures to interfere with the execution of my duty."

But the "Leopard" did not seem to be entirely reassured by this statement; evidently he had a very poor opinion of his companion's will to withstand the wiles of women.

Muttering something to himself, he put out his hand to take the map, but Von Rosenburg thrust him aside with a quick movement of his elbow.

"I'll look after that, Venner," he said firmly.

The "Leopard's" face flushed with anger.

"Why?" he asked. "It is just as safe with me!"

"Then it might just as well be in my pocket!"

The two men glared at each other across the table. Both were now getting angry, and regarded each other with a suspicion which neither of them attempted to conceal.

"It will be safer in my pocket, Von Rosenburg!" said Venner in thick accents.

"You think what you like, Venner," replied the other, folding up the map and putting it away. "It's in my pocket now, and there it's going to stay."

He took a swift glance at his companion and raised his voice.

"Who's boss here, Venner—you or I? You're forgetting yourself. Please remember whom you're speaking to. I don't think it's to your interests to fall out with me."

Venner bit his lip, but did not attempt to argue the matter further.

"Very good, Von Rosenburg!" he said, "I wash my hands of the whole affair. Only remember, it'll be the worse for you if anything should happen to it now that it is in our possession."

"You leave that to me!" rejoined Von Rosenburg. "And now listen, Venner. I am catching the boat-train this evening. We will not travel together, but I shall look out for you at Charing Cross at five o'clock. Once we get across we shall have nothing to fear. See that you leave nothing of any importance behind in your room. I'll settle the bill. Is everything clear?"

Venner nodded his head in assent.

"Very good, then, Venner! Five o'clock at Charing Cross, and mind you're not late."

With an angry scowl on his face the "Leopard" picked up his hat and left the room.

Von Rosenburg looked at his watch, then opened a small hand-bag, in which he proceeded to stow away his personal belongings. He had very few things to take away, for he travelled with as little baggage as possible. His particular enterprises necessitated sudden and swift moves, and luggage was only an encumbrance under such conditions.

He had only just finished packing-up when a knock sounded at the door, and the next moment a page-boy entered and handed him a slip of paper. Von Rosenburg could hardly repress a start of surprise as he stared at the missive then he crushed it in his hand and flung it on the floor.

"I will answer it now!" he said to the page, and strode to the door and ran swiftly down the stairs.

Reaching the hotel lobby, he entered the telephone-box and picked up the receiver.

"Hello!" he said. "Are you there?"

A woman's voice answered with a pleasing, musical accent.

"Is that you, Monsieur Rosenburg?" she asked.

A flush of pleasure mounted to Von Rosenburg's face, and the hand that held the receiver trembled with excitement.

"Yes, yes!" he said quickly, "it is Rosenburg. Is that Mademoiselle Julie?"

A little silvery laugh came from the other end, which seemed to increase Von Rosenburg's agitation.

"Yes, it is I, monsieur!"

The man hesitated a moment.

"What do you want?" he asked abruptly.

"But, really, that is unkind of you!" said the woman, with a slight tremor in her voice that made Von Rosenburg catch his breath. "What should I want, Monsieur Rosenburg, but to see you?"

The man did not reply for a few seconds; he seemed to be struggling to retain the mastery of his feelings.

"I can't, Mademoiselle Julie," he said huskily. "It is impossible."

"Impossible, monsieur! But why?"

"I cannot explain, Julie," he said hurriedly. "It is impossible now; some other time, perhaps."

A deep sigh, that sounded suspiciously like a sob, came to Von Rosenburg's ears, and in his agitation the receiver almost slipped from his fingers.

"You are too unkind, monsieur," said the woman again. "You will go away without seeing me. You do not care. If you will not see me, may I not come round to you for two minutes? Do, monsieur!"

"No, no!" said Von Rosenburg apprehensively. "Julie, don't do that! I'll come along now. But I must not stay; you understand? I dare not."

"Monsieur is too good," said the woman gaily. "It is a promise?"

"Yes! I am coming now."

Von Rosenburg replaced the receiver and returned to his room. His sallow face, which usually wore such a cold expression, was now flushed with excitement, and his eyes were sparkling brightly. He glanced at himself in the mirror and straightened his tie. Then, putting on his hat and coat, hurried from the hotel.

✳✳✳

Von Rosenburg had scarcely been gone an hour when The Leopard came suddenly into the room. He glanced round in surprise, not expecting that his companion would have left so quickly. Then he caught sight of a crumpled piece of paper lying on the carpet near-by.

Idly curious to know what it was, The Leopard stooped down and picked it up. He smoothed it out, and stood looking at it somewhat puzzled for a second or two. It was the printed slip of paper notifying Von Rosenburg of the telephone-call.

Suddenly The Leopard realised what had happened to his companion. A swift stab of jealousy and suspicion shot through him, and his face darkened with anger. With a muttered imprecation, he snatched up his hat and rushed madly from the room.

Chapter 11
A Woman's Toils

MADEMOISELLE JULIE replaced the receiver on the telephone, and stood for a moment looking thoughtfully down into the street. Presently the frown lifted from her pretty face, and, clapping her hands delightedly, she sped across to her boudoir, where she added a few brief touches to her toilet.

A few moments later she entered the daintily furnished sitting-room again, and sat down at the window to await the arrival of her guest.

When a woman attracted Sexton Blake's attention it was evident that she possessed something out of the ordinary, for the great detective was not much to emotionalism, and he had had too vast an experience of life to be affected by the sight of a pretty face.

But Mademoiselle Julie was no ordinary woman, as more than one man had been forced to admit. Her beauty was of that uncommon type that casts its spell over the strongest of men and compels them to commit deeds which, in their sane moments, they would never think of doing, and from which they would shrink with disgust.

In her toils the most resolute man found himself bereft of the will and power to gainsay her wishes, for she twisted the strongest round her little finger as if he were a mere baby.

Her beauty was famous throughout all the fashionable resorts of Europe, and her wit and elegance gave her the entree to the most select and exclusive circles of society.

Yet Mademoiselle Julie scorned the world of fashion and laughed at the pleasures and enticements that were held out invitingly to her if she would but take them.

She had placed her dazzling beauty and charm at the service of her country, and, although few suspected it, she was regarded as one of the most reliable agents of the French Secret Service.

It was this woman of whom The Leopard had warned Von Rosenburg, for the former was only too well acquainted with her activities. On two occasions he had measured his wit against hers, and had been fooled both times.

Von Rosenburg had met her in Paris and had immediately fallen a victim to her wiles; now he was hurrying to keep an appointment with her, and in his pocket was the key that would open the lock of a million and a half of money.

Mademoiselle Julie glanced nervously at the ormolu clock that ticked away merrily on the mantelpiece, then looked down into the street again.

She was suddenly apprehensive that Von Rosenburg would not come—that he had made the appointment merely to throw dust in her eyes.

She glanced across at the mirror facing her and eyed her reflection appreciatively, then gave a little smile of satisfaction.

Yes, Von Rosenburg would come right enough; there was no fear of that. She was only too well aware of the strange power she possessed over men to doubt that he would keep his word.

She watched a taxi as it came speeding up the road. Was he in there? she wondered. The cab began to slow down as it approached, and then drew into the kerb and came to a stop outside. The door opened and Von Rosenburg stepped out.

Mademoiselle Julie slipped across to a little wicker chair that stood in front of the fire, and, sitting down, rested her chin on her hands and gazed reflectively into the glowing coals. A moment later a knock sounded on the door.

"Come in!" she said in a low voice; but she did not move from her chair.

Presently she looked up, and gave a little cry of pleasure.

Von Rosenburg stood at the door staring down at her. His face was now white, but his eyes still glittered with a strange excitement and his silk hat shook in his trembling fingers. He shut the door and came swiftly towards her.

"Julie!" he said, taking her white, slender hand in both of his.

She laughed into his face.

"So you have come, Monsieur Rosenburg!" she said.

"How could I stay away, Julie?" he asked, and drew closer to her.

She gently pushed him away.

"You are strangely familiar, monsieur!" she said, with a little pout.

Von Rosenburg was breathing quickly, and the blood had rushed back to his face again.

"I beg your pardon, mademoiselle!" he said contritely, "but you make me forget myself."

"And you do not like to forget yourself, monsieur—eh?"

Mademoiselle Julie gave a little silvery ripple of laughter and motioned her visitor into a chair.

"No, mademoiselle!" he said as he sat down. "It is not always safe to forget oneself."

"Why not, monsieur?"

Von Rosenburg hesitated a moment.

"It depends, mademoiselle!" he said, with some confusion.

She turned and stared him in the face.

"On what does it depend, monsieur?" she asked.

Under the steady gaze of her dark violet eyes Von Rosenburg felt himself losing his control. He averted his head quickly and spoke in suppressed tones.

"It depends where one happens to be, mademoiselle—in what company one finds oneself."

She laughed softly, and laid her fingers on his arm.

"But why do you turn away, monsieur?" she asked. "Is it that you do not like to look at me?"

Von Rosenburg's hand closed on her fingers like a steel vice.

"You are playing with me," he said hoarsely. "You know that I would sit and look at you for ever."

Mademoiselle Julie tried to disengage herself from his grasp.

"You are hurting me, Monsieur Rosenburg," she said quickly. "Please do not be so violent.

"And now, monsieur," she said, when he had let go her hand, "tell me why sometimes it is unsafe to forget oneself."

Her eyes still held him entranced. It is thus that the serpent transfixes his prey. The man shifted uneasily, and a look of irresolution came into his sallow face.

"When one forgets oneself, mademoiselle," he said slowly, "one sometimes forgets one's honour, and one's friends, and one's country."

Her face clouded for an instant, and she bit her lip to hide her thoughts.

"And it is not well to forget those things, monsieur?"

Von Rosenburg looked at her inquiringly, as if he expected her to continue.

"No!" he said shortly, and waited expectantly.

The young woman turned to him swiftly and caught his hand.

"What is honour, and friends, and country, monsieur?" she asked, and he felt her breath fanning his face. "It is sometimes worthwhile to forget these things."

"How, Julie?"

She came closer so that her hair brushed his face.

"Am I not worth it, monsieur?" she asked softly.

Von Rosenburg drew back. His mouth twitched nervously, the perspiration stood out on his forehead, and she felt his hand trembling in her own.

"What do you mean, Julie?" he asked huskily. "What are you asking me to do?"

"Are you blind, monsieur?" she asked, and her eyes grew moist as she looked up at him from beneath the long lashes. "Or is it that you do not care?"

He stared at her incredulously.

"Is it possible, Julie?" he asked. "If I thought that, then everything would be worthwhile!"

"It is possible, monsieur!" she said coquettishly.

Von Rosenburg caught her in his arms. He had completely lost his head. Nothing mattered now—honour, friends, and country were mere trifles when placed against the allurements of this woman.

She submitted to his caresses for a few moments and then pushed him gently away.

"Listen, monsieur," she said. "You have something in your pocket—it means wealth beyond the dreams of avarice. I will get my price for it, then—well, there are other lands where one may live peacefully."

"And you will come with me, Julie?"

Von Rosenburg was panting from the strain of his emotions. He was just like clay in the hands of this slender, beautiful woman.

"I will come, monsieur," she said. "And you will give me the map?"

For a brief moment a tremendous struggle went on in Rosenburg's mind between his sense of duty and the desire to please this woman—and the woman won!

He fumbled in his inside pocket, and his hands shook so violently that it was some minutes before he could find the thing he wanted. Then he drew out the folded map and held it in front of her.

"This is it, Julie," he said hoarsely. "Remember, I am selling my soul for you. If you play me false I will kill you."

A smile of triumph came into her face. She held out her hand, and was about to take the map from his fingers, when a voice sounded from behind her.

"Stop!"

Von Rosenburg and the young woman swung round with exclamations of fear and surprise, and stood staring at the shiny weapon that covered them.

At the door stood the Leopard glancing swiftly from one to the other, his finger hugging the catch of the revolver, which he grasped in his hand. For a few seconds after his first rasping command, he did not speak, but glared fiercely at the man and woman with a murderous scowl on his face.

"A very pretty piece of love-making, Von Rosenburg!" he sneered. "A case where two is company, three is none!"

Von Rosenburg's fascinated eyes were still fixed on the weapon. He seemed to have lost all power of speech, and the Leopard continued in a harsh, metallic voice.

"So this is how you fulfill your trust, Von Rosenburg!" he said. "The Fatherland still knows how to reward the traitor! In the meanwhile you will hand that map over to me. At once!"

At these sneering words Von Rosenburg's face suddenly became livid, with a gesture of suppressed rage he took a step towards his opponent.

"You dare to speak like that to me, Venner!" he said thickly. "You—you low-down hireling! You scum! Look to yourself! The Fatherland will know what value to place on your words! You cannot injure my reputation. Lower that weapon!"

But the Leopard had no intention of obeying his superior this time. A murderous look crept into his eyes and his finger tightened around the catch of the revolver.

"Back!" he hissed menacingly. "That map, Von Rosenburg—quick!"

For a moment Von Rosenburg hesitated; then, filled with rage and mortification, he advanced threateningly on his opponent.

Mademoiselle Julie uttered a sharp cry of warning and attempted to drag him back. But it was too late. Two reports followed in quick succession, and, with a little gasp of pain, Von Rosenburg staggered back, twisted on his heel and fell prone on the floor.

Before the woman had had time to realise what had happened the Leopard had swooped down on the prostrate man, torn the map from his clenched fingers, and fled from the room.

For some seconds after the Leopard had vanished the young woman stood breathing quickly and staring down at the body of Von Rosenburg. She did not attempt to touch him. Something told her that the shot had been fatal, and that the man she had wheedled so successfully but a few moments before was now beyond all human aid. Then suddenly she became wonderfully calm and self-possessed.

She went swiftly into her boudoir to come out again five minutes later dressed ready for a hasty departure. But no one would have recognised in this dapper little man in the grey suit the charming and beautiful Mademoiselle Julie.

She was an adept at disguising herself, for many a time her life had depended upon it. During those few brief moments she had to all outward appearances changed her sex, even to the extent of growing a little brown moustache, and she looked her part to perfection.

In one hand she carried an attaché-case, in the other was a bundle of letters and documents, which she flung on the fire and watched until they burst into flame. Then, with one final glance at the man on the floor she closed it to behind her.

Mademoiselle Julie was used to swift changes—they were quite natural events in her exciting and dramatic life—and so she was always prepared to vacate her place of domicile at the briefest notice.

Chapter 12
The Kensington Flat

I SHOULD know the house again, guv'nor. It's impossible to mistake it. You trust me for that!"

The evening paper was spread open on Blake's desk, and the detective and his assistant were pouring over the scanty details of the Kensington tragedy. Blake had only been back ten minutes from his interview with Sir Vrymer Fane. While he made a hasty meal he had given Tinker a brief indication of the task on which they were engaged.

"Very well, Tinker!" said Blake. "We'll go along to this Kensington flat immediately and see what's doing. If it happens to be the flat you watched yesterday we may possibly be able to get on the track of this map again. That's our one and only task at the present moment; and it's by no means an easy matter—it'll be a race against time!"

"Well, I'm ready, guv'nor!" said Tinker enthusiastically. "This is getting rather exciting—it's about my mark!"

The detective smiled rather grimly at his assistant's boyish enthusiasm. Tinker was an invaluable companion; he always saw the bright side of everything, and his irrepressible spirits refused to be damped by the most gloomy of adversities.

Many a time when Blake had been almost compelled to admit defeat he had been spurred on to fresh endeavours by some quaint remark of his young assistant, which had made his master laugh in spite of himself.

They took the tube to Kensington High Street, and then directed their steps to the scene of the tragedy.

"This is the shop where I had tea yesterday, guv'nor," said Tinker presently. "The flat is immediately opposite."

"Then it is the same place, Tinker," said the detective. "See, the police are at the doors and a number of people are still hanging about outside. Hello! There's an ambulance just come up. Wonder if they've taken the body away yet? And who's that getting out? Why, I believe it's Inspector Brown, of all people! Come along, Tinker!"

They caught the inspector up just as he was entering the gate, and followed him into the house. The policemen on duty outside made no attempt to prevent their entrance, for the detective and his young assistant were only too well known among the rank and file and held in great respect by them.

Inspector Brown was somewhat surprised to meet Blake again—and not too well pleased. He was still smarting from their recent morning, and felt rather foolish at being so easily outwitted.

"Well I'm bothered! Mr. Blake!" he said. "Fancy meeting you again! I'm feeling rather sore over that affair this morning. I'll see you don't put it across me this time."

Blake laughed good-humouredly.

"No use worrying about that now, Brown," he said. "But you certainly put your foot in it there. Fortunately for you, you'll never know what a tremendous hash you made of things."

Inspector Brown looked rather huffed at Blake's candid statement.

"You're talking rather wildly, Mr. Blake," he said peevishly. "After all, I don't see what there's to make such a fuss about. Anybody would think that I'd lost a thousand pounds instead of a scrap of paper not worth a cent."

"It might surprise you, Brown, to know that that scrap of paper, as you call it, is worth a million and a half," said the detective quietly.

The inspector was so startled at Blake's cool statement that he slipped on the stairs and only saved himself from falling by clutching frantically at the banister.

"What in the name of goodness are you talking about, Mr. Blake?" he asked, when he had recovered from his first surprise. "I've never come across such a chap for making ridiculous statements."

"I don't suppose you have, Brown!" admitted the detective, with an ironical smile.

"But if there's anything in what you say," insisted the inspector, "what the deuce are you doing here, Mr. Blake? You're not the sort of man to let a chance like that slip by. The fact of the matter is that it's a bit too big for you to grapple with. But you're pulling my leg; you've been rotting me all the time."

Blake could hardly repress his amusement. Inspector Brown was so genuinely astonished and fuddled that he felt rather sorry for him.

"I'm not rotting, Brown," he said seriously. "And, as you say, I'm not the sort of man to let a chance slip by like that. That's why I've come along here tonight. You don't think I'm out for a picnic, do you?"

"That's why you've come along here tonight, Mr. Blake!" echoed the inspector, staring at his companion to see if he was joking. "But explain yourself. What on earth has this business to do with the affair at the British Museum?"

"That remains to be seen, inspector!" said Blake. "We'd better drop the subject now. Tell me, has the body been removed yet? I noticed that you brought an ambulance with you."

"No, it hasn't, Mr. Blake. I've just come here for that purpose. The fellow was stone dead when he was discovered, and we had orders not to touch the body until one or two pots had come down from the Yard to take the necessary dispositions!"

"That's rather a stroke of luck!" muttered the detective.

They had reached the second floor by this time, and, pushing open a door on the right, the inspector entered, closely followed by Blake and his assistant.

The body had now been removed to the couch and was covered up by a rug. Two policemen were stationed inside on guard over the body. Blake took a rapid glance round the room.

It was tastefully furnished and had a quiet air of comfort. The detective's keen eyes immediately noted the unmistakable feminine touches about it.

"Have you found out who occupied these rooms, Brown?" he asked.

"No; we're rather floored there, Mr. Blake," answered the inspector. "The owner of the premises lives at Clapham. We got into touch with him, but he can't tell us much. Seems that this flat was taken over a few days ago by an agent on behalf of a Mrs. Smith. A month's rent was paid in advance, and so not so many questions were asked. However, I'm following up the matter, and hope to discover something useful in the morning."

Blake went over to the couch and pulled back the rug from the dead man's face. The bullet had entered the left temple, and death must have been instantaneous.

"You don't happen to recognise him by any chance, Tinker, I suppose?" he asked.

Tinker stared intently at the man's face for a moment or two.

"I won't swear to it, guv'nor," he said at length, "but I'm almost certain he's one of the men I followed from the Cosmopolitan Hotel yesterday."

"Oh, we know all about that, Mr. Blake," said Inspector Brown, who had overheard Tinker's remark. "He was staying at the Cosmopolitan right enough. The trouble is that the hotel people can't give us much information. He has been staying there with another fellow for the last two days, but evidently they've been going under assumed names— Jones and Williams, they're registered as. And that's about all we can discover. The other fellow's disappeared and left no trace behind."

But Blake did not seem to be paying much heed to what the inspector was saying. His attention had been attracted to a little mark on the wall which he was facing, and, stepping close up to it, he examined it carefully for some minutes. Suddenly he turned to the inspector.

"Has any of the furniture been moved, Brown?" he asked.

"No; we haven't touched anything, Mr. Blake."

"Then you found those two chairs in their present positions by the fire?"

"Yes, just as they are now."

Blake gave a brief nod, and turned to one of the policemen.

"I want you to lie down on the floor in the exact position that you found the body," he said.

The man immediately complied with the detective's request. Brown and the other policeman stood looking on with deep interest.

Blake was silent for some minutes, his mind occupied with a swift process of reasoning.

"That will do, constable," he said at length. "I think we may safely assume that this man and another person occupied those two chairs, and that he was shot by a third person, who suddenly entered the room and fired from the door."

But Inspector Brown evidently did not follow Blake's reasoning.

"Aren't you rather jumping at conclusions, Mr. Blake?" he asked. "I don't see that it's necessary to introduce a third person at all. My impression is that only two people are concerned, and that they quarrelled over something, and one of them got shot as the result."

"Then how do you explain the presence of that bullet embedded in the wall over there, Brown?"

The inspector glanced swiftly in the direction indicated by Blake.

"I hadn't noticed that," he said, a little taken aback. "However, I don't see that that proves anything."

"But it does, Brown! The man who fired that had his back to the door—that's pretty evident. And what's more, he must have been as far away as it is possible to be in this room. You can see that by the fact that the bullet has only just penetrated the wall. Therefore, it's safe to assume that he was standing close up to the door."

"Well, supposing that's correct, Mr. Blake," said Brown, convinced in spite of himself that there was something in Blake's reasoning. "Why introduce a third person?"

"Because the position of those two chairs in front of the fire leads me to believe they were occupied, and that they were suddenly pushed back as the two occupants sprang to their feet in surprise at being interrupted. You can see that by the way the rug is rucked up underneath."

Inspector Brown was not a little impressed by this time. He glanced from the door to the wall and then back again at the two chairs, as if measuring the distances, and nodded his head understandingly.

"That certainly seems a feasible explanation, Mr. Blake." he said. "It hadn't occurred to me in that light. But what do you think the motive of the crime was?"

The detective did not answer. His attention was riveted on a little white point that stuck out from beneath the hearth-rug. He stooped suddenly and picked it up and stood silently gazing at the little object that lay in the hollow of his hand.

It was a tiny shred of paper in the form of a triangle. Two sides were cut straight and at right-angles to each other, the third was ragged and frayed as if it had been torn apart. And close up to this torn edge were the remains of the figure "5."

Tinker was watching his master critically. He knew that contemplative look on his face only too well; Blake had made some important discovery.

Tinker hadn't the vaguest notion as to what it could be—the tiny piece of paper laying in Blake's hand conveyed nothing to him; but evidently his master attached some importance to it, and sooner or later he would let Tinker into the secret.

But Inspector Brown could not conceal his impatience.

"What on earth are you staring at that for, Mr. Blake?" he asked, with a trace of irritation in his voice. "If you're quite finished here I'll get on with my work."

The inspector turned to the policeman:

"Might get the body into the ambulance now!" he ordered.

But the detective stayed him with a gesture.

"One moment, Brown!" he said; and, taking his wallet from his pocket, opened it and took a strip of photographic paper.

Much to the mystification of the inspector Blake then went over to the couch on which the dead man was lying, and pressed the fingers of each hand lightly against the sensitive paper.

"That'll do, Brown!" he said at last. "I won't delay you any more."

"Oh, don't worry about me, Mr. Blake!" said the inspector, now thoroughly convinced that the detective had made a scoop. "What's your latest theory?"

Blake ignored the question; he was standing in the centre of the room, slowly glancing around with an alert expression in his eyes. Then he went swiftly over to the fireplace and knelt down in front of the still-smouldering fire.

On the top of the dying embers were the black carbonised remains of the documents and letters that Mademoiselle Julie had hastily flung into the grate.

Since the flames had destroyed them they had not been disturbed, and one carbonised sheet of notepaper on the top still preserved its original shape and form. On its black surface the oxygenised ink showed up quite distinctly.

Blake took out his pocket-torch and carefully scrutinised the writing for nearly five minutes, while the others crowded round in silence. Then he blew on the frail remains and they immediately crumbled to ashes.

"Found anything?" asked Inspector Brown suspiciously.

The detective had taken out his pocketbook and was writing something in pencil.

"Nothing much, inspector!" he muttered, without looking up. Then he tore out the leaf from his book and handed it to Tinker.

"Tinker," he said, "I'm going on to the Cosmopolitan Hotel; I'll see you later on. I want you to hurry off to Fleet Street and get that message inserted in the personal columns of the morning papers. You'll have to be fairly slick—understand?"

Tinker took the piece of paper and glanced at the pencilled message:

"Abracadabra. Will be at Vendetti's at 12 a.m. Ask for Mr. Mappe."

Whatever astonishment Tinker may have felt on reading this strange message he did not show it. What Blake said was good enough, for his master had a very good reason for most of his actions; no doubt he would explain things to him later on. He looked up with a reassuring nod:

"I understand, guv'nor," he said.

Without another word Tinker hurried from the room.

A few moments later the detective also left the flat. He vouchsafed no further information to Inspector Brown, although the latter tried very hard to get him to talk.

But Blake was in one of his uncommunicative moods and seemed hardly to take any more notice of the Scotland Yard man, much to the latter's annoyance.

Chapter 13
Blake Explains

IT was about eleven o'clock that night when Blake got back to Baker Street. Tinker had arrived some time since, and was impatiently awaiting his master's return.

"Well, Tinker," said Blake, "were you in time for my advertisement to be put in the morning papers?"

"Yes, guv'nor," said his assistant; "I managed that all right. I was only just in time, though."

"Good enough!" muttered Blake. "The only thing to do now is to wait and see what happens."

He sat down at his desk, and, taking out his pocketbook, was soon deeply engrossed in making a minute examination by the aid of the magnifying-glass.

His assistant watched him in silence for some time, and then, being unable to restrain his curiosity any longer, commenced to put a few questions.

"What does that message mean that you've stuck in the papers, guv'nor?" he asked. "I've been trying to think it out, but I'm absolutely fogged."

Blake looked up with a flicker of amusement.

"I expect you are, Tinker!" he said. "Just wait a moment and I'll explain everything to you."

Blake bent over his desk again, while Tinker, with his store of patience nearly exhausted, was obliged to await his master's pleasure.

Presently the detective sat back in his chair and turned to Tinker with a look of satisfaction on his face.

"Now, Tinker!" he said. "I'll try to make things clear to you. The one and only reason why I went to Kensington this evening was to get on the track of this missing map; the shooting affair doesn't interest me a bit; it's up to Inspector Brown to explain that. You understand?"

Tinker nodded an affirmative.

"Right, then!" continued Blake. "Now, as luck would have it, I did manage to get on the track of the map, Tinker, in fact, I even managed to get hold of a part of it."

Tinker received this piece of information with an incredulous look.

"A part of it, guv'nor!" he echoed. "But I don't quite follow you. Where is it now, then?"

"It's here, Tinker!" said Blake, pointing to the triangular shred of paper that was lying on his blotting-pad. "It's not much use, for it's rather small; but it explains quite a lot of things."

"But how do you know that's a part of the map, guv'nor?" asked his assistant, with some surprise. "It may be anything you like."

"Come closer, Tinker!" said the detective. "That's better! Now can you see that figure with a piece at the bottom missing? What do you make of it?"

"It looks as if it might be figure '5,' guv'nor," said Tinker, after a brief glance.

"So it does, Tinker! And do you remember what was the number of the page missing from that book in the British Museum Library?"

"Page 465, guv'nor," said Tinker promptly.

"That's right, Tinker! And that leads me to suppose that this piece of paper is the corner of page 465. Added to that is the fact that, as near as I can recollect, this is the same paper that is used for the other illustrations in that book. But I can prove that beyond a doubt tomorrow, although I'm quite satisfied to take it for granted, in the face of what we already know."

By Tinker's manner it was quite evident that he also was prepared to take it for granted.

"Now there's something else that this piece of paper teaches me, Tinker," continued Blake, "and that is that the man who was shot at Kensington today had the map in his possession. In fact he was grasping it in his fingers at the moment he was shot, and he was holding it so tightly when it was snatched away that this piece was torn off."

"But how on earth do you know all that, guv'nor?" asked Tinker, now thoroughly bewildered.

"Because, Tinker, there are two distinct impressions on each side of this piece of paper, and when I compare them with the fingerprints of the dead man I find that they correspond exactly to the thumb and finger of his right hand."

"By Jove! that's clever!" muttered Tinker admiringly. "It sounds mighty easy, guv'nor, when you explain it. But how about the message you put in the papers? That's what's bothering me!"

"You just be patient, Tinker!" said the detective. "I'm coming to that in a moment or two. First we've got to reconstruct what happened in that flat this afternoon. Now it's pretty evident that the man who killed this fellow was the very man who paid me a visit this morning, and that they were both staying at the Cosmopolitan Hotel together. I've been along there and made a few inquiries."

"The same two men whom I followed there yesterday, guv'nor?"

"The same two, Tinker! And for one of them to have shot the other they must have had a violent quarrel over something. What do you think the row was about, Tinker?"

"The map, I suppose, guv'nor?"

"Not exactly, Tinker. They were evidently working together on that job. Try again."

Tinker scratched his head and looked puzzled.

"How about money, then, guv'nor?" he asked.

Blake gave an amused sort of chuckle.

"Wrong again, Tinker!" he said. "When two men quarrel, in ninety-nine cases out of a hundred it's over a woman. You'll understand that, Tinker, one of these days when you're a bit older. And so we've got the eternal triangle again—two men and a woman! I've not the slightest doubt as to who that woman is; she's the mysterious Mademoiselle Julie. And it was in yielding to her allurements that this poor fellow doubtless met his death. Perhaps it was his own fault—but that remains to be seen."

"Sounds a bit romantic, guv'nor!" said Tinker, eyeing his master with some perplexity. "But I'm still longing to hear all about that funny message you sent to the papers."

"Coming to that now, Tinker. It's fairly certain that the map was in that flat at Kensington this afternoon, and that it was also in the possession of one of the two persons who left after the shooting affray. Since it's absolutely essential that I should get on the track of that map I'm trying to communicate with one of the parties who were in that room this afternoon. That's why I've put that notice in the papers."

"But I still don't follow you, guv'nor!" said Tinker.

"No, but you will when I've explained. You saw me stoop down and stare into the grate this evening?"

"Yes, guv'nor!"

"Well, some letters, had been hastily thrown on the fire, evidently just after the man was shot. They were mostly reduced to a cinder, except one on the top, which was carbonised but still intact. The oxygenised ink showed up quite plainly in one part, and I was able to read a few lines of what was written. It was in French but quite easy to understand. I've copied it out in my book. Here it is. You can read it for yourself."

Tinker picked up the pocket-book and read the following lines, which his master had hurriedly scribbled down in pencil:

"…but I will use the word 'Abracadabra' if there is any urgent communication. Please watch papers. If you should…"

"Do you follow me now, Tinker?" asked the detective, when his assistant had read the lines through about a dozen times and had thoroughly grasped their significance.

"I see, guv'nor," said Tinker slowly. "But you seem to hit on things so quickly that it well-nigh takes my breath away. Fancy thinking all that out in a few seconds, and getting me to rush off to Fleet Street! It would take me months to put two and two together like that, and then I should very likely make the answer, five instead of four."

But Blake only smiled at his assistant's youthful enthusiasm.

"I called myself Mr. Mappe in order to give a realistic touch to the message, Tinker," he said. "I'm hoping our mysterious Julie will read that in the morning papers and come along to Vendetti's. I shall be very charmed to renew our last somewhat abrupt acquaintance if she does. However, we can't do any more tonight, and the best thing now is to get to bed and forget our troubles for a few hours."

Chapter 14
What Happened at Vendetti's

IT was some time before the appointed hour that Sexton Blake arrived at Vendetti's next morning. He had taken the precaution to book a private room by 'phone there earlier on in the morning, and directly he arrived he found the maître d'hôtel and instructed him that anyone calling for "Mr. Mappe" was to be shown up to his room at once.

Blake looked at his watch; it was only a quarter to twelve now; he decided to sit down in the lounge and smoke for a few minutes.

Vendetti's was a Bohemian little restaurant and famous for the variety and excellence of its cuisine; at its snow-white tables all sorts and conditions of people congregated, and one heard conversations being carried on around one in every known tongue.

It was for this reason that Blake had chosen it as a rendezvous; it was a likely place for such a meeting as his, and the brief notice that he had inserted in the papers would have a ring of sincerity about it when coupled with such a notorious place as Vendetti's.

Very few people were in the lounge at the present moment; the habitual frequenters of the restaurant had not arrived yet, for Vendetti's did not commence to get busy until the evening.

The detective puffed reflectively at his pipe; his active mind was going over the extraordinary events of the last two days and reviewing the strange position in which he had been so suddenly placed.

He wondered what was happening to Granite Grant. How many thousands of miles was he away at that precise moment? Was he really marooned on some unknown island in the Caribbean Sea?

The whole thing seemed like some fantastic fairy tale; yet he did not doubt that his theories were correct and that the main facts of the situation, which he had so masterly put together, were true in their essential details.

Yet there were some aspects of this drama of intrigue that still puzzled him. How had Granite Grant managed to reach this island? If he had left the West Indies in a boat, as he must have done, then what had happened to the vessel to have prevented him from getting away again? And why had he sent out that strange message to him in code? Why not have sent a call for assistance to a passing ship? Why——

But it was useless to puzzle over these questions; he would never get an answer to them until he met the famous King's Spy again, and heard the story from his own lips. But would he ever see Granite Grant again? Would he——

Blake refused to consider that side of the problem. At any rate, he wasn't beaten yet— he still had a card to play, and it all depended on the result of this meeting at Vendetti's whether or not he would be obliged to have recourse to it.

He glanced across at the clock; it wanted but two minutes to the hour. He sprang to his feet, and hurrying across the lounge, went swiftly up the stairs to his room.

The two or three minutes that followed seemed an eternity to Blake. Would his message in the papers be seen and recognised by the person for whom it was intended? And even if it were, would anything come of it? He strode impatiently up and down the little room, stopping each time he heard a footstep in the corridor outside and listening intently.

It was gone twelve now—a minute past—and grave doubts began to form in his mind. Suddenly he fancied he heard a gentle tap at the door. He went swiftly towards it.

"Come in!" he cried.

The next moment he was staring in surprise at a dapper little man in a grey suit, and with a brown moustache, who stood at the door eyeing him curiously.

"I beg your pardon," said the little man, in a low, soft voice that had a quaint accent with it, "but I seem to have made a mistake."

"Not at all!" said the detective quickly. "What room did you want?"

"Room 16."

"This is Room 16!"

The little man seemed confused for a moment.

"Then it is the commissionaire, monsieur," he said, "who has made this mistake. I beg your pardon!"

He seemed about to withdraw, but it had suddenly occurred to Blake that perhaps there was no mistake after all. He had expected to meet Mademoiselle Julie and had thus been taken off his guard for the moment, but this little man spoke with a French accent and it was quite possible that he might have come here in answer to his advertisement.

"One moment!" he said, and put his foot against the door so that the other could not open it. "Perhaps there is no mistake after all. Are you looking for a Mr. Mappe?"

The little man's eyes glittered dangerously. Suddenly he made a quick movement with his right hand and the detective found himself facing a little, jewelled revolver.

"It is a plot!" he said angrily. "It is as I thought. Let me out—quick!"

Blake shrugged his shoulders in a casual manner.

"Very well," he said, "if you wish it."

He made as if to open the door, then, in a flash, his left hand shot out and caught the other's wrist in a grip of steel, and the weapon went clattering to the floor.

The little man uttered a snarl of rage and pounced on it. But Blake was too quick for him. He put one foot on the weapon and then picked up his opponent in his arms as if he were a baby.

For a few seconds he held him above his head while the little man struggled violently but quite impotently. Then, when his struggles had ceased, he lowered him gently to the floor.

The next instant Blake stepped back in quick surprise.

"Mademoiselle Julie!" he gasped.

In her struggles Mademoiselle Julie's bowler hat and wig had become dislodged, and her thick, golden hair was now tumbling over her shoulders in a mass of curls. The young woman tossed her head petulantly.

"You are a brigand!" she said angrily.

In her mortification she stamped her little foot and seemed on the point of shedding tears of vexation. Then she shot a swift glance of admiration at the detective.

"It is too bad, monsieur!" she added, in an undertone. "But you are very strong!"

And, as an afterthought, she whipped off the little brown moustache from off her upper lip.

Feeling strangely embarrassed, Blake could find nothing to say for a minute or two.

"I am very sorry, mademoiselle," he said at length, "to have been so rough. Pray accept my profound apologies! But I was not aware of your identity, although I was expecting you to honour me with a visit!"

The woman's anger had returned again.

"You were expecting me, monsieur!" she said. "But how dare you! What right have you to inveigle me here?"

"The right of necessity, mademoiselle! I think even you will recognise that right. Besides, our last meeting had a somewhat abrupt and unsatisfactory termination, if you remember!"

The young woman looked searchingly into his face.

"Then it was you, monsieur," she said, "who was at the Hermon Hall!"

Blake nodded an affirmative.

"It was I, mademoiselle!" he said.

The woman's eyes wandered again towards the door.

"We are wasting time, monsieur," she said. "I do not wish to be detained."

The detective went over to the door and, turning the key in the lock, put it in his pocket.

"Before you go, mademoiselle," he said firmly, "there are one or two matters that we must discuss."

The woman bit her lip vexatiously and her violet eyes clouded with anger.

"There are no matters that I wish to discuss with you, monsieur," she said haughtily.

"I think there are!" said Blake quietly. "You are a French subject, mademoiselle, and the great French nation and my own are friends and allies. We do not quarrel together."

The woman's face suddenly became flushed and an eager light came into her eyes.

"Who are you, monsieur?" she asked quickly. "Are you of the English?"

"I am, mademoiselle. My name is Sexton Blake."

"Sexton Blake! But that is the name of your great English detective!"

"Then that is I, mademoiselle!"

Mademoiselle Julie caught his hand in hers impulsively.

"Tell me, monsieur," she said earnestly. "The big Englishman, Granite Grant—he is a friend of yours?"

"He is a great friend of mine, mademoiselle."

"Then where is he, monsieur?"

The detective hesitated a moment. Was it safe to tell this young woman all he knew? Hadn't he better go carefully before he committed himself to any rash statement? He did not know now how far he might rely on her honesty and goodwill. There were still many things to be explained.

But the young woman perceived the look of doubt on his face.

"Ah, monsieur, you are thinking that I am a spy, she said. "And so I am! But not with the English—they are my friends. I did not know that you were the great Sexton Blake. It seemed that you were working for The Leopard."

Blake noted the glint of hatred which came into the woman's eyes at the mention of the name.

"Who is The Leopard?" he asked.

"His name is Venner, monsieur. He is in the pay of Germany—but surely you know! He is called The Leopard, but he is more like a snake. He killed my friend Monsieur Jacques, and it was he who shot Von Rosenburg yesterday at my flat."

Blake listened eagerly to her words. He was hearing the truth now, and he found that he was fairly, correct in his suppositions.

"But how about the map, mademoiselle?" he asked quickly.

"It is lost, monsieur. The Leopard has taken it. Von Rosenburg would have given it to me—but it is too late!"

"Why too late, mademoiselle? There is yet time to track down this man you call The Leopard."

The young woman laughed disdainfully.

"He is gone, monsieur," she said, "he is already in Holland. I go myself immediately. It was only your message this morning that detained me."

"Gone to Holland!" echoed Blake. "But how did he manage that so quickly?"

"There are means that you do not understand; monsieur," said the woman drily, "for those who work for the secret service."

"But if it is too late, why are you following him across?"

"It is too is too late, monsieur, to save the map, but it may not be too late to discover their plans. Besides, there is my revenge! Did he not kill my friend, Monsieur Jacques?"

The look of intense hatred had crept into her eyes again and in her anger she clenched her little hands together. The detective watched her in silence for some moments; for some he was turning something over in his mind. He still had his trump card to play, and he had determined to use it.

"Then you do not know where Granite Grant is, mademoiselle?" he asked presently.

"No, monsieur! But it is a pity. He would have known what to have done. He is very big. He would have taken The Leopard in his arms and throttled him."

Blake smiled grimly at this artless expression of opinion. But the woman was right. The big Secret Service agent had rather a vigorous method of dealing with his foes.

"When did you last see him, mademoiselle?"

"It was over three months ago now, monsieur. I had an appointment with him; we spoke of this missing bullion. The German Secret Service had been making inquiries and we were suspicious. Then he suddenly vanished. It was only this week that we learnt that the secret of its hiding-place was to be found in your big national library, monsieur."

Slowly and surely Blake was beginning to piece together exactly what had occurred. The secret—which these Continental agents had only just found out—Granite Grant had discovered over three months ago.

For some reason or other, perhaps because he wished to make sure of his information first, he had gone off alone to discover the whereabouts of this unknown island.

And now he was in difficulties, and had sent Blake that urgent call for help. Well, it was a tough proposition to discover the whereabouts of a man marooned on an unknown island—but Blake would not fail him. The odds were heavy, but they were never too heavy but there was a chance of winning through.

"Mademoiselle Julie," he said, "it may not be too late yet. Whoever discovers this bullion will yet have to reckon with Granite Grant. He is not a man to be easily defeated.

Perhaps The Leopard will have a surprise when he does come across the hiding-place—he may even find me there also to welcome him."

The young woman's eyes sparkled excitedly.

"That is splendid, monsieur," she said. "It is as a man should talk. Then we shall meet again, for I also shall be there."

Blake laughed pleasantly.

"If that is so," he said, "then it will be a very happy meeting."

"It will, monsieur. But I must go now, for tonight I must be in Holland."

The detective watched her as she adjusted her wig and moustache. He was wondering if she had meant anything by that latest curious statement.

Had she, too, determined not to give up the chase yet? She was merely a young woman, yet her charm and beauty enabled her to venture into places where a man would stand not an earthly chance. Perhaps she also had a trump card up her sleeve.

She turned to him and held out her hand.

"Au revoir, monsieur!" she said gaily.

"Au revoir, mademoiselle!" said Blake, taking her hand in his. "Or, perhaps, it would be more correct if I said 'monsieur'!"

He held the door open for her to pass out, then picked up his hat and gloves. He also was off to play his trump card, and for that purpose it was necessary that he should have an audience with Sir Vrymer Fane—at once!

Chapter 15
Blake Shows His Hand

SIR VRYMER FANE did not wait for his chauffeur to open the door for him. As the big limousine slowed up in Whitehall Court the minister sprang out and strode swiftly across the pavement and up the marble steps in front of the massive grey building. A moment later he entered the unpretentious room on the second floor where so many grave affairs of State had been discussed and decided.

"Ah, Mr. Blake!" he said. "I have hurried away from a meeting of the Cabinet because my secretary informed me that you wished to see me. You have some news for me?"

"I have, Sir Vrymer!" said the detective.

The minister hung up his hat and coat and then sat down at his desk.

"Draw your chair up closer, Mr. Blake," he said. "That's better! Now we can talk without fear of interruption. You have something pleasant to tell me, I trust!"

"I am sorry to say that is it rather unpleasant news, sir," the detective answered. "The map of which I spoke to you yesterday has been taken out of the country. At the present moment it is very possibly in Germany.

The minister's face became very grave and stern.

"How is that, Mr. Blake?" he asked quietly.

"It was, stolen by a Continental agent, sir, yesterday morning. I succeeded in getting on his track, but I was too late. I have just learnt that he crossed over to Holland last night."

"But what could our men have been doing to allow him to have escaped so easily?" asked Sir Vrymer impatiently. "This is very grave news, Mr. Blake. It puts us in rather an awkward predicament. You are quite certain that you have not made a mistake?"

"I am quite certain of that, sir!"

Sir Vrymer Fane passed his hand wearily across his forehead.

"The position is somewhat critical," he said. "We cannot allow all that bullion to go into the Central Powers; and yet there doesn't seem any way of preventing it. If we take diplomatic action they will simply deny all knowledge of its whereabouts."

He turned to the detective despairingly.

"Cannot you suggest some way out of the difficulty, Mr. Blake?" he asked. "Perhaps it's rather unreasonable of me to put such a question to you, but I am really quite at a loss to know what to do for the best."

"Supposing, Sir Vrymer," said Blake slowly, "that one were able to locate this island where the bullion is hidden, but could not get the treasure away without a little friction with some other country? In short, supposing one had to put up a bit of a fight to get the bullion away! Would that create any difficulties?"

"Not at all, Mr. Blake!" replied the minister quickly. "We should wash our hands of the whole business. Neither side would admit any responsibility in the matter. That is how the Secret Service works. The whole matter would be hushed up; it would never get to the ears of the general public."

"Then, Sir Vrymer," the detective said gently, "the bullion shall be recovered—map or no map!"

Sir Vrymer Fane stared at the detective in bewilderment.

"What do you mean, Mr. Blake?" he asked abruptly.

"I mean, sir, that I will use a wireless direction-finder to discover the whereabouts of this island, provided, of course, that I have your assistance."

The minister jumped to his feet and grasped the detective by the hand.

"By Jove, Mr. Blake," he said excitedly, "you fairly take my breath away by your resource and daring. Whoever would have thought of such a thing as that? You may certainly rely on me to give you everything you wish. A wireless direction-finder? Yes, I have heard of those wonderful things. But how do you propose to set to work?"

"If you will be good enough to give me your attention for a few moments, sir, I will endeavour to explain my plans."

"Carry on, Mr. Blake!" said Sir Vrymer, sitting back in his chair and folding his arms in an attitude of keen expectation.

"I take it, Sir Vrymer," began Blake, "that immediately that map reaches certain hands in Germany instructions will be secretly issued to some vessel to sail for the Caribbean Sea!"

The minister nodded his head in assent.

"Very likely those instructions have already been given, Mr. Blake," he said.

"That is very likely!" Blake agreed. "Very well, then, I am going to ask you to treat us with the same liberality. In short, am asking you to let me have a vessel immediately with a dozen reliable men besides the crew; and I am asking you to place the vessel entirely in my command."

"You shall have it, Mr. Blake," said Sir Vrymer eagerly. "In fact, it is ready for you now—the *Nancy*, lying at Southampton docks. It is kept for such unofficial voyages as you contemplate. No questions will be asked—you can trust me for that!"

"That is excellent, sir! Then she must be ready to put to sea in the morning with her full supply of fuel. It will be a race against time, and every moment counts. I shall make straight for the Caribbean Sea."

"And what then, Mr. Blake?"

"That depends on circumstances, Sir Vrymer. Roughly, my idea is this: You remember that we came to the conclusion yesterday that the *Spitzbergen* must have left her wireless set behind on the island, and that Granite Grant was able thereby to send out his message to me?"

"I recollect, Mr. Blake!"

"Very well, sir! I am hoping to be able to pick up wireless signals from this island, and by means of the direction-finder locate its position."

"But supposing you do not succeed in picking up these signals, Mr. Blake?"

"I have thought of that, sir. The German relief ship will, of course, take its bearings by the map. But the map can only give the rough position; and when the captain considers himself somewhere in the vicinity of the island he will no doubt try to enter into wireless communication to locate his bearings. That will give me my opportunity. I shall cruise about for a time around the spot where the operator of the *Wildfly* picked up the message from Granite Grant."

"Quite so, Mr. Blake. That seems an excellent plan. As you say, where you have an archipelago like that of the Caribbean Sea, even a map is not sufficient to locate one solitary island."

"If I do not succeed in picking up signals, sir, then I shall try to enter into direct communication with the island, and see what happens. The *Nancy* is fitted with wireless, I presume?"

"Oh, yes, Mr. Blake; but not with a direction-finder."

"A portable set can be easily obtained and installed in a very short time, Sir Vrymer!"

"I will give immediate instructions to that effect, Mr. Blake; and see that you have a first-class operator as well."

"That is certainly necessary, sir; I'm afraid my wireless knowledge is very limited. In addition, I am hoping to take the operator of the *Wildfly* with me; he will be a very useful man to have.

"There are no other details that you have omitted to mention?"

The detective thought for a moment with contracted brows.

"There is the question of equipment, Sir Vrymer——"

"You leave that to me, Mr. Blake," the Minister hurriedly interposed. "I will look after that. You shall have everything for an emergency—arms, ammunition. You understand!"

"Very good, sir! Then I shall expect everything ready for my leaving Southampton by tomorrow afternoon at the very latest!"

Sir Vrymer Fane nodded his head, and got up out of his chair.

"Upon my word, Mr. Blake!" he said, and his keen eyes shone with excitement, "this is a most extraordinary task you have undertaken. It makes me feel quite young again to think of it. Really, it is more like a romance of the days of Drake. I only wish I could join you. However, I wish you the best of luck, and I can't help thinking you will pull through somehow or other."

Blake shook the Minister's hand heartily.

"I think I will, Sir Vrymer," he said quietly.

***

"We're catching the ten o'clock train tomorrow morning for Southampton, Tinker, and we're sailing straight away for the Caribbees. See that you have everything ready in time!"

Tinker stared at his master as if he thought he had taken leave of his senses.

"What?" he blurted, when he had somewhat recovered his breath. "Sailing for the Caribbees, guv'nor?"

"That's what I said, Tinker!"

Tinker took another glance at his master to see if he were serious; then, evidently convinced that Blake wasn't kidding, gave a wild whoop of intoxicated joy, and began to dance round the room like a madman.

"Well, I'm jiggered, guv'nor!" he gasped, after having exhausted his energies in this fashion.

"I should say it was a more serious complaint than that, Tinker," said the detective, with an amused expression on his face.

But Tinker took no notice of his master's satire; the prospect of a voyage to the Caribbees was much too exciting for that.

"You really mean it, guv'nor?" he asked. "We're going in search of this unknown island?"

"Don't you understand plain English, Tinker?"

Tinker executed another of his frantic heathen dances, and this time succeeded in knocking over two chairs and a table.

"That's quite enough of that, Tinker!" said Blake.

And then Tinker suddenly sobered down.

"Sorry, guv'nor!" he said contritely; "but I had just to let off steam; otherwise I should have burst. Are we taking Pedro?"

"Rather!"

Blake and his young assistant had no sleep that night; they were far too busy with other matters. Tinker couldn't, have gone to sleep, even if he had had the chance; he was much too excited for that.

Chapter 16
On Board the *Nancy*

YES, she's the same boat, sir. We passed her two days out from Jamaica. Seems to be steering a rather erratic course. Wonder what her game is?"

Sexton Blake took the binoculars from Captain Sampson's fingers and gazed long and earnestly across the glaring waste of sunlit waters.

"Your eyes are evidently better than mine, captain," he said presently. "I can just make out two little black specks on the skyline, and that's about all."

Captain Sampson gave a deep, throaty chuckle, and little crows'-feet appeared about his light-blue eyes.

"They're her twin funnels, sir," he said. "There's no mistaking 'em. Can't catch me tripping on a thing like that!"

"Well, I'll take your word for it, captain!" laughed Blake. "But what's the worry—anything wrong with her?"

"Oh, I'm not saying she don't know what she's about! But she's been zig-zagging like an old grampus. She's changed her course now—going on an easterly tack."

"Where's she making for?"

"If she keeps going long enough, sir, she'll make the Lesser Antilles sometime or other. Don't see why she should change her mind like that, though. Shall we alter our course and keep her in sight, sir?"

Blake looked thoughtfully at the distant horizon.

"What course are we steering?" he asked.

"Nor'-norwest, sir!"

"We're making for Panama?"

"Somewhere in that direction, sir."

"Very well, captain. Swing her round. It doesn't matter much, either way. But don't go full-speed; we don't want to overtake her."

"No fear of that, sir!" said Captain Sampson. "She's doing a good twenty-five knots. Below the horizon already. In any case, we couldn't catch her up and she may alter her course again during the night."

The detective stepped down from the bridge and made his way across the *Nancy's* white glistening decks. He stopped a moment by the wireless cabin, and poked his head in the door.

"Picked up anything yet, Charlie?" he asked.

Charlie Jones glanced up from the mysterious-looking gadgets which he was busy manipulating.

"No, sir," he said. "Nothing doing! Haven't heard a buzz since we left the coast."

He adjusted his earphones again, and tapped the delicate little valves of the amplifier that glowed like electric lamps.

The detective watched him with great interest. He had great faith in Charlie Jones's skill and dexterity.

"How are we for position?" he asked presently. "Anywhere in the vicinity of the spot where you picked up that other message?"

"Yes, sir! We couldn't have been more than a few miles off this morning."

Blake nodded his head, and closed the door.

In the bows of the vessel, Tinker, clad in white ducks, lay stretched in a camp-chair—in the shade of an awning. The great bloodhound lolled at his feet with his tongue hanging out.

"Enjoying yourself, Tinker?" asked Blake.

His young assistant glanced up with sleepy eyes.

"Not too bad, guv'nor!" he said lazily; "but it's beastly hot."

"Pshaw!" said Blake; "it's only just warm."

And as if to confirm his statement, the detective took out his pocket-handkerchief and mopped feverishly at his perspiring brow, then went and leant against the taffrail and gazed across the wilderness of tepid sea that surrounded them on all sides.

It was nearly a month since the *Nancy* had left Southampton docks. The voyage out had been more or less uneventful; they had passed through the Windward Passage and called at Jamaica to replenish their fuel and victuals.

For the last four or five days they had been steaming slowly across the Caribbean Sea towards Panama.

Blake was thinking of England as he hung over the side of the vessel. It seemed impossible that the "old country" should be all those thousands of miles away, and that he should be out in these tropical seas.

He was a mere speck on this infinite ocean; it was full of unknown dangers; its complicated currents and dangerous shoals necessitated considerable skill and care on the part of the navigator.

Fortunate for him that he had such a sturdy old sea-dog as Captain Sampson as his right-hand man!

The thought came to him that, after all, he had embarked on a wild-goose chase; that to search for an unknown island in this desolate waste of waters was like looking for a pin in a haystack.

Then he remembered that he had solemnly promised Sir Vrymer Fane to succeed in his mission; he could not go back on his word somehow or other, this unknown island must be discovered.

A look of great determination came into the detective's face. If nothing happened by noon tomorrow he would turn the ship about and cruise over the area where Charlie Jones had picked up the message before.

He would keep sending out signals by wireless, in the hope that the people on the island would pick up and reply. But that would only be as a last resource. If possible, he wanted his visit to be quite unexpected; he wanted to give no warning of his coming, for he did not know what kind of reception he would meet with.

He glanced up at the sky; it hung overhead like a great inverted basin, with the sun blazing like a ball of fire at its zenith. Its rays beat upon the waters so that they glittered like burnished silver, while the tar between the vessel's white planks was as soft as wax.

The heat was overpowering; everybody seemed to be asleep; even Captain Sampson, up on the bridge, was leaning against the rail, nodding dozily. Blake decided that that was the best thing to do; he would have forty winks; he could work during the long, cool, refreshing night. He crept beneath the shade of the dinghy, and immediately sank into oblivion.

***

Blake's "forty winks" must have lasted rather longer than the regulation time. The day was fast waning when he again opened his eyes. The sun was sinking beneath the rim of the sea, and a great blood-red carpet of shimmering water spread from the ship to the horizon.

It was cooler now; a refreshing current of air fanned Blake's face. He raised himself on his elbow and stared around. He seemed to have a vague recollection of having heard, someone call his name. Then he heard Tinker call again, and crawled quickly out under the dingy.

"Hallo, Tinker!" he shouted.

His assistant came running across the deck towards him, his face aglow with excitement.

"I say, guv'nor!" he exclaimed. "There's something doing at last. 'Sparks' has been asking for you—he's picked up some message on his wireless gadget."

Blake was alert in an instant.

"Has he, by Jove?" he muttered; and, without asking any further questions, sped across the deck to the wireless cabin.

Inside, Charlie Jones was standing in front of his instrument with the earphones on his ears. With one hand he was taking down a message in pencil, while with the other he kept gently adjusting various studs and reactance handles.

Blake watched him for a moment in silence, not venturing to interrupt him in his work. Then he took the spare pair of earphones from the hook and put them over his ears.

The familiar dot-dash of the Morse code was coming through in a high-pitched, musical note, punctuated every now and then with little breaks and pauses.

Charlie Jones was evidently reading it like a book, and while he wrote with one hand, with the other he was adjusting the index-finger of the direction-finder, which would show from which direction the wireless signals were coming.

Suddenly the sounds in the earphones ceased. For two or three minutes they listened intently to see if the signals would be renewed; then Charlie Jones turned to the detective and handed him the sheet of paper.

"Here's what I've taken down, sir," he said. "First thing I heard was a ship calling the *Spitzbergen*. She went on calling for nearly two hours without getting any reply; then I suddenly heard this other station answering her. Sure it's the same one that sent that message to you—sounded just like her note. The message seems to be written in German, worse luck, and I can't read it."

"I can, though!" said Blake; and, picking up the pencil, began to translate what Charlie Jones had written down. Presently he flung down the pencil and turned to Tinker excitedly.

"Read this, Tinker!" he said, in suppressed tones. "The whole thing is as clear as daylight; the island has been found without a doubt."

At that moment Captain Sampson had entered the cabin, and had overheard the detective's last remark. He leant his grizzled face over Tinker's shoulder, while Charlie Jones looked on from the other side.

On the sheet of paper in Blake's bold hand were written a number of code signals, which he had not attempted to decipher, and then in plain English followed these two messages, which were repeated three times:

"*Spitzbergen*—Relief ship *Fraulein* from Hamburg. Is there a safe anchorage?"

"*Fraulein*—Enter by north-east point; keep centre channel; five fathoms close up.—
Spitzbergen."

"Shakes alive!" muttered Captain Sampson, scratching his head; "but that ship's evidently found a lump of earth floating about in the ocean. But where the blazes is it? There's nothing on the skyline!"

"You're forgetting, captain," said Charlie Jones quietly, "that these signals might have travelled a hundred miles or more before they reached us."

"The deuce they might!" said the captain, in perplexity. "Then how in the name of reason are we going to find this comic island? It's like looking for a cork on the ocean!"

Captain Sampson's bewilderment was so genuine that Blake could hardly prevent himself from laughing.

"There's something else you've overlooked, captain," he said, "and that's the direction-finder. Just explain it to him, Charlie."

Nothing loth, Charlie Jones turned to his instrument-board.

"There you are, captain!" he said, pointing triumphantly to a little index-finger that swung across a gradual dial, "that's the direction from which those signals came. It's up to you now to do the navigating."

Captain Sampson bent over the little instrument and studied it intently for a few seconds. Presently he looked up with an air of great dignity.

"Well," he said, in slow, deliberate tones, "if you want me to put her nose in that direction I guess I'm the man to do it. I calculate that our present bearings are about ten degrees off that course."

"Then take your bearings by the direction-finder, captain," said Blake quickly, "and get every ounce of speed out of her you can."

"Leave it to me, sir!" rejoined Captain Sampson, as he hurried away to follow out his instructions.

"And now, Charlie," said the detective, "how far off is that ship, do you think? Have you the least idea?"

"I should say about fifty or sixty miles, sir, by the strength of the signals. But that's only a very rough guess—it's impossible to say exactly."

"Very well, then, we sha'n't sight the island before the morning, at the very least. You tumble in and get some sleep—you may have a busy day tomorrow. I'll get the other operator to sit up and listen in."

Followed by Tinker, the detective stepped out of the cabin and crossed the deck to the hatchway. This swift turn of events had filled them both with a strong sense of adventure; at last they knew they were hot on the scent; the vessel was steering straight for this unknown island, and in a short while now their efforts would either be crowned with success or failure.

But there were many things to be done first. They must be prepared for any emergency. The *Fraulein* had got there first, and she would not give up her priceless treasure without making a fight for it.

As Blake and his assistant disappeared below the hatchway the thin red rind of the sun was just dipping below the horizon. Already the brief twilight of those tropical regions was fading into the darkness of night, and the great dome of the sky was clustering with a myriad stars.

All through that night the *Nancy* sped ceaselessly on towards her unknown destination, her keen bows cutting through the waters and spraying her white decks with foaming suds.

There was no sleep for Captain Sampson: he stood on the bridge gazing ahead into the darkness and straining his ears for that tell-tale boom of the breakers that would warn him of the danger that lurked in the path of his tight little vessel.

There was very little sleep also for Blake and his assistant. Not until the faint tinge on the eastern horizon warned them of the approach of dawn did they sink into their bunks and drop straight into the land of, dreams.

Chapter 17
The Island

BY Jove, guv'nor, isn't that just too wonderful for words! Just pinch me to see if I'm awake!"

Blake ignored his assistant's request; he stood in the bows of the *Nancy* gazing in silent fascination at the gorgeous spectacle that confronted them.

The vessel was rolling lazily in a sluggish sea, and not a breath of wind stirred the stillness of the air. The sun hung in a white heat a few yards above the horizon, and its slanting rays threw a broad ribbon of sheeny satin across the restless waters.

But it was not this that was riveting Blake's attention, and had called forth Tinker's remark. Their eyes were fixed on something else. For straight ahead, lying like a casket of jewels in the lap of the ocean, was the unknown island, to seek which they had embarked on this strange adventure and had come all these thousands of miles.

The island rose like a hillock out of the ocean, its white glistening beach sloping gently up from the sea for a hundred yards or so until it met the great belt of palm, locust, and gum trees with which the whole island seemed to be covered.

Some little distance from the shore a coral reef stretched, from one extremity to the other, encircling in its wide embrace a lagoon of pellucid blue water.

On this magic scene the rising sun flung its dazzling rays, striking the coral reef so that it spangled with coloured fire, and glistening on the calm waters of the lagoon so that they sparkled and scintillated like a sheet of burnished metal.

And encircled by the gleaming white beach was the deep green of the forest, heavy with the morning dew and festooned with innumerable tendrils and other exotic plants of that tropic zone.

No wonder Tinker could not find words to express himself. The detective himself was so deeply impressed that it was some time before he could move his fascinated eyes from the object of their admiration.

Presently he turned to Captain Sampson, who had that moment come along the deck.

"It seems too wonderful to be real, captain," he said.

"Ay, sir, it's a pretty sight!" admitted Captain Sampson.

"But I do not see any signs of this other vessel, captain!"

"She's there right enough, sir! I saw her when we were some miles away; that was before you were awake. She's just the other side of that promontory on the extreme left. I purposely made a wide circle so as to get the other side. Them's your instructions, sir?"

"Quite right, captain!" said Blake. "Do you think they know we're here? I can't see any signs of anyone on this side."

"There's no saying, sir, but that they might have spotted us; can't tell for a cert. But I don't think so. I bet I saw them first, and I wasn't for advertising the matter; I soon stuck her helm over and tacked to leeward."

"Good!" said Blake. "Then we'll spring a surprise on them. Get the boat over the side and everyone take their places. We're leaving you here, captain, to look after the ship, but you know exactly what to do. Now Tinker, get busy, my lad!"

Very soon the boat was creaking on the davits, and the dozen reliable men, whom Sir Vrymer Fane had placed at Blake's command, were clambering into it.

They were all fully armed with rifles, for although the detective hoped there would be no necessity to use them, yet he did not know what resistance he might meet with.

As Tinker was just climbing over the side the great bloodhound came pattering along the deck.

"Come on, Pedro!" shouted Tinker, "This way, boy!"

The great dog crouched low and took a flying leap and landed with a thud in the bottom of the boat.

"Where's Charlie Jones?" asked the detective, looking round. "Ah, here he is; over you go!"

He took another brief glance around, then turned to Captain Sampson.

"Well, good-bye, captain!" he said. "Don't go too far away; and look out for my signal."

Captain Sampson grasped the detective's hand, and glanced anxiously at the distant horizon.

"Don't quite like the look of things, sir," he said, shaking his head dubiously. "Some dirty weather brewing, I'm afraid. The barometer has dropped over an inch, and the sea's getting choppy."

"That's rather bad news," said Blake. "However, we must take our chance. No good hanging around and waiting for something to happen. Cheerio!"

He climbed over the side and dropped into the boat. A moment later they were pulling rapidly for the shore, and the *Nancy* was slowly drifting further and further astern.

As Captain Sampson had said, the sea was now very choppy, and it was hard work pulling on the oars. The sound of the breakers grew louder and louder, but it was nearly half an hour before they were close enough to the outer reef to discern an opening through which they could pass.

Then suddenly Blake, who was on the look-out in the bows, saw a gap in the reef that seemed wide enough for their purpose.

"Back oars!" he shouted. "Now, round with her. That's the style, boys! Wait for this next roller. Here she is—pull as if your lives depended on it!"

Blake held his breath and waited. The boat rose higher and higher on the crest of the wave: the jagged line of coral was sweeping impetuously towards them and threatening their frail craft with instant destruction.

Then, with a deafening swirl of waters in their ears, they shot through the opening and floated gently into the calm waters of the lagoon.

The detective gave a great gasp of relief. They were safe once more! But he had to admit that it was more by luck than by judgment that they had managed to pass through the narrow passage unscathed.

It was easy work pulling now. The clear waters of the lagoon were teeming with strange aquatic creatures, at which Pedro barked furiously until, with a gesture, Blake silenced him. He was afraid that someone on the island would hear the dog and would thus discover their presence.

Soon the boat grounded gently on the sloping beach, and, springing out, Blake held her nose while the others clambered after him.

"Now, Williams," he said, turning to one of the men, "you know your instructions! You're left in charge! You're to wait here until my return. If you hear me give three blasts on my whistle you'll know that I'm in need of assistance. In that case, try and make your way round to the other side of the island. But you needn't worry about that; I am sure to be back before long. I should pull out into the lagoon if I were you. Is everything clear?"

"I understand, sir. You trust me for knowing what to do!"

"Good enough!" said Blake. "Come on, Tinker—off we go!"

Blake and his assistant, with their rifles slung over their shoulders, commenced to make their way up the sloping beach towards the fringe of trees that skirted the forest.

Pedro was already some hundred yards on ahead, running to and fro excitedly and glancing at his master from time to time to see that he was following.

When they had reached the edge of the forest they turned in a westerly direction, and, keeping the trees closely on their right, swung along at a good pace, keeping a sharp look-out all the while for any signs of a pathway that might seem to lead in a definite direction.

About half an hour passed in silence; they were both too interested in their surroundings, and the infinite variety and magnificence of the tropical vegetation which met their eyes, to enter into conversation. Presently Blake happened to glance seaward.

"Tinker!" he exclaimed, coming to a halt. "Just look at that haze which is hanging over the sea. The *Nancy* has completely vanished."

Tinker gazed in the direction of Blake's finger.

"You're right, guv'nor!" he muttered. "It certainly seems to be getting rather thick. It's only the heat, I suppose."

The detective looked rather grave.

"Perhaps you're right, Tinker!" he said. "But I don't like the look of it. Captain Sampson seemed to expect dirty weather, and he's generally right. However, it can't be helped; we'll push on."

They continued their way for about a dozen yards, when suddenly Blake discovered that Pedro was nowhere in sight.

"Pedro, Pedro!" he called, looking round for the animal. But no Pedro answered.

"I saw him just now when we stopped, guv'nor," said the assistant. "He was nosing among the trees."

"Let's go back and see then, Tinker!"

They began retracing their steps, and Blake kept calling the dog by his name. Then they heard Pedro give his familiar low growl, and they commenced to thread their way through the trees in the direction of the sound.

A moment later they came across him about twenty yards away. The bloodhound was creeping slowly up and down with his nose to the ground, sniffing the earth suspiciously.

"Come here, Pedro!" called Blake again.

The dog lifted his great head, and, wagging his tail, shot a significant look at his master, then dropped his nose to the ground again.

Feeling somewhat curious, Blake commenced to walk towards the animal. Pedro immediately began to move away deeper into the forest.

Blake stopped again.

"Now what the deuce is he up to, Tinker?" he asked, with a note of curiosity.

"Blowed if I know, guv'nor! Perhaps we'd better follow him for a bit. Seems to have picked up a scent."

"I believe he has, Tinker!" said Blake with a thrill of excitement. "But what on earth can it be? Old Pedro seems rather pleased—he's wagging his tail. This is mighty strange."

Blake and Tinker hurried after the animal; but Pedro seemed determined to keep in front, and increased his pace accordingly.

The dog seemed perfectly sure of himself now and went forward with steady deliberation and with his nose held close to the ground.

The trees were getting thicker and thicker and crowding out the light of the sun. There were towering palms and locust trees of immense girth, whose gnarled barks were overgrown with lichen and mosses; strange parasitic plants hung in festoons from the boughs of the trees, growing to a gigantic size in the steaming heat of that tropic forest, while numberless strange birds of brilliant plumage flitted about in the branches.

The forest got denser and denser, and an impenetrable gloom surrounded them, in which everything began to take on an unreal and fantastic appearance.

The sky was now entirely blotted out from view, and high overhead was a thick canopy of luxuriant vegetation, which shed around a dim greenish light.

"Shouldn't like to lose myself in this black forest, Tinker!" said Blake.

Tinker nodded his head and answered in an awed kind of voice.

"Nor would I, guv'nor," he said. "Gives one a sort of funny feeling as it is. Glad when we see daylight once more."

"But where the deuce is Pedro taking us?" muttered the detective. "This is a sort of natural path we're on, Tinker. Wonder where it leads?"

He stooped suddenly to the ground and stared intently at the thick carpet of moss.

"Someone's been along here, Tinker," he said, "and quite recently, too! That's the scent Pedro is on. But who can it possibly be—the dog seems pleased as if he had recognised someone. This is most extraordinary."

"There's a sort of Robinson Crusoe touch about this business, guv'nor," said his young assistant in a scared voice. "I don't freeze on to this trip—it's a bit too creepy. There's all manner of queer things crawling about in this thick undergrowth."

"Yes, you'd better keep your eyes skinned, Tinker," replied the detective. "There may be poisonous snakes in this rank vegetation."

They continued their way in silence again, walking in Indian file. The dog still kept about a dozen yards ahead, running forward in queer little spurts, then stopping and casting furtive glances around with his ears held back.

The gloom hung around them like a heavy pall, and the weird rustling noises that sounded about their feet seemed only to accentuate the deathly stillness that brooded over the dismal forest.

It seemed impossible that any living thing should have penetrated this ghastly place or perpetual night, yet as Tinker tried to peer through the dim shrouded trees he could not help feeling that all manner of cruel invisible foes were lurking in their depths waiting for the opportunity to spring out on him.

This idea became such an obsession with him that he kept treading on his master's heels in his anxiety to be as near him as possible.

It seemed to Blake that they had been walking for nearly an hour, when Pedro shot forward and disappeared among the trees. He hurried his steps, and a few moments later came out into the wide clearing.

He stood at the edge staring around him in some surprise, half-expecting to discover the strange thing which Pedro had been tracking so persistently ever since they had entered the forest.

But nothing unusual met his eye; the clearing was devoid of trees, but the ground was still covered with that rich carpet of rank vegetation which spread throughout the forest.

"What's that mound over there, guv'nor?" asked Tinker suddenly. "There seems to be something sticking out of it."

Followed by his assistant, Blake made his way towards the object that Tinker had pointed out.

"Why, it's a cross, Tinker!" he said suddenly, when they were about a dozen yards away. "It looks like the broken part of a propeller."

"So it does, guv'nor! And, see, there's a heap of twisted scrap-iron over there."

Filled with curiosity, the detective stood gazing at the rough wooden cross that stuck above the mound. Whose grave could this be? Who lay buried in this desolate spot?

A strange sympathy came over Blake. This rude wooden cross, standing there alone, seemed a very pathetic and tender memorial to that silent, unknown creature that slept peacefully beneath.

He looked down at Pedro. The animal was a few yards away, anxiously sniffing at some object that he had found buried in the tangled undergrowth. Blake walked over to the animal and knelt on the ground.

Presently he climbed to his feet and stood looking with an expression of puzzlement at the object he held in his hand.

It was a briar pipe, and, from the look of it, its owner had made good use of it; the marks of his teeth were on the amber mouthpiece. And, as Blake stared at it, he suddenly realised why it seemed familiar.

He had given Granite Grant a present of a case of briars on the occasion of his marriage—and this was one of them!

The recollection came as a stunning blow to the detective. There was not the slightest doubt about it; the pipe he held in his hand once belonged to Granite Grant. He had bought it himself, and he could not make a mistake.

"This pipe belonged to Granite Grant, Tinker," he said, in an unsteady voice, and a great lump came into his throat.

The detective and Tinker both turned and looked again at the rough wooden cross, and, as if they divined each other's thoughts, they both removed their hats and stood in silent reverence, each being too deeply affected to speak.

So this was the meaning of that rough wooden cross! It marked the grave of Granite Grant. No question crossed Blake's mind to the contrary: he held Grant's pipe in his hand, and the association of ideas was too strong to doubt the truth of his conjecture.

Then he was too late! Granite Grant was no more; all that remained of the famous King's Spy lay buried beneath this rude mound.

With a deep sigh Blake turned away, and glanced round for Pedro. Suddenly some startling fact seemed to occur to him.

"Tinker," he said sharply, "why is it so dark? It's as black here as in the forest."

He stared up above in alarm. The sky was blotted out; an impalpable black mist was swirling above the tree-tops. Suddenly a great arc of fire cut across the heavens.

A moment of deathly silence followed; then the whole island seemed to rock with the terrific reverberation of thunder. At the same moment the great trees swayed like saplings beneath a perfect deluge of wind and rain.

Blake grasped his assistant by the arm.

"The cyclone, Tinker!" he shouted. "Down, down!" And flung himself flat on the ground.

But Blake's words were lost in the pandemonium of noise. Even if Tinker had heard them it is doubtful if he would have taken any heed.

In the face of this awful hurricane even the youngster's stout nerves failed him, and, impelled by the instinct of safety, he fled like mad towards the cover of the trees.

Chapter 18
The Boa-Constrictor

FOR a few crazy minutes Tinker rushed on madly. The great trees at the edge of the clearing were snapping with reports like rifle-shots, and several had been rooted bodily from the ground. It was by sheer luck that Tinker got through the danger-zone without being crushed to death.

As he penetrated deeper and deeper into the forest the force of the cyclone seemed to lose some of its fury; the trees were crowded so closely together that their giant trunks acted as a screen to the driving wind and rain.

But the noise was still deafening, and the ground shook with the crash of thunder. High up in the tree-tops the tornado was raging with increasing violence.

Presently Tinker slowed down in his wild, impetuous career. He was panting quickly, and seemed almost on the verge of exhaustion. His face and hands were scratched and bleeding from his contact with trunks of trees, gnarled roots and hanging tendrils, for the gloom was so opaque that he could not see more than a yard or so in front of him!

After a time his eyes grew more accustomed to the darkness, and he began to peer around. The coming of the cyclone had disturbed numerous reptiles and small rodents, which darted to and fro or wriggled about in the undergrowth at his feet.

There were adders, lizards, and scorpions of strange variegated colours and of enormous size, and Tinker's blood ran cold as he looked at them.

Fearful of being stung by one of these loathsome creatures, he climbed into the forked branch of a locust-tree, and began to feel more secure.

The cyclone still raged high overhead, and the forest reverberated with deafening thunderclaps and the crashing of trees. Vivid streaks of lightning lit up the woods every now and then, and the furious tempest of wind shrieked and moaned as if ten thousand devils had been let loose.

But, except for his own fears and the terrors of his overwrought imagination, Tinker had no cause for alarm; the great forest of trees effectually shielded him from the fury of the storm.

He began to wonder presently what had happened to Blake. He could not quite remember what had occurred immediately after that first vivid flash of lightning. Had his master also sought safety in the shelter of the forest?

The sudden appearance of the cyclone had so unnerved Tinker that he had forgotten all about his beloved master. He was regretting his selfish impulse now of thinking only of his own safety; he should have stayed near him. Perhaps he was lying at that moment crushed beneath one of those uprooted trees!

Tinker grew anxious and concerned. Where could Blake be? He must go and find him at the first opportunity. He glanced up above at the green canopy of foliage. How long would this awful tempest last? he wondered.

His knowledge of cyclones was very limited, but he knew that they sometimes gained a velocity of some thirty or forty miles an hour, and that, if they were only on the outskirts, the tempest would soon sweep by.

Perched in the fork of the tree, he waited anxiously for signs that the cyclone was spending itself. But the thunder and crashes and shrieking of the wind still continued with undiminished violence; there were no signs of it ceasing yet.

Nearly an hour must have passed by when Tinker at last plucked up courage to climb down from his perch. The trees still rocked from the whirlwind that surged up above; but the storm was abating, the thunder was rumbling in the distance, and the cyclone passing seaward.

He stood a moment irresolute, being not quite certain which way to go.

The gloom was not so impenetrable now; the dim, greenish light that filtered down above told him that somewhere through that thick curtain of foliage was the white glare of daylight.

He chose his direction carefully, and commenced to make his way towards the clearing where he had separated from Blake an hour or more ago.

It was slow work making his way through this dense forest of trees and clustering mosses and ferns; to move forward a dozen yards he had to go fifty—there was no such thing as making a bee-line here.

Yet the clearing could not be very far away; that first wild rush of his to safety had only been a matter of ten minutes or so; then he had stopped, and climbed into the locust-tree.

He had been struggling on for nearly twenty minutes when the realisation came to him that he must be going in the wrong direction. He turned about, and commenced to make his way back to the locust-tree.

When he got there he would try again in another direction; he couldn't very well miss the clearing it must be a simple matter to find that.

But no locust tree with the two forked branches met Tinker's anxious gaze. Every tree seemed alike to him, and although he searched frantically for some familiar object that he might recognise as having previously passed, yet nothing met his eyes that he could remember before.

The forest was a dreadful maze of trees, and in the bizarre greenish light each one seemed to have some strange resemblance of a face leering down at him with an inscrutable smile of mockery.

Tinker suddenly came to a stop, and leant against a tree, breathing heavily. He had missed his way somehow; he had not the vaguest sense of direction; he was lost—lost in this dark, dismal forest of trees and strange exotic vegetation.

What should he do? It was impossible to stay here; the gloom and silence of the place appalled him. There must be a way out.

He started off again in another direction. He was growing frantic now, and hurried forward blindly, without much regard for where he was going so long as he kept on moving.

Many times he slipped on moss-covered lumps of rock, or tripped over protruding roots, and went crashing to the ground. But he clambered to his feet each time and rushed on again.

The full force of the cyclone had swept by the island now, although the great trees still trembled in the violent wind that raged in their tops.

But the storm had no terrors for Tinker now; his one desire was to find a way out of this fearful forest, and discover the whereabouts of his beloved master.

He tripped again presently over a creeping shoot, and went sprawling heavily at the base of a great gum-tree. There he lay for a while, half stunned, and too tired to move.

As his senses came slowly back to him, he realised the hopelessness of his plight; he was lost in this dreadful forest, and unless someone found him in time he would perish there of hunger and thirst.

Suddenly he felt the tree behind him trembling, as if something were moving. He sprang to his feet in alarm, and stepped back with a gasp of horror.

Around the massive trunk of the gum tree a great, slimy shape was slowly uncurling, and, as Tinker looked, a branch seemed to shoot out, and two little green eyes glittered venomously.

Too fascinated and horror-struck to move, the youngster stood staring at this loathsome thing as it unwound its coils from the tree. It was an enormous boa, of a size only found in those tropical forests, and must have measured nearly forty feet in length.

Evidently it had been coiled round the tree asleep, and Tinker's presence had disturbed the creature's slumbers.

Suddenly Tinker seemed to regain control of his limbs. With a gasp of terror, he turned and made a blind rush. The next moment his foot had caught in a prickly bramble, and he went crashing to the ground.

He half raised himself on his elbow, and glared fearfully at the tree. The serpent had reared its head in the air, and was poised motionless, with its little beady eyes fixed on him with deadly intent.

Tinker felt that his last moment had come; another instant, and that cruel head and slimy body would come hurtling at him with the force of a battering-ram; he would be caught in those long, sinuous coils and crushed to pulp.

But at that tense moment a savage snarl of rage sounded close behind him, and the next instant a dark, whip-like form shot over him straight at the reptile's head.

It was Pedro! Tinker realised it with a wild surge of unrestrained joy and thankfulness. Somehow the sagacious animal had tracked him down, and had been able to reach him in the nick of time.

Yet the next moment his sudden relief changed to a feeling of great fear for the brave dog's safety.

The bloodhound had bit savagely at the monster's head as he swung clear, and now he crouched a few yards away, lashing his tail uneasily at the fearful odds which confronted him.

For a few seconds the boa writhed in rage and pain. Then it reared its head cautiously in the air, and, as it sought to discover the whereabouts of this new enemy, its little eyes glinted balefully like live coals.

Tinker knew that the great dog could not hope to win a tussle with this fearful monster; once the boa got the bloodhound in its coils Pedro would be no more.

Then a fresh diversion occurred. The tall figure of a man broke through the undergrowth, and stood for an instant silently surveying the weird scene.

Then the stranger sprang forward, and, swinging his rifle over his head, brought the heavy stock down with a smashing blow that shattered the monster's head.

"Out of the way, man!" he shouted, and, grasping Tinker's arm, dragged him out of reach of the boa's furious death struggles.

Presently the stranger stopped, and, releasing his hold of Tinker's arm, leant, against a tree, with his breath coming in short gasps.

Tinker scrambled to his feet, and stood staring at his rescuer in silent amazement. In spite of his tangled hair and unshaven face, he felt somehow that he had seen this man before; that the quick resource and extraordinary strength he had shown in killing the frightful boa singled him out as a man among a thousand—a man of iron nerves and matchless courage.

"By Jove," muttered the stranger, when he had somewhat recovered his breath, "that was a near squeak! What are you doing here, youngster? And who the deuce are you?"

And at the sound of his voice Tinker knew immediately who he was. He held out his hand impulsively.

"It's Granite Grant!" he shouted, and gave a wild whoop of joy. "You saved my life, sir! We thought you were dead—that that was your grave in the clearing over there!"

Tinker was so filled with emotion that he almost wept with delight. He held the big hand of the King's Spy in his own, and stammered incoherent sentences of joy and surprise.

A puzzled look had come into Granite Grant's face; he stared at the youngster with amazement and curiosity.

"Are you Sexton Blake's assistant?" he asked slowly. "What the deuce is your name? I've forgotten it now!"

"Tinker, Tinker! Yes, that's me!"

"Then this is Blake's bloodhound?" exclaimed Grant. "What's the old fellow's name? Pedro, isn't it? I met the old chap in the forest. Put the wind up me when I saw him! He was frightfully excited, and seized me by the leg of the trousers and dragged me all over the place. Then I came across this rifle—it's yours, I suppose? I felt there was something wrong when I saw that."

"Yes, that's mine right enough," said Tinker.

"But how did you get here, youngster? And was that your vessel that I saw early this morning from the other side of the island? And where's Sexton Blake? Is he here, too?"

"Yes, he's here, Mr. Grant."

Suddenly Tinker remembered that he had not seen his master since the coming of the cyclone. What had happened to Blake? Had he also managed to escape? Or was he lying bruised and bleeding, and perhaps dead, at the edge of the clearing felled by one of those huge trees which had been tossed about like matchwood in the cyclone's furious blast?

"I left him in that clearing, Mr. Grant," he said anxiously, "where there's a mound of earth with a wooden cross stuck in it. We were caught in the cyclone."

"I know!" muttered the King's Spy quickly. "Come on! It's not a great distance away. We must find Blake at all costs."

Closely followed by Tinker, and with Pedro trotting at his side, Granite Grant hurried as fast as he could through the maze of trees.

Evidently he was fairly familiar with his surroundings, for he never seemed in doubt as to his direction, and went forward without stopping to consider what path he was taking.

After proceeding thus for about twenty minutes, they suddenly broke away from the trees, and found themselves in the open space where Tinker had parted from his master some hours before.

The sky was still overcast, and great masses of cloud were rolling overhead, but the cyclone was raging miles away by this time, and only the havoc which it had wrought remained to show how dreadful had been its violence.

The King's Spy shot a hurried glance around.

"Is this the place?" he asked anxiously. "He's gone, then!"

Tinker stared blankly into his companion's face. For the moment he was at a loss what to do; he had been so eager to reach his master again that it had not occurred to him that it was some hours since he had left him in the clearing, and that he could hardly expect to find him here now.

"What shall we do?" he asked, with a feeling of dismay.

Granite Grant bit his lip, and a look of irresolution came into his face.

"Don't know exactly!" he said. "Wonder what's happened to him! Hope he hasn't blundered into that hornet's nest down by the creek."

"Why?" asked Tinker in alarm. "Do you think he is likely to come to any harm?"

"There's Venner and his ruffians there, youngster," said Granite Grant, "and he'll stick at nothing now that he has succeeded in finding out where the bullion is hidden. I wonder what damage the cyclone's done; hope it's stove a hole in their boat; that will rather cramp their style."

"But how about the guv'nor?" said Tinker anxiously.

And at that moment he heard Pedro's sharp yelp from the other side of the clearing.

"Come on!" he said excitedly. "Pedro's on his scent. The old dog'll take us to him—trust Pedro for that!"

Tinker stopped suddenly and stooped to the ground. Laying at his feet was Blake's rifle.

Chapter 19
Saved by Pedro

FOR some time after Blake had thrown himself flat on his face he remained where he was, not daring to move. A kind of natural instinct told him that he was safer there, and that until the first fury of the cyclone had passed it would be perilous to move in any direction.

It did not occur to him that Tinker had not heeded his frantic warning, that he had not even understood it. There was no time to think; it was a case of each man looking to himself and his own safety first.

He was quite sure that Tinker had dropped to the ground with him, and was at that moment lying somewhere a few yards away.

The detective was familiar with the nature of these sudden cyclonic disturbances, and Captain Sampson's warning a few hours before had led him to expect some such occurrence.

He lay still, and trusted that they were not in the centre of the cyclone, and that the spiral of its course would soon carry it over the island.

Presently he took advantage of a brief lull in the storm to raise his head and glance around.

He could see no signs of Tinker anywhere at hand; but this did not occasion him much alarm. No doubt his assistant was not very far away, and it was too dark to see more than a few yards around.

He lay down flat again, as ominous crashings and rendings close at hand warned him of the danger of falling trees and broken branches. Torrents of rain were descending on him, and he could feel the water sousing through his clothes.

He began to wish that he was anywhere but in his present position; if he could only get beyond the danger zone of trees that circled the clearing he could quickly plunge deep into the forest and be comparatively secure.

He raised his head again presently, and peered anxiously around. Where was Tinker lying? He could not be very far away.

He shouted his assistant's name at the top of his voice, but it was quite useless; the noise of the hurricane was too deafening; he could not even hear his own voice.

The minutes fled by, and the cyclone still raged with undiminished fury. Blake's position was becoming desperate; he was sodden through and through, and his limbs were stiff with the cramp.

He determined to make one supreme effort to get into the forest, and commenced to wriggle forward to the nearest fringe of trees.

A moment later he saw his opportunity. An ear-splitting crash of thunder rolled across the sky, and before the next flash of lightning came Blake was on his feet.

He scrambled frantically over a huge tree that had been unrooted, and dashed for cover. As he plunged through the rising trunks a rending crash just behind him warned him that he had only just scraped through in time.

Blake did not penetrate far into the forest; he felt rather anxious as to what had happened to Tinker, and decided to keep as near the clearing as possible. At the first sign of the storm abating he would make a thorough search for his young assistant.

Then the thought flashed across his mind that Pedro was also missing. He felt somewhat reassured at that; no doubt the dog was with Tinker, and the faithful animal would see that the youngster came to no harm.

A considerable time elapsed before the detective thought it fit to venture out in the open once more; the hurricane of wind that was blowing was so strong that it nearly lifted him off his feet.

He thoroughly searched the clearing, peering anxiously at the fallen trees, and half expecting to see his young assistant pinioned beneath one of them. But there were no signs of him—Tinker and the bloodhound had absolutely vanished.

Then he thought of the boat he had left to await his return. What had happened to Williams and the other men? How had they managed to escape the fury of the cyclone?

Having missed his master, perhaps Tinker would try to make his way back to the boat again! That was certainly a reasonable thing to suppose, and if his assistant did not turn up presently, Blake determined to try and retrace his steps.

Blake sought the cover of the forest again, and waited expectantly for the storm to subside. Not until an hour or more had elapsed did he think it safe to venture out again.

It was lighter now, although a curtain of angry clouds still obscured the sky. Blake stood out in the open, wondering which way he had come. The fallen trees somewhat changed the look of the place, and he was not very sure of his bearings.

He made up his mind at length and took the direction that appeared to be the right one. There were indications of a narrow path threading its way through the trees, and he was certain that he and Tinker had come that way before.

He strode on as fast as he could, keeping a sharp look-out for any poisonous reptiles that might lurk in the thick undergrowth. The path began to get more distinct as he continued, but soon he became aware that he was climbing steadily higher and higher.

Blake knew then that he had taken the wrong direction; the side of the island where he had left the boat lay lower than the forest; he was certain of that.

However, he had gone too far to turn back. He would go on and see where this path led to.

About ten minutes later he suddenly came out into the open once more. In front of him stretched the sea, covered with angry, snow-capped billows which seemed to merge themselves into the leaden sky.

He was about five hundred feet above the sea-level, looking down into a narrow gully that extended inland for some distance from the waters of the lagoon.

Down below, absolutely sheltered from the wind and rain, was moored the *Fraulein*. The vessel had come through the cyclone unscathed; her natural harbour had enabled her to defy the roaring tempest that had raged above.

Blake gazed down on to her decks with great curiosity. This, then, was the ship which he had heard signalling to the island, the German boat that was making a bid for this million and a half of bullion.

He could not see anyone on her decks; no doubt they were safe under cover. There must be some sort of dwellings erected down below in the gully, but from where he stood he could not see the upper end of the cleft. Had they discovered the bullion? he wondered. They certainly could not have had time yet to have stowed it on board. It had been a little after sunrise when he had left the *Nancy*. It was quite early now; perhaps nobody was astir yet down below.

No doubt the cyclone had caught them unawares, and they had laid listening in fear and trembling to the furious uproar. Blake was wondering what exactly would be the best thing to do. It was useless staying there out in the open; at any moment his presence might be discovered, then his life would not be worth a moment's purchase with these desperate men.

He only had his revolver in his hip-pocket. Unfortunately he had dropped his rifle when he made his dash from the clearing.

What a pity Williams and the men he had left behind with the boat were not with him. He would have taken his chance then and made a sudden raid on the vessel. No doubt he could have taken the crew by surprise, and overpowered them before they could realise what had happened.

The detective suddenly decided to make a detour to the left and get down to the shore. He disliked the idea of retracing his steps through the dark and dismal forest again.

This was the north-east extremity of the island, and by following the shore along he was certain to arrive at the spot where he had left Williams with the boat. At any rate, it was his only chance; there was nothing else to be done.

He was about to carry his plan into operation, when suddenly he heard voices immediately in front of him. The next instant a man raised his head above the cliff and swung himself over. Following immediately behind him were three others.

For an instant he stood staring at Blake in amazement; then, half recovering from his surprise, he took a step forward.

"Who are you?" he asked in guttural German.

But it did not take Blake an instant to recognise who the stranger was. He knew immediately that he was Venner, the "Leopard," the man who had killed Monsieur Jacques and Von Rosenburg, and who had succeeded in getting away with the map.

He cursed himself for his folly in thus allowing himself to be caught. But it was too late. He saw by the man's face that a sudden suspicion had flashed across his mind.

"I think we have met before," he said in English. "This is an unexpected pleasure, Mr. Blake."

"I have no doubt it is unexpected!" answered Blake coolly.

In his mind he was seeking for some method of making good his escape. He could not but admit that the position was desperate.

The "Leopard" was still somewhat taken back at this unlooked-for meeting, and Blake could see that he was plainly uneasy and at a loss to account for his presence. He determined to try and bluff him.

"It may interest you to know," he said quietly, "that a score of my men have got this place covered from the trees over there. I was just coming to have a friendly chat with you about something in which we're both interested."

Blake watched the effects of his words with great anxiety. He saw Venner cast a swift glance at the trees, then mutter something to his companions. The next moment his face went livid with rage.

"I'll not be beaten now," he shouted. "We'll make sure of you, at any rate."

He made a savage lunge at the detective but Blake stepped nimbly aside and brought his left up under the man's chin.

With a gasp of pain and fury, the "Leopard" toppled backward, and went sprawling on his back. The other three men instantly threw themselves on the detective.

For some moments he struggled furiously, and managed to give a good account of himself. But the odds were too heavy, and presently he received a stunning blow between the eyes from the butt of a revolver, and remembered no more.

***

For a long time Blake lay staring up at the darkness overhead, and wondering where he was and what had happened. Then slowly, very slowly, memory began to peter back to him.

The last thing he remembered was that meeting with the "Leopard" at the top of the cliff; there had been a bit of a tussle, and then he had received that stunning blow between the eyes. His temples throbbed dreadful now from the force of the blow.

He tried to move himself, but his limbs seemed like pieces of stone; there was no life in them. He began working his arms about; then he suddenly came to the conclusion that it was impossible to move them. They were tied securely behind him. He made an effort to move his legs, but it was useless; cords were also bound tightly round his ankles.

He did not attempt to move after that, but tried to think out where he could be. He was lying on something hard and cold like stone. He could just make out the dim outline of the walls and ceiling; they gleamed faintly as if they might be formed of a white, chalky substance. It came to him suddenly that he must be lying in a sort of cavern.

Presently he wriggled himself over on the other side. His first impression had been correct; it was a cavern. Facing him, and about a dozen yards away, was a gaping hole of dazzling light. He fancied he could hear the wash of the sea sounding from some distance in front.

Blake was too utterly weary and exhausted to do ought but lie still and ponder idly on his position. He had not the energy to try to free himself. Something told him that it was quite useless; his enemies had seen to that. He wondered what time of day it was. How long had he lain there? And what had happened to Tinker?

He closed his eyes and lost interest in his surroundings for a while. Presently he became aware that water was running over the floor of the cavern. He was puzzled at first. Where could it come from? It was not there a short time ago when he first regained consciousness.

The water seemed to be getting deeper; he was lying in it now. Not that it mattered much, for he had very little feeling left. Then the reason for the water's presence suddenly dawned upon him. It must be the sea; the tide was coming in, and the cave was gradually being flooded.

So this was the fate to which his enemies had consigned him! He was to perish here like a rat in a trap. This was the end of all his brilliant schemes and plans. He was not even to have a chance to fight for his life. He was to lay there and wait while the water rose higher and higher. He would splutter and struggle for a few brief seconds, then all would be over.

Well, it was no good kicking against fate; what had to be would be, and he might just as well meet the end calmly. His enemies had got the better of him this time. When they had bound him so tightly and left him in this cave they knew what they were about; they had certainly made sure of their work.

He stared in fascination at the patch of daylight. Just out there was freedom; it seemed so near, and yet so unattainable. It seemed just then that a shadow passed momentarily across that patch of light, as if something had dropped from above into the mouth of the cavern, but that was no doubt merely due to his fancy.

The next moment he fancied again that something was at his side—some lean, warm, shaggy body. In spite of the numbness of his body he could not suppress a start of surprise; something was there, he could feel it standing on his chest—a hot, rough tongue that smothered his face with caresses.

Then Blake suddenly knew.

"Pedro!" he murmured huskily. "Is that you, old friend?"

The faithful animal was snivelling and trembling with excitement. For a few seconds he pawed frantically at his master's arm, as if to warn him of the impending danger. Then he seemed to understand why his master did not move.

He thrust his great snout beneath Blake's back and bit cautiously at the cords that bound his hands. Many a time had Pedro done that same trick in play. It was one of the things Blake had taught the animal; now it was a matter of life or death.

It did not take long for Pedro's sharp teeth to cut through the cords. Suddenly Blake felt his hands drop apart, and he knew that the faithful dog had done his work.

He tried to raise himself, but his arms were useless, and he fell back with a stifled groan. The animal was at his feet now, gnawing frantically at the ankles.

Soon they also were free. And still Blake could not move; his body was paralysed, his muscles cramped with exposure and cold. Pedro's rough tongue was on his face and hands again. The sagacious animal knew only too well the dreadful predicament his master was in; it would be a fight against time, for the water was slowly encroaching on the cave.

Presently Blake felt the blood commence to tingle in his finger-tips. He made a supreme effort and propped himself up. Then he began to chafe his arms and legs. Soon he was able to climb to his feet, holding on to the wall for support.

He began slapping his limbs, gently at first, then more vigorously as the blood began to circulate more rapidly. The pain was intense; but he did not mind that; he would make a bold bid for freedom.

Very cautiously he started to creep towards the entrance to the cave. The water was up to his ankles now; Pedro was only just in time, another ten minutes or so and he would have been too late.

He stood at the mouth of the cavern and cast a swift glance around. The sea seemed to reach out on all sides, and as he looked anxiously across the restless waters, Blake felt his chances of escape grow remote again.

But Pedro knew the way to safety. The dog dragged at his master's leg, then stood a moment on the extreme edge of the cave and leapt upwards. Blake craned his neck forward and saw that the dog had jumped on to a ledge of the cliff that jutted out to the left.

He pressed himself close to the face of the cliff and felt for the ledge with his hand. A moment later he scrambled up above into safety.

"Good old Pedro!" he muttered, stooping down and patting the animal. "Which way now, boy?"

The bloodhound gave a little yelp of joy, and began to move cautiously along the ledge, with the detective following close behind. A few yards further along the narrow path bent abruptly to the left, and on rounding it Blake saw that the cliff sloped upwards in a series of rugged terraces.

It was easy going now; soon he stood at the flat top of the cliff, and about a hundred yards away was the thick forest of trees through which he had come some hours ago.

Glancing back from time to time to make sure that his master was following, Pedro made straight for the trees, then turned sharply to the right and kept on the fringe of the forest. Presently Blake saw about five hundred yards away the gully where the *Fraulein* was anchored.

He glanced at Pedro anxiously. Where was the dog taking him? He did not want to be captured again; his newly-won freedom was too dear to risk another meeting with the "Leopard" and his ruffians.

"Pedro!" he said softly. "Come here, boy!"

The dog glanced round reassuringly at his master, then plunged into the trees. His nose was to the ground now and he seemed to be following up a scent.

Blake tried to keep up with the animal, but the hardships he had undergone were telling on him; he felt his steps flagging, and a mist seemed to rise in front of his eyes. Then he stumbled heavily and sank to the ground.

He made one last effort to call the faithful dog back. But he was conscious himself that his voice made no sound. He seemed to be floating away into oblivion.

Chapter 20
"Granite" Grant Explains

FOR a long time Blake could not think what was happening to him. He seemed to be bobbing up and down on something, and the trees were slowly dancing by on either side.

Then he came to the conclusion that the thing he was sitting on was alive, and that he was being carried along through the forest. He stared curiously at the mass of tangled hair that rubbed against his face.

Was this a man's head, he wondered. Yes, of course it was! He was sitting on the fellow's back and his arms hung limply round his neck.

Who on earth could it be? It wasn't Tinker! The stranger was far too big and strong to be mistaken for his young assistant; he carried Blake as if he were a mere featherweight.

He was still puzzling over the problem when he heard the stranger speak.

"You keep close to me, youngster," he said in a deep, gruff voice, that seemed strangely familiar. "I know the way. You won't meet any more boa constrictors, unless you wander deep into the forest and disturb them in their lairs."

There was silence for a moment or two. Then the big man spoke again.

"How many men are with you, youngster?" he asked.

"About a dozen," said a voice close behind, which Blake instantly recognised as Tinker's.

"By gum!" muttered the stranger. "I hope they're safe. We ought to make a fight of it. But we shall have to look pretty slick, those fellows in the creek are getting busy; they won't stay long once they get the stuff into their boat."

A sudden suspicion flashed into Blake's mind. He leant forward across the man's shoulder and tried to peer into his face.

"Who are you?" he demanded.

The stranger came to a sudden halt, and with a muttered exclamation let his burden slide gently to the ground.

"You've come round then, Blake!" he said quietly.

The detective stared in astonishment at the stranger's unshaven face, and then passed his hand wearily across his forehead.

"I suppose I'm wandering!" he said slowly. "That's not you, Grant, by any chance?"

The other gripped the detective's hand.

"That's me, sure enough!" he said. "Do I look like a ghost?"

Blake gave a queer little chuckle.

"I can't quite get the hang of things, Grant," he said. "I'm all at sixes and sevens. What brought you back to life?"

Granite Grant burst into a roar of laughter.

"Why, you're the second person I've met today who thinks I should be dead," he said. "But I've still got a few kicks left in me yet."

Blake cast an admiring glance at his big friend.

"You certainly seem to be very much alive," he said. "But how did you find me?"

The King's Spy knelt to the ground and took Pedro's great head in his hands.

"Ask this old chap!" he said. "This stout old dog is worth more than that million and a-half of bullion, Blake. What do you say, Tinker, my boy?"

"Same as you!" Tinker replied somewhat unsteadily. "Old Pedro always turns up trumps."

"But tell me what has happened?" said the detective, still rather confused over recent events. "Where are we going now?"

Granite Grant put his hand kindly on Blake's shoulder.

"No questions now, Blake, old man!" he said firmly. "We'll leave those until later; then I shall have a few to put to you. Our present job is to make a bee-line for the spot where you landed this morning and see what's happened to the men. Come on, off we go again!"

He picked up Blake in his brawny arms, and, in spite of his protests, hoisted him on his back.

"You're not strong enough yet, Blake," he said. "You just save your breath; you'll want it by and by."

For some moments they continued their way in silence. Gradually the haze was lifting from Blake's mind and he was beginning to take an active interest in things again.

This sudden meeting with Granite Grant had buoyed up his hopes tremendously; he was eager to hear the story he would have to tell.

"Can't make out how you got here, Grant," he said presently. "You might ease my curiosity."

"Right, Blake! While we're going along we'll exchange a few notes. Did you see that mass of scrap-iron in that clearing in the forest?"

"Yes."

"Well, that's how I got here!"

"But still I don't understand, Grant."

"Then I'll be more explicit. I flew over from Jamaica. I didn't intend to land here, I assure you, but we ran short of petrol and crashed there in the clearing. The machine caught fire, and poor old Stern, my pilot, was killed. That's his grave with the charred propeller stuck in the ground. Got me, Blake?"

"Yes, that rather explains things, Grant. But why did you come out alone? Why didn't you explain things to Sir Vrymer Fane?"

"Pshaw, Blake, you don't understand! That's my job—to do things off my own bat. How could I explain things when I wasn't sure myself that I was on the right track? I only had that map to guide me. It was a hundred chances to one against my finding the missing bullion. Besides, friend Venner and his gang were getting too busy for my liking. I determined to make a dash for it. But you don't know friend Venner, the 'Leopard,' Blake, do you?"

"Oh, yes I do, Grant. In fact we had a few words together this morning. He thinks I'm food for the crabs by this time."

"Ah, I see you've got a good story for me later on, Blake. However, if that aeroplane had not been unfortunate enough to crash here, but had taken us back to Jamaica, there wouldn't have been any story at all—everything would have been over now."

"But how is it Venner and the others were three months behind you, Grant?"

The King's Spy gave a chuckle of satisfaction.

"I arranged that, Blake," he said. "I had the fellow from whom I got the information shipped to Australia—by accident, of course. You see, that gave me a good start. But now it's my turn to ask you a few questions."

"Fire away, then!"

"I managed to send out a wireless message from the island, Blake. Did you get that by any chance?"

"That's why I'm here, Grant!"

"By Jove," muttered the King's Spy, "that was a stroke of luck for me! I didn't know what to do, Blake. These fellows of the *Spitzbergen* saw my machine circle over the island, and when I blundered out of the trees in their midst they had the shock of their lives. I was kept practically a prisoner. One night I managed to crawl into the wireless hut they had rigged up on the beach and was able to send off that message. How did it get into your hands, Blake?"

"Picked up by an English ship, and the operator brought it along to me when he reached port."

"And then you deciphered it, and began to get busy?"

"That's so, Grant! But didn't these fellows try to get in touch with a passing ship? And if so, how is it that they have remained here all this time without being discovered?"

"But they didn't, Blake. You must remember that they were minding a million and a-half of bullion, and they weren't taking any chances. They used to listen in on their wireless continuously for the relief ship that they were expecting any day. And she arrived yesterday—the *Fraulein*—she's anchored in the creek."

"What happened when she arrived? Did you meet this fellow, Venner?"

"Did I not! The hound recognised me directly. There was a bit of a shindy, and I knocked a few fellows out. But there were too many for me, and I was knocked sense-less. When I came to I found they had flung me into the hold of the ship and battered down the hatch."

"And how did you make your escape?"

"That's a bit of a mystery, Blake. During the night someone opened the hatch and came into the hold. The fellow told me to make a dash for it, so I jumped overboard and swam ashore, and here I am."

"That's rather strange, Grant. Wonder who it was who let you loose."

"I've not the slightest notion, Blake. He was a little man, but it was too dark to see much else. However, I owe him a good turn whoever he is."

Blake and the Secret Service man were still discussing their adventures when the trees began to open out and a few moments later they found themselves on the sea shore once more.

A curtain of cloud no longer obscured the sun; it was now high overhead and blazing down on the white beach in dazzling splendour. As Blake felt its warmth on his wet body he sighed with satisfaction.

"Grant," he said, "I'm going to take off my things and give them an airing. They want it rather badly, they're wringing wet."

"Right-o, Blake!" said Granite Grant. "You just carry on. Don't have to conform to convention out here—you can wear the proverbial fig-leaf if you like. But let us get round this bend first, that's the spot where you landed this morning, and we ought to find somebody there."

They pushed on along the shore to the spot indicated by Granite Grant. Tinker and Pedro were now in high spirits, and raced joyfully up and down the strand, delighting in the sun's warmth and brilliance.

As they came nearer to the place where the shore turned sharply to the left a man came running towards them.

"Hello, this is Williams!" muttered Blake. "The fellow seems rather excited. Wonder what's up!"

"Mr. Blake, sir!" Williams exclaimed breathlessly, when he was within speaking dis-tance. "I never expected to see you again. The boat's stove in, and four of the men are missing."

The detective was somewhat taken back by this piece of news. He had half expected some such thing would have happened, yet he was not quite prepared for the worst.

"Where were you when the cyclone burst, Williams?" he asked.

"We saw it coming, sir, and made shore. Good thing we did, otherwise there'd have been no one left to tell the tale. Just cast your eyes along there, sir!"

They had turned the bend by this time, and Blake saw that this side of the island had certainly seemed to have received the full force of the cyclone.

The beach was strewn with great trees and broken branches, which had been wrenched down by the hurricane and tossed high up on the foreshore was all that remained of the boat that had taken them off from the *Nancy* at sunrise that morning.

"But where are all the men, Williams? I don't see anyone about."

"They're scouring the woods, sir, in the hopes of coming across you. I thought you might be in need of assistance. Then there are the four chaps who are missing, I don't know what's happened to them; they rushed off into the forest directly the cyclone swept down. The other men will be back soon."

"I see," said Blake. "And how about the *Nancy*—have you seen any signs of her?"

"Not since the cyclone, sir. As a matter of fact it was quite impossible to see beyond the reef until about half an hour ago, when the sun came out again."

Blake turned his face to the sea and searched the horizon. Not a speck appeared anywhere on that vast expanse of sunlit waters to indicate the presence of a ship. The *Nancy* had disappeared as completely as if she had been suddenly swallowed up.

"This is a pretty pickle, Grant," he said, looking anxiously into his companion's face. "We seem to be stranded here. The *Nancy* has gone—she may be at the bottom for all we know. We haven't even got a boat."

"Don't you worry, Blake," said Grant reassuringly. "If Captain Sampson's in charge of the *Nancy* it'll take a lot to send him to Davy Jones's locker. He may have run before the hurricane and have been blown miles or more out of his course. But the *Nancy*'s a tight little craft and will weather most storms. I've been in her before. Besides, what's the matter with the *Fraulein*?"

"The *Fraulein*!" exclaimed the detective. "What do you mean, Grant?"

"Exactly what I say, Blake! You're not going to let that ruffian Venner get away with a million and a half of booty while you've got a dozen stout men armed with rifles to stop him, surely?"

"I'm game, Grant!" said the detective quickly. "But do you think we stand a chance? Aren't the odds too heavy?"

"All depends on what you call too heavy, Blake! It may be a case of three to one, but I'm counting on springing a surprise on them. Venner doesn't know how many men are here. He knows that I'm roaming about the island somewhere, but he thinks he settled your account in that cave this morning. I bet he'll have every man working like a slave to get that bullion on board his vessel. He won't expect any visitors."

"How long do you think it will take him to get the stuff in the ship, Grant?"

"All the afternoon, Blake!"

"And what's the time now? Got a watch on you, Williams? Mine has stopped."

"Yes, sir. It's nearly one o'clock."

"Great Scott, Grant! I thought it was at least four. Seems hours ago since we left the *Nancy*."

"It is, guv'nor," said Tinker. "You forget that we came away at sunrise."

"You're quite right, Tinker, we did! And now, Grant, what's the next move?"

"To have some grub, Blake. While we feed we'll talk over the business, and fix on some scheme for giving Venner a nasty jar."

A grave look suddenly came into Blake's face. Grant's words had reminded him of his famished condition, and he remembered that the provisions had been left in the boat.

"Did you manage to save the food, Williams?" he asked anxiously.

"Yes, sir! We took good care of that. It's stowed among the trees over there."

"Good!" muttered the detective, with a sigh of relief. "Then we'll get busy, Williams. By the way, Grant, how have you managed for food all this time—been living on locust-beans?"

"Not much, Blake—although I've often remembered that last dinner we had together at the Karlton, and wished I could have it over again. But the *Spitzbergen* left enough tinned provisions to last for years, so we had no anxiety on that score. You haven't seen the dug-outs they've fitted up down in the gully; they're quite snug—even got electric light, which is worked off the petrol motor that runs the wireless gadget!"

"I'm beginning to think this deserted island isn't such a bad spot, after all, Grant," said Blake. "If we ever get away safely I'll advertise it as a home of rest for weary London-ers."

"I don't think!" said Tinker, with a shiver. "Makes me feel creepy to think of that nightmare I met in the forest this morning, guv'nor."

"What's that, Tinker?" asked Blake curiously.

"Tinker met a nice little boa-constrictor, Blake," explained Granite Grant, with a laugh. "However, he'll tell you the story another time; there's some of your men coming back. Let's just make up our minds what the next move shall be."

Chapter 21
"Baiting the Leopard"

THROUGHOUT the whole of that day a scene of great bustle and activity was being enacted down in the creek at the north-east of the island. The little steam-crane on the *Fraulein*'s decks worked continuously, hoisting the heavy boxes of bullion and lowering them down into the vessel's hold to be stowed away.

Venner's one idea was to get the booty safely aboard and to get away from the island. The thought that at this very last moment, when success was within his grasp, he might be robbed of his prize filled him with feverish anxiety and fear, and he worked like a madman.

Blake's sudden appearance on the island had greatly astonished him. He was quite at a loss to explain his presence there, for although he had climbed to the highest point of the island and searched the horizon, yet he could discover no signs of a ship anywhere. It seemed as if the detective had dropped from the sky.

When Blake had told him that his men were hiding in the trees he had at first believed it, thinking that a ship must have arrived during the night and anchored on the other side of the island.

But when no one came to Blake's assistance he was utterly bewildered, and at a loss to account for the situation.

However, he gave up puzzling over the problem at last, and consoled himself by the thought that he had safely rid himself of Sexton Blake's unwelcome presence, and that the latter would never trouble him any more.

His one desire now was to get the bullion on board and sail away, and to this end he bent his energies, not considering for a moment the possibility of a sudden surprise attack being made, and taking no precautions to meet it.

It was late in the afternoon before the last bale was hoisted over the side and stowed away. The Leopard was standing on the *Fraulein's* deck, mopping his perspiring brow and shouting instructions in a hoarse voice to the men on the beach.

Presently the boat containing the remainder of the crew came alongside, and they climbed on the vessel's deck; the boat was hoisted up, and, with a shrill gasp of her siren, the *Fraulein* began to move slowly into the middle of the channel.

The Leopard rubbed his hands with satisfaction, and watched the waters of the lagoon creep nearer and nearer. A few more minutes and the vessel would be clear of the channel and making for the opening in the barrier reef. Once through that, and they would be out on the high seas again, with his priceless cargo stowed safely in the hold of his vessel.

He lit a cigarette, and, with a flush of elation on his face, stood silently watching the widening V-shaped gully as it grew larger and larger. Another two hundred yards, and the vessel would be out in the lagoon——

Suddenly, a deep, gruff voice rang out from the cliff that projected out on the left of the gully.

"Back you go, Venner, or you're a dead man!"

The "Leopard" started violently, and glared up the cliff. He could see no one there. A look of baffled rage came into his face, and his fingers clenched nervously; but he took no heed of the summons.

✳✳✳

It was Granite Grant who had shouted that challenge to the "Leopard." With four of the men, he had concealed himself in a crevice in the cliff at the extremity of the gully, and from that position he commanded the entrance to the channel.

Unbeknown to Venner, his enemies had been watching his movements for the greater part of that afternoon, and directly the *Fraulein* had left her anchorage and steamed out into the middle of the channel, Sexton Blake and Tinker, with the remainder of the men, had crept down into the gully and taken up their positions in the huts which the crew of the *Spitzbergen* had erected on the foreshore.

Thus, with Granite Grant commanding the entrance to the channel and the detective covering the only place of landing, the *Fraulein* was caught in a trap from which there did not seem any escape.

It was this plan which Granite Grant and the detective had carefully worked out, and by which they hoped to give the Leopard the surprise of his life.

Granite Grant gave a chuckle of great satisfaction as he peered down at the "Leopard" standing on the *Fraulein's* deck.

"By Jove," he muttered, "that's given him a nasty turn. But he hasn't quite got the hang of things yet."

Four rifles spat out in quick succession from the top of the cliff, and a number of splinters shot from the *Fraulein*'s deck.

The crew immediately bolted below, leaving only the "Leopard" and the man at the wheel on deck.

Venner's face was white with passion. He let fall a string of oaths, and, dragging out his revolver, fired blindly up at the cliff. A derisive laugh from above answered this futile outburst, and the next moment a rifle cracked out again.

The man at the wheel shot away from it as if he had suddenly grasped a red-hot poker. With a hoarse cry, the Leopard pushed him angrily aside, and grasped the wheel with his own hands.

There was another crack from above, and Venner uttered a gasp of pain and went dancing across the deck, with the blood streaming from one of the fingers of his left hand.

"Good shooting, boys!" said the King's Spy cheerily. "They've got the wind up now. What's their next move, I wonder?"

The "Leopard" had taken cover behind one of the boats, and was evidently discussing the situation with the captain of the vessel, while the latter bound up his hand.

Presently he came out from his hiding-place, and stood glaring up at the cliff, with an ugly scowl on his face. Then he took out a white handkerchief and waved it above his head.

"Carry on, Venner! I'm listening!" shouted Granite Grant.

"Who are you?" asked the Leopard.

"Come, Venner; I guess you've heard of Granite Grant before today," the King's Spy shouted back.

"And supposing I have? What do you want?"

"Can't you guess, Venner?"

"I'm not trying!"

"Well, then, I'll tell you. I'm going to trouble you to unload that stuff you've taken such pains to stow away."

"And what if I don't?"

"But I think you will, Venner; therefore I haven't considered the other alternative."

The "Leopard" bit his lip in fury, and was silent for a moment. Several of the crew, who had now recovered from their surprise, were cautiously climbing up from below; the vessel was swinging dangerously near the other side of the gully.

He glanced up above again.

"Don't try any tricks, Venner," replied Grant warningly. "We won't stand any nonsense."

There was a brief discussion on the deck of the *Fraulein*, and then a man took the wheel again, and the vessel began to back slowly up the channel.

"He showed less fight than I expected," muttered Grant, keeping a narrow watch on the vessel until it disappeared from view. "But I bet Venner's got something up his sleeve—he's a wily scoundrel. He doesn't know Blake's waiting for him from the other end, though. That'll be a pleasant surprise."

The Secret Service man climbed to his feet, and slung his rifle across his shoulder.

"Keep your eyes skinned, Williams," he said. "I sha'n't be long; I'm just going to see the fun from below."

He hurried back along the cliff-top, every now and then catching sight of the *Fraulein* backing slowly up the channel a hundred feet below. Presently he noticed that the vessel had stopped, and that they were lowering a boat.

There was only one place in the gully where a boat could possibly land, and that was the strip of foreshore held by Blake. Grant determined that he would hurry on and warn the detective, and help to give the "Leopard" a warm reception.

Ten minutes later he scrambled down the rocky path leading to the foreshore, and blundered into the rough wooden shanty that had served as the home of the *Spitzbergen* men for all these months.

"Get ready, Blake!" he said. "Venner's going to try to make a landing. The boat will be along in a few minutes now."

"We're ready for him, Grant," said the detective. "The five of us could stop fifty men from landing on that strip of ground. Well, what happened further along?"

"It was quite good sport, Blake; Venner's green with rage. He doesn't quite know what to make of it yet. No doubt he thinks there's only a handful of us above, and that if he lands here he can cut us off."

"If he lands here, Grant! But I'm thinking he'll have rather a job to. I only wish we knew what had happened to the *Nancy*. That's the only thing that's troubling me at the present moment."

"You don't happen to know anything about wireless, Blake, I suppose?" asked Grant presently.

"Not much, Grant—why?"

"Nor do I, worse luck! I can tap out the Morse code on a key, and that's about all."

"But why do you ask, Grant?" said the detective again.

"Why, because there are some wireless gadgets in that shed over there, and if we only had someone to get them going we could try and communicate with the *Nancy*—unless, of course, she happens to be at the bottom of the sea at the present moment."

"Good gracious, Grant!" exclaimed the detective excitedly. "That's the very idea! There's Charlie Jones, here; we'll get him busy on the box of tricks later on. What do you say to that, Charlie?"

"How about juice, sir?" asked Charlie Jones somewhat dubiously.

He had been sitting by Tinker in the further part of the shed, and had overheard Blake's conversation.

"Juice!" muttered the detective, looking perplexed. "You mean electricity, Charlie?"

"That's it, sir."

"Don't worry about that," interrupted Granite Grant. "There's a petrol motor and generator, and several cans of petrol."

"Then you leave it to me, sir! If the *Nancy's* anywhere within a hundred miles I'll get in touch with her. The other operator we left on board is bound to be listening in."

"Get ready, you chaps!" said Blake, the next moment; "there's the boat just coming round the bend. Don't fire until you get the word, and then only to frighten them; we don't want any killing if we can do without it."

They waited in silence while the boat came swiftly towards them, the oars rising and falling together with steady precision.

"Is that Venner sitting in the stern, Grant?" asked the detective suddenly. "He's got his hand in a sling."

"That's right, Blake. It's only a scratch, but I had to show him I was in earnest."

The boat was now almost within fifty yards and making straight for the landing-place.

"Watch me, Blake?" said the King's Spy. "That'll make him sit up."

He stuck his rifle through the crack in the timbers, took hasty aim, and fired. Almost simultaneously with the report Venner's soft hat leaped frantically into the air, to drop a moment later in the sea.

The "Leopard" gave a startled shout and cast a frightened glance at the puff of smoke that circled up from the shanty on the beach. At the sound of the shot the men had stopped rowing, and were now leaning on their oars, and looking over their shoulders nervously.

"Some shot, Grant!" muttered the detective. "Venner looks as if he had seen a ghost. Let's give him a volley—just to show there's more than one of us here. All together, boys! Let it rip!"

The five rifles cracked together, and the water spurted up in all directions round the boat. Several of the men seemed to be seized with a sudden panic, and tried to turn the boat round, and make off.

For a time all was confusion; then Venner succeeded in restoring a semblance of order. He dragged his handkerchief out again and waved it at the shanty.

"There goes the white flag," said the King's Spy. "Better say a few words to him, Blake. But I wouldn't show myself; it isn't safe when dealing with a blackguard like Venner."

Blake put his lips close up to the hole:

"Got anything to say?" he shouted.

"Yes; what are your terms?"

"Unconditional surrender!"

The "Leopard" looked round like an animal in a trap.

"Who the deuce are you?" he demanded, choking with impotent rage.

"I'm Sexton Blake! Surely, you remember me, Mr. Venner?" the detective shouted sarcastically.

The "Leopard" cursed below his breath. He did not doubt the truth of that last statement: somehow, the detective had escaped from the cave.

It was clear that he was greatly disturbed by the predicament in which he unexpectedly found himself. He had an earnest conversation with the man sitting in front of him; then raised his voice again.

"Let us come ashore and talk the matter over!" he said.

"Delighted, Mr. Venner!" replied Blake. "Take your men back to the ship, and then row back here alone. I promise you a safe passport."

The "Leopard" gave a quick word of command, and, casting a furious look in the direction of the shanty, shook his fist savagely.

"To hell with you!" he shouted.

The men leant on their oars, and the boat shot round and sped away swiftly up the channel again.

"That's another one to us, Blake!" muttered Granite Grant. "That fellow is beside himself with rage. Wonder what his next move will be?"

"Supposing they wait until it's dark, Grant! We sha'n't be able to see what they're doing then. They can slip quietly down the channel and be miles out to sea before it's light."

"You're right there, Blake. I quite overlooked that. We may be able to stop them from the cliff. However, we can only wait and see what happens. I had better get back to where I left Williams now. They might make another attempt during the daylight."

"Just show Charlie Jones where this wireless hut is first, Grant. He can get busy straight away on that."

On inspection it was discovered that the cyclone had blown down the wireless aerial, but this did not cause Charlie Jones any dismay. He found a coil of copper-wire and soon rigged up another aerial in place of the one destroyed.

When Blake came into him about half an hour later the little petrol motor was already throbbing merrily in the corner of the hut, and Charlie was busy adjusting the various gadgets.

The day was drawing to a close now, and the sun was low down on the western horizon. Soon the night would sweep swiftly across the sky, bringing with it fresh dangers and anxieties.

A look of preoccupation came into Blake's face. His position was beset with difficulties. During the hours of darkness this battle of wits would be brought to a climax. How would this strange and exciting adventure end, he wondered?

Chapter 22
Julie's Revenge

FOR nearly an hour Granite Grant had been stretched flat on the cliff with his head stuck cautiously over the brink. From the black chasm that loomed a hundred feet below only the gurgle and lap of the waters had come to his ears. His spell of watching was now nearly up. Soon Williams would be along to relieve him, and he would be able to stretch his cramped limbs.

He could make out the water that surged in the channel below by the faint silvery shimmer on its surface. The *Fraulein* was invisible, for the cliff jutted out and screened it from above. But he knew it was only just beneath him—he had made a careful note of her position while it was still light.

Presently he fancied he heard a commotion going on below. Then several orders were given in a thick, guttural voice. He listened intently while snatches of conversation kept floating up to him, but the words were not distinct enough for him to understand what was said. Then sounded the steady splash of oars in the water below.

He climbed to his feet just as Williams came up.

"They've got the boat out, Williams," he said. "Evidently they're going to attempt to drag her out of the channel. I'm afraid it'll be rather difficult to stop the rowing-boat; it's too small a mark in the darkness. However, it's no use stopping here now. Better get along to our original position at the entrance to the channel where the other men are."

"Right, Mr. Grant!" said Williams. "If we can get a glimpse of the boat we'll make it pretty hot for them."

"Yes, Williams, blaze away for all you're worth. I'll join you very soon."

Granite Grant hurried off to advise Blake of this latest turn of events.

As he was about to enter the shanty at the bottom of the gully Charlie Jones brushed by him and sprang through the door.

"Hi, sir!" he shouted excitedly, waving a sheet of paper above his head. "The *Nancy* is about thirty miles off. I've just been talking to her. She expects to make the island in about three or four hours."

It was with the utmost difficulty that Blake kept calm in the face of this piece of good news. But Tinker did not attempt to restrain his feelings; he uttered a wild whoop of joy and gave an exhibition of his latest fox-trot, and, not to be left out of the excitement, Pedro wagged his tail and barked furiously.

Blake waited for the noise to subside and then turned to Charlie Jones.

"Did she say what happened to her, Charlie?" he asked.

"Yes, sir. She had rather a rough time in the cyclone. Carried about sixty miles out of her course. Here are the messages, sir, if you'd like to read them."

"Thanks, Charlie! You're a clever chap—a sort of wireless wizard!"

Charlie Jones looked rather proud of himself at the detective's compliment.

"Well, I'll get back again now, sir," he said. "I've promised to keep in touch with her. If you want anything sent through, sir, just let me know."

"I will, Charlie. I'll be along to see you in minute."

Blake suddenly noticed Granite Grant standing by the door.

"What are you looking so glum about, Grant?" he asked. "Isn't that just the best piece of news we've had. I was beginning to think we were doomed to stay on this infernal island for the rest of our lives."

"Many a worse place, Blake!" said the King's Spy, with a chuckle. "But that's not the point. There's the bullion to be thought of, and Venner is likely to beat us yet. He's got the boat out and is going to tow the vessel out into the lagoon."

"Well, Grant, we must stop him at all costs! It'll be too bad to let him slip through our fingers at the last moment. In a few hours the *Nancy* will be along and we shall have him cold."

"Yes; but how are we going to stop him, Blake? The boat's too small a mark to pot at in the dark, and the fellows are certain to put up some sort of cover."

"At any rate, Grant, we'll get along the cliff and blaze away at anything we see. We may be able to hold them up for a few hours—it's worth trying! Come on, Tinker!"

Followed by Granite Grant and Tinker the detective snatched up his rifle and bolted out of the hut.

"Steady on, Blake!" said Grant warningly. "Let me go first. I know the way better than you."

They sped along the top of the cliff as quickly as possible. As they approached the cleft where Williams and the men were guarding the entrance to the channel the sound of firing smote on their ears. Evidently Williams had already spotted the boat.

He heard the sound of their footsteps approaching and came hurrying towards them.

"The boat's just got by, sir," he said. "We blazed away at it, but it was no use. We couldn't stop it. They evidently had a barricade of bags and blankets on this side."

"How about the *Fraulein*, Williams? They're towing her behind!"

"Yes, sir, she'll be along in a minute. If you listen you can hear the rope splashing in the water as it sags."

Blake peered down into the darkness below. He could see the whole width of the channel here by the simmering waters that reached to the further cliff.

By day the position was impregnable. A handful of men could command the entrance to the channel, but in the darkness it was all but impossible to stop a small boat from passing out into the lagoon.

He could hear the towing rope splashing in the water and sending out great ripples over its surface, then the dark shape of the *Fraulein* slowly loomed up in the middle of the channel.

Blake and his companions watched her in silence. It was impossible to do anything; there did not appear to be anyone on her decks. Evidently they had taken the precaution to lash the wheel.

Granite Grant ground his teeth in impotent rage.

"Hang it all, Blake!" he muttered. "This is too bad. There goes a million and a half of bullion, and we're standing here twiddling our thumbs."

Blake was about to make some reply when a slight movement on the vessel's deck attracted his attention.

"Don't fire!" he said breathlessly, as Williams' rifle went to his shoulder.

A dim form moved along the deck and leaned over the vessel's bows. A moment later a gurgling splash echoed up from down below.

The *Fraulein* immediately began to lose way, and from the boat some twenty yards ahead startled cries rang out.

Granite Grant grasped the detective by the arm.

"Great Scott, man," he said, "the rope's cut!"

But Blake's eyes were still fixed on the *Fraulein*'s deck. The shadowy figure had now sped up to the bridge and was unlashing the wheel. Suddenly the vessel swung over towards the opposite bank, and, at the same moment hoarse shouts rang out from down below.

The next moment the hatchway was thrown open and a man scrambled out. With a cry of fury he rushed across the deck towards the figure that was creeping down the companion-ladder.

Blake knew instinctively that he was the "Leopard." Venner had discovered at the last moment that someone had cut the towing-rope. His rage and mortification had got the better of him.

Snarling like a wild beast he grasped the little figure round the waist. A furious struggle ensued. Locked in one another's embrace the two figures swayed across the deck getting nearer and nearer to the vessel's side.

Then, with a shock that displaced everything on her decks, the *Fraulein* grounded on the shoal at the base of the opposite cliff, and the two figures toppled over into the water.

Above the din and confusion that followed a strange, piercing cry rang out from the water in a woman's high-pitched voice.

"Help! Help! Monsieur Grant, it is I!"

As the piercing accents died away the men on the cliff stood as if suddenly petrified. For a breathless moment Blake and Grant stared at one another with blanched faces. Although neither spoke both men had recognised that piercing scream. They knew now who it was who had cut the towing-rope and run the *Fraulein* on the sand bank.

Then Granite Grant pulled himself together.

"Blake," he said hoarsely, "somehow we must get down. It can be done. Lend me your hand!"

But Tinker intervened.

"I'm the lightest, guv'nor," he said. "Hold hands and lower me down first."

Before they could act on this suggestion the bloodhound, who had been running frantically to and fro, went scrambling over the side of the cliff.

Tinker flung himself down flat and peered anxiously into the depths below. Half way down the cliff Pedro's dark form suddenly shot out like a catapult, followed immediately after by a great splash as he hit the water.

"Pedro's after her, guv'nor!" he shouted excitedly. "Lower away! The cliff juts out at the bottom. I can stand on it."

Grasping Blake's hand Tinker disappeared over the side of the cliff, Granite Grant seized Blake's other hand and dug his heels in the ground.

"Link up, boys!" he shouted. "That's the style. Now—gently does it!"

Tinker peered anxiously below. There was a ten feet drop, and only about two feet of projecting cliff to save him from the water. He decided to chance it.

"I'm letting go, guv'nor!" he shouted, and released his hold.

He landed on the strip of cliff, staggered wildly for a second or two, then managed to retain his balance.

"I'm safe, guv'nor," he shouted. "Send someone for a rope."

Blake's voice sounded from above with a little break in it.

"Good lad, Tinker!" he said. "Mind what you're doing! We'll have the rope along in a minute."

Tinker peered out into the channel. Some dark form was floating on the water and he could hear the great bloodhound panting and struggling with grim tenacity.

"Pedro!" he called. "Good dog, Pedro! This way, boy!"

The dog came nearer and nearer to the cliff, grasping in his great jaws his unconscious burden. A few moments later Tinker reached out, and grasping him by the scruff of the neck, hauled him on to the ledge of rock.

Blake's anxious voice came echoing from above.

"Still there, Tinker, my lad?"

"I'm here, guv'nor. Pedro's got her! Let's have that rope and we'll hoist them up!"

"It won't be long now, Tinker!" shouted back Blake. "Hold on, my lad!"

***

"She'll be all right in a minute, Blake; she's coming round."

Granite Grant put the flask to the woman's lips and poured a few drops between her teeth. Her head was resting on his arm, and her wet, golden hair hung down in tangled profusion. But in spite of the ghastly pallor of her face Mademoiselle Julie looked strangely beautiful.

Presently a light of recognition crept into her dark, velvety eyes, and, half raising herself, she glanced swiftly round the shanty.

"Where am I?" she asked in French, and her eyes rested inquiringly on Granite Grant.

"Why," she added, with sudden recognition, "it is the big Monsieur Grant!"

"Yes, it is I, Julie!" said the King's Spy in an unsteady voice. "But do not talk, you will be better presently."

But Mademoiselle Julie's vivacious spirits were already returning, and the delicate colour was spreading over her pale cheeks.

"But I am better now, monsieur!" she said, with a little toss of her head, and her eyes travelled to the detective's grim face.

"Ah, Monsieur Blake!" she said. "Do not look so glum. Have I not kept my promise?"

Blake felt as if he had been wound up to a state of tension and then suddenly relaxed. He gave vent to his familiar quiet chuckle.

"You are a brave young woman, mademoiselle," he said, "and you have certainly kept your promise."

"One day you shall tell us the story, mademoiselle," said Granite Grant. "But not now. You are tired, and there are many things to do."

"Let us make a compact then, monsieur! We will leave these things untold until all is finished, then we will all meet in my beautiful Paris and each will tell his story. Is it not so?"

Grant looked inquiringly at the detective and then turned to the young woman.

"Agreed, mademoiselle!" he said.

"Ah, it is the splendid dog!" she cried, nestling her soft cheek against Pedro's cold snout and tears came into her eyes.

But Pedro only looked embarrassed and nervously wagged his tail.

Chapter 23
The *Nancy* Arrives

AT sunrise next morning when Blake looked out across the lagoon he saw the familiar lines of the *Nancy* glistening in a sea of shimmering silver. As his eyes rested on her white decks the detective felt a great surge of emotion sweep over him, and he realised then how acute had been the nervous tension which he had endured during the last twenty-four hours.

All through the night Charlie Jones had been keeping in touch with the *Nancy*, and Captain Sampson had been made acquainted with all that had happened on the island since he had been swept out to sea in the fury of the cyclone.

The *Fraulein* still remained stuck hard and fast on the sandbank, but it was not known if she had sustained any further injury. For this reason Blake had instructed Captain Sampson to stand by until he knew what Venner's intentions were. Granite Grant had gone along the cliff to speak to him and see if he were prepared to admit himself beaten.

Some ten minutes later he saw the King's Spy coming along the cliff.

"Splendid news, Blake!" he shouted, when he was still some distance off. "We've got them beaten to a frazzle. They've chucked up the sponge."

"Good!" exclaimed the detective, with a flush of elation. "How did you manage it, Grant? Did Venner see he was in a hopeless position?"

"The "Leopard" will never see anything again, Blake," said Grant quietly. "He's drowned. They couldn't find him in the darkness—his body has just been washed up on the reef."

Blake was silent for a moment.

"Well, perhaps it's best as it is, Grant!" he muttered soberly. "The fellow was nothing but a blackguard—the world's well rid of such as he. And so the captain has capitulated?"

"Yes, he hasn't a kick left in him. The fore plates of the *Fraulein* are buckled; it'll take them a week to get her seaworthy again."

"Then we'll tell Sampson to come ashore in the dinghy, Grant?"

"No, not yet, Blake! The *Fraulein*'s boat will be along in a few minutes with all their guns. I thought it best to draw their teeth. We've got them well covered from the cliff, but it's best to take no risks; without rifles they're pretty harmless."

"That's certainly a brain-wave on your part, Grant!"

"Thanks, Blake! Here's the boat just coming up the channel. Best thing to do now is to tell Sampson to bring the *Nancy* into the lagoon and run her alongside the *Fraulein*. Then we can start getting that bullion transferred straight away."

"I'll get Charlie Jones on the job now, Grant," said the detective, hurrying off to put the idea into execution.

Granite Grant went down to meet the boat. Only two men were at the oars, and the bottom was stacked with rifles and ammunition, which he soon had safely stowed away in the shanty.

A short time later Blake joined him, and they stood together on the cliff and watched the *Nancy* tack into the lagoon and steam towards the entrance of the channel.

Presently the dinghy came up the creek, as Captain Sampson stepped ashore Blake grasped the grizzled old sea-dog's brawny fist.

"Welcome to Granite Grant's Island!" he said.

The King's Spy gave a deep chuckle.

"Nothing doing, Blake!" he said. "I guess I'm quite willing to hand the property over to you."

"Well, gentlemen," said Captain Sampson, furiously combing his grizzly beard, "I can't say you've got much to fight about. If you call this lump of earth an island—well, the sooner you tie the proverbial mill-stone round its neck and drop it into the sea the better. I've seen these things floating about in milk."

Blake burst into a roar of laughter.

"I bet that's not your natural diet, captain!" he said.

Captain Sampson winked his bleary eye at the detective and wisely refrained from replying.

"Well, whoever owns the island," said Granite Grant, "we all seem mighty anxious to get away. So if it's all the same to you, captain, we'll get busy on that bullion right now."

"You're late, Mr. Grant," said Captain Sampson; "the boys are already hauling the swag. If there's anyone else who's looking for a job, just let me know—I'll find 'em something to do."

"Then we'll all come and lend a hand, captain," said Blake. "And there's Williams and his men; we'll get them busy."

Late that evening, as the sun was sinking in a great red flame of fire, the *Nancy* steamed out into the blue lagoon and made slowly for the opening in the reef.

All that day Blake and his companions had been busy transferring the bullion from the hold of the *Fraulein*. It had been strenuous work, for they had determined if possible not to stay another night at the island, and not until the last bale was lowered into the *Nancy*'s hold did they cease in their exertions.

The crew of the *Fraulein* was busy repairing her damaged plates. The injury was not as serious as had at first been supposed, and, having satisfied himself that she could come to no harm, Blake had not troubled himself further in the matter. Some months later Granite Grant told him that the vessel had reached port safely, and there the matter ended.

Blake stood in the stern of the *Nancy* watching the island gradually growing smaller and smaller. In the red glow of the setting sun it looked strangely beautiful and tranquil—a jewel set in the shimmering sea; yet on that same little isle he had experienced some of the most strenuous and exciting moments of his life.

He turned presently to Mademoiselle Julie, who reclined in a deck-chair close by, wrapt in a blanket.

"It is the most beautiful spot in the world, mademoiselle," he said, "and yet——"

"And yet, monsieur," she said quickly, "it is more jolly in my gay Paris—and even your London, perhaps!"

"I suppose it is!" admitted the detective, thoughtfully.

Chapter 24
Explanations

A TALL, bronze-faced man stepped out on to the balcony of a rather imposing-looking house standing in the Rue de Ravenne, and, leaning against the iron balustrade, gazed attentively up and down the broad boulevard. The street below him hummed and throbbed with the noise of countless footsteps and the sound of swiftly-moving vehicles, for it was here that the elite and fashion of gay Paris thronged and jostled each other for a place in the sun to display their satins and silks, their feathers and fancies, and all the other adornments of feminine desires.

Not that the Rue de Ravenne is exclusively feminine—nor exclusively fashionable; for along its broad pavements many a dandy beau may be seen waggling his cane and bowing his respects to some passing beauty, or desperately ogling with gladsome eye the pretty *grisette*, who, conscious of her charms, would not be denied her place in the sun.

An urchin came running along the street with a bundle of newspapers under his arm. As he came beneath the window the bronze-faced man leant over the balcony and dropped a coin on the pavement.

The boy swooped down on it, flung a paper up to the window, and continued his way down the boulevard again.

Opening the paper, the tall man glanced thoughtfully inside, then, turning on his heel, disappeared through the open window.

"Blake," he said, "Sir Vrymer Fane was right; already Throgmorton Street is feeling its effects. The American exchange has risen in our favour. The Stock Exchange quotations are two points higher than yesterday, and they are still rising."

Sexton Blake nodded languidly.

"Glad to hear it, Grant," he said, "although it's more or less Greek to me; I'm out of my depths directly you start talking high finance. However, I suppose it's all to do with the gold basis—and a million and a-half of bullion is quite a nice little sum."

Granite Grant did not reply; he was still immersed in the Stock Exchange quotations. The detective puffed appreciatively at his cigar and stretched himself in his comfortable chair.

It was three weeks ago now since the *Nancy* had reached Southampton; it was nearly two months since they had steamed away from the island in the Caribbean Sea.

The memory of that strange voyage was already less distinct in that world of swift changes in which the detective lived.

He glanced round the well-appointed apartment. This was Mademoiselle Julie's home—when she happened to be in Paris. Its luxury and magnificence betokened wealth and splendour and refinement.

Blake could not help contrasting it with a little wooden shanty standing in the creek of that desolate island in the Caribbean Sea.

He was still pondering over these things when Mademoiselle Julie entered. An opera cloak was flung over her shoulders as if she were prepared to go out; her hair was exquisitely coiffured, and even in the waning light glistened like yellow gold.

Blake rose from his chair and stood eyeing her attentively; her dazzling beauty rather puzzled and perplexed him; she possessed that irresistible something against which the coldest mind and strongest intelligence is powerless.

She touched Granite Grant lightly on the shoulder.

"You seem more interested in the paper, Monsieur Grant," she said, "than in taking me to the opera."

The Secret Service man crumpled the paper in his hand with a quick gesture.

"Never, mademoiselle!" he said. "Mr. Blake and I are only too sensible of the honour you bestow on us."

The young woman gave a gay laugh of contentment and turned to the detective.

"Come, Monsieur Blake," she said, "tell me if your big friend speaks the truth."

"As far as I am concerned, mademoiselle," said Blake gravely, "he but feebly describes our pleasure."

"Then, messieurs, if you are quite ready we will go!"

"But Mademoiselle Julie," said Granite Grant suddenly, "I have not yet heard your story!"

"Nor I!" chimed in Blake.

"La, la!" said Mademoiselle Julie, with a wave of her hand, "we have been talking all the afternoon. I am tired of hearing of your wretched island."

"Then tell me one thing, Mademoiselle Julie," said Grant. "Was it you who let me escape from the *Fraulein?*"

"It was, monsieur!"

"I also would like to ask you a question, mademoiselle," said Blake. "How did you manage to get on board the *Fraulein* without Venner being aware of the fact?"

"But he was aware of it, monsieur!"

"Then why did he not stop you?"

Mademoiselle Julie glanced at the detective significantly.

"Do you think you could have stopped me, monsieur," she asked, "if I wished it very much?"

As Blake looked into her dark eyes the meaning of her words became suddenly clear to him; it was that strange power over men which she possessed that had enabled her to smuggle herself aboard the *Fraulein* with Venner's knowledge.

"I don't think I should like to try, Mademoiselle Julie," he said earnestly.

"But why did you wish to come so much, mademoiselle?" asked Granite Grant.

The young woman's eyes clouded.

"You forget my good friend, Monsieur Jacques," she said in a low voice. "Tell me, did I not have my revenge?"

"You certainly did, mademoiselle!" muttered Granite Grant.

"And now let us be going, messieurs! You two silent Englishmen will never cease chattering, and I will not answer your questions any more."

The two men followed her out of the room and down into the street. A car was waiting outside, and a few moments later they were gliding swiftly along the boulevards in the direction of the Avenue de l'Opera.

THE TEED FILES #2: FOUR CLASSIC TALES
INTRODUCING DR. HUXTON RYMER AND PRINCE WU LING

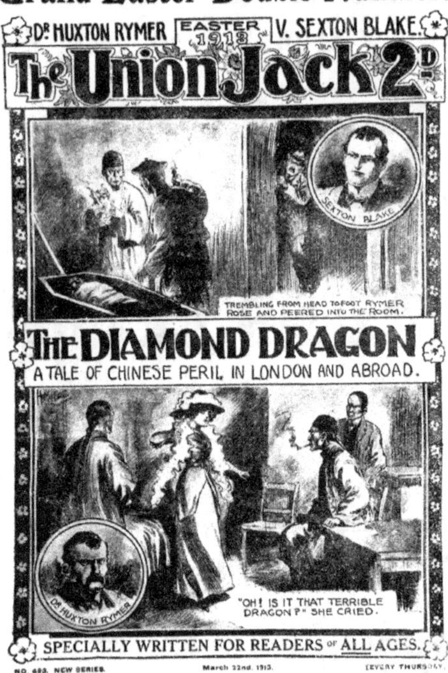

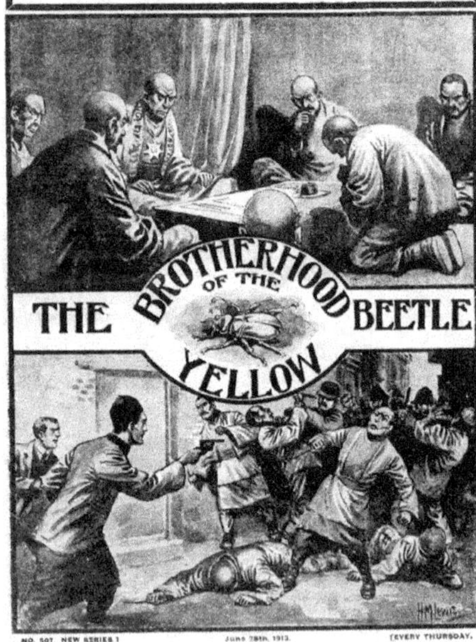

THE MYSTERY OF THE TURKISH AGREEMENT

A Grand and Stirring Story of Adventure in England and Algiers,
Introducing Sexton Blake, "Granite" Grant, Mdlle. Julie, and Tinker.
Splendidly Written by the Author of "The King's Spy," etc., etc.

SEXTON BLAKE
SCHOOLDAYS

SEXTON BLAKE AT SCHOOL
SEXTON BLAKE IN THE SIXTH
SEXTON BLAKE AT OXFORD

LOST WORLDS
40 Classic Tales
ROH PRESS
MASTERWORKS OF ADVENTURE

ATLANTIS & LEMURIA
16 Classic Tales
ROH PRESS
MASTERWORKS OF ADVENTURE

MASTERWORKS
OF
ADVENTURE

CLASSIC TALES FROM
THE GREAT AGE
OF STORYTELLING

ROH PRESS

Four new volumes of the SEXTON BLAKE LIBRARY are issued on the first Friday in every month. Please give your newsagent a standing order for them.

The Mystery of the Turkish Agreement.

A Thrilling Detective Novelette, Strong in Adventure and Plot, Introducing Sexton Blake, Tinker, "Granite" Grant, the King's Spy, and Mademoiselle Julie.

A Story of an International Complication.

Chapter 1
The Fight in the Dark

A THOUSAND twinkling lights were blazing in Leicester Square and its immediate vicinity and the long facade of imposing shops and restaurants stood out staringly in the white glare of incandescent and electric light. It was between ten and eleven at night and the chimes of innumerable belfries had a few minutes before struck the half hour.

Thronged as the famous thoroughfare is during most times of the day, it was now brimming over with dense masses of people. They were flocking from the theatres and restaurants and making their way slowly to the 'buses and tubes that would take them home to their beds, to sleep until the alarum should warn them that another day of toil was begun.

Others seemed less inclined to hurry away from this garish and dazzling centre of extravagance and gaiety. There were the habitual haunters of West End life—the showy, restless, pleasure-seeking crowd.

Their laughter, and merriment, and gaiety mingled with the strident shouts of newsboys, the steady, persistent rumble of thousands of feet, the noise of swiftly-moving vehicles; and the whole orchestration of sound rose on the night air like the heavy breathing of some strange, sleeping monster, surfeited with food and restless with nightmare.

In a side street, not more than a hundred yards from where this great artery throbs with quivering life, stand the famous Veuxpillo Galleries. But the building was now wrapt in silent gloom and darkness; the blazing lights of Leicester Square did not penetrate to its smuggled retreat, and only a confused, persistent murmur told of the human stream that ebbed and flowed but a few yards away from its doors.

The galleries stand in the backwaters of London's winding arteries, tucked away in a pocket of brick and mortar, and few people stumble on the building merely by chance.

Most people ask to be directed, even when they are but a few yards from its doors, and the policeman on point-duty in Leicester Square is tired of jerking his thumb over his shoulder and grunting: "Just round there—first on right!"

Yet the fame of these galleries is world-wide. Their name is on the lips of everyone who prides himself on being someone in artistic circles. They are noted for the fineness of their exhibits, and the greatest painters or the day vie with one another to have their pictures hung on its panelled walls. The aspiring artist reckons he has "made good" when he at last succeeds in having a picture hung in the Veuxpillo Galleries.

On this particular day in question all the artistic fraternity of London, and a good number of foreign art students, had flocked to the galleries to see a wonderful collection of "old masters" that was being exhibited.

It had been a private view day, and the demand for tickets had far exceeded the supply; even titled ladies and gentlemen eminent in political and diplomatic circles had applied in vain for admission.

It was with a sigh of thankfulness that Mr. Erasmus Mayn, the manager of the galleries, had seen the doors close on his fashionable clientele, and, after a careful glance around, had hurried off to keep an appointment he had made to dine with some friends.

The docks were now just striking the quarter. The south-room of the galleries was wrapt in impenetrable darkness; the line of stained-glass windows were shuttered and barred, and not a gleam of light crept in from the outside world.

Suddenly the silence was broken by the sound of a door creaking on its hinges, and almost immediately a thin beam of white light shot across the room.

Then stealthy, muffled footsteps began to pad across the polished floor, and the light moved slowly along the paintings that hung around the wall and presently came to rest.

In the white circle of the flash-lamp the portrait of a man showed up with startling distinctness. The picture was painted in oils, and on the grey military tunic several rows of foreign decorations and orders glistened in dull lustre.

The face was that of an old man: the skin was wrinkled and parched, and the hair that was brushed straight back from the furrowed forehead was sparse and straggly and driven white.

The strange intruder stood gazing at the portrait for some moments. Then he slipped beneath the oak balustrade that railed in the pictures and prevented people from touching and injuring them.

With a rapid movement he lifted the portrait from its hook, laid it flat on the floor, and set to work with quick, nervous energy.

Whatever his task was, he evidently had no fear of being disturbed. He did not pause once to listen or to glance around, but worked on silently and swiftly as if he had carefully planned his visit and had come with a very clear idea of what he intended to do.

Every now and then the thin steel blade of a knife gleamed in the light of the electric torch, and the sharp sound of its cutting through canvas followed.

Twenty minutes must have passed by like this. Then, with a grunt of satisfaction, the stranger rose to his feet, and, lifting the picture from the floor, replaced it on its hook.

He held in his hand what looked like a square patch of canvas. This he folded into a small, thick wad and carefully wrapped it in a sheet of brown paper.

After picking up various implements from off the floor and dropping them into his pockets, he slipped under the wooden balustrade again and made to cross the floor.

The next instant he had stepped back with a half-stifled exclamation. A few yards away from him another man was standing; the light from the torch shone full on his face. It was thin and angular, and the swarthy skin was drawn tightly over the high cheekbones. His nose was deformed, as if it had once been broken and had not mended properly.

As he stared at the other man's face his black, deep-set eyes glowed with a fierce, sinister light.

After that first exclamation neither man spoke; except for their laboured breathing the silence was unbroken. Then the newcomer moved swiftly forward, the torch dropped from the other man's fingers, and the next moment they were locked in one another's arms in a desperate struggle for mastery.

They slithered to and fro on the polished floor, their breaths coming in deep panting sobs. A hand was raised on high grasping a thin steel blade; the other man's fingers were gripping the wrist.

They lurched and staggered up and down and the knife was brandished backwards and forwards as each strove to force it from the other's grasp.

But the new-comer was the stronger; his fingers were closing round his opponent's wrist like a steel vice.

Slowly and surely the upraised hand was being forced down, while the beads of perspiration stood out on its owner's forehead and the fierce light of despair shone in his eyes.

Then the wrist suddenly grew limp, the blade swooped down impetuously, and with a gasping cry the man staggered back, crashed against the wooden balustrade, and crumpled to the floor.

For a few moments the other man stood breathing heavily. Then he stooped to the floor, and, picking up the torch, flashed it around.

The little brown-paper parcel was lying a few yards away, where it had been dropped in the desperate scuffle. He pounced on it eagerly, thrust it into his pocket, and, without glancing at his prostrate foe, hurried away.

***

The clock-tower at Victoria had just struck eleven when a man came hurrying out of the station, and, standing on the kerb, glanced quickly up and down.

He was a tall, muscularly-built man, and wore a dark, closely-cropped beard. His face was bronzed and tanned from exposure to many climes; he seemed to move as if he were on springs, and even beneath his rough tweed suit the play of his whip-like muscles could be noticed as he walked restlessly to and fro.

His name was James Grant, more commonly known as "Granite" Grant, the King's

Spy. In diplomatic circles throughout the world he was known for what he was—a tough fighter, a hard hitter, and a man who never knew himself beaten.

He moved in that secret network of diplomatic intrigue and international duplicity known only to those who pull the strings of foreign affairs.

In the fulfilment of his duties he pursued his ends unswervingly and relentlessly, mixing with all ranks of society and adapting himself without the slightest difficulty to the needs of the moment.

It was because of his daring and courage that he had earned the nickname of "Granite" Grant; and well it suited his strong, inflexible nature.

For a moment the King's Spy glanced impatiently around. By the restless movement of his queer blue eyes he seemed to be searching for something.

Then, seeing a taxi turn into the station approach, he ran swiftly towards it.

"To Leicester Square—quick!" he said sharply, and clambered inside.

The cab swung round and sped off up Victoria Street. Ten minutes later it pulled up outside the Empire. Granite Grant jumped out, paid his fare, and hurried across the Square.

Evidently he knew his way without stopping to inquire, for a few moments later he stood in front of the Veuxpillo Galleries.

He glanced up at the building somewhat doubtfully, then walked up the marble steps and tried the handle. He gave a grunt of surprise as the heavy door swung open.

"What the deuce!" he muttered, and stepped inside.

Two swing glass doors faced him, leading to the corridor that passed up the centre of the galleries. He took out his pocket-torch, pushed open the doors, and crept silently along the corridor until he came to the south-room.

The next moment he stood inside, sweeping the thin beam of light over the paintings that hung on the panelled walls.

"It's number forty-seven, I think!" he muttered, and began moving slowly along with his hand feeling the wooden balustrade.

Suddenly, his feet tripped over a body that lay sprawled across the floor. He clutched the rail and saved himself from falling, and, kneeling to the floor, gazed into the white upturned face and wildly staring eyes.

He placed his hand over the man's heart, and withdrew it again with an exclamation of consternation.

"Merciful heavens!" he muttered, and sprang to his feet.

The light rested on the painting of the grizzled old man in the military tunic. He looked at it curiously for a moment, then, stooping beneath the rail, lifted the painting away from the wall and carefully scrutinised the back.

"Pah!" he muttered with deep disgust. "I'm just too late."

He bit his lip with vexation, then turned his attention to the silent man on the floor. A brief glance told him that he was past all human aid; he was stabbed to the heart and death must have been almost instantaneous.

After a few seconds' scrutiny, Granite Grant rose to his feet and turned away. As he did so his foot kicked against something that went jangling across the polished floor.

He followed the sound with the light and picked up a bunch of keys. For a moment he seemed nonplussed. Then he gave a grunt of understanding, and, dropping them into his pocket, went across the room and down the corridor into the street.

All was silent outside. The murmuring life of the great city sounded vague and confused. A mere stone's throw away innumerable people were passing to and fro; but none was aware of the grim tragedy that had taken place in the Veuxpillo Galleries that night.

Not many were even aware that the building was situated in that mean, narrow by-street.

Granite Grant swung the heavy door to behind him, and tried the largest key of the bunch. The lock slipped into the slot with a sharp click.

"Best for him not to be discovered until the morning," he muttered, and, striding down the steps, disappeared into the night.

Chapter 2
Sexton Blake Gets Busy

JUST round the corner—first on right!"

The policeman took a quick glance at the man who had just asked him the way to Veuxpillo Galleries.

"I beg your pardon, Mr. Blake, he said hurriedly. "I didn't know it was you; people are always asking the way to the galleries."

Sexton Blake, the famous Baker Street detective and expert criminologist, nodded pleasantly.

"That's quite all right, constable," he said. "Thanks!"

He crossed the Square with Tinker, his young assistant, walking at his side, and made his way quickly up the narrow side street.

A number of people were already assembled outside the Veuxpillo Galleries—the usual crowd of curious folk who never seem to have any sort of occupation.

Two policemen were standing in front of the doors, keeping the people from coming too near the entrance. They recognised Blake and his assistant and gave a respectful "good morning" as he strode up the steps.

As he pushed his way through the swing-glass doors a gentleman came to meet him and held out his hand.

"I am glad you have come, Mr. Blake," he said, somewhat anxiously.

"Mr. Erasmus Mayn, I believe!" said the detective, taking the outstretched hand.

"That's right, Mr. Blake," answered the manager of the Veuxpillo Galleries. "The police have only been here a few minutes; I telephoned for you at the same time."

"Then the body has not been removed, Mr. Mayn?"

"Not yet, Mr. Blake. Inspector Frenton from Scotland Yard is just taking the necessary dispositions."

"Perhaps you will give me a full account of what has happened, Mr. Mayn? Your telephone message was very brief."

"I will, Mr. Blake," said the manager. "Excuse my agitation—I am somewhat unnerved. There is not very much to tell. I came here at nine o'clock this morning just to have a look round before the galleries open to the public. The outer doors were locked, and although I rang the bell I got no answer."

"Whom did you expect to answer, Mr. Mayn?"

"The caretaker, Mr. Blake. He sleeps on the premises."

"I understand, Mr. Mayn. Pray proceed!"

"After ringing the bell several times and getting no response I began to grow a little concerned——"

"One moment, Mr. Mayn," interrupted the detective. "Have you no key to the door yourself?"

"I have one, Mr. Blake, but I do not carry it about with me as a rule. It would have taken too long for me to have gone back for it, so I fetched a locksmith and had the lock forced. When I got inside there was still no signs of the caretaker. I went up to his room, but he was not to be found."

"You say he sleeps on the premises, Mr. Mayn?"

"That is so, Mr. Blake!"

"Then did his bed look as if it had been occupied?"

The manager shook his head.

"No," he said. "The bed-clothes were undisturbed."

"And you cannot account for his absence?"

"I am absolutely at a loss for an explanation, Mr. Blake."

"Then what did you do?"

"I made a hurried inspection of the galleries. Everything seemed all right until I got to the south-room. There I found the door unlocked, and directly I entered I noticed some dark object lying on the floor over to the left. I flung open the shutters of the windows, and made the dreadful discovery of which I have already spoken to you on the 'phone."

The manager was plainly very much shaken by what had happened. He took a cigarette from his case, but his hands trembled so violently that he had difficulty in placing the cigarette between his lips.

"Thank you, Mr. Mayn," said Blake. "That will be enough for the present; but I am afraid I shall have to worry you again later on."

"Do exactly as you think fit, Mr. Blake. I am only too anxious to get this dreadful mystery solved. I took the precaution of seeking your expert advice for that reason."

"Then we will go along to the south-room, Mr. Mayn, if you will be good enough to lead the way."

They went along the corridor and entered the south-room. A little group of men were bending over the body that lay on the floor. Inspector Frenton turned round as the detective approached.

"Hello!" he said, somewhat surprised. "You here, Mr. Blake!"

"Yes; Mr. Mayn telephoned for me, Frenton," said the detective.

The inspector shrugged his shoulders superciliously.

"Of course, the Yard has got the matter well in hand, Mr. Blake," he said.

"Mr. Blake is acting for me in a private capacity, inspector," interposed Mr. Mayn.

Inspector Frenton raised his eyebrows, but did not offer any further comment. At that moment the doctor, who had been kneeling on the floor, rose to his feet.

"That will do," he muttered, and picked up his bag.

Then he saw the detective, and added pleasantly:

"Good morning. Mr. Blake! So you've come along. Well, it's a queer business, to say the least. It will tax all your ingenuity."

"What's the cause of death, doctor?" asked Blake.

"Stabbed to the heart, Mr. Blake. Must have been instantaneous."

"Just one more question before you go, doctor. When do you suppose the poor fellow met his death?"

"Been dead some hours, Mr. Blake. Must have happened somewhere about midnight or a little before."

"Thanks, doctor! No other conclusions?"

The doctor shook his head and smiled drily.

"It's up to you to draw the conclusions, Mr. Blake," he said, and, nodding pleasantly, he walked towards the door.

Inspector Frenton was just giving instructions for the body to be removed. Blake laid a detaining hand on his arm.

"One moment, Frenton!" he said. "Is this the position in which he was discovered?"

"It is, Mr. Blake. He hasn't been moved yet."

The detective gazed long and earnestly at the dead man. Not a detail escaped those penetrating eyes of his. He was making a mental picture of the scene, and later on much might depend on the record furnished by his retentive mind.

"Have you established his identity yet, inspector?" he asked presently.

"No, we haven't, Mr. Blake. Doesn't seem to carry any papers about with him. But some of his linen seems to be marked with the initials 'G. F.'"

"Anything at all in his pockets?"

"Yes. Those things over there!"

Blake glanced in the direction indicated. A few miscellaneous articles were lying on the floor. He went over and examined them. There were a pair of forceps, a thin steel rule, some brass-headed drawing-pins, a small bottle of liquid glue, a roll of adhesive tape, and one or two other delicate instruments.

Blake's brows contracted thoughtfully as he gazed at this curious collection of articles. What did they mean? What were they doing in this man's pockets?

The crime seemed more mystifying than ever; there seemed nothing here to account for it. What had this dead man being doing here? How had he entered the galleries after they were closed?

He suddenly thought of the missing caretaker. Where was he? What had happened to him? He turned to the manager, who stood eyeing him doubtfully.

"Is there another way of entering the galleries besides the one I came in this morning, Mr. Mayn?" he asked.

The manager shook his head.

"No, Mr. Blake," he said. "The only other way is through the windows, and they were all shuttered and barred when I came here this morning. I am quite sure they had not been disturbed."

"And the door of this room was open, you say?"

"It was, Mr. Blake. I remember locking it myself last night before I left."

The detective's mind was working quickly. To have opened the door of the south-room someone must have had a key. In that case, doubtless the doors leading to the street had been opened in the same way. After committing his fiendish crime the murderer had fled from the building and had locked the outer doors before making good his escape.

But what was the motive of the crime? Who had committed it? And why? Things certainly looked rather black against the caretaker. The man was missing from his post; he had not slept in his bed. His absence, whatever the reason of it, must in some way be connected with this tragedy.

But perhaps he had been enticed away and robbed of his keys! That might certainly be an explanation. Blake turned to the inspector.

"You didn't find the key of the outer door in his pocket, I suppose?" he asked.

Frenton shook his head.

"No," he said. "That's all I found down there."

"It seems quite inexplicable," muttered Mr. Mayn.

Blake nodded his head, but did not reply. Inspector Frenton looked up sharply.

"Don't you worry, Mr. Mayn," he said. "Just wait until we lay our hands on this caretaker fellow. No doubt he knows all about it. Shouldn't be surprised if he committed the crime."

Blake smiled drily at the inspector's cocksure manner.

"You're more optimistic than I am, inspector," he said.

Frenton's eyebrows went up again.

"You trust the Yard for clearing the matter up, Mr. Blake," he said. "And now if you're quite finished, I'll get the body removed to the ambulance."

Blake stood aside and watched them pick up the body and carry it out into the corridor. Then he turned to Tinker.

"Now they're gone, Tinker," he said, "we'll get busy and see if there's anything to be discovered."

He knelt to the floor and began to scrutinize it very intently. The manager stood by and watched him in silence. Presently Blake picked up a black cloth button. He stared at it for a few moments; it looked as if it had been pulled off from someone's coat, and one edge of it was slightly flattened. Then he dropped it into his pocket and turned his attention to the floor again.

"There are a number of scratches here, Tinker," he said presently. "There must have been a furious struggle here quite recently."

He continued his scrutiny until he came close up to the balustrade. The lower wooden rail was only about an inch from the floor. Blake put his fingers beneath it and slowly drew them along. Then he dragged out something from beneath, and, holding it in the palm of his hand, gazed at it curiously.

It was a piece of paper so tightly folded that it only occupied about a quarter of an inch square of space. Yet the thing that impressed Blake was that it was perfectly clean, while his fingers were covered with the dust and dirt that had accumulated beneath the rail.

It was quite evident that it had not laid there long. It must have got lodged beneath the rail only recently.

He carefully unfolded it. It was bigger than he had supposed, about the size of a half sheet of notepaper. But it was quite blank. There was not a mark on either side.

Blake held it up to the light and looked for the water-mark. But there were no trace of any. He folded it up at last, and, putting it in his pocket-case, continued his investigation.

It was between the balustrade and the wall that he made his next discovery. A number of dirty white chippings were scattered about over the polished floor. At first Blake could not think what they were.

"When was this room last swept out, Mr. Mayn?" he asked.

"Directly the galleries were closed yesterday evening, Mr. Blake."

The detective stared at the strange particles again. Then, suddenly, it dawned on him what they were. They were fragments of hard paste—some special glue that was used for mounting pictures and photographs.

Even then Blake felt somewhat perplexed. How had they come there in the first place? What could they possibly mean? If the room was swept out yesterday evening, then they must have been lodged in their present position since that time. But they couldn't have got there by themselves; they must have been brought there by some human agency.

At that moment Blake happened to glance above his head. The portrait of the old man in the grey military tunic hung just above him. It occurred to him that the glue might possibly have become dislodged from the frame and fallen on to the floor.

He rose from his feet and lifted the painting away from the wall. For some moments he scrutinized the back of the picture, and as he stared at it a number of vague suspicions and lightning thoughts were speeding across his keen brain.

He knew then that he had stumbled right across the main plot of this strange mystery; that by a quick grasp and sifting of elementary facts he had made a discovery that was as startling as it was obscure.

But no signs of emotion showed on Blake's imperturbable face; it was as cold and as impassive as a mask. He had too great a control over his features for them to give any indication of what was passing in his cool, resourceful mind.

Only Tinker had a vague suspicion of the truth; he knew his master so well that he could read that something had happened by the cold gleam in his grey eyes. He listened attentively while Blake spoke to the manager.

"What painting is this, Mr. Mayn?" he asked quietly.

"That is Murillo's *Don Montino*, Mr. Blake."

"Can you tell me anything about it?"

"Not very much, Mr. Blake. The picture was hung, some time back, in the Paris Salon; I bought it two days ago through a French agent."

"Is it of any great value, Mr. Mayn?"

"I gave a hundred guineas[9] for it, Mr. Blake. But that is not a great price when dealing with old masters. There are pictures worth a great deal more than that hanging in this room; that Velasquez immediately on your right is worth ten times that sum."

Blake experienced a kind of mental jar. A theory had been quickly forming in his mind; but now he had to admit to himself that it did not quite fit the case.

His first thought was that the motive of the crime must have been robbery; that an attempt had been made to steal an old painting of great value.

But this particular picture by Murillo was only worth a hundred guineas, while the Velasquez on the right was worth ten times that amount. The thief would surely not have troubled about the Murillo when he could have stolen a much more valuable work of art.

Feeling more perplexed than ever, Blake sought about in his mind for some other explanation. The picture had obviously been tampered with, there was no doubt about that. And on the back of the frame Blake's keen eyes had spotted something else. There were two small smudges, faint, but quite clear to his expert eyes. He knew immediately what they were; they were bloodstained fingerprints.

What did they mean? Whose fingers had made those impressions? And what part did this picture play in this absorbing mystery? He gave up puzzling over the matter at last, feeling considerably baffled and perplexed.

"Would you trust this painting in my hands for a day or so, Mr. Mayn?" he asked.

The manager looked somewhat astonished by Blake's question.

"Why, if you wish it, certainly Mr. Blake," he said. "But I do not quite follow you. Do you think this painting is connected in any way with what happened last night?"

"I have my suspicions, Mr. Mayn."

"But in what way, Mr. Blake?"

"You must pardon me," said the detective, "if I cannot satisfy your curiosity at the present moment. For certain reasons I want to have this picture examined by Mr. Charles Osburn, the fine-art dealer of Charing Cross Road. It is very possible that I may be able to furnish you with further information later on."

The manager shrugged his shoulders submissively.

"Very well, Mr. Blake," he said, "just as you wish. Shall I send it along to Mr. Osburn?"

"No; I will take it myself, Mr. Mayn. It is not very big, and I can easily carry it."

"Then I will have it wrapped up immediately, Mr. Blake, if you will wait just a few moments."

---

[9] £100 in 1920 is worth about £5,700.00 in 2023

Chapter 3
The Woman in the Musquash Coat

TEN minutes later Blake and his young assistant left the Veuxpillo Galleries. The detective was carrying the painting by Murillo under his arm. He hailed a taxi that was turning into the square, and they both clambered inside.

As the cab began to move away from the kerb, Blake leaned out of the window and gave a swift glance behind him. Something had attracted his attention; almost intuitively he felt that his movements were being spied on.

The only person he could see was a woman wearing an expensive musquash coat; she was standing still in the middle of the pavement; he could not see her face, it was heavily veiled, but he felt sure that behind it her eyes were watching him curiously. An instant later the cab had swung round the corner.

Blake sank back in his seat with a thoughtful look on his face. But Tinker, unmindful of his master's preoccupation, began to ply him with questions.

"What's wrong with this picture, guv'nor?" he asked quickly. "Why are you so interested in it?"

"We shall see what Mr. Osburn says about it, Tinker," answered the detective. "It's been tampered with, I'm quite certain of that. I have my doubts whether it's a genuine Murillo. But we shall see."

"A genuine Murillo, guv'nor!" echoed Tinker.

"Yes, Tinker; I have a shrewd suspicion that it's a fake and not worth the canvas it's painted on."

Tinker whistled softly.

"Funny how you manage to stumble on these things, guv'nor," he said.

"But that's not all, Tinker," continued the detective. "There are two distinct impressions of fingerprints on the back of the frame, and I believe they were made by the person who killed this man in the galleries last night."

"What makes you think that, guv'nor?"

"Because they are blood-stained fingerprints, Tinker, and were evidently made quite recently."

"Well, I'm blessed, guv'nor!" said Tinker, getting rather excited. "That'll give old Frenton a nasty jar when he hears all about it."

"He won't hear all about it yet, Tinker. Once he gets certain fixed ideas in his mind, he'll stick to them until the bitter end; and I'm not going to attempt to enlighten him; it would be quite useless."

The cab stopped in Charing Cross Road, and the detective and his assistant got out. Mr. Charles Osburn's rather antiquated-looking shop was crowded with fine art treasures.

The detective was immersed in some old steel engravings when the art dealer himself came out of his office.

"Ah, Mr. Blake," he said, glancing at the frame that was tucked beneath his arm, "you are not going to tell me that you have changed your occupation?"

Blake gave vent to his familiar chuckle.

"No," he said, "I've got nothing to sell, Mr. Osburn. But I want your advice on a certain matter."

"Come in here then, Mr. Blake. Delighted to be of any service. And now, Mr. Blake, fire away!" he said, when they were seated in his snug little private office.

The detective cut the string around the painting and removed the paper covering.

"I want you to express your opinion of this painting, Mr. Osburn," he said.

The art dealer's critical eye rested for a few seconds on the portrait.

"It reminds me of the seventeenth century school of art," he said; "the work of Murillo, for instance."

"You are quite right, Mr. Osburn; it is supposed to be Murillo's *Don Montino*."

"Yes, of course, Mr. Blake! I recognise it now by the photographs I have seen. It is not worth much, you know; it is one of his very early efforts, and rather crude."

"Then you are quite sure that it is a Murillo, Mr. Osborn?"

"Ah, Mr. Blake, now I see what you are driving at! You wish to know if this is a genuine Murillo. I should certainly not stake my reputation on such a brief inspection. It looks like a Murillo, but I do not say that it is. It may be an imitation. In any case it is a remarkably clever one!"

"And how would you discover if it were an imitation, Mr. Osburn?"

"There are a number of methods of ascertaining that, Mr. Blake. A dark varnish may be put on a picture to make it resemble the patina of great age. That is a common trick of art swindlers. By cleansing the panel I could soon see if it were a genuine Murillo however."

"Very well then, Mr. Osburn! I am going to ask you to undertake that task for me. This painting was hung in the Veuxpillo Galleries. Mr. Erasmus Mayn has allowed me to take it away in order that you may examine it. And now I want you to look at the back of the frame and tell me what you think."

The art expert held the picture up so that the light from the window fell on the back. For two or three minutes he scrutinized it in silence. Then he turned quickly to the detective.

"This canvas, Mr. Blake, has only just recently been put on the wooden stretcher," he said. "In fact, the glue is even now not quite hard."

Blake's eyes narrowed thoughtfully. He remembered the queer implements that had been found in the dead man's pockets—the pair of forceps, the bottle of paste, and the other things—and he began to understand what they had been used for.

"I thought as much, Mr. Osburn," he said quietly. "And now, when can you let me know definitely if the picture is genuine or merely an imitation?"

"Sometime this afternoon, Mr. Blake. I will ring you up if you wish."

"Thanks, if you will! There is one other thing I must do before I go. I will lay the picture on this table, if you don't mind."

Blake took a small glass phial from his pocket containing French chalk. He very carefully sprinkled some of the white powder on the edge of the frame, then blew it gently away. But some of the chalk still adhered in the shape of two clear fingerprints.

"I am going to ask you not to touch the picture until a photograph has been taken of those fingerprints, Mr. Osburn," said Blake. "My assistant will see to that matter at once. Is that quite agreeable to you?"

"Quite, Mr. Blake! I will take care that it is not disturbed."

"Thank you!" said the detective. "I will expect you to ring me about four o'clock."

"I shall not forget, Mr. Blake."

A moment later Blake and his assistant were standing in the street once more.

"You go straight away and fetch the photographer, Tinker," said Blake. He paused abruptly and stood gazing intently across the road.

"That's dashed funny," he muttered, and grabbed his assistant by the arm. "Tinker," he said quickly, "follow that woman in the musquash coat. She's just disappearing round the corner. I'll attend to the photographer. Quick!"

He watched his assistant dash across the road and turn the corner, then began to walk slowly up Charing Cross Road. His mind was full of puzzling thoughts. Who was this woman in the musquash coat? Why was she following him about?

But was she following him about? He had certainly seen her twice that morning; and in each case his suspicions had been aroused. But after all it might be simply a coincidence; perhaps he was rather inclined to exaggerate a mere trifle. However, Tinker would soon find out if there were anything wrong.

At that moment a 'bus passed, going in Blake's direction. He sprang nimbly into the road, gripped the rail at the rear, and clambered inside.

Chapter 4
The Interrupted Message

EVEN Sexton Blake's habitual calm seemed to have forsaken him. He rose somewhat unsteadily to his feet, and his face was clouded with a look of incredible amazement. He held in his hand the photograph of the fingerprints on the Murillo painting and stared down at it as if he had seen a ghost.

"Holy Jupiter!" he muttered. "The fingerprints of Granite Grant!"

He picked up the glass again and minutely examined the proof, then compared it with a specimen that he had taken from his files.

There was no getting away from the fact. They were the fingerprints of Granite Grant, the famous King's Spy. Granite Grant had been in the Veuxpillo Galleries last night; he must have been there for those fingerprints to have got on that frame. He had been there when this crime had been committed. His fingers were stained with blood.

Was it possible that he had killed this unknown man?

For some reason Blake's mind revolted from the thought. Yet the evidence was clear. They were Granite Grant's fingerprints right enough; there was not the slightest doubt about that.

But what did it all mean? Blake was so astounded that it was some time before he could get his brain to work clearly.

He began striding up and down the room with his hands behind his back, and his brow wrinkled in thought. One thing was now certain. It was not merely a case of robbery; that could not be the motive of the crime. This latest discovery had proved that conclusively.

If Granite Grant was mixed up in this affair, then something vitally affecting the interests of the country must be at stake.

The King's Spy did not concern himself with the doings of art swindlers; such small fry were quite beneath his notice. He went in for the big scoops—the intrigues that affected nations.

The telephone pealed forth at that moment and put a stop to the detective's meditations. He went swiftly to his desk and put the receiver to his ear.

"Hallo!" he called.

"Is that you, Mr. Blake?" asked a voice. "Osburn, of Charing Cross Road."

"Oh, yes, Mr. Osburn! And what's the verdict?"

"The picture's an absolute fake, Mr. Blake. There's not the slightest doubt about it. Sorry I didn't ring up before, but I've been rather busy this afternoon."

"That's all right, Mr. Osburn. And so it's merely a clever imitation?"

"Exactly! I was sure of it directly I removed the varnish. But to make doubly certain I scraped some of the pigment into a test-tube, and made a chemical test. It was as clear as a pikestaff; the thing has been painted from a photograph—and quite recently, too."

"Thanks very much, Mr. Osburn. That's a very important discovery. I'll send round for the picture directly my assistant comes in."

"But it's gone, Mr. Blake. Only just been taken away; Mr. Mayn came himself from the Veuxpillo Galleries to fetch it. I understood from him that you had sent him along."

"Really! As a matter of fact I didn't. But if Mr. Mayn came himself, I suppose it's quite all right."

"Well, good-bye, Mr. Blake; I've got an appointment."

"Good-bye!" said Blake, and replaced the receiver.

He stood thoughtfully stroking his chin. What did the art dealer mean? He had not given any instructions to Mr. Mayn to fetch the picture. He must have made a mistake. But, after all, it didn't matter very much. If Mr. Mayn had come for it himself there was nothing to worry about.

His thoughts turned to Tinker. What on earth could have happened to him? Why hadn't he returned? He had not seen him since he had dashed across the road after the lady in the musquash coat. And that was about eleven o'clock. It was now nearly seven. It seemed rather strange that his assistant should be away all that time.

As the detective was puzzling over the matter he heard the sound of footsteps hurrying up the stone steps. Very likely this was Tinker, he thought. He would know in a moment or two exactly what had happened.

He heard the housekeeper answer the bell, and turned expectantly as his door was flung open. Then a look of startled surprise crossed his face.

"What in the name of Heaven are you doing here, Mr. Mayn?" he asked.

It was some moments before the manager could recover his breath. He had evidently been hurrying more than was good for him, and was panting heavily.

"The Murillo, Mr. Blake!" he gasped. "It's been stolen!"

The detective knitted his brows and eyed the other with faint bewilderment.

"Been stolen, Mr. Mayn!" he said. "But I do not quite understand. Pray compose yourself. Here take this chair!"

The manager sat down heavily in the chair. In a few moments he became more calm and collected.

"And now, Mr. Mayn," said the detective, "please tell me exactly what has happened."

"The picture has been stolen, Mr. Blake," reiterated the manager. "I was just crossing the pavement to the galleries when someone came up from behind, the picture was wrenched from my grasp, and before I could recover from my surprise the person had vanished."

"But what were you doing with the picture, Mr. Mayn?"

The manager looked at the detective in mild surprise.

"Doing with it, Mr. Blake!" he echoed. "But I had just brought it away from Mr. Osburn's in Charing Cross Road. You telephoned me——"

"But I didn't!" interrupted Blake.

The manager's bewilderment increased.

"You didn't telephone me, Mr. Blake!" he gasped. "Are you quite sure? It was only about an hour or so ago. I could have sworn it was your voice. Are you certain you didn't ask me to fetch the picture from Mr. Osburn's?"

"I can assure you on my solemn oath, Mr. Mayn, that I did no such thing. I was speaking to Mr. Osburn a few minutes before you arrived. He told me that you had just taken the picture away. I was quite surprised to hear it."

"But what is the meaning of it, Mr. Blake?"

The detective shook his head vaguely.

"It is extremely puzzling, Mr. Mayn," he said. "Of course, it was simply a trick on someone's part to get possession of the picture. But I must confess that I cannot understand the motive. You see, the picture is quite valueless—it is not worth the canvas on which it is painted."

"What, Mr. Blake! But the picture is a Murillo—a crude work, I admit! But it is worth a hundred guineas—or even more."

"It is not worth a hundred pence, Mr. Mayn. It is an imitation—a pure fake. I have it on the authority of Mr. Osburn."

"But this is absurd!" muttered the bewildered manager. "The picture was hung in the Paris Salon. There is not the slightest doubt that it is a genuine Murillo."

"The picture that was hung in the Salon may have been, Mr. Mayn. And so was the one that was hung in the Veuxpillo Galleries yesterday. But the one I took to Mr. Osburn this morning was a fake. It had been substituted for the genuine Murillo some time during the night."

"You astonish me, Mr. Blake. If Mr. Osburn says it was a fake then, of course, it must have been. That may throw some light on the dreadful tragedy that occurred in the south-room during the night."

"It certainly does," said Blake. "But it does not explain why you should have been robbed of the worthless imitation. I do not see what possible use that can be to anyone. Have you no idea who the thief was?"

"It all happened so suddenly, Mr. Blake. I was taken absolutely by surprise; and for the moment I was too flurried to think what had happened. When I turned there were only a few people in sight, and there was a lady just getting into a taxi———"

"Was she wearing one of those heavy fur coats—musquash I think they're called?" asked Blake hurriedly.

"Yes; she was, Mr. Blake. I only saw her for a moment; then the door was slammed behind her and the cab sped off and vanished round the corner."

"Ah, I thought so, Mr. Mayn. Then it is the same woman———"

"The same woman!" echoed the manager. "Then you know her?"

"No, I don't know her, Mr. Mayn. But I have seen her twice before today. Her movements aroused my suspicions. What her game is I can't think; but she seems to have a finger in this mystery."

"But what———"

The telephone-bell pealed forth again and cut short the manager's further statement.

"Who the deuce is that?" muttered Blake, grasping the receiver and placing it to his ear.

"Hallo! Are you there?" he called.

A familiar voice answered him, speaking in excited tones.

"Hallo, hallo! Is that you, guv'nor? I'm at Robespierre———"

The voice ceased abruptly, the sound of the receiver clattering to the table followed, then a sharp click as it was replaced on the hook.

Now thoroughly aroused Blake rattled the instrument violently.

"Hallo, hallo!" he shouted.

But there was no reply.

He kept shaking the lever savagely. After a few minutes the operator at the Exchange answered.

"Are you calling?" she asked.

"Yes, miss!" said Blake excitedly. "I have been cut off."

"What number, please?"

"But I do not know the number, miss!"

"Sorry they've rang off then," said the operator curtly.

With an angry exclamation the detective jammed the receiver back in its place.

What on earth did it all mean? Why had he been so suddenly cut off? What amazing adventure had befallen his young assistant?

For he had not the slightest doubt as to who had spoken to him from the other end of the wire; he had recognised the voice immediately; it was the voice of his young assistant, Tinker.

Chapter 5
Tinker on the Track

IT was Tinker's quick wit and his readiness to act on the spur of the moment that had made him such an invaluable assistant to his master. When Sexton Blake gave him the hurried instructions to follow the lady in the musquash coat, he did not stop to question his master's motives. If he had done so he might have lost sight of his quarry. Blake had told him to go, and so he hastened to do his master's bidding without further discussion.

He followed the strange woman up Shaftesbury Avenue, keeping about fifty yards behind, and watching her movements very carefully. Even Tinker's unsophisticated eyes could not help admiring her slender figure and the graceful manner in which she walked. Somehow there was something familiar about her which he could not quite understand. He could not help thinking that he had met her before somewhere or other.

He hurried his steps as he approached Piccadilly Circus; the street was becoming crowded, and he was afraid of losing sight of his quarry. Then he saw her suddenly disappear into the Tube station.

Tinker hastened in after her, procured a ticket at the slot-machine, and managed to scramble in the same lift just as the attendant was closing the gates.

The lift was crowded with people, and the lady was standing over the further side from Tinker. Once she turned her head in his direction; but he could not make out her features, the veil she was wearing partially obscured her face. He noted the flash of her dark eyes, however, and had a momentary feeling that she was aware of his presence.

Presently the lift stopped and the people crowded out. The lady caught a train on the Bakerloo line. Tinker got in the same compartment, but sat at the other end. He did not wish to make his presence too obtrusive.

His quarry got out at Waterloo and went upstairs to the South-Western station. Then Tinker saw her enter a public telephone-box. After a few minutes had elapsed she came out again and walked across to the booking-office.

His first impulse was to hurry over to the office and try to discover where she was going. But his natural caution suggested that his movements might then appear rather too obvious, and that by so doing he might give himself away.

As he stood there hesitating what to do next he saw the lady leave the booking-office and walk across to Number 4 platform. Tinker's ready wit immediately suggested a way out of the difficulty. From platform 4 the trains took a wide, circular route back to

Waterloo again. He would take a ticket to Teddington, which being the furthest station on the loop, would allow him to get out at any station on the route that he wished.

A moment later he was hurrying across to platform 4 with the ticket to Teddington in his pocket.

The lady in the musquash coat was some distance down the platform. Tinker did not attempt to approach her; he thought it best not to take any risks of betraying his purpose. When the train came into the station he watched her enter a first-class compartment, then clambered into a third-class one that was adjoining.

As the train stopped at each station Tinker kept a keen look-out for the woman in the musquash coat. But he did not see her among the passengers who alighted. Over half an hour passed like this; then at Hampton Wick he caught a glimpse of her as she went swiftly past his window.

He opened the door and sprang out. The woman was speaking to two men who had met her on the platform. They seemed to be listening intently to what she was saying; then they raised their hats, and, with a nod of her head, she left them and hurried through the barrier.

The two men passed Tinker as he walked quickly towards the gates. But he did not stop to pay much attention to them—he was too eager not to lose sight of the woman in the musquash coat.

When he got down to the street he saw that she had taken the road to the left. There were very few people about; the one or two passengers who had left the train were hurrying away, and the place was soon deserted.

It was necessary for him now to be very cautious; if the woman saw him following behind she was bound to have her suspicions aroused. He allowed her to have a good start, then took the same direction, keeping as near to the cover of the houses as possible.

Tinker was not very familiar with his surroundings, but he knew that they must be close to the river, and going towards it. At the end of the road the woman turned to the left again and disappeared. When Tinker reached the corner he saw her walking along about two hundred yards ahead. The name-plate, bore the words, "Robespierre Gardens."

On one side of the road were fields and allotments, and on the other side was a row of large detached houses, standing in their own grounds and evidently fronting on the river. Except for the woman he was following not a solitary person was in sight, and a great quietness seemed to brood around. Tinker crossed the road, and, keeping in the cover of the trees, continued shadowing the strange woman.

He had not gone more than about thirty yards when he suddenly heard the sound of hurrying footsteps behind him. He glanced quickly over his shoulder. Two men had just rounded the corner and were coming swiftly towards him. He knew immediately who they were; they were the two men to whom the woman had spoken at the station a little while before.

Feeling a little apprehensive Tinker slowed down and decided to let them get in front. They were close behind now—another moment, and they must pass by. Then he felt himself grabbed on either side and a hand was clapped over his mouth.

He struggled violently and succeeded in wrenching himself away. But his assailants were too strong for him. The next moment his legs were dragged from under him, the other man seized his wrists, and still struggling feebly he was being frog-marched along. A gate was opened, and they passed up a white gravelled path.

Tinker could have cried with vexation. He saw it all now; it was a trap that had been carefully set for him. He was a fool not to have suspected it before. The woman must have known she was being followed when she arrived at Waterloo. She had got on the telephone and asked these two confederates to meet her at the station. They had waited behind and watched to see if her suspicions were correct. Since he had left the station his movements had been spied on.

What a fool he was to have been so easily caught! Why hadn't he been a little more on his guard? However, it was no use his bemoaning the fact now; he must make the best of a bad job. He gave up trying to free himself—the odds were too heavy. Better to save his strength until an opportunity arose of effecting his escape. The two men carried their burden along the path that skirted the side of the house, and then went down a flight of steps at the rear. Tinker was lowered to the floor and released. A door clanged to behind him, a key turned in the lock, and all was silence.

Tinker climbed to his feet and glanced around. The room was in the basement, and only partially lit by a little grated window that was very high up and close to the ceiling. The floor was stone-flagged, the walls of solid brick, and the door heavy and studded with iron.

Evidently the place had once served as a pantry, for there were marks on the walls where shelves had been removed. But the place was now bare and destitute of furniture.

Tinker leant against the wall and began to think over his position. What did his captors mean to do with him? he wondered. Why had they brought him here—and what mysterious plot were they hatching?

They had not treated him with any great violence; in the scuffle they had not handled him more roughly than they could help. If they had wished they could have easily knocked him over the head, and none would have been the wiser.

They seemed more anxious to prevent his interfering with their plans than to wish to do him any injury. He had not the vaguest notion as to their identity, and from first to last neither of them had spoken a word. But somehow or other he must effect an escape. Blake would be wondering what had become of him. He began to inspect his surroundings, going round the room and carefully examining the walls and door. It did not take him long to discover how slender his chances of escape were; the room was too strongly built to offer any great hopes of getting away without some outside assistance.

He turned his attention to the window. It was too high up for him to reach and was heavily barred. Even if he could have wrenched the iron grating away he very much doubted if he could have squeezed himself through.

He sat down on the stone floor and gave himself up to silent meditation.

Chapter 6
"We Are Too Late!"

TINKER had guessed right in thinking he had fallen into a cunningly laid trap. As a matter of fact, the woman he was following had noticed him when he got into the lift at Piccadilly. At Waterloo she had immediately got on the telephone to her two friends, with the results already known.

After Tinker had been captured she began to retrace her steps, and a few minutes later entered the house where he had been taken. She let herself in with a latchkey, and crossed the wide, lofty hall to a room that overlooked the river.

There she removed her hat and veil, and stood gazing reflectively out of the window at the broad, sweeping lawn that reached down to the water.

Her face, which was very youthful, was also strikingly beautiful, for she was none other than Mademoiselle Julie, one of the cleverest agents of the French Secret Service.

This amazing woman was famous in Paris and in nearly every fashionable resort on the Continent for her beauty and wit and accomplishments; she was admitted to the most exclusive circles of select Society, and when she happened to be staying at her fine residence in Rue de Ravenne numerous admirers were constantly flocking to see her and to pay their respects.

Yet very few had any suspicion of the nature of the work that necessitated her sudden and frequent absences from Paris. She was thought to be passionately fond of travelling—that was all. But in the inner councils of secret diplomacy her name was mentioned with reserve, and her whereabouts treated with an atmosphere of mystery.

But because of her charm and beauty she was often able successfully to carry out the most difficult of enterprises, and her fearlessness and courage had won her the respect of those with whom she came into contact.

As she stood staring pensively in front of her, footsteps sounded in the hall outside, and the next moment the door opened and her two companions entered.

"Ah, Mademoiselle Julie!" said one of them in French, "we have got the youngster safely under lock and key. And now we will talk."

The young woman turned to him swiftly:

"You have not been too rough, Monsieur Maurice?" she asked.

The man laughed pleasantly.

"No," he said, we treated him very gently. But you seem very concerned about this youngster, mademoiselle."

Julie's dark eyes flashed resentfully.

"But he must not come to any harm," she insisted. "He is the assistant of Monsieur Blake, the great English detective. We can trust him implicitly."

"Trust no one, Julie!" said the man firmly. "You may be quite right, but we must take no risks. The matter is too important to take any notice of sentiment. For some reason or other you were being shadowed. We work too much in the dark to distinguish between friend and foe, and we do not want anyone prying round here just yet. It is not safe."

The man spoke with an air of authority. Evidently he held some high post in the service of his country, for his companion followed his words attentively, and kept silent. Mademoiselle Julie gave a little petulant toss of her head.

"Very well, monsieur," she said, "it shall be as you wish."

The man nodded approvingly.

"And now we will discuss the other matter, mademoiselle," he said, with a note of eagerness in his voice. "Have you found out what has happened to the picture?"

"Yes, monsieur; it was taken from the galleries this morning to a place in Charing Cross Road."

"Do you mean that it has been sold?" asked Maurice sharply.

"No, Monsieur Maurice; I do not think so."

"Then why has it been taken there?"

"Listen, monsieur, and I will tell you. Last night something happened in the Veuxpillo Galleries—a man was killed——"

"Killed, Julie! Good heavens! But who was he?"

"It was Gustave Fulk, the painter, monsieur," said Julie quietly.

Maurice drew in his breath quickly.

"Ah!" he muttered, "then it is as we thought: Gustave Fulk was a traitor—he sold himself to the enemies of his country."

"But he has paid the price, monsieur!"

"You are right, Mademoiselle Julie! Yet I do not quite understand. How is it that this Gustave Fulk was killed and what was he doing here?"

"I cannot answer your questions, monsieur," said Julie. "But it is clear that Gustave Fulk knew of the whereabouts of the stolen cipher. When it was discovered that the document had been stolen from the Foreign Office suspicion immediately fell on Kalib Pasha, the Turk. He was followed to the house of Gustave Fulk, and a search was made. But nothing of an incriminating nature was found."

Her companion was silent for a moment. A look of perplexity had come into his face.

"I cannot understand what has happened, Julie," he said presently. "But we are sure now that the cipher was glued to the back of the Murillo. That is why we could not find it when we made our search. Somehow, we must gain possession of the painting—and quickly, too."

"The English police evidently suspect something, monsieur," said Julie. "Sexton Blake has taken the picture to an art expert named Charles Osburn."

"They will spoil everything!" rapped out Maurice sharply. "They are trying to find out who killed Gustave Fulk. And it does not matter to us. We are playing a bigger game. Soon everything will be in the papers, and we do not want that to happen. Somehow, we must get hold of the picture—there is no time to lose."

A thoughtful expression came into Mademoiselle Julie's face. She began twisting her glove in her delicate fingers while her companions watched her anxiously. Presently she looked up.

"You will leave it to me, Monsieur Maurice," she said quietly. "Somehow, we will get hold of the picture before it is too late. I will go now, and I will take Bervais with me. He may be useful."

A look of relief swept across Maurice's face. He held out his hand impulsively.

"It is well, mademoiselle," he said. "I know you will not fail. Bervais will go with you, and I will stay here until you return or send me some message. It is quite clear?"

The young woman nodded her head.

"Quite clear" she said. "You may rely on me monsieur."

Half an hour or so later Mademoiselle Julie and her companion, Bervais, were in the train on their way to Waterloo again.

For a considerable time after they had gone Maurice prowled restlessly up and down the room. He was plainly ill at ease and very anxious as to the outcome of the venture on which Julie had embarked.

Presently he became more composed, and, sitting down at a writing-table in the corner, took out a bundle of letters from his pocket and went carefully through them. Then he began to write industriously, making frequent references to the letters at his elbow.

Whatever his task was, he was evidently absorbed in it to the exclusion of everything else; he did not pause again until the waning light told him that the afternoon was drawing to a close. Then he glanced at the clock, and rose abruptly to his feet.

Carefully putting the papers away in his pocket, he crossed the hall and entered a little room on the opposite side. On a bracket in the corner stood a telephone; on the other side was a dresser containing a few kitchen utensils, and nearby was fitted a gas-ring. A table stood in the centre, and three or four chairs. The window was heavily barred.

Maurice switched on the electric light and took a loaf of bread, some butter, and a tea pot from the dresser. For some minutes he busied himself with the gas-ring. Presently a sudden thought seemed to occur to him; he gave vent to a muttered exclamation.

"Quite forgotten the youngster!" he murmured.

He took a shiny little automatic from his pocket and went swiftly down into the basement.

All the afternoon Tinker had been making strenuous efforts to escape from his prison. But his struggles had been in vain. Somehow or other he had managed to climb up to the little grated window; but the iron bars were too firmly fixed for him to move them.

It was when he had sunk to the floor exhausted and in despair that the sound of the bolts being withdrawn from the door made him start to his feet with renewed hope.

He peered anxiously into the stranger's face as the door was pushed open, and although it was nearly dark, recognised him as one of the men he had seen at the station that morning.

His first instinct was to make a dash for liberty. But the weapon in the other's hand had him well covered, and he decided it was better to bide his time.

"Hungry?" asked Maurice, in a pleasant tone of voice. "Come this way. But do not try any tricks. We do not wish you any harm, but I shall fire if you attempt to escape!"

He stood aside and allowed Tinker to pass in front. Together they went along a stone-flagged corridor and up a flight of steps into the hall.

"The door on your right!" said Maurice curtly from behind. And Tinker had no alternative but to obey.

Still facing his prisoner, Maurice locked the door behind him and motioned Tinker into a chair.

"Now," he said with a dry smile, "there is not much to eat, but you are welcome to what there is. Remember that I am armed, and shall not hesitate to fire if necessary."

Tinker did not think it was necessary to reply to this threat. He was ravenously hungry; the loaf of bread and the butter seemed priceless luxuries to him in his present state. He set to work with a will, and did not pause until his keenest pangs of hunger were somewhat appeased. His companion joined him in his meal, but did not offer any further comment.

Presently Tinker began to take an interest in his surroundings. His first thought was of the window; he took a swift glance over his shoulder at it. There was no chance of escape that way, even if the opportunity arose; it was too heavily barred for that. There only remained the door which led out into the hall. He might make a dash for it there if the chance offered.

He wondered if there was anybody else in the house. There did not seem to be; although he listened carefully, no other sounds smote on his ears. He glanced across at his companion; he was sitting at the other end of the table, and the pistol lay in front of him, just within his grasp. Tinker decided that the supreme moment had not yet arrived.

Five minutes or more passed in silence. Tinker was getting in a state of nervous tension; he could not stand it much longer; he must make his dash soon, or else it might be too late. And at that moment the front door shut with a slam, and hurried footsteps sounded outside in the hall.

His companion sprang to his feet, hesitated a moment, then hastened to the door.

"I'm only just outside," he said, with a threatening gesture. "Keep where you are."

The door shut behind him, and the key was turned in the lock. Tinker sat listening intently for a moment or two. The footsteps crossed the hall, and then the sound of voices followed.

This was his chance; it was a case of now or never. He crept to the door and tried the handle. It was securely fastened, and he dare not attempt to force it—his enemies were too near for him to risk making a noise. Then he turned his attention to the window again; but a very brief examination told him how hopeless that was.

Tinker felt his chances slipping by; somehow, he must get away. Then his glance rested on the telephone standing on the bracket in the further corner.

In a moment he had sped across the room and had snatched the receiver from its hook. Although it only occupied a few seconds, it seemed an interminable time to Tinker before the operator at the exchange answered. He gave Blake's number in a voice that shook with excitement.

"Quick, please, miss!" he said. "It's urgent."

It seemed as if he would never get through in time; each second seemed more like an hour to his excited imagination. Then his master's familiar voice spoke at the other end of the wire, and Tinker gave a sigh of overwhelming relief.

"Hallo, hallo!" he said, in suppressed tones. "Is that you, guv'nor? I'm at Robespierre——"

But he got no further in his brief statement. The door was suddenly flung open, a hand grasped him roughly by the collar and dragged him away, and the receiver dropped from his fingers.

Struggling violently, he was grasped by the hands and feet and carried downstairs into the basement. A moment later he found himself back again in the little stone-flagged room, with the door securely fastened behind him.

Tinker nearly wept with despair and mortification. To have been so near to telling Blake of his whereabouts and then to have been beaten at the last moment was almost more than he could stand.

He flung himself at the door, and raved and shouted in a paroxysm of anger, bruising his hands in a futile effort to drag it open.

Presently his rage subsided, and he commenced to ponder over his position. How much had Blake heard? Had he been able to give his master the name of the road before he had been torn from the instrument? He knew that the name was just on the tip of his tongue, but whether Blake had heard or not he could not say.

But his master would know something was wrong. Tinker wondered what he was thinking at that moment. Blake would not leave a stone unturned to discover his whereabouts; Tinker was sure of that. Perhaps already he was hurrying to come to his assistance! But what could he do? How could he find him when he had no idea where he was?

Tinker leant against the wall, a prey to gloomy thoughts. At that moment he felt the bitterness of defeat more than he had ever done before. It was pitch dark inside the room now: only a little square luminous patch showed high up on the wall where the window was placed.

A feeling of great loneliness came over the youngster; he was too tired to make any further effort to get out of his prison, and he knew it would have been quite useless if he had. He remained where he was, hoping against hope that something would happen to render his escape possible.

Meanwhile, the two men had hastened upstairs to the room that overlooked the river. Mademoiselle Julie was standing by the table, on which lay the painting that had hung in the Veuxpillo Galleries that morning, and which Blake had subsequently taken to Mr. Charles Osburn in Charing Cross Road.

Maurice's face was flushed with excitement, and he did not attempt to conceal his satisfaction.

"It is an excellent piece of work, mademoiselle," he exclaimed. "I congratulate you on your cleverness."

He turned the picture over and scrutinised the back, while his two companions watched him in silence. Presently he looked up with a shade of perplexity on his face.

"It is strange," he muttered. "The document was supposed to be glued to the back of the canvas."

He turned the picture over in his hands and eyed it suspiciously, then took up a clasp-knife and began making little cuts all over the canvas. The look of perplexity on his face deepened, and a stern look crept into his eyes. He laid the picture down at length, and drew in his breath sharply.

"We are too late," he said, and his voice shook with anxiety; "the cipher is not here. This picture has been tampered with. See, the varnish has been cleaned off the surface and some of the pigment scraped away."

A moment of intense silence followed the man's remark; the three of them stood casting glances at one another as if this discovery had taken them wholly by surprise. Then Maurice suddenly became galvanised into action.

"Quick!" he said: "there is no time to waste! Somehow Kalib Pasha has managed to get hold of the cipher. The position is serious. I must return to Paris immediately. You will get instructions from me tomorrow, mademoiselle. Now we will catch the next train to London; we will discuss our plans as we go along.

As Monsieur Maurice was speaking in short, authoritative accents he was cutting the portrait from the wooden frame. He rolled the canvas up and put it in his attaché-case, then put on his hat and coat.

"Do not stop for anything," he said quickly. "Everything now depends on speed."

Evidently his companions had nothing to stop for. They were used to these rapid changes; it was all in the day's work as far as they were concerned. A moment later they joined Maurice in the hall, and, without further talk the three of them left the house.

As they were just stepping into the street Mademoiselle Julie caught hold of her companion's arm.

"How about the boy, monsieur?" she asked quickly.

Maurice stopped abruptly, then, shrugging his shoulders, continued on his way.

"I had forgotten," he said. "But it does not matter. Tomorrow we will send somebody to release him. We will take no risks now, his chatter might interfere with our plans."

Julie seemed about to remonstrate, but evidently thought better of it, for she did not refer to the matter again. When the train came into the station they chose an empty first-class carriage, and passed the time up to town in earnest conversation.

Chapter 7
Pedro Lends a Hand

FOR some minutes after he had heard Tinker's voice on the telephone Sexton Blake stood with a puzzled frown on his face. For the life of him, he could not think what to do. His young assistant was in trouble somewhere; something extraordinary must have happened for him to have been cut off so abruptly: and yet he had no way of going to his assistance.

He knew it was no unusual event to be cut off on the telephone in the midst of a conversation; the same thing had happened to him many times before, much to his annoyance.

Yet this was different. Tinker had been forcibly dragged away from the instrument; he was sure of that; he had heard the receiver hit against something as it dropped from his fingers.

What could it possibly mean? Tinker was being detained somewhere against his will; he had managed to get through on the telephone to let Blake know where he was; then at the last moment he had been discovered.

The detective felt a sudden thrill of anxiety; somehow, he must find out where his young assistant was confined, and go to his rescue. That now was the uppermost thought in Blake's mind.

What had Tinker said? "I'm at Robespierre——" Yes, that was the place he had mentioned—Robespierre something! It suddenly occurred to the detective that he might find some such name in the Directory.

He turned to the manager, who had not spoken since the telephone-bell had rung out.

"Excuse me, Mr. Mayn!" he said. "I have been called up about some matter of importance."

Blake took down the directory and began to search through it. Eventually he found what he was looking for in the Suburban part; the place was named "Robespierre Gardens," and was situated up the river, near Teddington.

He closed the Directory with a sharp snap.

"I shall have to hurry away, Mr. Mayn," he said. "Some urgent business has suddenly demanded my attention. Perhaps you will give me your private address, then, if I wish to see you before tomorrow, I shall know where I can find you."

"Very well, Mr. Blake," said the manager; "here is my card. In any case I shall expect to see you in the morning. The whole business is worrying me to death. I rely absolutely on you."

"Try to dismiss the matter from your mind, Mr. Mayn. You may depend on me to see the thing through. And now I must wish you good-night."

The detective ushered his visitor out with some haste. Directly he was gone he opened the back door.

"Pedro, Pedro!" he called softly.

The dog gave a joyful whimper in answer to his master, and came bounding into the room.

The detective stooped down and patted the animal's great head.

"Got a job for you, Pedro!" he said.

The bloodhound's intelligent eyes rested on his master's face, and his ears pricked up expectantly. Blake gave an appreciative chuckle.

"Not much you don't understand of the King's English, old dog!" he muttered. "Where's Tinker, boy?"

The dog began to grow restless, and ran round the room, whimpering softly. Then he sank back on his haunches in front of his master, and stared up in his face with a wistful expression.

Blake put the animal on the lead, opened the door, and stepped out into the street. At the further end of Baker Street he picked up a taxi.

"To Teddington!" he said. "Double fare!"

Blake leant back in his seat as the cab began to thread its way through the busy London streets and gave himself up to his own thoughts. Pedro placed his paws on the window-ledge, and, hanging his great head over the side, gazed with mild curiosity at the passers-by.

The cab soon shook off the more crowded thoroughfares and sped along silently and swiftly through the night. Immersed in a brown study, the detective forgot all about the passing of time.

He was going over all the details of this strange case; it was one of the most baffling mysteries that had ever taxed his ingenuity. He could not quite get a grip of the affair yet, but he did not doubt that he would unravel the problem before many more hours had passed.

"What part of Teddington do you want, sir?"

Blake sat up with a start. The cab had slowed up; he had got to his destination long before he had expected.

He poked his head out of the window.

"Ask the way to Robespierre Gardens," he said, "and drop me just before you get there."

"Right you are, sir," said the man.

He climbed down from his seat and crossed the road. A few seconds later he came back again.

"'Tain't far now!" he said.

The cab went on again slowly for about ten minutes. Then it stopped.

"It's about a hundred yards further on down the road, sir," said the driver. "Just on the right; you can't miss it."

Pedro did not wait for the door to be opened, but clambered through the window. The detective stepped out after him and paid the fare.

"Good-night!" he said.

"Good night! Thank you, sir!" said the man.

Blake called the dog in a low voice. The animal came obediently to his side. He slipped the lead on his collar, and then made his way slowly down the road.

The place was wrapt in silence and very dimly lit. Once the detective caught sight of the river shining through a gap in the trees. This occasioned him some surprise, for he did not know he was so near.

Presently he came to a turning on the right. On the river side a row of large detached houses loomed up in the darkness: the right side of the road had not been built on. A line of wooden palings edged the pavement. Blake peered at the name-plate that was fixed at the corner; in white letters were painted the words "Robespierre Gardens."

He stared across at the gaunt-looking houses with a feeling of curiosity. Had he come to the right place? Was his young assistant shut up in one of these? At any rate, he would see what Pedro could do: if Tinker had been here the dog might possibly pick up his scent.

Blake crossed the road, and then stooped down to the dog and held his great head in his hands.

"Pedro, old fellow," he said, "we're after Tinker—Tinker; find him, boy!"

The bloodhound seemed to know exactly what his master said. He cast a swift look of understanding up at Blake, then struggled to get away. The detective let go of the dog's collar, but still held tightly to the lead. With Pedro straining eagerly a yard or so in front, he made his way slowly along the pavement.

Blake did not underestimate the task he was setting the faithful animal. Even if Tinker had passed down the road a short time before, it would have been no easy matter to pick up his scent. Some hours, however, must have elapsed since his assistant came this way, if, indeed, he had come here at all—and under those circumstances the task seemed almost impossible.

But he had great faith in Pedro. The dog possessed an amazing sense of smell, and some of the feats he had performed in tracking down criminals had seemed well-nigh incredible. If there was the slightest possibility of picking up the scent, Pedro would not fail.

They had gone some distance down the road by this time. The animal did not seem to take much interest in the business; he trotted on in front with his head held high and his ears back.

Blake was just beginning to think that he was on a wild-goose chase, when the bloodhound sank his head to the ground, and began sniffing suspiciously.

They were just outside a large house. Blake glanced up at the windows. The place was in total darkness; not a ray of light showed from any part of the building.

"What is it, Pedro?" he asked sharply.

The dog lifted his head momentarily at the sound of his master's voice, then sank his nose to the ground again. He seemed now to be thoroughly excited, and the hair along his back was bristling in a thin line. For a few moments he sniffed a few yards up and down, then began to move slowly up the road.

Still holding the lead, Blake followed after the animal. He was somewhat puzzled by Pedro's manner; it was strange that he should have picked up the scent so abruptly, and have then moved away down the road. Was this really Tinker's scent that he was following? And, if so, where was he taking him to?

The dog was now slowing down; he seemed to have difficulty in going any further. Presently he stopped altogether and nosed eagerly around. Then, with a soft whimper, he began to retrace his steps. As they approached the house he grew more impatient, but he came to a halt where he had previously picked up the scent, and seemed plainly disconcerted.

For the space of a minute or two the detective was as puzzled as the bloodhound. The scent evidently stopped abruptly here. If Tinker had been this way, then he must have suddenly vanished at this spot. At first he could not think what had happened. The dog was plainly excited, and his eyes were blazing with anger.

Then an explanation suddenly flashed across Blake's mind. Tinker must have been set upon here and taken by surprise. His assailants had picked him up and carried him off somewhere. That would explain why the scent had so abruptly finished. He had been carried into one of these houses; it was from one of them that Tinker had telephoned to him.

He took a swift glance around. A telephone-post stood a few yards away, and the wire ran straight across to the roof of this very house. It did not take Blake long to make up his mind. He pushed open the gate, and, with Pedro close on his heels, crept up the gravel path to the front door. At the top of the steps he stood listening for a moment or two. Not a sound came to his ears to disturb the silence. He knelt down and placed his eye to the keyhole, but he could see nothing; the place was in darkness.

It suddenly occurred to him that he had arrived too late. No doubt Tinker had been caught at the telephone, and taken from the house before help could arrive.

Spurred on by this thought, Blake abandoned his usual precaution. He took a bunch of skeleton-keys from his pocket and fumbled with the lock. In a moment the door swung open and he stepped inside.

He closed the door gently behind him, and stood listening intently, but, save the panting of the bloodhound, there was not the slightest sound. Then he took out his pocket-torch, found the electric switch on the wall, and flooded the hall with light.

The spacious hall was somewhat tastefully furnished; a thick Axminster rug covered the floor. At the further end a door stood half open. Blake went quietly across, and, entering the room, switched on the light. Then he gave a quick intake of breath, and stood staring in surprise at the table.

On it was lying a faded gilt frame. He knew in an instant that it was the frame of the faked Murillo that had been stolen from Mr. Mayn, an hour or so before. But the painting was now gone. It had been cut out with a knife; the frayed canvas still adhered to the inside edge.

Feeling more mystified than ever, the detective glanced curiously round the room. Then the low growl of Pedro came to his ears. He hurried out into the hall again; the dog was sniffing suspiciously at a door on the left and scraping at it with his great paws. Blake tried the handle; it yielded to his grasp, and Pedro sprang inside.

Wondering why the dog was so excited, Blake peered about the room. The light from the hall was sufficient to see everything clearly. In the centre stood a table on which were the remains of a meal; evidently someone had been there quite recently.

Pedro was over in the corner nosing around in the same excited manner. Then Blake saw the telephone on a bracket just above.

Then this was the room from which Tinker had telephoned! There could be no doubt about that; it explained why Pedro was so excited. But where was Tinker now? What had happened to him after he had been dragged away from the instrument?

Pedro was now making for the door again. The dog seemed pleased and his tail wagged joyfully. Blake followed him across the hall and then down into the basement. They went along a stone-flagged corridor, the detective sending a thin beam of light ahead from his flash-lamp.

Outside a door on the left the bloodhound suddenly stopped, took one or two deep sniffs, and then began to scrape furiously with his paws. Blake pushed back the rusty bolts and swung open the heavy door.

In the circle of light from his torch Tinker's white face stared out at him with mingled surprise and joy.

Chapter 8
The Mysterious Message

THE detective was the first to find his voice.

"By Jove, Tinker!" he said, "I thought I should be too late."

Tinker caressed the great dog as it bounded joyfully about him. For a few seconds he seemed to have lost the power of speech.

"Golly, guv'nor," he said at last, "it seems too good to be true. I was just settling myself for the night in this beastly hole."

Blake gave a dry smile.

"Well, you'll have to deny yourself that pleasure, Tinker," he said. "But let's get out of here; we'll talk the matter over upstairs."

Nothing loth to get away from his unpleasant surroundings, Tinker followed his master along the corridor and went up the flight of steps that led into the hall. Blake walked over to the front door and put the chain up.

"Doesn't seem to be anyone at home, Tinker," he said; "but we'll be on the safe side. That'll give us a chance to get away if we're disturbed. Come into this room here, and I'll switch off the light in the hall."

They passed into the room that overlooked the river. Blake had now put Pedro on the lead. The dog seemed satisfied at having found Tinker, and lay quietly down on the carpet at his master's feet.

"Now, Tinker, be as brief as you like! Tell me just what happened."

"That's soon told, guv'nor," said Tinker, and proceeded to give his master an account of what had happened from the time when he had left him in Charing Cross Road up to the telephone episode.

Blake listened in silence until he had finished, but he was evidently not a little surprised and perplexed by Tinker's adventures.

"You did not see the woman in the musquash coat enter this house, then, Tinker?" he asked.

"No, I didn't, guv'nor. But it was evidently a put-up job."

Blake nodded his head thoughtfully.

"Yes, you're right there, Tinker," he said. "But it seems a very queer business. Several things have happened today while you've been away. For one thing, the picture we took along to Mr. Osburn this morning has been stolen."

"Stolen, guv'nor!"

"Yes, and brought to this house. The frame is lying on the table over there."

Tinker stared in astonishment in the direction of Blake's finger.

"But what does it mean, guv'nor?" he sked. "If that's the frame, then where's the painting?"

"It has been cut out, Tinker: you can see that for yourself. But, listen! The picture I took to Mr. Osburn this morning was a fake, as I thought; it had been substituted over-night for the genuine thing."

"Then why should this one have been stolen, guv'nor?"

"It was snatched from Mr. Mayn's grasp by the woman in the musquash coat, Tinker. And apparently she did not know that the picture was a fake; she thought she had hold of the genuine thing."

"But I can't quite get the hang of it, guv'nor! Why are all those people after that picture? Is it worth a lot of money?"

"No, not much, Tinker; about a hundred guineas!"

"That's not much to make all this fuss about, guv'nor."

"It's not, Tinker; but I've come to the conclusion that something was concealed in the original picture that certain people would stick at nothing to get hold of."

"What on earth makes you think that, guv'nor?"

Blake walked across to the table and picked up the frame.

"Do you see those two smudges on the edge there, Tinker?" he asked, pointing with his finger.

"I see them, guv'nor!"

"Well, those happen to be the fingerprints of Granite Grant."

"Granite Grant!" echoed Tinker. "The King's Spy!"

"Exactly, Tinker! The marks are bloodstained. Granite Grant must have been in the Veuxpillo Galleries last night when this man met his death—or immediately after."

"But do you think he killed him, guv'nor?"

"I do not know what to think, Tinker. But the fact that Granite Grant is connected with the crime convinces me that there is more in it than meets the eye. Grant plays for big stakes, and he's not mixed up in this affair merely for the sake of amusement."

Tinker looked decidedly bothered and bewildered.

"Well, I leave it to you, guv'nor," he said. "It's just got me beaten. I can't understand how you make head or tail out of these things."

Blake shook his head doubtfully.

"I'm almost as stumped as you are, Tinker," he said. "However, we'll get away from this place as soon as possible. But I'll just have a look round first, although I don't think I shall discover much."

Blake's latter remark proved quite correct; although they went over the whole house, nothing was found to throw any light on the identity of the present occupants.

The house was furnished throughout with an air of quiet luxury, but, apart from the heavy, costly furniture, there were no small articles and ornaments of any value.

Strangely enough, although there were a number of bedrooms upstairs, yet not one of them contained a bed. In this respect they were all incomplete, just as if they were dummy rooms.

"It's quite evident, Tinker," said Blake as they crossed the hall again to the room they were in at first, "that no one sleeps here. It's one of those silent houses that are used very occasionally by people on secret business from the Continent; a sort of recognised meeting-place in case of emergency."

"But couldn't you find out who owns it, guv'nor?"

"I expect you could, Tinker, after a great deal of trouble. But, you'd get no further then. The owner would be a somewhat retiring sort of gentleman who spent most of his time abroad on account of ill-health. His London agent would know very little about him, and would be inclined to tell you less. And that's about all the satisfaction you'd get."

"Well, I'm jolly glad you turned up, guv'nor. Goodness knows how long I should have been stuck in that cellar if you hadn't: I expect I should have been starved to death."

Blake's face clouded resentfully.

"Yes," he said; "that was a low-down trick. It would have been impossible to have escaped from that hole without assistance from outside. I should like to make someone suffer for that. At any rate, we'll get away from here now."

He stopped abruptly just as he was moving towards the door, and stood looking at the little writing-table that stood over in the corner. Then he went quickly over to it and picked up the blotting-pad that lay on the top.

The paper was scored with ink marks made by Monsieur Maurice a few hours before. Blake's keen eyes saw at a glance that they had been made quite recently. If the blotting-pad was anything to go by, then someone had sat at that table this afternoon and written a number of letters.

Tinker watched Blake closely as he held the blotting-pad in his hand and carefully scrutinised it. He knew his master too well to ask any questions until he had finished, but he felt instinctively that something important was to happen. It was like Blake to make some fresh discovery just at the last moment.

Blake presently walked over to the mirror that hung above the mantelpiece, and held the blotting-pad up in front so that he could see its reflection in the glass. He turned it about several times and stood surveying it with contracted brows, then, without taking his eyes off the mirror, he spoke to Tinker.

"Got a pencil and paper on you, Tinker?" he asked quietly.

"Yes, guv'nor!"

"Then copy this down as I read it out."

He began to spell out very slowly various words and phrases, sometimes asking Tinker to erase one, and then going back and repeating himself.

It was no easy task on which Blake was engaged. The centre of the pad resembled a huge blot of ink more than anything else; it was only round the sides that the marks could be recognised as writing. The letters were so jumbled together as to be almost unintelligible, and with the exception of one letter in English, the writing was in French.

But the detective was not easily defeated, and after much stumbling he managed to read out quite a number of words and phrases which Tinker took down.

He came to a pause at length and took the paper from Tinker's fingers. For some five minutes he studied it in silence, making various jottings on the margin of the paper. Then he copied something out on a separate piece of paper and handed it to his assistant.

"What do you make of that, Tinker?" he asked.

"With growing perplexity Tinker stared at the following unintelligible jumble of letters and words:

"…with fai . He a ked or We ter XXI, oreig Se vi e, and ga e he e-wo d 'Twe ty fat o s eep and t ent le gus a ay.' Hi o fici nu ber is f fty fi It is im or an to eme b r sha…"

Tinker smoothed back his hair with a bewildered expression.

"Is this a Chinese puzzle, guv'nor?" he asked blankly.

"Looks like it, Tinker," said Blake, with a low chuckle. "Now, I'm going to see if I can make sense of it."

He picked up the pencil again and began to fill in letters every here and there. Over some of the words he brooded for quite a long time, and it was only after several repeated efforts that he succeeded in discovering the missing letters.

Finally he wrote the whole message out again and handed it to Tinker.

"Can you make anything of it now, Tinker?" he asked.

Tinker stared at the paper again. Written down in Blake's clear hand was the following message:

"…without fail. He asked for Western XXI, Foreign Service, and gave the keyword 'Twenty fathoms deep and twenty leagues away.' His official number is fifty-five. It is important to remember that…"

"It's certainly readable now, guv'nor," said Tinker, after a moment's pause. "But it simply gets me stiff how you manage to find out all that. What are you going to do now? After all, it doesn't seem to convey much."

Blake did not answer. He was still gazing at the message, and there was a curious glint of suppressed excitement in his eyes. Then he suddenly jumped to his feet.

"By Jove!" he exclaimed. "I'll try it!"

"Try what, guv'nor?" asked Tinker, more bewildered than ever.

"Where's the telephone, Tinker? In the next room, isn't it?"

"Yes, but——"

"Don't stand there arguing, Tinker," said Blake. "Come on, this way——"

Followed by his astonished assistant the detective hurried across the hall to the room where the telephone was installed. Snatching the receiver from its hook he placed it to his ear and waited impatiently.

"Western XXI, please, miss!" he said presently.

After waiting for about half a minute a voice said:

"Western XXI!"

"I want Foreign Service," said Blake.

The familiar sound of a switch being plugged in followed, then a man spoke in sharp, crisp tones:

"This is Foreign Service," he said.

The moment had arrived for Blake to try the effect of his chance shot. His reply came firmly and without a moment's hesitation.

"Twenty fathoms deep and twenty leagues away!" he said.

"What number?" asked the voice immediately.

"Number fifty-five!" said Blake.

"Hold on!" said the voice curtly.

Blake experienced a strange thrill of excitement. His quick brain had immediately grasped the significance of the message which he had so cleverly deciphered.

On the spur of the moment he had decided to put his conclusions to the test; but the results so far had been quite beyond his expectations. He waited anxiously now to see what would happen. A moment later the voice at the other end of the wire spoke again.

"Hello, fifty-five! The chief will see you tomorrow morning at half-past eleven. Is that clear?"

"Where?" asked the detective quickly.

"At thirteen, Kursan Place!" said the voice.

Before Blake could make any further remark a click sounded in his ear as the receiver at the other end was replaced on its hook.

Blake's pulses were now beating quickly as he turned to Tinker:

"I'm in it now with both feet, Tinker," he said.

Tinker had a feeling that he was a little beyond his depth. His head was in a turmoil, Blake seemed to be playing with black magic.

"I don't know what you're getting at, guv'nor," he said. "I don't even know what has happened. If you'd only begin at the beginning and explain it slowly I might be able to understand what the game is."

Blake could not help laughing at his young assistant's bewilderment. He put his hand kindly on the youngster's shoulder.

"But I'm almost as mystified as you are, Tinker," he said. "So how can I explain? However, I'll tell you as much as I can. You heard what I said on the 'phone just now?"

Tinker nodded his head.

"Well," continued the detective, "I've not the slightest notion as to who was speaking at the other end of the wire, but I've arranged to meet the chief at eleven-thirty tomorrow morning at number thirteen, Kursan Place."

"The chief, guv'nor!" echoed Tinker. "Who on earth is the chief?"

"Goodness only knows, Tinker! I don't!"

"But are you going there, guv'nor?"

"I certainly am, Tinker. The chances are that I shall put my foot in it with a vengeance. But that doesn't matter; the chief will have a nasty shock, whoever he is."

"But haven't you got a ghost of an idea what it's all about, guv'nor?"

"Not much, Tinker! We seem to have blundered into a veritable hornet's nest of secret-service activities—I'm sure of that. But I'm bothered to know what it all means. That picture by Murillo is at the bottom of the whole mysterious business—that's pretty evident. But what the mystery is goodness alone knows."

"Perhaps you'll be able to find out tomorrow morning, guv'nor, when you keep this strange appointment."

"Perhaps I shall, Tinker! At any rate, I shall either find out or be slung out—one or the other. However, we've been here quite long enough; we'll get back to Baker Street, if you're quite ready. And we'll take this frame along with us. It may come in useful yet."

With Pedro on the lead Blake and his assistant opened the front door and stepped outside. When they had traversed the narrow gravel path that led down to the street Tinker immediately turned to the left.

"Which way are you going, Tinker?" asked Blake sharply.

"This is the way to the station, guv'nor," said Tinker.

"Is that the way you came, Tinker?"

"That's right, guv'nor!"

"Ah," said the detective. "That rather explains why Pedro didn't pick up your scent until he got to the house. I was rather puzzled about it at the time. You see, we came from the other direction."

Nothing else happened on their way to the station. It was now getting late and very few people were abroad. From Waterloo they took a taxi to Baker Street, and, feeling somewhat tired after their day's exertions the detective and his assistant soon retired to bed.

Chapter 9
Frenton is Suspicious

SEXTON BLAKE had another surprise next morning. While having breakfast he briefly scanned the morning papers, as was his usual custom. It was the following item of news in the "stop-press" column that caught his eye:

"ART DEALER'S SHOP BROKEN INTO.

"A mysterious raid occurred late last night on some premises in Charing Cross Road. Full details are lacking."

Blake did not have to think twice to realise the significance of this brief item of news. Although no name was mentioned he knew immediately that the premises referred to were those of Mr. Charles Osburn, the art expert.

This, then, was another knot in the extraordinary web of intrigue which he had set himself to unravel. He might have expected some such thing to have happened; yet he could not help feeling perplexed at this latest development of the mystery.

That this raid on the art dealer's shop was in some way connected with the mystery that surrounded that Murillo he had not the slightest doubt. But why had Mr. Osburn's shop been raided? What were these unknown marauders searching for?

He was sure of one thing. The person or persons who had stolen the faked Murillo from Mr. Mayn earlier on in the day had also been responsible for this latest affray in the Charing Cross Road. And if that were the case, then they must have discovered that the painting in their possession was a fraud.

But even then it did not explain everything. Why should they raid Mr. Osburn's shop? What were they searching for? Did they expect to find the genuine Murillo? Surely they did not think that Mr. Osburn had both copies in his possession!

These problems occupied the detective's mind while he finished his breakfast, and during that time he did some intensive thinking. When he at last pushed back, his plate and rose to his feet he had got a fairly workable idea of the nature of the task before him.

The genuine Murillo must have contained some important secret—he could not think what it was, but very likely it was a document of some sort and certain people would go to any risk to get hold of it.

The fake had been stolen under the impression that it was the original, and when it was discovered that the document—or whatever it was—was missing, suspicion had fallen on Mr. Osburn, and his premises had been broken into and a search made.

The next thing was to put his theory to the test. He would go along to the art dealer and find out if anything was missing from the shop. If nothing had been stolen, then it pointed to the fact that the marauders had gone away disappointed.

The detective turned to his assistant.

"I'm going along to Charing Cross Road, Tinker," he said. "Perhaps you'd better come with me!"

"I'm ready, guv'nor," said Tinker.

They left the house together and took the Tube to Leicester Square. As they approached the art dealer's shop Blake saw that the place was shut up; but the shop was exciting little interest from passers-by; evidently the brief item of news in the stop-press column had attracted little attention.

The door was opened to the detective by Mr. Osburn himself.

"Ah, Mr. Blake," he said, "I was expecting you. And what have you to say for yourself?"

The detective cast a swift look of surprise at the art expert, feeling somewhat puzzled by his manner.

"I don't quite follow you, Mr. Osburn," he said.

The art expert laughed a little nervously.

"Come into my private office, Mr. Blake," he said, "We can talk the matter over quietly there."

"And now," said the detective, when the three of them were seated in the comfortable saddle-bag chairs, "I'll put the same question to you, Mr. Osburn. What have you to say for yourself?"

Mr. Osburn looked a trifle disconcerted.

"But it's up to you to explain, Mr. Blake!" he said. "You telephoned me last night——"

"I telephoned you, Mr. Osburn?"

"Yes—— At least, I thought it was you."

"At what time?"

"About half-past ten."

"As a matter of fact, I didn't, Mr. Osburn," said Blake quietly. "However, go on!"

"Well, Mr. Blake, at the time I thought it was you, but after what happened I certainly had my suspicions."

"And what did happen, Mr. Osburn?"

"I'm just telling you. I was 'phoned up at my private address about ten-thirty. I didn't answer the telephone myself; the maid took down the message and handed it to me. It was an urgent request to meet you here at eleven o'clock."

"And what happened then?"

"Well, I thought it was rather funny, I must confess. But I was taken off my guard somewhat. That business about the faked Murillo made me think that something serious had happened. So I came along."

Blake nodded his head appreciatively and the art expert continued.

"I arrived here about ten minutes past eleven and looked around for you. A policeman was just strolling past, and when he saw me he stopped and said, 'Mr. Blake says he won't be a moment, sir; he's just gone up the road.'"

"Really!" said Blake, in surprise. "And did you know the policeman, Mr. Osburn?"

"Certainly, I did, Mr. Blake! That's just what took me in so completely. I've tackled the fellow since; he is quite innocent. A man did come up to him a few minutes before I arrived, told him he had promised to meet me here and asked him to give me that message."

"But the policeman must have known it wasn't me."

"Yes, but you're not the only person who has a right to the name of Blake. Mind you this, he didn't say Mr. Sexton Blake. The policeman might have smelt a rat if he had."

"Just so, Mr. Osburn! It was a cunning piece of work; it not only took you off your guard but also made everything right with the police."

"Exactly, Mr. Blake! Feeling quite unsuspicious I unlocked the shop and came inside; in fact I didn't even trouble to lock the door behind me. I went upstairs and told the caretaker not to worry, and came down again. The next moment I was grabbed from behind, thrown on my face, and bound and gagged before, I could collect my scattered wits or even realise what was happening."

Blake whistled softly.

"That's one of the cutest things I've ever come across," he said.

"A bit too cute for my liking, Mr. Blake," said the art expert somewhat ruefully. "However, to finish the story, they searched my pockets as if they were expecting to find something valuable. Then they took my bunch of keys and thoroughly ransacked my office upside down. All this time I was lying on the floor helpless; I couldn't even see who they were. They had thrown the table cover over my head."

"There were more than one, Mr. Osburn?"

"Yes: two or three, I think; but I don't know exactly. At any rate, after continuing their search for about half an hour they quietly left the shop. Fortunately for me the housekeeper came down about ten minutes later to ask me if I'd like a cup of tea; if it were not for that, I should have lain here until this morning."

"What time was that?"

"About twelve o'clock, Mr. Blake."

"And has anything been stolen?"

"That's the most extraordinary part about the whole strange business, Mr. Blake. I've checked everything and not a single item is missing. Goodness knows what they expected to find. But at all events, they didn't find it. What do you make of it, Mr. Blake?"

The detective did not answer. To him the matter was not so inexplicable as it was to Mr. Osburn; but he had no intention of telling the art dealer of his suspicions.

It was as he thought. The story fitted in with the theory that had been forming in his mind. The original Murillo had held some secret, and on the night of the crime at the Veuxpillo Galleries the fake had been substituted. These unknown persons, who had raided Mr. Osburn's premises, had for some reason suspected him of having the secret in his possession.

"You have communicated with the police, of course, Mr. Osburn?" he said at length.

"Immediately, Mr. Blake! They were here last night. Inspector Frenton of Scotland Yard has been asking a number of questions, He was very surprised when I told him what happened yesterday and seemed rather anxious to see you. I understood that he was going to call on you early this morning."

"I expect I left just before he arrived then," said Blake. "But did you know that the picture was stolen from Mr. Mayn after he left here yesterday?"

"Yes; Mr. Mayn rang me up and told me all about it. That was what seemed to surprise Inspector Frenton so much; he was frightfully excited when I told him."

A ghost of a smile flitted across the detective's face. As he turned to his assistant, who had been closely following the conversation, there was a suspicious twinkle in his eyes.

"I can just imagine Frenton getting excited, can't you, Tinker?" he said. "No doubt he thinks he's brought off a big scoop."

Tinker nodded his head.

"I bet he does, guv'nor," he said. "He'll be chasing clues like a donkey with a carrot stuck in front of his nose."

Blake laughed heartily at his young assistant's humorous remark, and at that moment footsteps sounded outside, the door was flung open, and the subject of their conversation burst into the room.

"Ah!" he exclaimed, puffing breathlessly and mopping his perspiring brow. "You're the very man I'm looking for, Mr. Blake."

Blake winked his eye at Tinker.

"I hope, inspector," he said innocently, "you haven't come to tell me that anything I say will be used as evidence against me."

Inspector Frenton's face went the colour of beetroot.

"Come, come, Mr. Blake!" he said hastily. "You're only joking now."

The detective's features resumed their habitual calm again.

"Well, a joke's a joke, Inspector!" he said. "And now we will try to be serious for a little while. We're all just thirsting to hear your explanation of what has happened, so fire away, inspector!"

Inspector Frenton snorted violently and cast a feverish eye at each member of his audience in turn.

"Explanation!" he stammered. "That's coming it a bit too thick! I think it's up to you to do the explaining, Mr. Blake."

"But you can do it so much better than I, inspector! To tell you the truth, I'm absolutely stumped."

The Scotland Yard man assumed a business-like attitude and took his note-book out of his pocket.

"Very well, then, Mr. Blake!" he said deliberately. "But before I start explaining I should like to ask you a few questions."

"Let's have them, inspector! Don't mind me!"

"First of all then, Mr. Blake, I should like to know why you rang up Mr. Osburn last night about half-past ten and arranged to meet him here?"

Blake was too highly amused at the inspector's pompous manner to make any reply, but the art expert broke in quickly:

"That's all right, inspector," he said. "It wasn't Mr. Blake who rang me up at all; it was a clever trick on somebody's part to catch me napping."

Frenton looked rather disconcerted at this remark; but it was evident that he was in no wise convinced. Certain ideas had formed themselves in his mind and it would take a lot to shake him from them.

"Then I suppose you didn't ring up Mr. Mayn and ask him to take that picture away from here yesterday afternoon," he said. "That was another trick, I suppose."

Blake was getting just a little bit ruffled by the inspector's affected manner. He answered him rather sharply.

"You are right again, inspector," he said. "I congratulate you on your smartness and ingenuity."

Inspector Frenton waved his hand airily.

"That's all very well, Mr. Blake," he said, "but I should like to know why that picture was brought here yesterday from the Veuxpillo Galleries. I have reason to believe that it has some bearing on the crime that took place there on Tuesday night."

"I congratulate you again, inspector," said Blake. "As for my reasons for bringing the picture here, they are quite obvious to Mr. Mayn, Mr. Osburn, and myself. I don't mind in the least letting you into the secret; we wished Mr. Osburn to examine it and give us his expert advice as to its value."

"Just so, Mr. Blake. The picture was worth a lot of money. On Tuesday night an attempt was made to steal it, and that is how that fellow got killed. But it should never have been taken from the Galleries; I had the matter well in hand, and if it had been left to me all this would not have happened—the picture would not have been stolen."

Blake stifled a yawn; he was getting a little weary of the discussion.

"So you've found out everything, inspector," he said. "You've solved this mysterious crime that took place on Tuesday night!"

"I don't say that there's nothing else to be explained, Mr. Blake. But I know more than you think, and before very long I hope to make an arrest. At any rate, there'll be some rather awkward questions for a certain person to answer."

The detective took out his watch; it was nearly five minutes past eleven. Suddenly he remembered the strange appointment he had with the "Chief" at 13, Kursan Place. He had promised to be there at half-past eleven; he only had twenty-five minutes left to get there.

"You must excuse me," he said, hurriedly getting up from the chair. "I must hurry away to keep an appointment."

He glanced at the Scotland Yard man. Frenton was eyeing him with distrust and suspicion. It suddenly occurred to Blake that he had been ragging him rather severely; perhaps he had rather overdone it!

"Well, good-morning, inspector!" he said, holding out his hand in a friendly manner. "Perhaps I shall see you later on; then you may have cleared up the mystery."

But the inspector stuck his hands in his pockets and pretended not to see Blake's outstretched hand.

"I shall clear it up, Mr. Blake," he said. "You can bet your life on that!"

Without a word Blake turned on his heel and left the shop.

He was not a little puzzled by Frenton's manner. The detective was on very good terms with the Yard, and was great friends with most of the officials there. But Frenton had evidently "got his goat out" about something: Blake felt rather sorry for pulling his leg as he had done.

"I'm afraid Frenton's rather sick with me, Tinker," he said, when they were outside once more.

"You certainly seemed to rub him up the wrong way, guv'nor!" said Tinker.

Blake looked thoughtful for a moment.

"Well, we won't worry about him," he said. "I'm going on to Kurson Place now. I don't suppose I shall be away long, and I shall expect to find you at Baker Street when I get back. I dare say I shall have something interesting to tell you."

"Right-ho, guv'nor! I wish I were coming with you. I shall be anxiously awaiting you to know what has happened."

A moment later Blake left his assistant to climb on a passing 'bus. He was still feeling rather puzzled over the inspector's strange manner. Why had Frenton regarded him with such suspicion? What on earth could the man be thinking of?

He glanced at a passing clock; it was now nearly a quarter past eleven. Blake forgot all about Frenton, and the art dealer, and everything else in the excitement of his approaching mysterious appointment.

Later on, however, he was to have a startling explanation of the queer thoughts that were passing through Inspector Frenton's ponderous brain.

Chapter 10
"Return to Paris!"

ABOUT the same time that the foregoing events were being enacted, the beautiful Mademoiselle Julie was seated in the lounge of a West End hotel.

In spite of her strenuous duties, and the fact that she had been able to snatch only a few hours' sleep—for it was her quick and resourceful mind that had planned the raid on the art dealer's shop—yet she showed no signs of fatigue.

Mademoiselle Julie was one of those women who live on excitement and adventure; her natural charm and beauty required no artificial aids to support them, and she seemed always to be aglow with health and vigour.

She was wearing a plain costume of blue serge, which, although it was not elaborate of itself, did not conceal her slender figure and the grace of her movements.

The rings, which so often glittered on her white fingers, were no longer there; she had taken them off as if she wished to avoid attracting attention. Julie was expecting to make one of her quick journeys abroad again, and she was dressed for the occasion. As she sat sipping her coffee, her dark eyes flashed impatiently every now and then towards the big glass doors, and an expectant look came into her face every time someone entered.

But an hour or more elapsed before the person arrived whom she awaited with such impatience. Then Bervais appeared at the door, glanced swiftly round the lounge, and came towards her.

She motioned him into the opposite chair, and they began to talk in low, earnest tones across the little wicker table. Now that Monsieur Maurice was no longer present, Bervais seemed more at ease, but he still treated Mademoiselle Julie with the respect due to a superior.

"Then you have been over to Robespierre Gardens, Bervais?" asked the young woman.

The man nodded his head.

"I have come straight from there, mademoiselle," he said.

"And you have released the boy?"

"He was not there, mademoiselle," said Bervais. "He must have escaped during the night."

Mademoiselle Julie uttered a little exclamation of surprise, but she did not seem to regard the information as of much consequence.

"It does not matter," she said, shrugging her shoulders. "It was too bad to keep the poor boy locked up there all night. If it had not been for Monsieur Maurice I should never have permitted it."

Bervais smiled somewhat drily.

"Sometimes you are very sympathetic, mademoiselle," he said, "and sometimes——"

He waved his hand airily and left the sentence unfinished.

The young woman took him up sharply.

"And sometimes I have a heart of stone. Is it not so, Bervais?" she asked, with a flicker of amusement in her dark eyes.

"It is, mademoiselle," he said, "since you say so!"

"But I do not forget my friends, Bervais," Julie continued quickly. "And Monsieur Blake, the big, cold Englishman, he is my friend. This boy, who followed me yesterday, is his assistant. He is called Tinker. I did not like to shut Tinker in that nasty, dark place."

A sudden thought seemed to strike her. She laughed softly to herself, took a sheet of notepaper from the papeterie, tore off the address, then commenced to write a message in block letters.

Her companion regarded her with silent curiosity. This slender, charming young woman was a puzzle to him. He occupied one of the minor positions in the diplomatic service; Mademoiselle Julie, on the other hand, moved in the inner circles of the profession: she was known to be in the direct confidence of that mysterious figure who planned and schemed and pulled the strings from behind the scenes but who never showed himself.

He sat watching her as she addressed an envelope and stuck it down, and wondered all the while that this young and beautiful woman could possibly possess those qualities of courage and daring that had raised her so high in her profession.

He waited until she had, finished, then picked up the thread of their conversation where it had been broken off a few minutes previously.

"In our profession, mademoiselle," he said quietly, "it is sometimes better to have no friends."

The young woman pursed her lips, and a frown showed on her white forehead.

"You are saying exactly what Monsieur Maurice has said, Bervais," she replied. "But he means right—and so do you. If I had not known that better than you both I should have asked Monsieur Blake to come and see me."

"It was wise not to," said Bervais. "Blake is trying to discover who killed Gustave Fulk. That does not matter to us: but we do not want to be dragged into inquests and post-mortems and such things. We must avoid those by every means in our power."

A moment's silence followed. Then Bevais asked abruptly:

"Was not the frame of the Murillo left in that room overlooking the river?"

"It was, Bervais!"

"Then it has gone, mademoiselle. I thought the boy could not have escaped by himself; some other person must have entered the house last night and taken the frame away after opening the door of the cellar."

But Julie did not seem to be very much impressed by this piece of news.

"The frame is quite useless, Bervais," she said: "and we shall not go back to the house again. It will change hands through the usual channels. And now, tell me about Monsieur Maurice; has he left yet?"

Bervais nodded an affirmative.

"Yes," he said; "he flew over from Hounslow early this morning."

"Then he should be in Paris by now?"

"Some hours ago, mademoiselle!"

"In that case, Bervais, his message should arrive soon. I think it will tell us to return. The cipher has left the country; I am sure of that. Our men will know what has become of Kalib Pasha, and he is the man we should carefully watch."

"Was Monsieur Maurice to communicate with you here, mademoiselle?" asked Bervais.

"Yes, that was our arrangement," said the woman.

"Then perhaps it has already arrived?"

"I do not think so, Bervais. I have told the maître d'hôtel that a message would arrive for me, and he has promised to let me know immediately."

"He may have forgotten, mademoiselle," said Bervais. "What name did you give?"

"It will be addressed to Madame Duvain."

"Then I will go out into the vestibule and make inquiries, mademoiselle!"

Bervais got up from his chair and crossed over to the doors. He was not gone many minutes before he reappeared again. In his hand he held a buff-coloured envelope.

Julie held out her hand eagerly.

"Then it was there all the time, Bervais?" she said, with a gesture of displeasure.

"It had but just arrived, mademoiselle," said Bervais.

Julie tore the envelope across and took out the slip of paper. It was the cablegram from Monsieur Maurice that she had been expecting. The message was brief, and would have conveyed nothing to the ordinary person; but to Mademoiselle Julie, who knew the code, it had quite a different meaning to that openly expressed.

She read it in silence, then glanced quickly at her companion.

"It is just as I thought, Bervais," she said. "Tonight we must be in Paris."

She got up from her seat without further discussion, and together they left the lounge.

Chapter 11
"House Number Thirteen"

IT wanted about two minutes to the half hour when Sexton Blake turned the corner into the quiet and select neighbourhood in which Kursan Place was situated.

He glanced up at the numbers on his right, then noticed that they were even, and crossed the road. The houses were tall and stately, and of the Hanoverian style; there was an air of quiet dignity about them, and they gave the impression of being owned by well-to-do people, who kept them as town residences for use during a few months of the year only.

The detective could not repress a tremor of excitement as he strode along the pavement and drew nearer and nearer to Number 13. There was an atmosphere of mystery and uncertainty about his approaching appointment which appealed to his adventurous disposition; even the number of the house suggested something sinister and fascinating.

He wondered what would happen to him when he got inside. But would he get inside? Perhaps their suspicions had been aroused by this time; perhaps they had discovered since that he was an impostor!

In that case he might meet with a warm reception. His hand went almost unconsciously to his hip-pocket, and his fingers closed reassuringly over his trusty little automatic.

"Who was the 'Chief'?" he asked himself for the hundredth time. But he could find no reasonable answer to the question. The whole extraordinary business was an enigma; it was mystery from start to finish. Blake was baffled to know what to think.

About half-way down the road the detective suddenly stopped and stood for a moment silently looking up at the house in front of him. On the fan-light over the door was painted in white letters the number 13.

Blake's pause was sufficient only to assure himself of the number; it was not his way to hesitate at the last moment; he had already made up his mind and decided on his line of action. He opened the gate, walked quickly up the tiled pathway, and gave a sharp rat-tat at the knocker.

Almost immediately the door was opened by a man in brass buttons. He stood aside, and, without making any remark, seemed to expect his visitor to enter. The detective stepped inside, and the door closed quietly behind him.

One of Blake's mottoes was, "When in doubt, say nothing!" He acted on it now. He found himself standing in a wide, gloomy hall, which was partitioned off from the further part of the house by a green baize door. On the right was another door. The commissionaire opened it, and, silently motioning the detective inside, closed it behind him.

Blake's keen eyes took in his surroundings at a glance. The room was furnished plainly, like an office; a table, some leather chairs, a few shelves, on which rested one or two financial journals, were all that it contained. The blinds were half drawn, and the room was as gloomy and depressing as the hall.

The detective suddenly experienced the unpleasant sensation that someone else was in the room besides himself. He glanced round sharply, and found himself face to face with a suave-looking man in black, who had entered so quietly as to have made no noise.

For a moment Blake felt just a little taken back: he stared at the stranger suspiciously and sized him up. The man inclined his head as if in acknowledgment, and returned Blake's stare with a look of mute inquiry.

The silence became rather strained; suddenly it occurred to the detective that the man was waiting for him to speak. It was a critical moment; instinctively Blake felt that the fate of his enterprise hung in the balance, that everything depended on his saying precisely the right thing.

A swift process of reasoning went on in his mind; his hesitation was only momentary, then with lightning speed he had reached a decision.

"Twenty fathoms deep and twenty leagues away!" he said, in cold, deliberate tones.

The man before him betrayed not the slightest emotion; but Blake felt intuitively that he had said the right thing. Then for the first time the stranger spoke.

"And your number?" he asked, in a quiet, dispassionate voice.

"Number fifty-five!" came the quick response.

Without a word the man turned on his heel and left the room.

Blake felt a little thrill of triumph. His faculties had not played him false he felt sure of that; his instincts had led him aright. He had risen to the occasion through his usual cleverness and ingenuity. Whatever happened now, he had passed the first critical test.

At that moment the door opened and the suave-looking man reappeared.

"The Chief will see you now," he said. "Follow me, please!"

He led the way outside and crossed the hall, with the detective following close on his heels. They passed through the green baize door, which shut to behind them of its own accord.

Blake's keen eyes noticed that the house was immediately transformed. An air of great munificence seemed to pervade the place, in direct contrast to the bare hall and ante-room that he had just left; a thick pile carpet covered the floor, on which their feet made no noise, and in the centre of the embossed ceiling was a dome of coloured glass, which threw a soft, subdued light over the well-appointed vestibule.

The detective noticed all these things in a few swift seconds. He found himself wondering who this man was in the black coat: there was a quiet air of authority about him, as if he were a well-trained servant occupying a rather important position.

There was something impressive and solemn about the place. It seemed to go by clockwork. Blake had the strange feeling that he was surrounded by some hidden organisation which was controlling and directing a secret, but all-powerful machine.

Then he found himself following his guide up a wide, curving staircase, covered by the same thick pile carpet. Presently the man stopped at a door facing them, knocked gently, then turned the handle and motioned Blake inside. The door closed softly behind him.

A short, stout man in a black frock-coat was standing over the other side of the room staring out of the window. At Blake's entry he turned swiftly and took a step forward. The next moment he gave a startled exclamation, and a look of utter astonishment swept over his face.

The surprise was mutual; even the detective's imperturbable face lost for a moment its habitual calm and self-assurance. Then almost simultaneously, the words dropped from their lips:

"Sexton Blake!"

"Sir Vrymer Fane!"

Chapter 12
The "Chief" Explains Things

AFTER their first quick exclamations the two men regarded each other in a dead silence for the space of half a minute.

Blake's mind was working swiftly. The significance of his position was now clear to him; in a flash the mystery of No. 13, Kursan Place, was explained.

He had wondered who the "Chief" could possibly be. Now he knew. The "Chief" stood before him. It was Sir Vrymer Fane, the great head of the British Secret Service, the Minister to whom the tangled skein of European politics was nothing but a game of chess, and who fingered his pieces with such consummate skill and cunning.

He had blundered right into one of the hidden cloisters of the British Secret Service. He knew that he had gained admittance by a pure accident; that without the chance discovery of the secret countersign he would never have been able to have penetrated this jealously-guarded sanctum.

It was Sir Vrymer Fane who broke the strained silence; and behind his obvious bewilderment there was a faint note of displeasure.

"What is the meaning of this, Mr. Blake?" he asked in a quiet, cold voice.

There were not many men who would have dared to beard Sir Vrymer Fane in his own secret den: the Minister was held in profound awe and commanded such immense respect that casually provoking his anger was unthinkable.

But Blake did not feel in the least dismayed. Now that he had got thus far he was determined to see the matter through; the somewhat peculiar and embarrassing position in which he was placed rather appealed to his venturesome nature.

"The meaning of my presence here, Sir Vrymer," he said deliberately, "is not quite clear to me; I think that perhaps you may be able to disclose that. But I can certainly explain to you how I came here."

The Minister darted a searching look at his cool visitor. He was evidently somewhat impressed by Blake's calmness, but his bewilderment seemed to increase.

"How you came here, Mr. Blake!" he echoed. "Then by all means explain; for it's quite beyond my comprehension."

"And yet the explanation is very simple, Sir Vrymer. I caught a 'bus to Marble Arch and walked the rest of the way."

Sir Vrymer Fane staggered back as if he had received a blow; his face flushed crimson, and he seemed like having an apoplectic fit. For a moment or two he struggled with a whirl of emotions, then his sense of humour got the better of his anger, and he bit his lip to prevent himself from laughing.

"Upon my soul, Mr. Blake," he said, with his mouth twitching suspiciously, "you're about the coolest customer I've ever met. You blunder into this house of secrecy as if it were a barber's shop, and when I ask you how you got here you calmly tell me that you caught a 'bus and walked the rest of the way."

He still felt constrained to laugh, and turned his back on the detective to hide his face. Then he swung round again with a grave and serious expression.

"How did you know I was here, Mr. Blake?" he asked.

"I did not know you were here, Sir Vrymer."

"Then why did you come here?"

"To see the Chief, Sir Vrymer!"

"But I am the chief!"

"I did not know that, Sir Vrymer."

The Minister seemed more perplexed than ever; his face was a study in bewilderment.

"But what is the object of your visit, Mr. Blake?" he asked.

"I came here to keep an appointment," replied the detective.

"To keep an appointment, Mr. Blake! Tell me, who let you in?"

"The commissionaire at the door."

"Yes, but didn't you see anyone else—my private secretary?"

"I saw a gentleman dressed in black, Sir Vrymer. It may have been your secretary.

The Minister seemed to hesitate a moment as if carefully framing his words.

"What did you say to him?" he asked.

"I said: "Twenty fathoms deep, and twenty leagues away.'

Sir Vrymer Fane drew in his breath sharply.

"Then you knew the countersign!" he muttered, and his face was troubled and anxious. "Did you say anything else? Did you give a number?"

"I gave the number fifty-five, Sir Vrymer."

The Minister had got beyond feeling surprised now; if the detective had suddenly turned into an elephant it would not have added to his confusion.

"Then it was you, Mr. Blake, who rang up Western XX1 last night?" he asked.

Blake nodded an affirmative.

"It was," he said. "And may I ask whom you expected it to be, Sir Vrymer?"

"You seem to know so much, Mr. Blake that I shall not be taking any risk if I answer your question. I thought the man who rang up Western XX1 last night would be the man I should meet here this morning at half-past eleven; that is, number fifty-five. And number fifty-five is Granite Grant."

Blake had got himself well in hand now; he had recovered from the first surprise of this unexpected meeting. When he had discovered that strange message on the blotting-pad at Robespierre Gardens it had been due merely to a sudden impulse on his part that he had 'phoned up Western XX1.

Yet his impulse had led him right; fifty-five was Granite Grant's official number, and Grant had been in the Veuxpillo Galleries on the night of the crime.

"That is a very interesting piece of news, sir," he said. "Strangely enough, Granite Grant is the very man I am most anxious to meet."

"You are, Mr. Blake! And for what reason, pray?"

"To ask him what he was doing in the Veuxpillo Galleries on Tuesday night, when a certain man was stabbed to death."

Sir Vrymer Fane passed his fingers through his hair with great agitation. He seemed to be getting more and more confused.

"You have got me completely muddled, Mr. Blake," he said. "Let us start at the beginning. You mentioned this crime at the Veuxpillo Galleries. Of course, I have heard about it; but what has Granite Grant to do with it? What are you doing here? What the dickens does it all mean?"

He waved his hand about in despair, then sank down in a chair.

"Sit down!" he said. "Sit down and tell me all about it. I don't know whether I'm on my head or my feet."

The detective sat down as he was requested, then began again.

"You know what happened on Tuesday night, sir, and I will not go over the details again. There are certain facts of the case, however, which are known only to me and one or two other people. One is that on the night of the crime a certain picture in the South-room was tampered with."

"Tampered with, Mr. Blake! In what way?"

"The painting was taken from its frame and a fake substituted, sir."

"Really, Mr. Blake! Then the crime was concerned with robbery? The painting was worth a great deal of money?"

"You are wrong there, Sir Vrymer; the painting was worth very little compared with other old masters. In fact, it was worth about one hundred guineas."

"Then why was the fake substituted, Mr. Blake?"

"I can only guess at the answer to your question," said the detective, "but I think I can make a very shrewd guess. The picture was valued not for itself, but for the secret it contained; and there are certain people who will stick at nothing to gain possession of that secret."

The minister leant suddenly forward; his hands were trembling a little as he gripped the arms of his chair, and his face was grave and set.

"One moment, Mr. Blake!" he said quietly. "You say this picture contained some secret. Why do you connect Granite Grant's name with the crime?"

"Because, Sir Vrymer, I discovered two blood-stained fingerprints on the frame of the picture. And they were the fingerprints of Granite Grant."

Sir Vrymer Fane rose to his feet and walked to and fro for some moments to hide his agitation. When he turned to the detective he had almost regained his composure.

"Mr. Blake," he said slowly, "I apologise if I were discourteous a short while ago; I was so astonished at seeing you here. That has still to be explained. But you have stumbled on something of the utmost importance. From what you tell me I have not the slightest doubt that on this picture was concealed the secret cipher which was stolen last week from our Embassy in Paris."

"Ah," exclaimed Blake, "now I begin to see things more clearly! But will you give me your reasons for that statement, sir? It may explain several points that still baffle me."

"Certainly I will! Immediately we learnt of the loss of the cipher we placed the matter in the hands of Granite Grant. He went over to Paris immediately. Two days later I had a communication from him to the effect that the cipher had been stolen by a man named Gustave Fulk, a painter who had been employed at the Embassy on some job or other."

"And you have not heard from Grant since?"

"Not a word, Mr. Blake!"

"Did he speak to you on the telephone, Sir Vrymer?"

"Yes, he did! But he did not say where he was."

"What day was that, sir?"

"On Tuesday—the day of the crime!"

"We are unravelling the problem bit by bit, sir. The man, who was killed in the Veux-pillo Galleries on Tuesday must have been Gustave Fulk; his handkerchief was marked with the letters G. F. Evidently Granite Grant followed him across from Paris that day. He must have 'phoned you directly he arrived at Dover."

The minister nodded his head, and Blake continued.

"That brings me to another point. How did you know it was Granite Grant speaking? Did he give his name?"

"No!"

"Then he used the counter-sign and gave his number—fifty-five?"

"That is so, Mr. Blake. But how on earth did you know that?"

"When Granite Grant 'phoned you up, Sir Vrymer, he must have been spied on by someone; perhaps he spoke from a public telephone box. At any rate, part of his conversation was overheard. While following up this mysterious crime I came across a blotting-pad containing a portion of a letter. The statement that aroused my interest was: 'He asked for Western XX1, Foreign Service, and gave the key-word twenty fathoms deep, and twenty leagues away. His official number is fifty-five.'"

"Then that explains how you came here—you acted on the information contained in that letter?"

"Just so, Sir Vrymer!"

"You are a clever man, Mr. Blake. I was startled when I saw you enter. The real meaning of this house is an absolute secret. When I come here I always enter by the back; and it is only used when we suspect that our movements are being watched. The counter-sign must be changed immediately."

"You have heard nothing further from Granite Grant since Tuesday then, Sir Vrymer?"

"Nothing at all, Mr. Blake. I am puzzled to know what has become of him."

"Do you understand the significance of those fingerprints, sir?"

The minister looked at the detective with narrowed eyes.

"I do," he muttered. "They rather point to the fact that Granite Grant killed Gustave Fulk."

"That is certainly the obvious explanation, sir. But we do not know all the facts yet; there may be another explanation."

"There may be," agreed Sir Vrymer. "But I am not concerned so much with that. If Granite Grant killed this man he did it in self-defence—I am sure of that. What is troubling me is the present whereabouts of Grant and this secret cipher."

"That is the thing which is baffling me," said Blake. "If Grant did kill Gustave Fulk, what has happened to the picture? If Grant has it, he would have reported to you directly—would he not?"

"Certainly he would, Mr. Blake!"

Blake was silent for a few moments. There was a missing link somewhere; if he could only discover it the solution of this baffling problem would be within his grasp.

"Do you know if this man, Gustave Fulk, was acting for anybody, Sir Vrymer?" he asked presently. "What was his object in stealing the secret cipher?"

"I will tell you, Mr. Blake. Just before the loss of this cipher was discovered a highly confidential communication was sent us by our Paris Embassy. The communication reached London after being strangely delayed on route; and we have reason to suspect that during that time the envelope was opened and a copy made of the contents."

"May I ask what was the nature of that communication, Sir Vrymer?"

The minister hesitated a moment before replying.

"I trust you implicitly, Mr. Blake," he said, "therefore I will answer your question. I have not forgotten the important services you were able to render me on another occasion. The communication contained the text of the Anglo-French agreement on the Turkish question."

"And it was in code?"

"It was in code, Mr. Blake; but the stolen cipher is a key to the code, and anyone having it would be able to read the agreement."

"You say the communication was highly confidential, sir?"

"So highly confidential, Mr. Blake, that we must prevent its disclosure at all costs. The position is fraught with anxieties; if a premature disclosure of the agreement were made it would possibly lead to grave international complications."

"You say it was the text of the Anglo-French Agreement on the Turkish question, Sir Vrymer. In that case, would not the Turkish Government be prepared to pay a big price to gain possession of this stolen cipher?"

"Precisely, Mr. Blake! I may tell you that we suspect a certain Turkish official named Kalib Pasha, who came over for the Peace Conference, of being concerned in making a copy of the Agreement."

"And do you know his present whereabouts?"

Sir Vrymer shook his head.

"Unfortunately we have lost trace of him," he said.

"One other question, Sir Vrymer. The French authorities are naturally acquainted with all that has happened; it will be to their interests, as well as ours, to regain possession of the stolen cipher."

"Naturally, Mr. Blake!"

"And are you aware of what efforts they are making towards its recovery?"

"No; their Secret Service works as silently as ours, and they would not inform me of its movements. Of course, directly they recovered the cipher they would advise me of that fact. But why do you ask?"

"For several reasons, Sir Vrymer. One is, that the faked copy of the picture was stolen yesterday, and it has just occurred to me that the French Secret Service might be responsible."

The two men lapsed into silence again. The minister's face was grave and anxious; he watched the detective narrowly, as if he hoped he might suddenly solve the problems that were agitating him.

But Blake's face was cold and impassive; if he had any startling explanation of the mystery that confronted them he gave no indication of the fact. Only by the thoughtful look in his grey penetrating eyes did he show that his quick mind was busy sifting out the evidence before him. Presently he got up from his chair.

"Then, if there is nothing else, Sir Vrymer," he said, "I will ask leave to depart."

"And what are you going to do, Mr. Blake?"

The question was asked with forced indifference; but the anxiety behind the minister's words did not escape Blake's keen observation.

"A tragedy occurred in the Veuxpillo Galleries on Tuesday night, Sir Vrymer," he said quietly; "Mr. Mayn, the manager, has placed the case in my hands. Since Granite Grant was in the South room about the time the crime took place, I naturally suspect him of knowing something about it. My next step, therefore, is to find Granite Grant."

The minister held out his hand.

"Then you can kill two birds with one stone, Mr. Blake," he said; "for if you find out what has happened to Granite Grant you will doubtless also discover the whereabouts of the stolen cipher. At any rate, I place that commission in your hands; in pursuing your own private work I ask you also to look after the interests of your country."

Blake gripped the outstretched hand in his own.

"I understand, Sir Vrymer," he said.

"And now, Blake, I am going to ask you to leave by the back entrance. It will be safer. We do not know who may have followed you here; and as I am leaving now myself I will give you a lift in my car. If you should want to see me again you had better come to Whitehall Court."

A few minutes later a closed limousine came purring softly past Kursan Place and made in the direction of Marble Arch. But no one who noticed the vehicle troubled to take a second glance.

No doubt they would have betrayed greater curiosity if they had known that in it were seated side by side the head of the British Secret Service and one of the most famous criminologists of the day.

Chapter 13
The Blank Paper Speaks!

I SAY, guv'nor, here's a pretty kettle of fish! Old Frenton's been here and pinched the frame."

Blake gave his assistant a stony stare and slowly proceeded to divest himself of his hat and coat.

"Now," he said, "let's hear what you've got to say. And don't say 'pinched,' or I shall have to show you exactly what it means, my lad."

"Well, he's stolen it, guv'nor," said Tinker, evidently not very anxious for his master to start explaining the process of 'pinching.'

"Who's stolen it, Tinker?"

"Frenton—Inspector Frenton, guv'nor!"

"Stolen what?"

"Why, the frame!"

"The frame?"

"Yes; you know—the frame of the Murillo, or whatever the beastly thing's called."

Blake became suddenly interested.

"Do you mean to say, Tinker, that Frenton has been here and taken the frame away?"

"That's it, guv'nor. Just what I've been trying to tell you!"

"But why did you let him?"

"I didn't let him. He came here this morning just after we had left."

"Who let him in?"

"Mrs. Bardell. She didn't know we were both out."

"Call her in, Tinker."

Tinker did as he was told. A moment later the housekeeper appeared, seeming somewhat perturbed at the unexpected summons.

"What's this about Inspector Frenton, Mrs. Bardell?" asked Blake.

"He called this morning, sir," began the housekeeper, in a state of great trepidation. "I thought Master Tinker was in, so I asked the inspector to step inside."

"And what happened then, Mrs. Bardell?"

"Well, I saw that no one was here, so I turned to go. Then the inspector suddenly stops, and stands staring at something against the wall."

"Yes, Mrs. Bardell!"

"Well, sir, next he walks across the room and picks up a frame that stood in the corner, and stands turning it over and over in his hands. Then he says to me quite sharply, 'What's this doing here, ma'am?'"

"And what did you say, Mrs. Bardell?" asked the detective with a flicker of amusement in his eyes.

"I says as how it was Mr. Blake's property, sir, and as how Mr. Blake didn't allow no one to come and meddle about with his things."

"That was very well said, Mrs. Bardell. And what did the inspector say then?"

"He says as how he was going to take charge of it, sir; and when I says 'You just put that frame down,' he got kind of dignified, and replies in a high and mighty sort of way, 'I'm an officer from Scotland Yard, and anything you say will be taken as evidence against you.'"

Blake trembled with suppressed merriment.

"And so Inspector Frenton went, taking the frame with him, Mrs. Bardell?"

"I couldn't very well stop him, sir."

"Of course not, Mrs. Bardell! You acted quite right. That will do; thanks very much!"

Feeling greatly flattered by the detective's praise, Mrs. Bardell turned and swept from the room.

Directly the door shut behind her Blake began to shake with laughter. His assistant regarded him in mild surprise for a moment or two, then seemed to see the humour of the situation and joined in the mirth.

"Why, Tinker," exclaimed Blake, when his merriment had somewhat subsided, "that explains everything. I was wondering what was the matter with Frenton this morning. Now I know. I'm under suspicion; he regards me as a sort of accessory to the fact."

"But it's like his cheek, guv'nor, to come in here and meddle with our property."

"It's not really our property, Tinker. Besides, Frenton evidently thinks the end justifies the means."

"But he didn't mention the matter when we saw him this morning, guv'nor—didn't even say he had been round here first."

"No, he didn't. But he was evidently not quite sure of himself—trying to feel his way. You remember how riled he got when I asked him for an explanation—got quite huffy, and said it was up to me to do the explaining."

"That's so, guv'nor. I wonder what his game is!"

A thoughtful look came into the detective's face.

"He must be in a deuce of a stew, Tinker. You see, now he's found this frame he must think I've been fooling him all the time. Perhaps he thinks the whole thing was a put-up job yesterday, and that I'm at the bottom of it."

"But he may make it rather awkward, guv'nor—especially if he starts fooling around."

"I was just thinking the same thing, Tinker. However, we won't anticipate trouble; I've got more important things to occupy my mind at the present moment than Inspector Frenton's feelings."

"Yes; that reminds me, guv'nor. How about this mysterious appointment? I'm just bursting to hear what happened. Did you see the Chief?"

"I did, Tinker."

"And who was he, guv'nor?"

"Sir Vrymer Fane."

"Well, I'm blowed, guv'nor! If that doesn't just put the lid on it!"

Blake went over to his desk.

"Sit down, Tinker," he said, "and I'll tell you all about it."

He sat down himself in the swivel-chair, and glanced over his desk. Then he suddenly caught sight of an envelope addressed to himself and picked it up.

"What's this, Tinker?" he asked.

"Oh. I clean forgot about that, guv'nor," said his assistant. "I found it in the letterbox a short time ago."

"It's got no stamp on it, Tinker," said the detective, staring at it curiously; "it must have been delivered by hand. We'll see what's inside."

He tore the envelope across and drew out a piece of notepaper. On it was written in block letters the following brief communication:

"Greetings to Monsieur Blake.—It was a shame to lock the poor Tinker in the cellar. But he would follow me, and I could not throw him off. He is like the brave Pedro, that boy, he takes a grip and will not leave go. I hope Monsieur Blake will have the good success."

Blake read the missive through in silence, then handed it to his assistant.

"Just cast your eyes over that, Tinker," he said.

Tinker's mouth dropped open as he read the strange communication.

"What on earth does it mean, guv'nor?" he asked.

"A polite little note from our lady friend in the musquash coat, I think, Tinker."

"But it's a rummy thing to say, guv'nor! Wonder who she is—and where was this sent from?"

"The address has been torn off—you can see that. Tinker. And the writing is in block letters. Our lady friend is evidently not very anxious to disclose her identity."

"But she seems to know all about us, guv'nor. Haven't you the slightest idea who she can be?"

A look of abstraction had come into the detective's eyes. Across his mind had flashed the vision of a woman with a mass of wavy, golden hair. She was slender and graceful, and even the strongest of men had fallen victims to her strange beauty and charm.

Once before Blake had come face to face with her. He remembered how impressed he had been then; how irresistible was her charm, and the soft appeal of her alluring yes. He remembered also the other side to her versatile character; her daring and courage, and the cleverness that had raised her so high in the services of her country.

Yet, if Blake was thinking that the mysterious woman in the musquash coat and this dazzling, golden-haired woman were one and the same person, he did not say so. All he said was:

"By the way she writes English, Tinker, I should think she must be a French woman."

Tinker still held the slip of paper in his hand.

"Seems quite a friendly little note, at any rate, guv'nor," he said.

"Yes, it does, Tinker. You'd better give it to me. I'll put it away in my pocket-case. It's not much use, but I'll keep it as a souvenir."

He took out his pocket-case, and, folding the note up, pushed it in the cover. As he withdrew his fingers he dragged out another half-sheet of notepaper.

Blake glanced casually on either side; the paper was quite blank. He crumpled it in his hand, and was about to throw it in the waste-paper basket, when he hesitated, as if something had occurred to him. Then he unfolded the paper again, and, smoothing it out flat on the desk, sat eyeing it critically.

He remembered now what it was. It was the piece of paper he had found in the South room of the Veuxpillo Galleries, on the morning after the crime. It was lodged beneath the wooden rail; and the reason why it had so interested him was because it was perfectly clean, while his fingers had been covered with dust. Evidently the paper had fallen there quite recently.

Had this piece of paper any connection with the mystery of the stolen cipher? he wondered; had it been dropped during that fierce struggle that had taken place in the south-room, and been kicked beneath the rail? If that were so, what a tale this piece of paper could tell if it could only speak—what a dramatic disclosure it could make!

The detective turned it over and over in his hand.

"If it could only speak!" he muttered below his breath, and stared at it with a frown on his face. He ran his fingers over the surface several times, feeling the texture critically, then smelt it to see if it had any scent.

And as he did so, a queer light came into his eyes. "If it could only speak!" Yes; but would it speak? Could he make this blank piece of paper tell him what it knew? Could he, by some strange magic, force this piece of paper to disclose the mystery of its presence in the south-room of the Veuxpillo Galleries on Tuesday night?

It seemed impossible! It seemed utterly absurd to expect a piece of paper to talk, to give up the secret it contained. Only a madman, surely, would conceive of such a folly! Might as well attempt to extract sunbeams from cucumbers as to expect a blank piece of paper to speak!

And yet, that was what was in Blake's mind; what was apparently impossible seemed to him to be possible. Nothing was impossible to him; his life was too full of extraordinary happenings and amazing coincidences for him to admit that anything was beyond the realm of possibility.

He turned swiftly to his assistant; and only the faint note of eagerness in his voice betrayed the excitement he felt.

"Tinker," he said sharply, "ask Mrs. Bardell for a lemon—quick!"

"A lemon, guv'nor?"

"I said a lemon, Tinker."

Something in his master's voice warned Tinker that it would not be wise to argue at the present moment. He hurried outside, and returned also immediately with the required lemon.

"Right, Tinker. Now bring me the test-tube rack and the chemical cabinet."

Again Tinker hastened to obey.

The detective took out his pocket-knife, and, slicing the lemon in halves, squeezed a little of the juice in a test-tube. Then he busied himself with a number of bottles of various shapes and colours, adding a few drops out of this one, and pouring a little more out of another. Every now and then he shook the solution vigorously, and allowed the effervescence to subside before proceeding.

Finally, he seemed satisfied with the result, and, standing the test-tube in the rack, waited while the solution cleared into a pure amber liquid. His assistant stood by his elbow, watching his master in silent wonderment, and not daring to ask any questions.

Presently Blake picked up a camel-hair brush, dipped it into the liquid in the test-tube, and, with a few quick passes, painted over the surface of the piece of paper.

For a few minutes he sat staring at it intently. But nothing happened—the paper still remained blank. A shade of disappointment passed over Blake's face. He turned the paper over and repeated the process on the other side.

The result was almost instantaneous! The piece of paper acted like a photographic plate when placed in the developing solution in the dark-room. Before the eyes of the detective and his astonished assistant there appeared on the white surface a faint scrawl, which grew more and more distinct every moment.

Sexton Blake had performed the seemingly impossible—he had made the piece of paper speak!

Chapter 14
"Frenton Threatens"

S HAKES alive!" muttered Tinker, staring at the strange, illegible writing as if loth to believe his eyes. "If that don't just knock Maskelyne and Devant's mysteries[10] into a cocked hat!"

But Blake was oblivious of his assistant's bewildered surprise. He was carefully scrutinising the writing, and he saw immediately that it was in some foreign tongue. For the moment he was nonplussed, then he recognised that the characters were those of the Arabic language.

The detective had a sufficient smattering of the tongue to be able to make himself understood in Arabic, but when it came to reading the language it was quite another thing—especially as the writing itself was none too legible. He ran his eyes swiftly down the page and gave a slight start as his glance rested on the signature that was scrawled at the bottom.

Crabbed and ill-formed as the letters were, he could not fail to recognise what they were. It was the signature of Kalib Pasha!

Even Blake's impassive face lost for a moment its imperturbability. It was impossible

---

[10] John Nevil Maskelyne (1839–1917) and David Devant (1868–1941) were popular magicians and illusionists in the early 20th century.

for him to over-estimate the importance of his discovery. What amazing piece of information was contained in that letter? What was the secret nature of this communication that had led the writer to take the precaution of using invisible ink?

The signature was that of Kalib Pasha. And Sir Vrymer Fane had said that Kalib Pasha was the Turkish official who had come over for the Peace Conference, and who was suspected of obtaining a copy of the secret Anglo-French Agreement on the Turkish question.

Somehow he must discover the contents of this letter. He did not doubt that it was concerned with the disappearance of the Murillo on Tuesday night—perhaps it might even explain the whereabouts of the stolen cipher! Here, perhaps, was a clue to the whole amazing mystery—the most invaluable clue! And, by a mere stroke of luck, it had fallen into his hands.

But there was no time to waste. The surface of the paper was getting dry, and already the ink was fading away into invisibility again.

"Tinker," he said breathlessly, "don't ask questions. I'll tell you everything afterwards. Get a sheet of paper, quick, and make a copy of this letter. I'll do the same."

Blake set to work at high speed. As near as possible he made an exact copy of the document. But the writing was becoming very faint by the time that he got to the signature.

Tinker was not yet finished; he was not so expert with the pen as his master. The writing was almost unreadable before he got to the last line, and before he could complete it the ink had quite disappeared. The sheet was blank again; on its surface was no sign of the secret that it contained.

"That'll do, Tinker," said Blake. "I asked you to make a copy so as to check mine. If I happen to have taken anything down wrong, no doubt it'll be all right on yours. Understand?"

"I've got you so far, guv'nor. But I don't know what it's all about. I've never been so fuddled as I am in this case. Things keep happening so quickly that I can't keep up with them. I'm absolutely in a flat spin."

Blake gave a short chuckle.

"Then you'll have to commit crashery, Tinker, as our flying friends say. I can't stop to pull you out now. By-and-by I'll explain the whole situation to you. I've got a job for you now; just get into your hat and coat while I write a short note to Professor Bailey."

Blake was just sticking down the envelope by the time his assistant was ready.

"Now, Tinker," he said, handing him the envelope, "this contains the two copies of the invisible writing. I want you to take it to Professor Bailey and wait for a reply. I've put a note inside explaining everything; but I'll get on the 'phone to him immediately, and tell him you're coming. You know where to find him—the School of Modern Science, at Hampstead."

"I know, guv'nor; I've been there before."

"Off you go, then!"

Blake got through to the professor a few minutes after his assistant had left.

"Is that Professor Bailey?" he asked.

"Yes," came the familiar high-pitched voice; "I'm Bailey right enough. Who are you?"

"This is Blake speaking—Sexton Blake."

"Sexton Blake! Ah, yes! How are you? I know why you've rung me up, Blake."

"Do you, professor? Then why?"

"You're going to ask me to do a job for you. I know you, Blake. That's the only time you remember Professor Bailey, when you want him to do something for you."

The detective chuckled appreciatively.

"You're quite right, professor," he said. "You must be a thought-reader. But I know you rather like my little jobs."

"I do, Blake—always delighted to be of any assistance! What's the latest difficulty?"

"I want you to translate a letter written in Arabic, professor."

"That's easy!"

"Is it? You just wait until you've seen the writing. I'm sending my assistant over with it; he'll be along there shortly. I've explained the matter in my letter, but I thought I'd just ring you up and let you know he was coming."

"That's all right, Blake. Just leave it to me; if I can't make head or tail of it, nobody else can."

"Thanks, professor! One other thing—the matter is absolutely confidential. Understand?"

"Exactly, Blake! It always is. You seem to be bristling with secrets—in fact, you're a sort of human hedge-hog."

"But this is more than secret, professor—it's holy!"

"Is it, by gum! Well, you can trust me, Blake. Good-bye!"

"Good-bye, professor!"

Blake replaced the receiver, and leant back in his chair. He could hardly restrain his impatience. Everything depended on the contents of that letter.

The mystery had reached a stage now when he wanted some fresh clue to help him to solve the problems that confronted him. He hoped to find that clue in this secret letter written in the invisible ink.

He fell to pondering over the whole strange business, going through every aspect of the case in detail, and seeing if he had failed to take into consideration any essential fact.

But always his mind seemed to come round to that absorbing question: Where was Granite Grant? What had happened to the famous King's Spy? What part had he played in the crime at the Veuxpillo Galleries; what was the meaning of those bloodstained fingerprints?

He was still wrestling with the problem when he was aroused from his preoccupation by a knock at the door.

Blake sat up with a start.

"Come in!" he called.

The door opened and the house-keeper appeared.

"I thought I'd make sure you were in this time, sir," she said. "He's come again."

"Who's come again, Mrs. Bardell?"

"Why, the inspector, sir!"

"Inspector Frenton, Mrs. Bardell? Ah, yes; show him in!"

Blake felt a little surge of irritation. The inspector was the last man he wished to see at the present moment; his presence was somewhat disturbing at a time when he wished to be alone and to think. What did the man want now, he wondered? At that moment the inspector himself was ushered in.

"Good afternoon, Frenton!" said Blake cheerfully. "Make yourself at home; there's a seat here."

But the inspector did not take the proffered chair. He still remained standing and seemed plainly ill at ease.

"Oh, I'm not stopping, Mr. Blake," he said, "thanks! Just thought I'd call in, that's all!"

"I see, Frenton. And what's the trouble now?"

The inspector shifted from one foot to the other.

"No trouble, Mr. Blake," he said, with an attempt at indifference. "Thought I'd like to talk the matter over."

Without appearing to do so Blake was eyeing him narrowly. Frenton had come there with the express purpose of telling him something, he felt sure of that, and now that he was here he was rather nervous how to begin.

"Well, are there any fresh aspects of the case, Frenton?" he asked.

The inspector seemed to seize on Blake's question as a loophole out of an awkward predicament.

"That's just what I came to tell you, Mr. Blake," he said quickly. "There's been a fresh development of the case—the missing caretaker has turned up."

Blake was not deceived by the inspector. He knew that he had not paid him this visit especially to tell him that; there was some other reason that he did not like to state openly. But he was quite interested in this piece of information.

"You mean the caretaker of the Veuxpillo Galleries, Frenton?" he asked. "And what reason did he give for his absence?"

"Said he received an urgent message from the manager to meet him somewhere or other. Somebody asked him to have a drink and then he remembers no more until he woke up last night and found himself in a common lodging-house off the Euston Road."

"Then he was evidently drugged, inspector!"

"So he says! But I'm rather doubtful about him—there's more in this case than meets the eye."

"I'm sure of that, Frenton! But you don't doubt that this man is speaking the truth, do you?"

"I'm not expressing any opinion at the present moment, Mr. Blake. I want to hear what another person has got to say for himself first."

The two men looked each other full in the eyes for the space of a few seconds.

Then the inspector's gaze wavered and his fingers played with his coat-button.

"And that other person happens to be me, Frenton?" said Bake quietly.

Frenton did not answer.

"Come on, Frenton!" continued Blake sharply. "Out with it, man! You know you didn't come here to tell me about the missing caretaker."

"Well, supposing I didn't, Mr. Blake?" said the inspector doggedly.

"There's no supposing about it, Frenton. You came here to tackle me on the subject of that frame which you were good enough to take from this room this morning. So why beat about the bush?"

"Very well, then, Mr. Blake! Since you've mentioned the subject yourself I'll ask you a plain question. I want to know how that frame, which was stolen yesterday evening from Mr. Mayn, found its way into this room?"

"By the same method as it found its way out again this morning, Frenton—that is, by hand!"

The inspector's face became a little pink, but he still stuck to his point.

"You're simply quibbling now, Mr. Blake," he said; "and it won't do. This is no laughing matter. I'm asking you a plain question and I want a plain answer."

"And supposing I do not choose to answer, inspector?"

"I think it will be to your interests to answer my question, Mr. Blake. This picture is connected with the crime at the Veuxpillo Galleries. Yesterday it was stolen from Mr. Mayn under somewhat suspicious circumstances; and afterwards I find the frame in your possession. It's certainly up to you to explain how it came here."

"I follow your reasoning, inspector; and yet, I am sorry, but I cannot oblige you. For certain reasons I do not feel disposed at the present moment to disclose how that frame came into my possession."

"I'm sorry you should take up that attitude, Mr. Blake. As you know, the case is in my hands, and if I find it necessary to adopt unpleasant measures to uphold the course of justice, you must not blame me, the fault is entirely yours."

"And what do you mean by unpleasant measures, Frenton?"

"I mean this, Mr. Blake! The inquest today on this man was adjourned until tomorrow. Since you refuse to answer my question, you will be subpoenaed to attend. Then you may find the coroner's questions more difficult to answer than mine."

"I see, Frenton. Thanks for telling me. If that's all, then I'll wish you good-afternoon."

The inspector hesitated a moment, as if he hoped Blake would change his mind at the last moment; then, seeing that the detective had taken up his pen, he turned on his heel, and, without a word, strode from the room.

Blake put down his pen and folded his arms. Although he had appeared indifferent to the inspector's threat, he could not help feeling a little disturbed. He did not doubt that Frenton would carry it into effect.

In a way he sympathised with his attitude; the man was naturally curious to know how the frame had come into his possession—the case was in his hands and it was up to him to find out all he could.

But it might be rather awkward if he had to attend the inquest. Sir Vrymer Fane trusted him implicitly; it would be the last thing he would desire to have the real facts of the case stated at the inquest and published broadcast in all the papers. What a sensation it would produce! How eagerly the Press would take up the matter, and exaggerate it until it became an international scandal!

Somehow that must be prevented. He must avoid attending this inquest tomorrow at all costs. Presently he got up, and, hurrying outside, bought an early edition of the evening paper from a news-boy who was passing down the street.

Then he carefully read the account of the day's proceedings. The case was already attracting great interest; various fantastic explanations of the crime were given; the reporters were seizing on every available piece of tittle-battle in order to dish it up to the hungry public in bold, sensational headlines.

He imagined what would happen tomorrow if he attended the inquest. Already he saw the sensational placards staring him in the face, with their thick, black lettering:

VEUXPILLO GALLERIES CRIME.
SEXTON BLAKE'S AMAZING EVIDENCE AT INQUEST.

No; that must not happen! At the risk of coming into conflict with the law he must somehow avoid attending the inquest. He rested his head on his hand and sought about in his mind for a loophole of escape from his awkward predicament. He was still puzzling over the matter nearly two hours later when his young assistant returned from Hampstead.

"Ah, Tinker!" he said. "Have you done the needful?"

"Yes, guv'nor! Here's Professor Bailey's answer."

With a feeling that everything hung in the balance, Blake opened the blue envelope and took out the enclosures.

One was a brief covering letter from the professor:

"Dear Blake," it read—"Your writing is degenerating. I had the greatest difficulty in reading it. Pull yourself together—or I shall have to give you some lessons in calligraphy. However, by the aid of both copies, I was able to translate the missive, which is attached herewith. It is rather an interesting document—my curiosity is aroused. I suppose I sha'n't hear from you again until you want something else done! Good-bye.—Bailey."

Blake smiled to himself as he came to the end of the letter.

"The professor ought not to grouse about my handwriting!" he muttered. "His own is nothing to write home about."

He picked up the other sheet; and as he read it through that queer, set expression came into his face, which always indicated to Tinker that his master had made some extraordinary discovery.

On the sheet of paper, in Professor Bailey's handwriting, was written this strange message:

"Watch Gustave Fulk very closely. He is no longer to be trusted. The picture has been taken to London. It is at present hanging in the Veuxpillo Galleries, and its number is forty-seven. You will know best how you can gain possession of it. They are observing my movements closely; everything I do is known, so once you have the picture in your possession, follow me immediately to Algiers. You know where we met before—the Ak-el-baran—at the foot of the Kasbah. Again, I say watch Gustave Fulk! Do not fail me! You know the penalty!"

"Kalib Pasha."

Blake handed the missive to Tinker in silence. It was clear to him now. This letter had explained the whole thing.

So there was a third person in the Veuxpillo Galleries on Tuesday night—there must have been for this letter to have got in the south-room. It did not belong to the murdered man, and it certainly wasn't sent to Granite Grant.

And it was this unknown third person who had killed Gustave Fulk; there could be no doubt of that. Gustave Fulk had attempted to betray his comrades. Very likely some other country had offered him a big price for the secret cipher and he had determined to gain possession of it.

Being a clever painter, he had made a copy of the Murillo while it hung in the Paris Salon. He had crossed to England and succeeded in substituting the fake for the genuine picture. Then, at the last moment, this third person had intervened with such a tragic result.

But where did Granite Grant come in? What was the mystery of those bloodstained fingerprints? That matter still wanted clearing up; the part Granite Grant had taken in the tragedy had yet to be explained. Perhaps he would never find out that until he met the King's Spy again and heard the story from his own lips.

One thing, however, was certain. Granite Grant was after the stolen cipher. And where the stolen cipher was, there he would find Granite Grant. Sir Vrymer Fane was right— it was a case of killing two birds with one stone!

Then Blake suddenly thought of the inquest tomorrow and of Inspector Frenton's threat. Very likely the writ of subpoena would be served on him tomorrow morning if not before. Once he got that, there was no help for him—he must attend the inquest.

That decided him. He would steal a march on Frenton. He would follow up this latest clue that fortune had thrust into his hands. And the latest clue would take him to Algiers. He would get the laugh of Frenton after all; when the writ of subpoena was served he would not be here to receive it. He would be away, and no one would know where to find him.

Blake turned to his assistant, who was still staring at the letter.

"We're leaving London in two hours, Tinker," he said quietly. "See that you have everything ready, and travel as light as possible. We're taking Pedro with us."

"Leaving London, guv'nor!" echoed Tinker, not quite sure that he had heard right. "Where're we off to?"

"To Algiers, Tinker!"

"Algiers, guv'nor! But——"

The detective placed his hand on his assistant's shoulder.

"Tinker," he said, in a deliberate voice, "get busy! Don't talk! You shall know everything after we've started. Now, I've got one or two matters to attend to. You know exactly what to do. Don't waste time! Get on with it!"

Tinker knew his master too well to argue with him further. When Blake said "Get on with it!" that was enough; there was nothing else left but to get on with it. Without another word he hurried from the room and began to busy himself with the arrangements for the journey.

He was used to these sudden emergencies. He knew exactly what they should take. Blake always left these details in his hands. And as he worked silently and swiftly in the back room, making his preparations for the sudden journey, he could hardly repress his excitement at the adventure in front of them. They were going to visit the wonderful city of Algiers—the place of mystery and enchantment and strange oriental customs!

It was certainly an adventure after Tinker's own heart!

Chapter 15
The "Gare de Lyon"

GAY Paree" was resplendent in the brilliant rays of the midday sun. The invigorating touch of spring was in the air, and along the wide boulevards the trees pushed out new shoots and buds of emerald green towards the warm sunshine, and revelled in the perennial awakening of life.

The sun shone on church spire and kiosk, on the rich man and the beggar, on the just and the unjust, and spangled all with its burnishing rays—impartial of religion and creed, colour and race and all the idle pretensions to which men lay claim. It shone, too, on the Gare de Lyon, and coruscated its glass-domed roof with a sheen of fire.

Beneath its lofty dome the Gare de Lyon was an animated scene of bustle and activity. Its gangways, platforms, and approaches were seething with eager passengers; there was much excited running to and fro, a confusion of cries, a rumbling of hand-lorries laden with portmanteaux and pushed by gesticulating porters, and above all the hissing of steam and the shrill, impatient scream of the engine.

For this was the great terminus of the "Chemin de fer" that wound snake-like across France to Lyons, Marseilles, and the Mediterranean; and already the express that was to take the more fortunate and worthy of mankind to bask in the pleasures of the "Sunny South" was steaming at its siding in a fever to begin its headlong rush.

While the doors were yet banging, and white handkerchiefs were fluttering their farewells, two late arrivals came hurrying along the platform and made for a carriage labelled "Dames," which, in English, means "Ladies only."

"One of them seized the handle of the door, politely helped his companion inside, and closed it to behind her. The lady let down the window and leaned out.

"*Juste Ciel!*" she exclaimed breathlessly. "But it was a rush! It is a pity, Monsieur Maurice, for there was much to say. You were saying that Bervais was to follow on—were you not?"

"Yes!" jerked her companion, mopping furiously at his brow. "Listen, Mademoiselle Julie! Today is Friday. On Sunday Kalib Pasha communicated with a certain man; we do not know his name, but he had a broken nose. On Monday that man went to England; on Wednesday he was back here in Paris. Perhaps there is nothing in it, but it is well that he should be watched."

"And you have put Bervais on his track, monsieur?"

"Yes, Mademoiselle Julie! If we find that our suspicions are unfounded Bervais shall be sent after you immediately with instructions to place himself at your disposal."

"I follow you, monsieur. And this Kalib Pasha—what news of him?"

"This morning we were informed that he has embarked at Marseilles for Algiers. At all costs track him down, Julie; we are relying absolutely on you."

"You may trust me, monsieur."

"I know we can," said Maurice quickly. "If anybody can succeed, you will. If there is any further news, we will wire you at Marseilles. But do not wait for anything. It is a question of speed."

"I understand that, Monsieur Maurice."

The shrill whistle of the guard cut short their further conversation. The man took a step back as the train began to move slowly down the platform.

"Au revoir, mademoiselle!" he said. "Bon voyage!"

"Au revoir, monsieur!"

He stood silently watching the carriage window recede with increasing swiftness into the distance, then, with a parting wave of his hand, turned and strode from the station.

For the remainder of that day the great Gare de Lyon throbbed and hummed with animation and bustle. Sometimes there were little rills in the ceaseless storm of activity; short intervals of respite in anticipation of the next scramble and rush, to be followed again by the rumbling and din and confusion of a departing train.

One of these lulls of comparative quietness occurred later on in the evening, after the sun had set in a red glory and bathed the boulevards of Paris—its institutes, conservatoires, and its Champs-Élysées—in a deep, vermilion stain.

The station was still crowded with expectant people; they were waiting for the train that was to cover the identical route that Mademoiselle Julie had embarked on some seven or eight hours before—the night express to the "Sunny South" of France.

Fresh arrivals were coming into the station every minute, bustling anxiously over their portmanteaux and baggage and worrying blue-bloused porters to the verge of distraction.

Outside one of the platforms various little groups of people were standing, talking together excitedly and embracing one another as if their pent-up affections had at last found expression. They were little family parties, who had come to see their relatives and friends off on their journey and to wish them "God-speed."

One of these little groups was rather different from the others. It only comprised three persons—or, to be more correct—two persons and a dog. The two persons were dressed as tourists, with knee-breeches, Norfolk jackets, and knapsacks slung over their backs. The third member of the party, being merely a dog, had not troubled to get himself up especially for the occasion.

The elder man of this little party had a lean, ascetic face, and keen, penetrative eyes. He seemed to be taking no very great interest in what was going on around him, his face betrayed no emotion, yet, if anyone had suddenly questioned him as to what he had observed, his answer would have surprised them. As a matter of fact, there was very little that his quick eyes hadn't observed and noted.

His companion was a youth, and he made no attempt to hide his curiosity and interest in his surroundings. His eager eyes were taking everything in, and every now and then he made some little exclamation of astonishment and gave a short, excited laugh.

The bloodhound lolled at his master's feet, first sitting up on his haunches, then sprawling out flat on his belly. His great head moved slowly from side to side, his tongue hung out, and altogether he seemed bored stiff with his present situation.

The youth presently turned to the elder man.

"I say, guv'nor!" she said, in an audible whisper, "just look at those two old buffers. They're hugging and kissing each other like a pair of school-girls."

Sexton Blake, for it was none other than the famous detective, glanced idly over at the two emotional Frenchmen.

"They're only shaking hands, Tinker," he said.

"Shaking hands, guv'nor! I like that. Why, they're biting each other—look!"

But the detective's attention had been attracted elsewhere, and, after vainly endeavouring to arouse his master's interest again, Tinker subsided into a silent contemplation of the scenes that were being enacted in front of his eyes.

A few minutes later the detective grasped his assistant's arm.

"Come on, Tinker!" he said. "They're opening the gates: we'll try and find an empty compartment."

They passed through the barrier, and made their way along the platform, with Pedro walking between them on the lead. Soon Blake was in the midst of an animated discussion with a voluble conductor who objected to Pedro's occupying a first-class carriage.

Not being able to follow the argument, Tinker thought it up to him to encourage his master by a few words in plain English.

"Let him have it, guv'nor!" he cried excitedly. "Go in and bash him. Don't stand any of his old buck."

"Shut up, Tinker!" said Blake sharply, and, turning to the conductor, continued in French: "Very well, my man; you shall take the dog to the luggage-van yourself. Here—catch hold of the lead!"

"Tickle him up, Pedro, boy!" he said, in a low voice.

The conductor put out his hand to take the strap. But Pedro had understood his master's brief injunction; with a growl of anger, the great dog sprang into the air, and his jaws snapped together barely a fraction of an inch away from the conductor's wrist.

The man gave a gasp of fright, backed precipitately, then turned and fled down the platform as if a thousand devils were at his heels.

Blake gave a short laugh, and pulled open the carriage door.

"In you get, Tinker!" he said. "I don't suppose we shall be worried again. Come on, Pedro, old chap!"

As the door closed behind Sexton Blake and his two companions a man came hurrying along the platform with a porter at his side. He had a dark, swarthy face and high cheek bones; but his most salient feature was his nose, which had an unsightly crook in it; evidently it had been broken, and the fracture had badly mended again. In his hand he carried a small leather case, which he seemed to clutch convulsively.

The porter stopped at a sleeping-car which was labelled "Compartiment reserve," unlocked the door, and locked it again after his companion had entered.

Immediately afterwards another man, who had been standing by the barrier watching what had happened, walked quickly down the platform, paused just before he reached the reserved compartment, then clambered into the next carriage.

The last comer was Bervais, a minor official of the French Secret Service and confederate of Mademoiselle Julie and Monsieur Maurice.

The guard blew his whistle, there was a final slamming of doors, a last hurried scramble, and the night express began to move on its long journey to the "Sunny South."

Chapter 16
While Dawn was Breaking

IT was now about midnight. For nearly five hours the express had been rushing on through the night, tearing up mile upon mile of its long journey across France to the south and the Levantine.

The "Chemin de fer" threaded its way like a huge, winding serpent through field and forest and across broad acres of waving corn; it passed by hamlet and village, town and city, and still the "iron horse" did not check its impetuous career that brought it nearer and nearer to the warm sunshine of the Mediterranean.

The countryside had long since hushed in slumber; in spite of the persistent thunder of the train, a great quietness brooded around; in the scattered hamlets and villages only a few dim lights kept watchful sentinel throughout the long night. The inhabitants had long since retired to their beds to sleep the sleep of the just.

Even Blake and Tinker, and the faithful bloodhound, had at last succumbed to the fatigues of the day. Coiled up in their narrow bunks the detective and his assistant slept peacefully, and forgot the toils and troubles of their strenuous lives. The dog slumbered restlessly at his master's feet.

Except for the thin edge of light that still crept beneath the blinds of two adjacent compartments, the long line of sleeping-cars was wrapped in darkness. Evidently all the passengers, except those two, had followed Blake's example, and had taken themselves to their bunks.

In one of these compartments was the Arab with the broken nose. He sat in the corner of the coupe with his back to the engine, and for the last hour or more he had not moved.

Only the smouldering fire in his dark, sinister eyes showed that he was awake and watchful. He still clasped in his hands the leather case, as if its contents were too valuable for him to let it go from his grasp.

Silent, morose, and taciturn, he sat there like a graven image; and except for the occasional flicker of an eyelid, not a muscle of his face moved, and from one hour's end to another he never shifted his position from the corner of his coupe.

He was a fanatic, imbued with but one thought. And that was to fulfil his mission, to do his master's bidding, to carry the thing that was in his case safely to Kalib Pasha.

In the adjoining coupe sat Bervais, the French police agent. He also sat in the corner, but facing the engine, so that only a slight wooden partition separated him from the stranger next door.

But Bervais was as restless as his neighbour was still and tranquil. He had just rung the bell for the third time in the last hour.

"A coffee!" he asked of the steward who answered the summons.

"You will want nothing else tonight, sir?" asked the man, as he laid the tray on the seat beside his passenger and stifled a yawn.

The request was more of the nature of an ultimatum than a question. Bervais saw the man's meaning; he yawned himself through utter weariness.

"No," he said. "You can turn in. I shall—after I've drunk this."

The steward nodded and left the compartment.

But, weary as he was, Bervais had no intention of turning in. Fortune tonight had placed in his hands too big an enterprise for him to ruin his chances by giving way to such weaknesses of the flesh.

Already there flitted before his eyes the alluring prospects of a speedy promotion if he would but play his cards right. There must be no sleep for him tonight—not until his work was done, at all events.

He left his coffee untouched, and, getting up from his seat, stepped out into the corridor. He had done this quite a dozen times already; he did it again. He glanced swiftly up and down, and saw the corridor was deserted, then crept stealthily to the next compartment, and peered for a moment beneath the blind.

The stranger had not moved from his corner; he still grasped the leather case in his hands; but he was not yet asleep; his eyes were wide open.

Bervais crept back to his coupe again.

"Not yet!" he muttered. "But there is still time."

He took out another cigarette and lit it from the end still glowing in his mouth. Then began to sip his coffee in silent abstraction.

Many thoughts passed through his mind during those still hours of the night. Bervais was a young man, and his short experience of life had not yet taught him to mask his feelings beneath a calm exterior.

His face was a study in changing moods and expressions, and every now and again that self-satisfied smile played about the corners of his mouth.

Bervais was thinking of his coming promotion. Already he was congratulating himself on the achievement of his task. He had envied Monsieur Maurice and Mademoiselle Julie; they had "made good." In their presence he had kept silent, for they were his superiors.

But how he envied them—their assurance and their undisputed authority. Now fate had thrust this chance into his hands. Separated from him by a thin wooden partition was the man who had the stolen cipher in his possession. He was quite sure of that.

It was his opportunity—the opportunity that only comes once in a man's lifetime. He must not let it slip between his fingers. If he could but get possession of that painting, what a scoop it would be! He would be made; there was no position in his profession to which he could not climb. Yes—at all costs he must keep awake!

And yet, strangely enough, while Bervais was urging on himself the necessity of keeping awake, he was already asleep. Outraged Nature had at last come by her own. Bervais slept! And while he slept in the corner of his coupe he dreamt pleasantly of his promotion, and thought that he was awake.

The train still rushed onwards, its speed unchecked. And behind it trailed the long line of carriages with their precious burden of silent, sleeping humanity. It passed through tunnels, and sped across bridges with the water gurgling a hundred feet or more below, to the accompaniment of that monotonous rhythm of iron-shod wheels on the metal rails.

And Bervais still slept on, dreaming that he was awake, and all unconscious that the opportunity that Fate had thrust into his hands was slowly slipping from his grasp.

Not until the night was passing away and the first faint flush of dawn was quivering in the eastern sky did he stir in his corner. Then he suddenly sat up with a start.

For the moment he would not—could not—believe that he had been asleep. Surely he had not been guilty of such a gross betrayal of his trust! He rubbed his eyes and stared blinkingly around. Then, for the first time, he noticed the faint tinge of dawn in the eastern sky that crept through the corner of his blind.

Then he had slept! He must have slept for some hours!

Bervais sprang frantically to his feet, dragged open the door and stepped into the corridor. He had flung precaution to the wind now: his one idea was to retrieve this disgraceful error of which he had been guilty. He stepped quickly to the next compartment, took a key from his pocket, and unlocking the door, entered without a moment's hesitation.

The stranger had not moved since he had last peered beneath the blind; he sat in the same corner with his back to the engine, and in his hands he still grasped the leather wallet. But at Bervais' entry he did not look up; his eyes were closed. He, too, had at last succumbed to Nature's demands—for he was asleep.

Luck was on Bervais' side—in spite of the fact that he had been caught napping in the real sense of the word. Nobody was astir yet; it was too early for that. For an hour or so more he could depend on being undisturbed.

He was prepared to go to any lengths to get possession of the stolen cipher; he would have killed this man without the slightest hesitation. But Fate had been kind to him—the man slept, and the leather wallet was in his grasp. There was no need of violence.

Very stealthily Bervais crept towards the sleeping man. His nerves were in a state of tension; the creak of his boots sounded to him like a pistol-shot. Then he put out his hands to the leather wallet.

Inch by inch he raised it from the nerveless fingers. He could feel the man's breath fanning his hands; he dared not breath himself, for fear of waking him. Slowly, and with infinite care, he lifted the wallet from the other's grasp. Presently his patience was rewarded—the wallet was his!

With the wallet in his hand, Bervais crept quietly out of the compartment back into his own. There he unloosened the strap and opened it with trembling fingers. The thing he sought was there; he drew it out—a thick wad of canvas, folded, with the painting of Murillo inside.

Bervais lifted his attaché-case from the rack and took out another wad of canvas. It was the faked Murillo that Monsieur Maurice had cut from the frame. He would put the fake back in the leather wallet and then replace it in the hands of the sleeping man.

It was a clever ruse on the part of Bervais. The stranger next door would never find out what had happened until it was too late, and by that time Bervais would be back in Paris with the stolen cipher in his possession.

It was certainly a cunning move; and if Fate had continued to smile on Bervais this story might have had a different ending.

But at the very moment when he was most in need of it Bervais' luck deserted him. As he was in the act of inserting the faked Murillo in the leather wallet the door of his coupe was flung violently open, there was a snarl of rage, and before Bervais could do anything he was grasped round the waist by two lean, wiry arms.

The man with the broken nose had suddenly awakened to discover his loss. Like a tiger robbed of its prey, he was now driven to fury to recover it.

Backwards and forwards the two men swayed to the rocking of the train. Bervais was a good athlete; he could hold his own with most men in a rough-and-tumble. The surprise attack had taken him at a momentary disadvantage; his foe had grasped him from behind; but by squirming violently he managed to throw him off, and for a moment they faced each other.

Then Bervais whipped out his revolver; but before he could level it his adversary had sprung on him again, and a desperate struggle began, while the train still thundered on through the cold, silent night.

Writhing and twisting, they fought up and down the narrow coupe. No words were exchanged; there was no quarter asked or given; each man knew that he was fighting for dear life. Both were panting breathlessly; the sweat was pouring down their faces; yet neither paused in the fierce, deadly contest.

Bervais was strong. But his foe was a fanatic; he fought with the instincts of a tiger, and used his hands, nails, teeth, and feet like a wild cat at bay. The revolver had fallen to the seat. Presently Bervais managed to snatch it up again. The cold muzzle touched the other man's forehead; the Arab's sinewy fingers grasped at Bervais' wrist and jerked it up. There was a flash and a report that was lost in the thunder of the train, and the furious struggle still continued with undismayed frenzy.

Now they were on the floor, twisting over and over like two eels, then on the seat. Sometimes one seemed to gain the advantage sometimes the other. Both men's faces were now lacerated and torn and bloody. But they did not pause for breath; the fight still went on.

They were up against the door now. The Arab was gripping his adversary's throat, and his eyes gleamed like two live coals. Bervais was gasping for breath; his strength was failing him.

The Arab suddenly relinquished his grasp, and gave a deft twist to the handle of the door. The wind caught it and flung it open. The next moment, with a despairing cry, Bervais went hurtling backwards, and disappeared.

The Arab dragged the door to, and stood there, breathing heavily. Then he turned and looked for the leather wallet. It had been kicked beneath the seat. He picked it up, and, seeing, the dispatch-case on the seat, that had belonged to Bervais, flung it out of the window. After straightening up the compartment, he stepped out into the corridor and silently returned to his own coupe.

The train still rushed on its journey. The grey dawn had now broken over the broad bosom of the earth; presently the red rim of the sun appeared in the east.

Yet another two or three hours were to elapse before any occupants of the train had a suspicion of the grim tragedy that had been enacted at the break of dawn.

Chapter 17
The Black Cloth Button

TINKER sat up with a yawn and blinked around in a dazed sort of fashion. At first he could not think where he was or what was happening. Then everything came crowding back into his mind.

He glanced out of the window. The sun was some yards above the horizon, and blazing like a white ball of fire. The broad, undulating fields of France—its vineyards and orchards—lay glistening in the morning's dew.

He clambered out of his bunk and stuck his head out into the corridor. Blake was already dressed. He was standing by the window, smoking a cigarette and contemplatively watching the passing landscape. Pedro was there, too, standing on his hind legs, with his paws on the window-frame, and with his great head waving to and fro in the rush of air.

The detective turned his head, and, seeing his assistant, nodded pleasantly.

"Had a good sleep, Tinker?" he asked.

"I should say so, guv'nor!" replied Tinker, feeling a little ashamed of his laziness. "Didn't know you were up. What's the time?"

"Quite early yet, Tinker. You can sleep for another hour, if you like!"

"Not me, guv'nor! Feel as fit as a fiddle. But isn't this just glorious?"

"Not bad, Tinker. We're getting into the Rhone Valley now. We ought to reach Lyons just after breakfast, where we have to change."

"Talking about breakfast, guv'nor, I could just do with a cup of tea. Pity we can't ask Mrs. Bardell to bring us one up."

"Don't know about tea, Tinker, but you can have some coffee. I could do with a cup myself. Just get into your things; I'll ring for the attendant."

It did not take Tinker long to dress. As he came along the corridor, rubbing his face with the towel, he almost collided with the steward, who was carrying the tray of coffee. He followed the man into Blake's coupe.

The steward cast an anxious look at Pedro, hurriedly deposited the tray in the corner, and backed towards the door.

"It is a big dog, monsieur!" he said, standing half in the corridor.

"It is!" agreed Blake.

"It is what we call 'un limier,' monsieur."

"That's right. In England we call them 'bloodhounds.'"

The man thought a moment.

"He finds people when they are missing, monsieur, is it not so?" he asked.

Blake nodded his head in agreement. He was becoming just a little curious at the man's persistence. He watched him beneath his brows, and noted that he seemed somewhat perturbed and agitated.

The steward hesitated at the door, then came back into the coupe. He seemed suddenly to have forgotten the existence of Pedro.

"It is very strange, monsieur," he began, in a confidential tone, "but there is a gentleman missing from the train."

Blake felt suddenly interested. Then, after all, there was a reason for the man's strange questions.

"Missing!" he said. "How?"

The steward glanced quickly over his shoulder, then continued in the same confidential tone.

"He was up very late last night, monsieur. At twelve o'clock I took him a coffee. He seemed very strange then. This morning he is not in his coupe, and his bed has not been slept in."

"But he may be on the train somewhere," said Blake.

The man shook his head doubtfully.

"He may be, monsieur," he said. "But I do not think so."

The detective regarded him in silence for a moment.

"You had better make a few inquiries," he said. "Let me know if you cannot find him on the train."

"Very good, monsieur!" said the man, and, stepping out into the corridor, closed the door softly behind him.

Tinker had not been able to follow the conversation, but he saw that something was amiss.

"What's the trouble, guv'nor?" he asked.

"Passenger mysteriously disappeared during the night," said the detective, slowly sipping his coffee.

"Disappeared, guv'nor!"

"Yes—so the steward says! He took him a coffee at twelve o'clock; this morning he is not to be found anywhere, and his bed has not been slept in."

"That's rummy, guv'nor. Mysteries seem to chase us wherever we go. Wonder what could have happened!"

"May be still on the train, Tinker. At any rate, the man's going to make a few inquiries and let me know."

They drank their coffee in silence, and turned their attention to the window again. The sun was getting higher now, the sky was blue, and the dry, bracing, exhilarating air that came through the open window soon dispelled any lingering touch of mystery. Blake had almost forgotten the incident, when the steward silently entered the coupe again.

"It seems that he is missing, monsieur," he said.

"You have made inquiries?"

The man nodded positively.

"He is not on the train, monsieur."

"Which is his compartment?" Blake asked.

The steward answered with a trace of eagerness in his voice, as if he hoped Blake would investigate the circumstance.

"It is the twelfth coupe down, monsieur," he said; "number eight."

"Then I will have a look at it!"

Blake turned to Tinker.

"Come on, Tinker!" he said. "This is getting interesting."

They stepped outside and closed the door behind, them.

"Good dog, Pedro!" said Blake. "Stay there, old fellow." And he began to follow the steward along the corridor.

At coupe number eight they stopped. The steward opened the door, and they passed inside.

Blake glanced curiously around the small compartment. As the steward had said, the bed had not been slept in. To the unexperienced eye, however, there were no other signs to arouse suspicion that anything untoward had happened.

But Blake knew immediately that something was amiss. There was no deceiving his keen, observant eyes. He noted the little jagged tears in the floor-rug, the ripped-up blind, and several other evidences of the fierce struggle that had gone on at the break of dawn.

At that moment the steward left the compartment to attend to a call. Blake turned to Tinker.

"This may prove interesting after all," Tinker, he said. "If I am not greatly mistaken, something dramatic happened in this coupe after the steward left it at twelve o'clock last night."

He began to make a careful scrutiny of his surroundings, closely examining the partitions and woodwork. There was no doubt about it, a struggle of some sort had occurred here quite recently. The smears of the woodwork were caused by someone's fingers clutching at it for support. The meaning of the marks was quite apparent to Blake.

He stared up at the white-painted ceiling then gave a quick exclamation.

"See, Tinker!" he said. "That hole was made by a revolver shot: the bullet is still embedded in the woodwork."

"By Jove, guv'nor, you're right!" said his assistant. "What on earth could have happened? Wonder who fired it!"

"Goodness knows, Tinker! But that's evidently not been there long."

Blake suddenly noticed something lying in the shadow of the door. He stooped to the floor and picked it up. It was a button—just a disc of metal covered with black cloth. But the peculiar part about it was that in one place the edge was a little flattened, as if the machine had worked too near the edge of the sheet of metal from which the disc had been stamped.

After minutely examining it, Blake handed it to his assistant.

"Anything remarkable about that, Tinker?" he asked.

Tinker turned the button over reflectively.

"By the look of it, guv'nor, it's evidently been torn violently from somebody's coat."

"You're quite right, Tinker; that's an important point. Anything else?"

His assistant shook his head, and Blake continued:

"Do you remember my finding a button like that, Tinker, in the Veuxpillo Galleries on the morning after the crime?"

"Ah, yes, guv'nor: you're right there! It was certainly identical with this. But it's not a very uncommon sort of button; it may be simply a coincidence."

"It may be, Tinker. But there is one other small detail about it that you haven't noticed. One edge is a little flat. Do you see?"

"So it is, guv'nor!"

"Yes; and so was the other button, Tinker. Pity I haven't got it on me now. But it looks as if they were stamped out of the same sheet of metal."

Tinker whistled softly.

"It's a cinch, guv'nor!" he said. "But I must be a thick-head. When you point these things out they seem so simple."

Blake gave a thin smile.

"There may be nothing in it, Tinker," he said. "But it's certainly a coincidence."

He knelt down on the floor and began to grope under the seat. Then his fingers closed on something crisp like a thick piece of brown paper. He dragged it forth and rose to his feet. Then even Blake's habitual calm left him, and he gave a quick gasp of amazement.

In his hands he held the faked copy of the Murillo!

The detective stared at the painted canvas as if unable to believe his eyes. What did this astonishing discovery mean? How had the faked Murillo got there?

Then the finding of the black cloth button was no coincidence! It had been torn off a man's coat, and that man had been in the south room of the Veuxpillo Galleries on the night of the crime.

But who was this man? And where was he now?

Was he the man who was now missing from the train? And, if so, what had he been doing here? What had happened to him during the night? There had been a struggle of some kind in this coupe; someone had fired a revolver. There was, therefore, a second man to be accounted for. Had he also left the train, or was he still on it?

The more Blake probed the problem the more mysterious it seemed to become. He was still deep in thought when the steward returned a few minutes later.

"You have not found anything, monsieur?" he asked anxiously.

Blake shook his head. He had hastily concealed the painting under his coat for certain reasons of his own.

"I am afraid it is a case of suicide," he said. "What was the gentleman like? Was he a countryman of yours?"

"Ah, yes, monsieur; a young man—about thirty, I should think. But very highly strung. I could see that."

"And how was he dressed?"

"In grey serge, monsieur. But I did not observe very closely."

"You are sure it was grey serge?" asked the detective.

"Quite sure, monsieur!"

Blake thought of the black cloth button that was in his pocket. Somehow his reasoning was at fault; the evidence did not tally. One would not expect to find black cloth buttons on a grey serge coat. But there was a second man to be accounted for; possibly the button had been wrenched from his coat.

"Do the occupants on either side know about this?" he asked.

"Yes, monsieur. I have asked them if they remember being disturbed in the night, but they heard nothing strange."

"Then the matter had better be reported!"

The man nodded.

"Nothing can be done until we reach Lyons, monsieur," he said. "It is no use stopping now."

"When do you expect to reach Lyons?"

"Three quarters of an hour, monsieur, or even less."

"Then we'd better get some breakfast while there's time," said the detective. "Come on, Tinker; we're both pretty hungry."

As they passed number nine coupe on the way to the restaurant-car, Blake caught a glimpse of the occupant. The man was in his shirt-sleeves, but his face did not impress Blake very favourably. He noted the swarthy features, the high, prominent cheekbones, and the ugly, broken nose, and decided to renew his observations later on.

He did not get the opportunity, however, of pursuing his inquiries. He lingered rather longer than he should have done over breakfast, puzzling over this latest development of the mystery he had set out to solve. They were still in the restaurant-car when the slowing-up of the train warned Blake that they were approaching Lyons.

He got up immediately and returned with Tinker to their coupe. The next ten minutes or so were fully occupied with packing their haversacks and attending to the innumerable little formalities that arise after a lengthy train journey.

Although Blake was still greatly preoccupied with the mystery that surrounded coupe number eight, he was too busy to investigate the circumstances any further. They had only just completed their arrangements when the train drew up at its sidings.

Then followed the usual scramble of leaving one train and catching another. Besides their haversacks they had two portmanteaux in the luggage-van. The formalities of registration had to be gone through again before proceeding on their journey, and this caused some delay.

It was while Blake was hurrying across the station-approach to catch the Marseilles train that the next event occurred. A man was just getting into a fiacre, and as Blake passed he recognised his face. It was the man with the broken nose, who had occupied coupe number nine.

But there was another important detail that the detective's keen eyes had noted almost unconsciously, and even then he did not appreciate its significance until he had gone a dozen steps or so. Then he suddenly halted and swung round on his heel. The man was wearing a black coat, and it was fastened with one button only; the two lower ones were missing.

The detective stood there in doubtful hesitation. The fiacre had already drawn away from the kerb and was moving out of the station. For an instant he was minded to follow it. Then he thought of Tinker and Pedro and the train he was to catch, and decided to let the matter drop.

But while the train was on its way to Marseilles Blake's mind was busy with a hundred-and-one harassing questions.

Who could this stranger have been? Where was he going? And what part had he played in the tragedy that had taken place that night in coupe number eight?

Then there was the strange fact of the faked Murillo which he had discovered under the seat. How had that come there? What was it doing in the carriage? And had the struggle taken place for its possession? Yet that could hardly be the case, else why should it have been left under the seat? But there had been a struggle, that was quite clear, and they must have fought over something. What was this thing which they had striven so fiercely to obtain?

Next, Blake thought of the black cloth button which he had found that morning in the south room of the Veuxpillo Galleries. It must have been dropped there by the man who had occupied coupe number nine. And that man had killed Gustave Fulk, and had stolen the genuine Murillo.

Blake began to wish, after all, that he had followed the fiacre out of Lyons Station.

The man who had climbed inside was the very man he had set out to track down; he was sure of that now. Then he remembered the message written in the invisible ink. This man was to meet Kalib Pasha somewhere in Algiers. If those instructions meant anything, then he was certain to make his way there.

Very likely he would follow by the next train; he had missed this one in order to throw possible pursuers off the scent. Blake decided that his most obvious course was to get on to Algiers as soon as possible.

At that moment Tinker, who had kept silent for quite half an hour, felt it was up to him to say something.

"I wonder what old Frenton's doing now, guv'nor?" he said.

And, in spite of the problems which he was trying to solve, Blake had to laugh.

"Chasing about for me with a writ of subpoena, I expect," he muttered.

"He must be frightfully sick, guv'nor."

"I dare say he is, Tinker."

No other event of importance happened on their journey. They had to spend the night at Marseilles, and were able to pass a few interesting hours in seeing some of the sights of "Europe's great gateway to the East." Tinker was so much fascinated by this cosmopolitan, town that he could hardly drag himself away.

Early next morning they embarked on their steamer, and a little after mid-day entered the harbour of Algiers—exactly a week after the crime at the Veuxpillo Galleries had taken place.

Chapter 18
The Veiled Lady

THERE are two hotels in Algiers almost exclusively patronised by wealth and fashion. They are in the French quarter of the town that surrounds the harbour. One overlooks the harbour; the other is more central.

This district is in strange contrast to the people who flock down its spacious boulevards. It is a miniature European city of electric cars, gay Parisian shops, and open-air cafés. But behind it is the old town, a place of mystery and enchantment and strange Oriental customs. The native quarter is a secret land, as yet undiscovered by the civilisation of the West.

In its streets and market-places mingle turban and fez, Moor and Arab, with, perhaps a few doubtful Europeans. But although they mingle, they never mix, for each element still preserves its traditions and the customs that have been handed down through the centuries. The women are veiled, and peer furtively at the world through two narrow slits in their yashmaks.

On the day of Blake and Tinker's arrival one of these veiled women sat on the verandah of the hotel that overlooks the harbour. Her costume was European, and cut stylishly so as to show the youthful curves and symmetry of her figure to the best advantage.

Only the native veil that concealed her face led one to suppose that she was not European, but the wife of one of the Arab or Moorish officials resident at Algiers.

She sat in a secluded corner of the verandah, and slowly sipped an iced drink through a long straw. Besides herself there was only one other person on the verandah. He stood some distance away, and was leaning on the balustrade, gazing reflectively across the harbour as the steamboat from Marseilles slowly approached the landing-stage.

His face was thin and arrogant, his forehead high, but narrow, and as he watched the approaching vessel his fingers kept up an impatient tattoo on the ornamental pillar of the balustrade.

Apparently he awaited the arrival of some person from Marseilles with considerable anxiety; and yet did not know when to expect him, and was not even sure that he would come.

As a matter of fact, this was exactly the case, for the man was Kalib Pasha, the Turkish official who had attended the Peace Conference. And the man whose arrival he awaited with such impatience was the man whom Sexton Blake had seen getting into the fiacre at Lyons station, and who had occupied coupe number nine.

Although Kalib Pasha was not aware of it, the woman's dark eyes were regarding him very attentively through the two slits in her veil, and there was not a movement of his that escaped her observation.

Presently she gave a quick turn of her head and glanced across at the French windows that opened out from the dining room; then, with a little amused shrug, she turned her attention to the Turk again.

Behind the French windows stood one of the hotel waiters. He, too, seemed greatly interested in the movements of Kalib Pasha. But although he was dressed as a waiter, and carried a white napkin over his arm, yet he seemed strangely out of place in his present garb.

He was a strongly built, big-boned man, his face was clean-shaven, as a waiter's should be, but every now and then he put his hand to his chin like one not quite certain if a beard were there or not. He had queer blue eyes which gave one the nasty feeling of reading one's thoughts.

He noticed the quick movement of the veiled lady, and the little amused gesture, and immediately drew back from the window. But from the interior of the room his eyes still watched Kalib Pasha's movements.

For some time the Turkish official did not move from the verandah. The vessel was nearing the jetty now; soon the hawsers were thrown out, she was brought to her moorings, and the passengers began to crowd across the gangways.

From the hotel the distance was too great to recognise anyone leaving the boat, yet something seemed to induce Kalib Pasha to watch the disembarkation. Not until the gangways were clearing and the people were disappearing behind the quay did he remove his reluctant eyes from the vessel.

Yet if his eyes had been keen enough he might have seen a bloodhound following two figures across one of the gangways, to emerge later on from the customs-house, and make their way towards the central hotel.

If he had noticed the incident, the chances are that he would not have attached any significance to it. Yet that small factor was to play a very big part in Kalib Pasha's schemes later on, as he found out to his cost.

The Turk stood for a moment lost in thought. Then, with an impatient gesture, he turned, and strode into the dining-room. The veiled woman was now alone on the verandah. She, too, seemed to have fallen into a pensive mood. Presently she cast a swift glance at the French windows, then rang the small table-bell.

In answer to her summons the big waiter appeared, and came quickly towards her.

"Madame will have another iced sherbet?" he asked in a voice that seemed more used to giving orders than receiving them.

He had spoken in French, the language mostly used there, and the woman replied in the same tongue.

"Perhaps monsieur, from the lengthy experience of his profession, can recommend something more cooling for such a very hot day?" she said.

There was a trace of mocking laughter behind the words, and the man flushed up angrily. He was about to make some angry reply, then seemed suddenly to recollect his present position.

"No, I cannot!" he said abruptly.

"Come, come, monsieur," she twitted him, "surely you are proficient enough in your calling to know of a more cooling beverage than iced sherbet?"

The waiter surveyed his customer beneath lowered brows. He could not see her face, but the lurking humour in her dark eyes told him only too plainly that she was poking fun at him. He paid her back in her own coin.

"Madame has already consumed three iced sherbets," he said, with forced politeness. "Its cooling properties can receive no better recommendation than madame's own testimony."

The woman gave a little silvery peal of laughter. Then she spoke in English,

"Now Meester Grant is becoming impertinent," she said.

The man bit his lip. But his face betrayed no surprise; not a muscle moved. Only the little tremor of his fingers as he played with the thin straw in the glass betrayed the iron will that checked any expression of his feelings. He glanced furtively over his shoulder, then bent his head.

"Who are you?" he asked, in a low whisper.

The woman gave a little shrug of her finely modelled shoulders.

"Ah, now monsieur is becoming inquisitive as well," she said.

The man gave another glance over his shoulder; then, before she could stop him, he made a quick movement and lifted her veil.

"Julie!" he exclaimed; and still he held himself in check, and stood there as if deferentially awaiting her order.

Mademoiselle Julie—for it was she—pouted resentfully as she adjusted her yashmak.

"You are too rude, Monsieur Grant," she said. "I have a good mind to report your insolence!"

"I shouldn't," he said curtly. "It might lead to inquiries. Madame Korofa, the wife of a Moorish official, will suit your convenience better at the present moment than Mademoiselle Julie of the French Secret Service."

The woman nodded; and Granite Grant continued:

"But we are wasting time, mademoiselle. Tell me, is it Kalib Pasha you are watching?"

"Yes, monsieur. And you also! We are working for the same end."

"You recognised me in the hotel?"

"Yes; just now. But I was not surprised. I expected to find you in Algiers. Last week I followed you across from Paris. You spoke from a telephone-box at Victoria Station."

"Yes?"

"I was in the next box!"

"Ah," he said, "I wonder what you know. But it does not matter—we do not work at cross-purposes. So you followed me here?"

"No, no! I missed you in London. It was from Paris that I was instructed to follow Kalib Pasha."

"Then you do not know what has happened to the stolen cipher?"

"Unless Kalib Pasha has it, monsieur!"

Granite Grant shook his head.

"He has not," he said. "I am sure of that. We left Marseilles together. I have searched his room; it is not there. He seems to be awaiting someone's arrival."

"So it seems, monsieur. Last night I followed him to the Ak-el-baran."

"You did, mademoiselle! But not alone, surely? It is no place for a lady."

The young woman raised her head proudly.

"There is no place where I would not go, monsieur," she answered.

"I know that, mademoiselle," he said quickly. "I know that you have no fear. But there are some places where even you dare not go alone. It is in the mosque at Ak-el-baran that Kalib Pasha has spent the last two evenings, and you dare not go in there."

"Then you think he goes there to await someone's arrival, monsieur?" she asked sharply.

Granite Grant nodded.

"I have watched him," he said. "He stays there very late, and all the time he seems to be expecting someone."

Mademoiselle Julie was silent for a moment. Presently she glanced up at him determinedly.

"I will go to this mosque," she said. "I must find out why Kalib Pasha is there."

"But you cannot go alone!

"I shall," she insisted. "Nothing shall stop me."

He laughed a little awkwardly.

"I'll wager ten pounds that you do not get in," he said. "But it is useless to argue, mademoiselle," he added, "when you have made up your mind. But you do not quite understand. However, I shall be there if there is any trouble."

The young woman shrugged her shoulders again.

"That is very kind of Monsieur Grant," she said; "but I am quite able to take care of myself. And you will have to pay me that ten pounds."

Granite Grant gave vent to a deep chuckle.

"You are very independent, mademoiselle," he said; "but you are only a girl, after all."

She was about to make some sharp retort, when one of the hotel guests came out on the verandah.

"Shush!" he whispered, and then raised his voice.

"Madame will have another iced sherbet!" he said, and quickly disappeared through the French windows.

Mademoiselle Julie watched the King's Spy vanish, and then gave an amused sort of laugh.

"The big Englishman as a waiter!" she muttered. "It is very drôle!"

Chapter 19
"In the Arab Town"

S EXTON BLAKE and his assistant had too many things to occupy their attention on their arrival in Algiers to see much of the town that day. By the time that they had seen their portmanteaux safely deposited at the hotel, booked their rooms and had something to eat, they were too tired other than to have a quiet walk around the harbour and then retire to bed.

On the next morning they were both up early, and went for a stroll along the wide boulevards. In their interest in the strange sights and sounds that they saw and heard the detective and his assistant almost forgot the brooding mystery that had brought them to this wonderful cosmopolitan city.

"We've only seen the French quarter so far, Tinker," said Blake, as they began to retrace their steps to the hotel in time for breakfast. "Wait until we get into the old town and the Arab quarter, then you'll see things that'll make you sit up."

"Where does the old town lie, guv'nor?" asked Tinker.

He spoke in an awed kind of voice, for the youngster was greatly impressed by the strangeness of his surroundings.

Blake pointed over his shoulder to where the old town climbed up the steep hillside, terrace by terrace, to the Kasbah, fortress.

"That's it, Tinker!" he said. "And that's where we shall find the Ak-el-baran. We're in for a little excitement there later on."

They walked back in silence. As they were approaching their hotel a native clothed in a bundle of rags slunk up to Tinker and began talking to him in a strange jargon that set Tinker's teeth on edge.

The youth cast a swift look of perplexity at his master. But Blake stood a few paces away looking on, and seemed to be enjoying the joke. Tinker suddenly determined not to be outdone when it came to a matter of talking. He turned to his disreputable accoster again.

"Well, and how's your father?" he asked politely.

Blake's merriment increased, and so did the native's flow of language. Tinker suddenly found that the man was getting too close for his liking.

"Here, old sport!" he said, pushing him aside with his hand, "don't get between me and the wind. It doesn't smell too healthy."

The native slunk back, and, gesticulating wildly, poured forth such a flood of rhetoric that Tinker was astounded at his eloquence.

"What's he saying, guv'nor?" he asked, in bewilderment. "Sounds like a scratched gramophone record. Can't we bust the spring somehow?"

But Blake only laughed the louder.

"He's swearing at you, Tinker!" he spluttered. "He's cursing you by the beard of your father."

Tinker was so impressed by this piece of news that he was speechless for a moment or two. He took out his watch and gazed at it critically, as if he were timing a race.

"Is he still swearing, guv'nor?" he asked presently.

"Yes, he's still cursing you, Tinker. He's started on your mother now."

Tinker suddenly became furious.

"Here, old bird," he said wrathfully, "that's quite enough of that."

And with a swift movement Tinker twisted the native round, planted his foot smartly on a certain part of his anatomy, and sent the bundle of rags sprawling into the gutter.

"Don't you meddle with my family affairs again," he growled, "you—you unredeemed pledge-shop!"

"What's the joke, guv'nor?" he asked innocently, as he rejoined his master a moment later.

"He was only asking you for alms, Tinker," said the detective.

"I thought you said he was swearing, guv'nor?"

"So he was, Tinker—afterwards, when you pushed him away."

Tinker thought for a few minutes.

"I must learn Arabic, guv'nor," he said suddenly.

"Why?"

"Can't beat it, guv'nor. It's perfect. Knocks English into a blue fit."

As they turned into their hotel Tinker glanced back over his shoulder. The bundle of rags was still standing in the gutter, waving his arms frantically, and hurling curses at his head.

As they crossed the foyer of the hotel they heard sounds of commotion proceeding from the floor above. Feeling a little apprehensive, the detective hurried through the glass doors and came face to face with the concierge, resplendent in red fez, blue trousers, and embroidered vest. The man was greatly excited, and was wringing his hands in despair.

"Monsieur," he gasped—"the dog—the dog!"

Blake pushed him roughly aside, and raced upstairs with Tinker close behind. The door of his room was open, and a crowd of frightened waiters and attendants was collected outside in the corridor.

From inside a number of low threatening growls were proceeding from Pedro. The crowd made way for the detective and his assistant, and they strode into the room.

Huddled in one corner was a swarthy-faced, Jewish-looking little man, with the bloodhound crouching in front of him and showing his great teeth menacingly. The little man's eyes were rolling in fright, and every time he made a movement the great dog gave a ferocious growl and made as if to spring at him.

Blake took the situation in at a glance. The French windows leading on to the verandah were wide open; he had omitted to put up the catch when he had gone for his stroll. The little man was only a common or garden thief, who had taken advantage of his negligence to swarm up the verandah and enter his room.

It was just like Pedro to wait until the thief had got to work and then to emerge from under the bed and catch him in the act. Blake could imagine what a fright the man had had. Pedro was a sagacious animal; he always secured the evidence to hang his man before he arrested him.

The detective took a step forward.

"Steady, Pedro, old fellow!" he said. "He won't run away."

The dog wagged his tail understandingly at the sound of his master's voice, but he still kept a keen watch on his prisoner.

"What are you doing here?" Blake asked sternly in Arabic. "Just hand over what you have stolen. Come on! Out with it!"

The man wept and gnashed his teeth, and talked with such vigour that Tinker began to grow suspicious.

"What's he saying, guv'nor?" he asked. "Is he casting aspersions on my family history? For if he is I'll tweak his nose for him."

"No, it's all right, Tinker. He's calling on Allah to bear witness to his innocence. When he finds that Allah doesn't answer he'll finish up by bringing out the swag."

Blake was right. The man kept up his voluble flow of language for some minutes; then, finding that Allah was deaf to his invocations, he suddenly delved into the recesses of his tattered garments and flung a number of small objects at the detective's feet.

"There you are, Tinker!" said Blake. "My gold sleeve-links and watch-chain. Pedro evidently didn't give him time to sneak anything else. Now he's asking Allah to prove that some evil spirit made them walk into his pockets."

He turned to the concierge, who had by this time summoned up enough courage to enter the room.

"Take him away!" he said. "Give him a bath—that will be sufficient punishment."

Still strenuously protesting his innocence, the man was seized by the attendants and dragged from the room.

But after this little incident Pedro became quite a popular hero, and although the domestics still kept out of his way they treated him with every respect and consideration.

"That's our second little affair this morning, Tinker," said Blake, as they went downstairs to get something to eat. "Interesting place, isn't it?"

"I should say so, guv'nor! Makes you wonder what's going to happen next."

The walk had given them both a keen appetite, and they ate their breakfast with a relish. After having a quiet smoke on the verandah Blake got up from his chair.

"I'm going out to make one or two purchases, Tinker," he said. "I sha'n't be gone more than an hour. This afternoon we'll both go into the native quarter and try and find out what's on at the Ak-el-baran."

"Right-ho, guv'nor!" replied his assistant. "I'll wait here until you come back. I've got one or two things I want to do."

After walking for about ten minutes he came into the boulevard that led down to the quay. Quite a number of people were approaching from the further end, and for the moment Blake was puzzled to know where they had sprung from. Then he saw that they were new arrivals from the Marseilles boat that was now at her moorings in the harbour.

Presently he found himself studying the face of a man who was coming towards him. Not until he had passed did it suddenly dawn on Blake who he was. Then he knew it was the man with the broken nose whom he had last seen at Lyons, and who had occupied coupe No. 9.

Swiftly making up his mind, Blake determined to keep him in sight and find out where he was going. He turned immediately and quickened his pace until only about a dozen yards separated him from his quarry, then began stealthily to dog his footsteps.

Evidently the man in front was familiar with his surroundings, and had a definite object in view, for he strode on quickly without once hesitating as to what direction he should take.

For nearly a quarter of an hour they proceeded like this, the man Blake was following seeming to have no suspicion of the fact that he was being shadowed. Then the detective began to notice the change in their surroundings.

The wide, spacious boulevards of the French quarter had given place to narrow squalid streets of ramshackle dwellings, amongst the garbage of which dirty, half-naked children scrambled and played. Sprawled about and sitting at the doors of their houses were Arab men and women clad in filthy ragged garments, who eyed him suspiciously as he passed, and wondered what he was doing there.

One or two of them went so far as to accost him, but before the detective's stern gaze they quailed and slunk away, muttering imprecations on his head.

For a moment Blake was half minded to retrace his steps. Although he had never visited the place before, he knew very well where his quarry was leading him. He was getting into the heart of the Arab town where few Europeans dared to penetrate alone—a strange secret den of eastern life and mystery.

Not that Blake had any qualms on account of his own personal safety; but he would have preferred to have been dressed more in keeping with his surroundings than in the Norfolk tourist suit, which made him so conspicuous.

Besides, there was Tinker to think of. Not being able to speak the language his assistant, would be in rather an awkward predicament if he were left alone for very long.

Then Blake decided that now he had gone thus far he might as well see where his quarry would lead him. He could take careful stock of his surroundings, and return again with Tinker should he so desire.

He continued his way, therefore, keeping one eye on the man he was following, and the other on the look-out for any signs of trouble.

Soon he plunged into what seemed more like a rabbit warren than anything else. The streets had entirely disappeared; he found himself feeling his way down narrow, precipitous passages, in comparison with which an English lane or alley would be quite a broad thoroughfare.

On either side were the squalid wooden and baked mud dwellings; sometimes they met overhead and the narrow defile burrowed underneath. This human ants' nest was as dark as night, and only occasionally did Blake catch a glimpse of a thin streak of sky overhead.

People seemed to swarm all about him, yet only once or twice did they actually get in his way. They appeared to be burrowed in the earth on either side like so many rabbits. The smell of the place sickened Blake, and he shut his mouth tightly. Once he had to stand flat to the wall in order to let a tiny donkey pass with panniers; no horse or cart could ever enter those narrow fissures.

It was too dark for Blake to see his quarry now; more by intuition than anything else he knew that he was somewhere ahead. He felt that it was too late to withdraw now, and that having got into these subterranean galleries he would see the thing to a finish.

A hundred yards further on he came to a place where the passage divided to right and left. He hesitated a moment, in doubt as to which path he should take.

Then, with a start, he was aware that two eyes were peering out at him from the gloom.

Chapter 20
The Fight in the Burrows

ONLY for a breathless instant did Blake stand there gazing into those dark, malignant eyes. But it was sufficient to tell him that he had been discovered; that the man he had been following through the tortuous passages of the Arab town had become aware that he was being shadowed and had hidden in wait for his unknown pursuer.

Then, with a furious snarl of rage, the Arab sprang towards him, and in his upraised hand Blake saw a wicked little blade glitter as it poised ready to strike.

But the detective was no novice in the art of self-defence: he had had too much experience in these matters to be caught napping. Quick as lightning his right hand shot out and caught his adversary's wrist; with a sharp twist that made the Arab scream with pain, he sent the knife flying from his grasp, and at the same time his left swung up and crashed with terrific force on the Arab's chin.

With a gasping cry the man crumpled up, and sank to the ground all of a heap.

Blake gave a swift glance at his prostrate foe and decided that the best thing he could do was to make his way back as quickly as possible. He turned on his heel and plunged into the passage again; he did not doubt that he would be able to keep to the path he had come.

But he was not to be unmolested long. Hardly had he gone a dozen yards than a perfect pandemonium of noise broke out behind him, and as if by magic the gully began to vomit forth brown wriggling forms, which crowded on him menacingly, but as yet did not dare to venture too close.

Blake still kept on his way. Sooner or later he knew there was fresh trouble in store: the screaming, gesticulating hordes that were following him would not let him escape without he made a fight of it. He was rather glad now that the passage was so narrow, he would only have to reckon with one or two foes at the same time: not more than that could get at him.

Then the fun began. One dirty Arab, bolder than the rest, made a sudden dart at him and grabbed at his coat. But Blake was ready for him; he nipped round and let fly with his terrible left again. The man made a funny little gurgling noise, turned a somersault, and went hurtling into the ragged swarm that pressed close behind.

A hushed silence followed, and the detective pushed on again. But the respite was only momentary; an instant later the shouts were renewed with greater intensity, and the swarm swept forward again.

But this time it did not stop; forced on by those behind, the foremost of the riffraff were driven into reach of Blake's arms. Then followed one of the most energetic displays of fisticuffs that the detective had ever indulged in.

It was more like having a round with the punch-ball than anything else. Blake plugged away like a machine, and against his scientific skill the rabble stood no chance. The Arabs went down like nine-pins, and as fast; as one was bowled over another was pressed forward to meet with the same swift punishment.

But Blake knew that it could not last much longer. His knuckles, hard as they were from constant practice, were becoming bruised and raw; and, apart from that, his line of retreat was being cut off; new adversaries were appearing from the other side and he was forced to stand with his back to the wall and hit out left and right.

For some moments more the fight went on—the quick intake of breath, the crunch of bone and gristle, the gasping cry, and, above all, the crazy hubbub of noise—then something dramatic happened.

Blake was hemmed in by a barricade of living, writhing bodies; they seemed to drop from the roof and wriggle out of cracks in the wall to pile themselves up beneath the hammer of his fists. One brown body dropped clean on Blake's head; he caught him by the legs and swung him like a battering ram at the strained, furious faces that surged on him.

And at the same moment the bottom of the wall heaved and suddenly crumbled away, and the detective, with a heap of struggling bodies, disappeared below.

The thin shell of the human hive had burst beneath the unwonted strain and precipitated him into one of the rude dwellings.

It was only a drop of about six feet. Blake quickly sorted himself out from the wriggling forms and started hitting out again. But the rabble had had enough of his terrible fists; they scrambled as fast as they could out of the opening again, and Blake was thankful to get a few moments respite.

He took a hasty glance around. It was too dark to see anything distinctly, but he was evidently in the basement of the dwelling above. It was only a small square cavity and the atmosphere was fetid. But even outside the odours were thick enough to cut with a knife, so Blake decided that that was no reason for quitting his present refuge. For a time, at any rate, he was safe here. He commanded the opening, and not more than two could get through at a time. There must be a door somewhere, but he could not see it. Outside a furious din was going on; he drew back against the wall and waited.

Presently a pair of bare legs began to wriggle cautiously through the hole. Blake drew out his automatic from his hip pocket and fired. The bullet grazed one of the bare legs, and, with a sharp cry of pain, they were hastily withdrawn.

A minute passed by while the noise outside rose to a perfect frenzy. Then simultaneously two pairs of legs began to descend. The detective fired again.

This time the bullet passed through the fleshy part of one of the bare legs. Its owner immediately grappled with his companion and the two wriggling bodies dangled for a moment above the floor. Then they were dragged out by those up above. After that no one else ventured to become a target for Blake's revolver practice.

Still keeping a vigilant watch on the hole, the detective sat down on the floor with his back propped against the wall, and slowly recovered his wind. The uproar outside had not abated, it was worse if anything. It seemed to Blake as if half the Arab town were swarming about his ears.

He tried to think over his present position. He had to admit that he had got himself into a pretty pickle; he began to wish he had returned to the hotel instead of following the man with a broken nose. At any rate, he had given the man a gruelling, he wouldn't recover in a hurry from the punch he had given him—that was some satisfaction.

But somehow he must get away from this evil-smelling hole. He thought of Tinker. The youngster would be very concerned when he didn't return. He had told him that he would only be gone an hour.

At that moment he heard a noise immediately overhead. He got up hastily, and, striking a match, looked up at the roof. There was a square trapdoor above, evidently the only means of egress from the chamber, and his foes were dragging some heavy object over it. Apparently they didn't intend to let him escape that way.

Blake sat down again and listened to the cries outside. He tried to do some hard thinking, but the hours sped by and still he could think of no way of escaping from his unpleasant predicament.

He felt for his pipe, and heaved a sigh of relief as his fingers closed over the beloved object. Thank goodness he still had that never-failing solace to fall back upon. He lighted up and puffed away in silence, and hoped something would happen.

Yet another hour or so passed by and still nothing happened. The frenzied cries outside had somewhat abated now. But in their stead was a low confused jabbering of many tongues, as if some plan of action were being discussed and formulated. Blake was beginning to feel a little anxious; what was their next move to be, he wondered.

But he was to know shortly. Another half an hour or more passed, and then the dim opening in front of him was suddenly blotted out. A heap of sacking had been flung over it; he was now in impenetrable darkness.

Wondering what was to happen next he waited expectantly. Then a strange smell of burning assailed his nostrils.

And suddenly Blake understood!

They were going to smoke him out. He was to be slowly suffocated. From some crevice in the wall they were filling the room with smoke fumes. He was caught like a rat in a trap.

Blake gritted his teeth. So that was to be his fate! He was to meet an ignominious death at the hands of these dirty tatterdemalions. Rather than that he would make a bold dash for liberty. The odds were too heavy to hope to escape, he would be borne down by sheer weight of numbers, but he could at least sell his life dearly.

He drew back against the wall and held himself ready for the spring. Outside the din had suddenly increased again; strange frightened shouts and panic-stricken cries smote upon his ears. He wondered what all the confusion was about, then made a short run and sprang up at the sacking that covered the hole.

Chapter 21
Pedro in Pursuit

IT was not until lunch-time that Tinker really began to grow uneasy over Blake's absence. Then the prospect of going into the dining-room alone and being served by waiters who spoke an unknown jargon somewhat appalled him.

He began to wonder what had kept Blake so long. His master was a great stickler for punctuality; it was quite unlike him not to keep his word in the matter of appointments. Tinker went down into the lounge and kept one eye on the clock and the other on the door, hoping every moment to see his master's familiar face appear at the glass screen.

But the moments sped by and still no Blake appeared. Tinker's anxiety increased so that he could not keep still, but commenced to walk impatiently up and down the floor. He was oppressed by a feeling of great loneliness, for the first time he realised how helpless he was in a foreign town without his master's reassuring presence and quiet confidence.

He glanced up at the clock again. Blake had been gone for over three hours now, and he had promised to be back in an hour. Luncheon was now served, but Tinker had no inclination to go in and feed alone; he had no appetite unless Blake was there.

At last he could stand the suspense no longer. He ran and got his hat from the cloak-room and wandered out into the street. He dared not go too far from the hotel for fear of losing his way, there were no familiar London policemen he could ask to direct him.

For some time he roved about, hoping to see his master approaching every minute. But half an hour went by and there were still no signs of Blake. He hurried back to the hotel and grabbed hold of the arm of the first man he came across, which happened to be one of the waiters.

"I say," he began breathlessly, "have you seen Mr. Sexton Blake?"

The man stared vacantly at the youth for a moment, then beamed politely and began to rattle off a string of uncouth phrases.

Tinker grew frantic.

"Monsoor Blake!" he said impatiently. "For goodness' sake stop chewing your false teeth and answer a civil question. Ave a voo seen Monsoor Blake? Don't you understand plain English?"

The man gave a low bow, beamed still more expansively, and, waving his arm towards the dining room, rattled off again.

Tinker was now getting furious.

"Cut out that rough stuff!" he cried warningly. "I know what you're saying. You just leave my father's beard alone, or I'll pull your long nose for you."

He made as if to put his threat into action. The man stepped quickly out of arm's reach, bowed lower still, beamed so that his mouth met his ears, and began to froth at the lips with a perfect blast of eloquence.

Tinker passed his hand through his hair in despair, then turned and fled upstairs to Blake's room.

His master was not there, he had not expected to find him. He was sure by this time that something unexpected had happened. But Pedro was there. Scenting something amiss, the great dog came up and buried his nose in his young master's hands.

Then a sudden thought flashed through Tinker's mind.

"Pedro, old boy," he said, caressing the animal, "where's Blake—where's the master? Find him, there's a good dog!"

The bloodhound lifted his head and pricked up his ears. Tinker picked up the lead from off the dressing-table.

"Pedro," he said again, "the master's gone. We've got to find him, boy. D'you get me?"

Tinker spoke in low, earnest tones; his voice trembled in spite of himself. Pedro grasped the situation immediately; instinctively the faithful brute knew what was wrong. An eager light came into his keen eyes, he uttered a little impatient yelp and began to leap up at the door. At that moment Tinker felt that he was not alone in the world after all.

"Old Pedro," he said thickly, "you understand plain English, boy. These other scally-wags make a meal off their gums every time they speak. It's up to you and me to find Blake."

He opened the door and went downstairs, with Pedro tugging on the lead. Outside he paused a moment wondering which way he should go. He chose the direction that led to the harbour. It was the only way he was sure of; besides, Blake had gone out to make some purchases, and Tinker knew that the shops lay in that quarter.

Many curious eyes glanced at the youth and the dog as they hurried along the pavement, but Tinker took no notice of anyone. He had extraordinary confidence in the bloodhound, and somehow he felt that already they were hastening to Blake's assistance.

Tinker was not very long in getting to the precincts of the harbour. There was not a great number of people about now, for it was the middle of the day, when most of them were partaking of the mid-day meal.

He passed along the wide boulevard of fashionable Parisian shops until he approached the quay, then began to retrace his steps again. Tinker had no clear idea as to what his next move would be, he simply felt that he must keep on walking. The dog went eagerly forward in the direction his young master liked to choose; he, too, seemed to think that the chief thing was to keep moving.

After retracing his steps several times, Tinker suddenly realised the futility of his task. Even if Blake had been here it was hopeless to expect Pedro to pick up the scent; too many people had gone over the same ground for that. He came to a standstill and looked helplessly at his dumb friend.

"What in the name of goodness shall we do, Pedro?" he asked in despair.

But the dog only wagged his tail and pulled at the lead. Tinker started to walk on again.

Presently he came to the end of the shops further from the quay. He had turned here and retraced his steps several times before. He did so again. But Pedro held back; this time he refused to follow his young master. Instead, he hung on his collar with his nose pointing in the opposite direction and refused to budge.

Tinker looked doubtfully at the animal.

"What's the matter, old fellow?" he asked.

The dog glanced up impatiently and strained forward on the lead. Then, with a thrill of joy, Tinker realised that the bloodhound's almost uncanny instinct was urging him to go in the opposite direction.

He gave the animal the lead and let him go his own way.

"Good dog, Pedro!" he said excitedly. "Find the master, boy!"

The dog went on deliberately. He did not appear to be following any scent, his nose was held high. But by some unerring instinct the bloodhound was taking the direction Blake had taken earlier on in the day.

Tinker kept close behind, breaking into a little trot every now and then in order to keep up with the animal. Presently he noticed the change in his environs. The wide boulevard with its handsome shops had given place to narrow, mean streets of tumble-down dwellings. Dirty native women and children paused at his approach and slunk out of the way of the great dog with muttered threats and evil glances. Pedro was making straight for the centre of the Arab town.

Tinker had no doubt now that Pedro was on the right track. If his master, for some reason, had wandered into this part of the town, then anything might have happened to him. As Tinker looked into the sinister brown faces around him he felt glad that the dog was with him. Almost unconsciously his hand went to his pocket and felt for his pistol.

A little later Pedro sunk his nose to the ground and went more slowly; his hair was bristling angrily along his back, and he kept up a low sullen growl. Tinker knew then that the bloodhound had picked up his master's scent.

Presently they plunged into a narrow defile, more like worm-holes and burrowings underground than anything else. It was so dark that it was some time before Tinker could see anything; the smell and heat was almost unbearable, he had to gulp down a feeling of nausea.

Vague dark forms flitted to and fro, or flattened themselves against the wall with frightened cries at Pedro's approach. Sometimes one would attempt to obstruct the path, then the bloodhound would give a snarl of fury and crouch for the spring; the figure would vanish with a yell of fear.

Soon a low murmur began to make itself heard from in front, like the buzzing of wasps around the jam-jar. And when the bloodhound heard it he could not restrain his anger; baying furiously, he leapt forward and left his young master to follow as best he could.

As Tinker sped in the direction of the sound the noise increased, a confused jabbering smote on his ears, as of a swarm of people talking at once. A moment later startled cries were raised, hoarse shouts of rage and terror, and, above all, came the baying of the great bloodhound. Tinker knew then that Pedro had arrived—that somewhere ahead the dog was in the midst of a grim struggle.

Tinker had never run so hard as he did those last dozen yards or so; the thought of finding Blake lent wings to his feet. For that Pedro had come across his master just at the critical moment he did not doubt. Then, as he shot round a bend in the passage, a strange sight met his eyes.

The dim, narrow passage was swarming with lean brown bodies—twisting, writhing, and struggling together in utter confusion as the bloodhound flung himself into the melee and bit and tore at the naked limbs.

And in the midst of the scuffle was Sexton Blake, hitting out as hard as he could with his fists, and sometimes varying the procedure by picking up a wriggling body and hurling it into the fracas.

It was just like a scene from the Inferno, and the terror-stricken cries of the natives sounded like Bedlam broken loose. As Tinker sprang to the help of his master, Blake broke away from the struggling mass of men and slowly backed towards him.

It was not an attack now, but a rout. Driven to frenzy, by Pedro's relentless persecution, and pushed on by those in the rear, the natives scratched and tore at each other, fighting like demons to get out of reach of the dog's savage jaws. Blake simply used his fists to keep them back, and to prevent them from swarming over him.

Tinker had joined his master by this time. No words were exchanged between them— it was useless to try and make oneself heard in that appalling din. Fighting side by side and keeping back the terror-stricken crowd, they slowly retreated along the passage.

Then a new diversion occurred. Pedro had wormed his way some distance through the forest of struggling legs. The men who had been pushing on from behind suddenly found themselves attacked by the great dog. The confusion that ensued relieved the pressure in front, and the rabble wavered and began to hold back.

Blake shouted something in his assistant's ear, and although Tinker could not hear what he said, he understood his meaning immediately. They both turned simultaneously and dashed back along the passage.

No attempt was made to follow them; the terrified crowd was too busy struggling amongst itself to heed their escape. Those who were coming from the other direction either scrambled out of their way, or were bowled over by Blake. Presently he stopped and leant against the wall, panting from his exertions.

"By Jove, Tinker," he gasped, laying his hand on his young assistant's shoulder, "that was a near thing. You just arrived in the nick of time."

Tinker was too full of emotion to speak; he felt like weeping for joy at finding his master safe and unhurt. Blake remained listening to the pandemonium of noise for some minutes.

"Old Pedro's putting in some stout work," he said. "That rabble won't attack again in a hurry, I think we'd better call the beggar out."

He took a whistle from his pocket and blew three shrill blasts. A few moments later the bloodhound came bounding towards his master, still baying excitedly, as if he rather enjoyed the rough and tumble.

"Bully boy!" said Blake, fondling Pedro's great head. The dog licked his master's hands and whimpered with delight.

The outcry from along the passage had not abated, the Arabs were still struggling amongst themselves, and shouting frantically.

"Come on, Tinker!" said the detective. "Let's get away from this fetid den while we're safe."

They continued their way once more, walking in Indian-file, and eventually emerged out into the open. There Blake, who was somewhat anxious as to how Pedro had fared, carefully examined the animal. But although he was a little lame, and was bruised about the body, the dog had sustained no very serious hurt.

The detective himself had not escaped entirely unscathed. The knuckles of his hands were raw and bleeding, his face was scratched and bruised, and his Norfolk jacket torn and ripped in a number of places. Tinker felt rather concerned at first.

"You look as if you'd had a rare pummelling, guv'nor," he said anxiously. "Better let me help you along."

Blake gave a short laugh:

"I'm all right, Tinker," he said reassuringly. "But I should have been pulverised into pulp if you and old Pedro had arrived a few minutes later."

"Thank old Pedro for that, guv'nor."

"Yes; and you, too, Tinker. But we'll compare notes later on. I'm hanged if I know how you managed to find me—I had quite given up hope. Let's get back to the hotel as quickly as possible. We're not in an exactly healthy neighbourhood now; the sooner we're out of it the better."

They passed down the mean, narrow street that led to the boulevard, while dirty Arab men and women gaped at them in wonder and surprise. But no one dared to molest them again. Blake felt thankful when they came into the French quarter once more.

"Makes one appreciate civilisation, Tinker," he said, "to be in that stinking den for a few hours. A short while ago I never expected to see an open-air café again, or even the blue sky."

They managed to stop a growler and persuade the driver to take them to the hotel, which saved them the ordeal of passing through the busy thoroughfares and attracting attention to their strange plight.

Once at the hotel the detective and his assistant hurried up to their rooms and began to remove the traces of their recent stirring adventure.

But even Blake's iron constitution had felt the effects of his severe mauling. He felt somewhat refreshed after a hot bath, but for the remainder of that evening he rested in his room, with Pedro asleep at his feet. It required a good night's rest before he again felt like tackling the problem that had brought him to Algiers.

"Tomorrow, Tinker," he said, "we'll pay a visit to the Ak-el-baran. But we won't go as English tourists this time. It's not a healthy costume for these parts; it's far too conspicuous."

Chapter 22
The Mosque of Ak-el-Baran

WHEN Blake awoke next morning he was feeling his old self again. His limbs were still somewhat stiff from the strenuous events of yesterday, but a little exercise soon put him right in that respect. His knuckles were the chief source of trouble; they were still very tender, and it would take some days for them to get back to the normal.

Over breakfast he discussed the problem that faced them with his assistant.

"There is no doubt, Tinker," he said, "that the final act in this drama will be played out at the Ak-el-baran. Whether this fellow has the stolen cipher or not, he is bound to keep the appointment contained in that letter written in the invisible ink."

"But he may have gone there last night, guv'nor?"

"I don't think so, Tinker. He only arrived yesterday, and it'll take him some time to recover from that knock-out blow I gave him. He's feeling none too chirpy at the present moment, I'll be bound."

"But what is the Ak-el-baran, guv'nor? Is it a street, or what?"

"I'm not quite certain, Tinker. I'll ask the concierge in a minute. If you've finished eating we'll make a move."

"They got up from their table and passed out into the vestibule. There the detective found the concierge, in his gorgeous blue trousers, red fez, and embroidered waistcoat, standing majestically at the entrance to the hotel. Blake beckoned him aside and began to question him.

"Tell me about the Ak-el-baran!" he said.

"Ah, monsieur," said the man, only too ready to hold forth on his favourite topic, "it is very good. At the Mosque of Ak-el-baran one sees the dancing girls, and the Marabout's wonderful sword."

"Then there is a mosque at Ak-el-baran?" asked the detective.

"But the mosque is called Ak-el-baran, monsieur. There is no other."

"And do they allow visitors to enter?"

The concierge looked rather dubious.

"It may be that I can get you a guide, monsieur," he answered. "But even then it is doubtful."

"But I do not want a guide," said Blake, "I want to go alone."

The concierge shook his head decisively.

"It is not a nice place," he said. "And monsieur is not dressed for the part."

The detective thought for a moment.

"At what time does the performance commence?" he asked presently.

"Not until the evening, monsieur—at eight o'clock."

"And could you get me a native costume? You shall be well paid."

The man's eyes lighted up at the last words.

"Why, yes, monsieur," he said eagerly; "that is a very simple matter."

"Then get two costumes—one for my friend," said the detective.

"Very good, monsieur; it shall be done at once. I will see that they are sent up to your room in an hour or so."

"Thanks!" said Blake, and slipped some money into the concierge's ready hand.

***

Punctually at eight o'clock two turbaned figures, clad in loose burnouses, and with a bloodhound following close to their heels, passed down the narrow little side street of Ak-el-baran, and entered the gaudily-painted mosque.

Although nobody would have recognised them, one of these swarthy looking Arabs was Sexton Blake, the famous Baker Street detective, while the shorter of the two was Tinker, his assistant. They entered the mosque without being questioned, and Pedro, who was too cunning to make himself conspicuous, crept in between his masters' legs.

The place was dimly lit, and it was a few minutes before they could accustom their eyes to their surroundings. Then Blake perceived that the mosque was already crowded with dark figures, who squatted slipperless on the floor, but kept the centre of the place clear.

"Let's squat down here, Tinker," whispered the detective; "then we can get a good view of what's going on."

He sat down himself, and Tinker followed suit, with Pedro crouching between them.

"What a weird-looking place, guv'nor!" Tinker whispered. "Sort of gives one the creeps."

"You wait until the fun begins, Tinker; you'll find it creepy then."

Tinker was silent for a few minutes, gazing curiously around at the strange scene.

"Who's that fat fellow over in the corner there, guv'nor?" he asked presently.

"That's the Holy Man, or Marabout, I suppose, Tinker. He's the Johnnie with the wonderful sword."

"Rather antipose, isn't he guv'nor?" said the irrepressible Tinker. "And who's the skinny guy in the white night-shirt with the hooked nose?"

"He's the priest, Tinker. He runs the performance."

"And is that the refreshment-bar over there, guv'nor?"

"No, Tinker; it's the orchestra. They're not beer barrels, they're tomtoms."

"Well, I'm blowed!" exclaimed Tinker. "We're going to have some jazz music. When's the show going to start, guv'nor?"

"Shut up, Tinker!" said Blake suddenly. "It's starting now."

Blake was right; at that very moment the orchestra started up. The din was ghastly; the barbaric-looking drums struck up a fierce, rhythmic tattoo to the accompaniment of a number of squealing flutes and whistles. Pedro was so moved that he lifted his head and howled in unison. But Blake silenced him with a gesture of disapproval.

Then a number of half-naked dervishes rushed out from a room at the further end and began dancing up and down the space in the centre with frenzied cries and strange squirmings of their bodies. The barbaric music grew louder and quicker until it sounded like a fiendish racket, and the dancers worked themselves up into a state of madness, writhing and shaking and waving their arms as they spun round in the centre of the floor.

Then the white-robed priest picked up a handful of long steel skewers and began to stick them into the flesh of the dervishes as they danced up and down. Yet they still kept twisting and squirming to the rhythm of the tomtoms, although presently all of them had skewers sticking out of their faces, arms, legs, and bodies.

Tinker turned away from the horrible spectacle in loathing and disgust. He could stomach most things, but this was too much of a joke for his liking. Soon after, the music suddenly ceased with violent crescendo, and the mad dervishes disappeared into the room at the end.

The squatting audience remained silent and unmoved, as if the scene that had just been enacted was quite an ordinary everyday affair. As Tinker looked round at the crowd of dark, intent faces he experienced a feeling of violent repulsion. He could never have believed such things could have happened if he hadn't just witnessed them.

"Enjoying yourself, Tinker?" asked Blake, in a whisper.

"Getting a bit too meaty for my liking, guv'nor," rejoined his assistant. "What's the next item on the programme?"

But the detective did not reply. His gaze had wandered over to the door, and as he looked his mouth became compressed and his eyes narrowed.

"See that man who's just entered, Tinker," he whispered, "he's the man with the broken nose who occupied coupe No. 9, the man I followed yesterday. There'll be something doing, after all. See? He's just squatted down over yonder!"

Tinker glanced over in the direction indicated.

"That's the man right enough, guv'nor," he said excitedly. "Wonder what his game is now."

"We'll keep our eyes skinned, Tinker."

The Arab with a broken nose took a swift glance round the room, as if he was searching for somebody. Then his eyes came to rest on a spot over on Blake's right. The detective turned and looked in that direction. Just beyond the shadow of light a man was sitting at a little trestle table. By that fact, Blake judged he was someone of importance. His face was thin and arrogant, and his forehead high but narrow. He appeared to be dressed in a European costume, but on his head he wore a bright red fez.

The Arab was staring across at this man intently, as if he desired to attract his attention. Blake suddenly remembered the message contained in the invisible writing. Was this man Kalib Pasha? he wondered—the Turkish official who had written that letter making an appointment at Ak-el-baran? If so, then he must keep a sharp look-out. Things were going to happen tonight.

The music started up again at that moment with such suddenness that Pedro could hardly be restrained from repeating his last performance. This time a number of dusky maidens glided out from the room at the end and began to pirouette in the centre of the floor, brandishing their snakelike limbs to and fro, and wriggling up and down like eels.

Then, as the music grew more frenzied, the dancing girls abandoned themselves to an excess of fervour. One of them snatched up the Marabout's sword, and clasping the naked blade in her hands, ran them up and down the keen edge, then began to pierce her body with it.

But Blake was not interested in this bloodcurdling spectacle; his attention had been attracted to the door from which the dancers had emerged. Standing there, looking on unconcerned at the gruesome sight, was the slim, graceful figure of a woman. He could not see her very distinctly, but he knew immediately that she was different from the rest.

Something about her calm, imperious air seemed to fascinate the detective. He wondered who she was and what she was doing in this ghastly den of barbarous rites and devilment. She was clothed in soft, flimsy draperies; her rounded arms were bare, and—unlike the other coppery women—snow white; she was shod in silver sandals, and her silken stockings were of the same colour; as the dim light shone on her golden bronze hair a cusp of jewels flashed forth innumerable points of fire.

At that moment Blake felt Tinker's fingers gripping his arm. He turned his attention again to the weird scene that was going on in front. The beat of the tomtoms was now almost deafening; the priest was giving out wild, guttural incantations; and, as the dancing girls squirmed up and down they held burning twigs against their hands and feet and bare bodies. Then, one by one, they collapsed and dropped to the floor, and the priest dragged them off into the room at the further end.

The music sank to a hushed, murmur, and the audience rocked to and fro in an ecstasy of religious fervour. A tense atmosphere brooded over the dimly-lit mosque as if something unexpected was now to take place.

Blake glanced down at Tinker; in spite of the brown pigment on his face, the detective could see that the youngster was strangely affected. Even the bloodhound seemed to be subdued by this strange nightmare.

Blake looked round for the Arab with the broken nose. The man had risen from the floor and was stealthily approaching the trestle table, at which the man in the bright red fez was sitting.

The music suddenly rose to a crescendo again, and then sank to a low, melancholy thrumming. The woman in the flowing draperies and the silver sandals came slowly into the centre of the ring, and then, began to glide gracefully to and fro in Salome fashion.

The priest eagerly watched her every movement, as if this were some new turn for which he was responsible, and as if he were not quite certain of the result.

But as the detective's gaze now rested on the woman before him there flashed across his mind for the second time the vision of another woman—a woman of slender grace and charm, and with a mass of wavy, golden hair crowning her white forehead.

The vision of his imagination seemed to merge into the figure of the woman who danced before him. Was his imagination playing him false? Had the shrouded mystery of the place and the grotesque scenes he had witnessed got on his nerves? Was he really awake and not passing through a nightmare of dreams?

Or could this slender, graceful woman be Mademoiselle Julie, the French Secret Service agent?—the woman with the dark, alluring eyes, whose irresistible charm and beauty had overcome the strongest of men, and whose daring and courage had risen her so high in the services of her country?

And at that moment the woman began to sing. She sang in French—a low, plaintive love-song, which thrilled Blake strangely, and even seemed to affect the audience of stolid, doltish natives. Her voice was soft and musical, like the hushed playing of a viola. The song came to a finish, and the woman glided slowly round the circle of dark faces to the subdued thrumming of the tomtoms.

Blake glanced round for the Arab with the broken nose. He had just joined the man with the red fez. And at that moment the detective saw something pass between them— something that looked like a large leather wallet.

The woman was slowly gliding towards the trestle table. In front of it she stopped and held out her white arms alluringly towards the man in the red fez. His eyes were burning brightly, and a faint flush had mantled to his sallow face. Blake could see that he was in a state of mad infatuation. He beckoned the woman and smiled, and she came and sat down by his side.

The tomtoms still kept up the rhythmic thrumming: the audience seemed to have reached a state of hypnotism; the natives were rocking themselves to and fro with a low, crooning moan. Blake decided that it was time to act.

"Tinker," he whispered, "Pedro and I are going to do a turn. See that fellow in the red fez? He's got a leather wallet. While I keep the pot boiling make your way over to his side. When you see me bring out the faked painting, grab that wallet. Don't wait for me. Get it somehow, and make a bee-line for the hotel. Got me?"

Tinker nodded his head. He was trembling with excitement, and the perspiration was streaming down his face. The prospect of something doing appealed to him—anything to break the frightful tension to which his nerves were strung.

Blake spoke a sharp word to Pedro, rose suddenly to his feet and sprang into the centre of the floor. The bloodhound's body hurtled through the air at the same time, and landed by the side of his master.

The priest gave a startled exclamation, and half-rose from the floor; then he sank back again and stared stupidly at the strange Arab with his great savage dog. The orchestra seemed to regard this as quite a legitimate turn, and the tomtoms and flutes broke out into an infernal racket again.

Tinker watched his master in open-mouthed wonderment. Blake was getting Pedro to go through some of his familiar tricks. Tinker had often seen the dog perform in this way; but tonight it seemed novel and unnatural—the strangeness of the place added a glamour to the performance.

For a time Blake contented himself with exhibiting Pedro's cleverness and cunning to his strange admiring audience. The dog knew his master's every movement and expression and entered into the spirit of the thing with zest and keen enjoyment. They played together in the centre of the floor—leaping, turning, and twisting about one another, while the drummers kept up their monotonous tattoo.

Then the detective began his star turn. He stepped back a few paces from the dog, then began to creep slowly towards him with his hands held out threateningly. Tinker, who could not keep his eyes from the spectacle, knew immediately what Blake was about. Pedro and his master were to have a sham fight.

As Blake slowly approached the animal the dog crouched down on his belly and watched his master intently, with the rough hair along his spine bristling angrily and his great fangs bared. Then, with a roar of fury, he sprang straight at his master's throat.

A deep sigh of frenzied excitement went round the ring of staring faces. Even Tinker for the moment felt that something had gone wrong; that Pedro's anger was far too realistic to be a fraud. Unable to move a hand or stir to Blake's assistance even if he required it, Tinker's astonished eyes took in the scene that followed.

Blake and Pedro rolled over and over each other on the floor first one of them seeming to gain the advantage and then the other. They writhed and twisted and grappled with one another as if they were engaged in a struggle for life or death, and all the time the furious baying of the great dog sounded above the devil's tattoo of the orchestra.

Presently the detective disengaged himself from the scrimmage, and, springing to his feet, raced frantically round and round the outside edge of the ring with a look of utmost terror on his face. Pedro's teeth were buried deep in his burnous, and as he tied to shake off the dog's grip he swung the animal high over the sea of dark faces that spread around.

But Tinker knew now that, real as the fight appeared to the onlookers, it was all a sham. For as his master passed him he deliberately winked his eye, as much as to say, "How's this for a show, Tinker?" The youngster gave a grin of appreciation and then suddenly remembered Blake's last injunction. He immediately began to wriggle himself in the direction of the table at which the man in the red fez was sitting.

Blake was now in the centre of the floor again and had assumed the defensive. The bloodhound circled around his master watching warily for an opening to make another attack; every now and then he leapt in and made snarling snaps at Blake's legs, his great jaws closing together like spring traps.

Then Blake made a dash at the bloodhound's head, and again they rolled over and over on the floor. A furious struggle ensued; for a time it was difficult to see which was man and which was dog. In the dim yellow light it was impossible to think that those two writhing forms were merely shamming.

At any rate, the audience did not think so: the crowd of dark, sinister faces was alive with intoxicated excitement, the squatting natives panted and twisted their hands as if they, themselves, were taking part in this titanic contest.

Once again Blake shook off the dog and sprang to his feet. He stood in the centre and spoke a quick word of command to Pedro. The bloodhound immediately came to his side and crouched down submissively at his feet.

Blake lifted his right hand above his head, while his left went into the folds of his burnous. The barbaric music immediately hushed and died away, and a deathly silence brooded over the place.

Blake's eyes roved slowly over the sea of dark, tense faces until his gaze rested on the face of the man in the red fez. He was staring at the detective in silent fascination, while the woman at his side seemed just as deeply impressed. But, just behind, Blake had also seen the face of his young assistant, and although no sign passed between them, he knew that Tinker was waiting for the signal agreed upon.

Then the detective spoke in a calm, clear voice in Arabic:

"If Kalib Pasha is here," he said, "then in the name of Allah I command him to step forth, for here is Murillo's painting of Don Montino."

And as he spoke the last words he dragged from the folds of his burnous a wad of canvas, and, shaking it out, displayed the faked copy of the Murillo.

The effect was electrical. The man in the red fez gave a gasp of surprise and his face went livid. Then he rose unsteadily to his the feet and stepped towards the detective. But at the same moment a tall, big-boned man clad in a flowing burnous, who had been looking on from the rear, made a great spring and landed in the centre of the floor.

Then the woman in the silver sandals and the broken-nosed Arab also rushed forward, and in a moment Blake found himself the centre of an excited crowd struggling for possession of the painting.

In order to give his assistant time to get clear Blake hid the Murillo in the folds of his burnous and tried to shake himself free from the hands that grabbed at him.

For a few seconds the audience remained squatting on the floor, evidently thinking that they were now witnessing another turn; then, suddenly, scenting that something was wrong, the crowd of dark-faced men began clambering to their feet and jostling one another around the little group in the centre.

Then the struggle suddenly became furious. The big-boned man picked up the broken nosed Arab as if he were a mere baby and dashed him violently into the face of the Turk with the red fez. Then he turned swiftly to the detective.

"Just hand over that picture, you dirty, heathen humbug!" he exclaimed in English, "or I'll knock the sawdust out of you."

He gripped Blake by the throat with one hand, and with his other tore open his burnous and dragged out the faked Murillo.

The detective struggled to get away, but the man's fingers were like steel springs and his grip never relaxed. Dimly he saw two queer blue eyes staring fiercely into his own, and an irregular featured face that seemed strangely familiar in spite of the brown stain that covered the skin.

In those few tense moments Blake had seldom thought more quickly.

"Twenty fathoms deep and twenty leagues away!" he gasped.

With a quick cry of surprise the man dropped his hold and stared at Blake as if he had seen a ghost.

"Who the deuce are you?" he asked in bewilderment.

Before Blake could make any reply the lights were suddenly extinguished, and he found himself knocked over and being swept backwards and forwards in the crowd that surged in the centre of the mosque.

The confusion was indescribable and the noise deafening. Still intoxicated with religious enthusiasm the crowd shouted and screamed and fought each other in the darkness in an effort to find their way to the door.

Then, to add to the terror of the scene, a little burst of flame suddenly sprang from the inner chamber and spread fiercely along the dry wooden walls.

The mosque was on fire!

Chapter 23
The Burning of the Mosque

THE scene that followed was appalling to behold. The panic-stricken crowd fought with the frenzy of despair to escape from the burning building. A mad stampede was made for the narrow doors, and in a moment the mob of crazy men was crushed together in a living wedge, tearing each other with their nails in a paroxysm of terror.

Then, into this seething wall of human bodies sprang the big-boned man with the queer blue eyes. Lying across his left shoulder was the slender figure of the woman in the silver sandals. Using his strong right arm as a battering-ram he began to hew a path towards the door.

Before his incredible strength the living barricade seemed to melt like butter. Slowly but surely he carved his way through the dense mass of bodies towards the doors. In those few moments his right arm seemed to work like a great steel tentacle—sawing, cleaving, and rending a path for himself and his unconscious burden.

And then once more he stood out in the open!

He stood for a moment taking great deep breaths and filling his lungs with the fresh air. Then, with the woman still lying across his shoulder, he strode swiftly down the little side street and made his way in the direction of the French quarter of the town.

As he walked down the wide boulevard of brilliantly-lighted shops and gay cafés, many people turned to stare at this big man in the turban and the flowing burnous carrying on his shoulder the graceful figure of the woman. But he took no heed of their idle curiosity, and something in his manner warned them to steer clear of his path.

He approached the hotel overlooking the harbour, but did not enter by the main entrance. Instead, he made his way round the back of the building, and, passing through a small wicket-gate into the courtyard, mounted the outside iron spiral staircase, put there in case of fire, and entered a room on the second floor.

There he deposited his burden on a bed and began sprinkling her face with water. In a few seconds the woman opened her eyes and stared up at him wonderingly.

"Where am I?" she asked.

"Have no fear, Mademoiselle Julie," he said, in a low voice; "you are quite safe—you are in your room in the hotel."

The young woman glanced round the room and then rested her eyes on the man's face again.

"It is the big Monsieur Grant!" she said, with the light of recognition in her dark eyes.

"Yes, it is I right enough, mademoiselle!" he answered.

She stared at him incredulously, then her eyes brimmed with tears and she caught his hand impulsively and kissed it.

"Then it is the big Monsieur Grant who has saved my life!" she exclaimed.

Granite Grant flushed self-consciously and withdrew his hand.

"You are a brave young woman, mademoiselle," he said tenderly, "but you are a woman after all."

She raised herself with a little laugh, as if she recognised a familiar phrase.

"It is certainly useful sometimes, monsieur, to be a man," she said. And added, in an undertone, "If he is a big, strong man!"

"You are feeling better now, mademoiselle?" he asked.

She nodded her head reassuringly.

"It is nothing," she said. "But tell me what happened, monsieur! There was a fire, was there not?"

"There was, mademoiselle. You were knocked over in the rush. They fought like demons. I am afraid not many of the poor devils escaped."

"Yes, it was very dreadful," she said, and gave a little shiver at the recollection. "But I have won my bet, Monsieur Grant. Did I not say that I would go to this mosque?"

"You did, mademoiselle; the bet shall be paid. Yet when I saw you dance and sing I could scarcely believe it was you. How did you manage to get taken on as dancing girl?"

"Ah, monsieur, that is my affair. There are many things I can do that you do not know. But there was something else. Ah, I remember! You have the picture, monsieur?"

"I have, mademoiselle!"

The young woman rose to her feet excitedly.

"That is splendid!" she exclaimed. "Let us look at it, monsieur. Now it does not matter; you work for the English, I work for the French—it is all the same!"

"That is certainly so!" he agreed, and feeling in the folds of his burnous, brought out the faked copy of the Murillo.

He opened out the square of painted canvas and they both surveyed it in silence. Then he ground his teeth in anger and the young woman gave an exclamation of surprise.

"It is a cheat, monsieur," she said excitedly. "It is not the picture—it is a copy. The stolen cipher is not there."

Granite Grant clenched his fist.

"By the powers, Julie!" he exclaimed. "We have been sold. What does it mean?"

"Listen, monsieur! That painting was substituted for the Murillo when Gustave Fulk was killed. I obtained it in London, myself, as they were taking it into the Veuxpillo Galleries. It was taken to Paris, where it was proved to be a fraud. It was in the possession of our secret service when I left Paris."

Granite Grant's bewilderment increased.

"Then how has it come here, mademoiselle?" he asked. "What was it doing in the possession of that crazy fellow with the mad dog?"

"I cannot think, monsieur. It is all too extraordinary."

"But who was that fellow, Julie? One thing I had forgotten. I had him by the throat when he spoke to me in English."

"He did, monsieur?"

"Yes; but it was not that fact that startled me so much, as what he said. He gave the secret countersign that, I thought, was only known to two persons in this world—myself and the head of the British Secret Service."

"And what is that secret countersign, monsieur?"

Naturally, I cannot tell you that, mademoiselle."

"Then I will tell you, monsieur. It is 'twenty fathoms deep and twenty leagues away'— is it not?"

Granite Grant drew a deep breath.

"Ah! How did you know that, Julie?" he asked in astonishment.

"You forget, monsieur, that I was in the next telephone-box at Victoria Station."

"And you overheard?"

"I did, monsieur."

Granite Grant bit his lip in vexation.

"Then this must have been one of your men in the mosque tonight, mademoiselle," he said. "There is no doubt of that."

"And yet I cannot think who it could have been. Unless, indeed, it was Bervais. But, then, Bervais is not clever enough to act like that."

"Then who, in the name of thunder, was he, mademoiselle?"

"That is more than I can say. But it is useless to bother with than now; it is more important to know what has become of the stolen cipher."

"You are right, Julie. But what can be the explanation? I was watching Kalib Pasha all the time. I am certain that I saw a villainous-looking Arab give him something that looked like a large leather wallet."

"And so did I, Monsieur Grant. You saw me sit down beside him?"

"Yes, I did. I knew what you were up to. You are certainly a witch, Julie—you could have twisted Kalib Pasha round your dainty little finger."

The young woman laughed gaily.

"And would have done, monsieur," she said, "if this man with the mad dog had not spoilt everything."

"Then you think that stolen cipher was in that wallet, mademoiselle?" asked Granite Grant quickly.

"I am sure of that, Monsieur Grant."

"But if that is so, why did Kalib Pasha seem so eager to get possession of this fake?"

"It all happened so suddenly, monsieur; he was taken by surprise, I, also, was taken off my guard."

"And so was I, mademoiselle! It was a hoax. Something must be done quickly. That wallet must have contained the Murillo; and it is still in the possession of Kalib Pasha."

"But where is he, monsieur? You remember the fire——"

"Yes," interrupted Grant." I was forgetting that, mademoiselle. Perhaps Kalib Pasha did not——"

He paused abruptly, and, holding up his hand to enjoin silence, looked towards the door, listening intently. Then he went swiftly across the room, and grasping the handle, suddenly pulled it open.

With a grunt of surprise a man, who had been bending with his ear to the keyhole, stumbled forward and then sprang to his feet. In spite of his dishevelled appearance, and the fact that his clothing was burnt and torn and hanging in ribbons, Grant and Mademoiselle Julie immediately recognised in the thin, arrogant features the face of Kalib Pasha, the Turk.

He stood for a moment darting swift glances of surprise and anger from one to the other, then turned to escape from the room. But Granite Grant was too quick for him; he jerked the door to with a slam and put his foot against it, then turned to his visitor.

"We have not yet had time to appreciate your company, monsieur," he said in French. "Pray do not leave us so hurriedly."

"The Turk gave vent to an angry oath and tried to open the door. But the King's Spy was in no mood to stand any nonsense; he made a quick movement with his elbow and Kalib Pasha went spinning into the middle of the room.

"And now, monsieur," continued Granite Grant politely, "we are entirely at your service."

The Turk gave him a malignant scowl and addressed himself to the young woman.

"You were at the mosque tonight, mademoiselle?" he asked.

"I was, monsieur."

"Then you know why I am here?" the Turk asked quickly.

Mademoiselle Julie gave a little smile of contempt, and pointed to the King's Spy.

"Was it not Monsieur Grant who brought you in?" she asked. "But you do not know him—let me introduce Monsieur Grant of the British Secret Service!"

The King's Spy bowed gravely. He had not yet taken off the long, flowing burnous, and his face was still stained a coppery hue. Kalib Pasha cast a quick glance in his direction, and was plainly disconcerted and uneasy.

"Then this is a trap!" he hissed. "It was you who stole the wallet!"

Grant nodded, and made a little gesture to the young woman. She understood immediately and kept silent.

"You seem to attach a great deal of importance to this wallet, monsieur," he said. "Supposing I suggested coming to terms!"

The Turk turned to him eagerly.

"You will sell it," he said quickly. "I will give you a big price."

"For the wallet, monsieur?"

"For what it contains—the Murillo painting!"

Granite Grant had obtained just the information he required. He shook his head with an air of finality.

"We will not discuss the matter further," he said, and, pointing to the door, added, "Kindly relieve us of your company!"

Kalib Pasha's face went crimson with rage and his hand slipped into the pocket of his coat. But the King's Spy was quite prepared for any emergencies. In a trice he had sprang forward and lifted the Turk off his feet; then, pulling open the door, he flung him out in the corridor, and closed it behind him.

Mademoiselle Julie gave a ripple of laughter.

"That is excellent, Monsieur Grant," she said; "the haughty Turk has had a fall."

"He must have followed me from the mosque, Julie. Or else he recognised you there tonight and knew you were staying at this hotel."

"But evidently Kalib Pasha has not got the stolen cypher, monsieur."

"No," he said thoughtfully; "it is more mysterious than ever. We know now that the stolen cipher was in that wallet. But where is the wallet? That is the question. Two things may have happened. He may have dropped it, and in that case it has doubtless been burnt in the fire. I hope it has; that will relieve us of a difficulty."

"And if it hasn't, monsieur?"

"Then it has been stolen from Kalib Pasha. And the man we must find is that strange fellow with the mad dog. I wonder who he could have been, mademoiselle?"

"That is just what puzzles me, monsieur!"

Granite Grant stood some moments silently frowning at the faked Murillo. Then he folded it up and put it beneath his burnous.

"I am going back to the mosque, mademoiselle," he said. "Something must be done quickly."

"Then I will come, too, Monsieur Grant!"

"No," he said. "You forget, Julie, that although we work for the same end, yet we both work independently."

"Very well, Monsieur Grant!" she laughed. "Then I will do as I think best."

The next moment the King's Spy had passed through the French windows, and was making his way down the iron escalier by which he had come with Mademoiselle Julie on his shoulder.

Chapter 24
Tinker Meets a Lady

TINKER had found no great difficulty in carrying out the task his master had assigned to him. Directly Blake had made that dramatic exhibition of the faked Murillo in the centre of the mosque, Tinker's light fingers had dived into Kalib Pasha's pocket, and had whipped out the leather wallet.

In the confusion that followed he was easily able to squirm through the crowd and make good his escape. As he got outside he heard sounds of commotion coming from within the mosque. But he did not stop; he knew Blake was quite able to take care of himself.

He ran swiftly down the narrow street, and found suddenly that Pedro was gambolling by his side. He felt rather pleased with this discovery. At that moment Pedro's company was very acceptable. Very likely, he thought, Blake had sent the dog after him to see him safely to the hotel.

When he reached the end of the street he turned round and looked back at the mosque. It was too dark to see very distinctly, but something extraordinary seemed to have happened. Not a light appeared anywhere in the building, and yet even from where he stood he could hear a confused sound of shouting and wild cries.

However, it was no use stopping; Blake's instructions were that he was to get back as quickly as possible to the hotel with the wallet. He had distinctly told Tinker not to wait for him. He therefore started off again.

The thoroughfare gradually widened as he approached the French quarter; he had stopped running now, and contented himself with a sharp walk. Presently he glanced back again over his shoulder in the direction of the mosque.

The building was now hidden from view, but the sight that met Tinker's eyes made him come to a sudden halt with a little thrill of anxiety. From where he knew the mosque was situated a dense volume of smoke curled up to the sky, lighted up every now and then by little spurts of flame.

He knew immediately what had happened. The mosque, had caught fire!

For a moment Tinker hesitated. His master was in the building when he left; most likely he was in there now. Would he be able to escape? Tinker could picture the frightful confusion that was going on inside the blazing mosque; he could imagine the wild panic of the crazy Arabs and their frantic efforts to escape through the narrow doors.

Should he go back to the assistance of his master? He had almost made up his mind to retrace his steps, when he remembered Blake's instructions again. He had better not go back; his master would be angry if he arrived at the hotel before his assistant.

Then he thought of Pedro!

"Pedro!" he said quickly. "Go back to the master, boy! Good dog, Pedro! Find Blake!"

The bloodhound looked up at Tinker half doubtfully, wagged his tail two or three times in acknowledgment, then turned and cantered off up the street.

Tinker felt somewhat relieved after the dog's departure, and did not pause again until he had arrived at the hotel. There, for half an hour or more, he waited impatiently for Blake's arrival, filled with all manner of vague anxieties and fears on account of his master's safety. Yet the time went on and still no Blake appeared.

Tinker had discarded his turban and burnous now. He decided to climb to the top of the hotel and see if he could get a view of the blazing mosque from there. He sped along the corridor and went up two or three flights of stairs. Then he came to a little window at the end of a passage that faced the direction of the Kasbah.

A red glow hung above the Mosque of Ak-el-baran, and a black pillar of smoke crawled up above the buildings. Sometimes showers of sparks shot up into the sky, and little jets of flame flickered above the surrounding dwellings. Although the hotel was some distance off from the old town, yet from where he stood Tinker could understand what a blazing furnace the mosque must now be.

He watched the scene in silent fascination for some time, seeming to hear the moans of the poor wretches who had not been able to escape from their awful doom. Then, feeling sure that Blake must have returned by now, he hurried downstairs again to his master's room.

But still there were no signs of Blake. For some reason his master had not yet returned. And as Tinker glanced anxiously round the room a great fear suddenly seized him. Something seemed to tell him that his master was imprisoned in the blazing mosque.

Tinker had more than the average share of courage. He could stand most troubles and trials without flinching, but when it was a question of Blake's safety he was driven to distraction. And he knew for a certainty now that some grave peril threatened his beloved master, that perhaps Blake had already perished in the fire, and he was too late to render any assistance.

With trembling hands he slipped on a light rain-proof coat, and, seizing his cap, rushed downstairs and out into the street. He was familiar with the way back to the mosque by this time; even if he had been uncertain of it, the red glow in the sky would have directed him. He rushed madly along the boulevards, impelled by that overwhelming desire to find his master.

When he at last reached the scene of the conflagration it was only to find the mosque a great heap of flaming wreckage. It had been burning for some hours now, and, once lighted, the fire had not been slow to catch the inflammable material and set it well ablaze.

When the roof had fallen in every effort had been made to prevent the fire from spreading to the surrounding buildings, and the French fire-brigade was still directing the crowd of toiling natives and helping them to beat back the flames.

Tinker went frantically through the crowd searching for his master, hoping vainly that he might discover Blake assisting in the work of extinguishing the fire. But, his search was fruitless; there were no signs of Blake anywhere—even Pedro seemed to have vanished.

In his anxiety he began to question every person he met, grabbing hold of their arms excitedly, and demanding if they knew what had happened to "Monsoor Sexton Blake." But they could tell him nothing. None of them knew what he was saying; he spoke a foreign tongue to them. And if they did trouble to reply, Tinker could not understand what they said.

It was while he was frantically questioning a man who had rushed towards him with a bucket of water in one hand and an axe in the other that a slim figure wrapped in a dark mantle suddenly intervened.

"What is that you say?" asked a soft, musical voice.

Tinker turned eagerly to his unknown questioner. He could not see her very distinctly, but he knew by the voice that it was a woman who had asked the question. And, in spite of the quaint accent, she had spoken in English. Tinker had never realised until that moment how beautiful his own language sounded.

And as he hesitated, the figure in the mantle spoke again.

"Is it of Monsieur Sexton Blake that you inquire?" she asked.

"Yes; Sexton Blake—that's him!" said Tinker eagerly. "Where is he? Have you seen him?"

The woman came closer and peered into his face.

"Why, can it be the Tinker?" she exclaimed in surprise. "Tell me, is it not the Tinker you are called?"

Tinker's mouth opened in astonishment.

"Yes, I'm Tinker," he said. "But how do you know? Who are you?"

The woman laughed gaily, and pulled back the hood which half-concealed her face.

"Surely the Tinker has not forgotten Mademoiselle Julie?" she exclaimed.

Tinker drew a deep breath as his eyes rested on the mass of golden-bronze hair and small symmetrical features of his fair questioner.

"Crumbs!" he stammered, "if that don't just beat everything. It's the French lady we met on that island in the Caribbean Sea."

Mademoiselle Julie seemed highly amused at Tinker's bewilderment.

"We have met since then, Tinker," she said. "It was I you followed to Robespierre Gardens last week. But tell me about Monsieur Blake. Where is he now? And was the brave Pedro in the mosque tonight?"

Then Tinker remembered why he was there, and all his former fears of his master's safety came crowding back into his mind.

"Yes," he said, with renewed anxiety, "Blake was dressed as an Arab; that fight with

Pedro was simply a sham. He was in the mosque when it caught fire. He may have been burnt to death."

The young woman caught her breath in dismay, and grasped Tinker's arm agitatedly.

"Oh, it cannot be," she cried; "it is too dreadful. But where is the brave Pedro? Was he not with Monsieur Blake?"

"No; he was following me to the hotel. When I saw the mosque was on fire I sent him back to look for the guv'nor."

Julie clasped her hands together.

"It is dreadful," she exclaimed again. "But Monsieur Blake—he is so collected and clever. He is certain to have escaped. What can we do!"

"But he has not come back to the hotel," insisted Tinker. "He must have met with an accident or something. Where would he be? He is not here anywhere. Can't you ask somebody, Miss Julie? I don't know what they're talking about."

"Ah; the Tinker cannot speak Arabic! Very good; I will see what can be done. Stay here and I will be back directly."

The young woman hurried from one group of men to another, questioning each in turn as to whether they had seen "Monsieur Blake and his dog." Filled with harassing doubts, Tinker watched her pass in front of the flickering fire and disappear in the darkness on the other side.

After about ten minutes had elapsed he saw her slim cloaked figure coming in his direction again.

"Any news?" he asked anxiously, as she drew near.

"Listen, Tinker!" she said. "A few minutes after the mosque caught fire a big dog was seen trying to force his way through the doors. But the brave dog did not get in; the doors were jammed tightly with struggling men. They say it was very horrible."

"Then what happened to him?"

"The Tinker is impatient! I have not yet finished. The dog was not seen again until about half an hour ago. Then it was seen disappearing down the street, and the brave dog was following a big man in a turban and burnous."

"Then it must have been the guv'nor," cried Tinker excitedly.

"It was a very big man, Tinker, bigger than Monsieur Blake. They say he carried something in his arms, but they do not know what it was he carried."

"But it must have been the guv'nor," Tinker insisted. "Pedro wouldn't follow anyone else, especially when his master was in danger. I'm going straight back to the hotel. Very likely the guv'nor's there, wondering where I've gone."

"Then I will come there, too, Tinker," said Julie.

"Come on, then!" said Tinker abruptly.

Later on they both arrived breathless and perspiring at the hotel. Straight up to his master's room Tinker ran, and flung open the door. But there were no signs of Blake nor Pedro. As far as he could see no one had entered the room since he had left it to return to the mosque.

He turned despairingly to the young woman.

"You can talk the lingo," he said. "Ask them if anyone has seen the guv'nor."

They went downstairs again, and Julie closely questioned the concierge. But the detective had vanished; nobody knew what had become of him.

"Come, Tinker," said Julie. "We will go along to my hotel. Perhaps the big Monsieur Grant will know what should be done."

"Grant!" echoed Tinker; "do you mean Granite Grant, the King's Spy?"

"It is so, my friend," rejoined the French woman. "The big Monsieur Grant was in the mosque when the fire broke out."

"But Pedro knows Grant," said Tinker quickly. "Perhaps he was the big man in the turban whom the dog was seen following!"

"That is true, Tinker. We will go there at once."

With renewed hope Tinker followed the woman across the foyer and out into the street. There they hired a fiacre and drove as fast as possible to the harbour hotel.

Chapter 25
Blake's Thrilling Experience

SEXTON BLAKE had only a very hazy idea of those first few terrible moments in the blazing mosque. When Granite Grant's iron grasp had relaxed from his throat he had stumbled back gasping for breath, and been swept hither and thither in the panic-stricken crowd. Then he received a violent blow on the head, and sank down unconscious.

He could only have remained insensible for a few brief moments, however, for he suddenly came round to find himself lying in the centre of the mosque, staring up at the blackened ceiling. He climbed unsteadily to his feet and began to take stock of his position.

The place was like an inferno; the heat was terrific. The wall on one side was now a sheet of flame; the ornamental pilasters and the tinselled finery that was draped between them were wreathed in fire, and flung out showers of sparks, which threatened every moment to envelope the whole mosque in flames from floor to ceiling.

Blake hugged his burnous tightly around him and turned towards the doors. Escape was impossible that way. The entrance was blocked with human bodies; they were piled one upon the other. Most of them had already perished of suffocation; only those on the top still struggled feebly to find an escape from their dreadful doom.

Yet, somehow he must find a way out. His position was critical; at any moment the ceiling might cave in and bury him in a tomb of flames. If he were to escape at all it must be now. The smoke and fumes were getting thicker. It was difficult to breathe; his throat was parched with the dry, intense heat.

He looked about him eagerly, searching for some loophole that might hold out some small hope of escaping from this dreadful vault of fire. And at that moment he came face to face with another figure that had suddenly risen from the floor.

He recognised him instantly, in spite of the crazy look in his face and the wild, staring eyes. It was the man with the broken nose, the man he had followed yesterday into the winding labyrinth of the Arab town, and who had come here tonight to keep the appointment with Kalib Pasha.

The Arab, too, had seemed to recognise in the man before him his late foe of yesterday. He peered into the detective's face for a few tense seconds with a look of fierce hatred in his eyes, then, with a howl of demoniacal rage, flung himself on him.

Blake beat him off with a stinging blow in the face.

"Fool!" he cried fiercely, "save yourself! In a moment it will be too late."

But the madman took no notice of the detective's warning cry. The blow had momentarily dazed him, but the next moment he sprang forward again with blazing eyes, and, although Blake did his best to ward him off, he could not prevent his coming to close quarters.

Biting, tearing, snarling, the Arab dragged Blake to the floor, where they rolled over and over among the burning embers which were now dropping from the blazing pilasters. In vain Blake tried to tear the frenzied man's fingers from their tenacious grasp. The man clung to him like a limpet and fought with the fury of a wild cat.

Blake struggled to his feet again with his foe still clinging desperately to him. Up and down the blazing room they staggered, with the flames licking zig-zag above their heads and all around them, and throwing out showers of sparks and dense volumes of smoke. Then, with a superhuman effort, the detective wrenched himself from the Arab's grasp and flung him off.

The madman went staggering backwards across the floor of the mosque, and crashed up against a blazing pilaster, which immediately broke under his weight. Then the architrave above, now without any support, caved in with a great burst of fire and engulfed him in a blazing mass of wreckage.

Then, for a second time that night, Blake remembered no more. The overpowering heat and the frightful exertions he had undergone were too much even for his iron constitution. He dropped to the floor insensible.

When he came to again it was some moments before he could realise where he was. The events of a few minutes ago, and his terrible fight with the crazy Arab, seemed distant and remote in the present confused state of his mind. His body felt, one huge blister, his tongue was swollen so that it seemed to occupy the whole of the space of his head.

He gazed vacantly up through the sweltering heat and smoke. A tornado seemed to be raging above his head—a tornado of hissing red fire. He appeared to be moving; the floor was slowly scraping against his cracked, blistered hands.

Suddenly his brain cleared of the fog that enveloped it. He knew instantly that he was moving, that he was being dragged over the floor of the mosque. Something was gripping him by the collar of his burnous; he could feel the cloth tightening under his armpits each time his hands scraped the floor.

He wriggled himself over and scrambled to his knees. A hot, rasping tongue rubbed against his face like a flint file. He reached out his hand, and felt the great shaggy head of Pedro.

He could not see the dog; the hot, blinding smoke choked him. But he could feel his teeth tearing frantically at his burnous as the faithful animal sought to urge his beloved master forward. Crawling on his hands and knees, Blake allowed his trusty guide to direct him where he chose.

The floor of the mosque was like a hot plate; innumerable glowing embers pierced and blistered his hands, but he still went on through the choking smoke. He trusted Pedro implicitly, yet he could not help wondering where he was going. In front was a great flame of fire; they were getting nearer and nearer to it.

Then Blake suddenly put his hands on mere emptiness. He lurched forward, felt a wooden rung beneath him, tried to save himself, and ended up by rolling down a flight of steps. A moment later he was brought up with a jolt at the bottom.

He felt the dog tugging at his burnous again, and, began to crawl towards him. And as he started to move a great rending noise sounded from up above, there was a series of ear-splitting reports, then a mass of blazing debris came hurtling down the steps.

He had escaped from this dreadful blazing furnace only a moment too soon. The blazing roof of the mosque had caved in!

Still led by the bloodhound, Blake crawled slowly along the dark tunnel. Presently the thick smoke fumes began to lift, cool wisps of fresh air smote against his parched, blistered face. Then he felt a flight of wooden steps leading upwards immediately in front of him, and, crawling up them found himself out in the open once more.

It was then that Blake realised to the full the nerve-racking experience he had undergone, it was only by a miracle that he had escaped being incinerated in the burning mosque. Had not Pedro turned at the fateful moment he would have been lying now amongst the blazing wreckage, and nothing would have been left of him but a charred cinder.

He tried to reach out to the brave dog, but fell back again with a dry, feeble sob. He was too weak and exhausted to move any further; he felt half roasted, as if his body was desiccated of moisture.

The bloodhound lay at his side, panting desperately, his flanks heaving like bellows as he struggled for breath. The great hound was almost as exhausted as his master.

The burning mosque was now about a hundred yards away. Dense volumes of smoke still swept skywards, pierced by tongues of red flame. As he lay there Blake could hear a confusion of hoarse shouts and cries, and vague forms flitted about around the blazing debris, like so many demons, vainly trying to stop the flames from spreading.

The secret entrance to the mosque came up in a little cobbled court, where the detective was now lying. He was comparatively safe where he was; the wind was blowing the other way, and the flames were not likely to advance in this direction.

He lay there as if in a waking dream, not attempting to move after that first painful effort, while random thoughts passed idly across his brain.

He might have lain thus for over an hour; he had no idea of the time. But without seeing him go, he somehow knew that Pedro was no longer at his side. He began to wonder where he had gone. Poor old Pedro! What a brick he was! In that last supreme effort to save his master he had all but perished himself.

Then Blake thought he heard footsteps approaching across the cobbled court. A moment later he felt the dog's nose gently rubbing against his parched face. Then a dark, turbaned figure bent over him and peered into his face.

Very tenderly the stranger put one arm under his shoulders and the other beneath his legs, and lifted him up as if he were an infant. He did not speak a word. Neither did Blake; he only wanted to lie still and dream.

They began to move across the cobbled court and through a winding passage out into the narrow street. Then the strange man in the turban and burnous went more swiftly. Blake did not take much heed of the rest of that journey; the gentle rocking motion seemed to soothe him; he closed his eyes, and his mind became a blank.

Chapter 26
"A General Meeting"

BLAKE suddenly felt something stingingly cold touching against his parched lips. It brought him to his senses with staggering abruptness. Then a gentle trickle of icy water began to ooze down his dry throat.

It gave him a sensation of exquisite pain; but he gulped the cool, refreshing liquid eagerly, and already began to feel a new man. For some moments he did not open his eyes; he was lying on a soft, downy bed, and the feeling of complete restfulness was too delicious to be disturbed.

Then a man spoke in a deep base voice very close to him:

"By George," he muttered, "it's old Blake, right enough. What a wonder the fellow is!"

Blake tried to smile, but did not succeed very well; the muscles of his face seemed to require oiling. Then, almost mechanically, something prompted him to murmur:

"Twenty fathoms deep and twenty leagues away!"

The man gave vent to a deep chuckle.

"Blest if the fellow hasn't got it on the brain!" he said.

Then Blake opened his eyes.

A turbanned head was very near his; two queer blue eyes were looking at him tenderly from a familiar, irregular-featured face.

"You'd have it on the brain," he said, "if a great, hulking lump of a fellow was throttling your windpipe."

The big man laughed rather nervously, and impulsively held out his hand, then drew it back quickly.

"I won't shake your hand, old Blake," he said, with a little tremor in his voice, "but you can take it for granted."

The detective suddenly raised himself with an effort, and sat up.

"Why, what's the matter with my hand, Grant?" he asked, gazing at it curiously. "Is it too dirty?"

"It's not too dirty, Blake, but it wants lubricating. You've been sitting too close to the fire. By gosh, man, but you'd have been nothing but a lump of desiccated soup if you'd remained there much longer. Here, take this pot of vaseline and rub it into your skin."

"I certainly seem rather sunburnt," laughed the detective, as he took the vaseline and began rubbing it into his hands.

"Don't talk, Blake. Keep quiet and rest yourself."

"But I'm going to talk, Grant. I've got lots to say, and I'm quite fit to say it. Just give me another drink, there's a good fellow. Not the glass, the jug—and fill it to the brim."

Blake took a long pull, and heaved a sigh of intense satisfaction.

"Where's Pedro?" he asked suddenly.

The dog crawled out from under the bed, and, resting his great head on the counterpane, blinked up at his master, with a feeble wag of his tail.

Blake looked into the faithful brute's eyes, and could not find words to express himself. He glanced quickly at Grant; the two men eyed each other in silence for a moment. Then Grant spoke.

"He's the goods!" he said simply.

Pedro sank down contentedly on the floor, quite satisfied to have done his duty according to his own canine code of "playing the game."

"Tell me what happened, Grant?" said Blake, as he gently smeared the vaseline over his face.

"Not much to tell Blake. I was in the mosque when it caught fire, and managed to save my skin. I returned there about an hour ago. This old dog suddenly pounced on me and began tearing at my burnous. I tried to beat him off, but he wouldn't leave me alone, so I followed him. And—to cut it short—found you lying in a little brick court at the back."

"You were in the mosque this evening, Grant?"

"Yes; and watched your thrilling performance. Snakes alive, Blake, but I was never so taken in before in my life. I never dreamt it was you. You were about the last person I expected to see in Algiers."

"D'you know why I'm here, Grant?"

"That's just what I'm bursting to know, Blake. Don't tell us the whole story now; that'll take too long. And I know it's much too interesting to spoil. Put it in a nutshell."

"Right, Grant! I'm here killing two birds with one stone."

The King's Spy looked perplexed.

"For mercy's sake, don't talk in paradoxes!" he said.

"The first bird," continued the detective, unmindful of the interruption, "happens to be the bird who killed Gustave Fulk in the Veuxpillo Galleries last Tuesday week."

"Ah: now we're getting to it! So they've dragged in the famous Sexton Blake to solve the baffling mystery?"

"Precisely, Grant! And the famous Sexton Blake would like the equally famous Granite Grant to explain how he came to leave two blood-stained fingerprints on the frame of a certain painting that hung in the south room on the night of the crime."

Granite Grant looked somewhat startled.

"Good gracious, Blake!" he exclaimed. "What a sleuth-hound you are! But you don't suspect me of being implicated in the crime, do you?"

"I'm merely asking you for an explanation, Grant."

"Well, I'm not bound to tell you that, Blake; but I will. I went to the galleries for a certain reason, which I won't mention. But I was just too late. I tripped over this fellow in the dark, and must have got some of the blood on my fingers. Then, for the reason already mentioned, I lifted the picture away from the wall. And that's how those fingerprints came to be there."

"That's exactly what I thought, Grant. As for your reason for being there, you needn't keep that a secret, because I already know it. You were after the secret cipher that was stolen from our Paris Embassy."

"The deuce, Blake, but you seem to know everything!"

"Well, naturally, Grant, since that happens to be the second bird to my stone," remarked the detective drily.

"What do you mean?" asked Grant sharply.

"Wait until I've done with the first bird, Grant. It may interest you to know that the man who killed Gustave Fulk perished himself tonight in the fire at the mosque."

"He did?"

"Yes; but I'll tell you that story later on. And now for the second bird! I think my stone has killed that also. It was to find out where a certain Granite Grant had hidden himself, and, incidentally, to discover what had happened to the stolen cipher. I received those instructions from the lips of Sir Vrymer Fane himself."

Grant gave a cry of astonishment.

"Phew, Blake," he exclaimed, "we shall have to call a special bull-session to listen to your story."

Then, as an afterthought, he added quickly:

"But you haven't quite killed the second bird, Blake!"

"How?"

"You've found me!"

"Yes?"

"But you haven't found the stolen cipher!"

"I think I have, Grant. At least, I'm hoping that Tinker, my assistant, has it in his pocket at the present moment."

"Where is he, Blake?—we must get hold of it quickly."

"What's that, row outside in the corridor?" asked Blake suddenly.

"Somebody's coming!" said Grant, and turned to the door just as it was thrust violently open, and Tinker and Mademoiselle Julie burst into the room.

"It's the guv'nor!" shouted Tinker breathlessly, and in his relief and joy he would have flung himself on Blake if Granite Grant had not put out a restraining hand and held him back.

"Steady, youngster!" he said: "The boss is not shaking hands today."

Then Tinker saw his master's blistered hands and scorched eyebrows, and his mouth dropped.

"You're not badly hurt, guv'nor, are you?" he asked anxiously.

"No, I'm all right, Tinker," said Blake. "A little bit scorched, that's all."

But, Mademoiselle Julie's womanly sympathy was not content with that. She lifted the detective's hand tenderly and pressed it to her lips.

"Did I not say Monsieur Blake was too cold to be roasted?" she said. "But the poor Tinker was so distracted."

Blake could not help laughing at the young woman's quaint way of expressing herself.

"So that is what you said, mademoiselle!" he laughed. "But even an iceberg will melt, if it's too near the fire. However, I've had time to freeze again since."

"Ah, but Monsieur Blake, the Tinker really thought you were dead!"

"You did, Tinker?" asked Blake.

"I certainly had the wind up, guv'nor, when you didn't come back. I went back to the mosque afterwards. Then I met Miss Julie."

"I see, Tinker. Well, I've got to thank old Pedro here for not being frizzled to a cinder at the present moment."

"Then he found you, guv'nor? I sent him back."

"You sent Pedro back, Tinker?"

"Yes, guv'nor; he followed me out of the mosque. When I got some distance down the road I saw flames shooting up; so I told Pedro to go back and find you."

"You're a good lad, Tinker," said Blake quietly. "You certainly saved me from being burnt to death."

Julie knelt down and hugged the dog in her white arms.

"The brave Pedro!" she murmured; "but he is just too splendid!"

The detective glanced at the young woman's slight, graceful figure as she knelt on the floor caressing the great dog, and his eyes narrowed reflectively.

"I think, Mademoiselle Julie," he said, "that we were playing hide-and-seek together in London last week—were we not? You were our mysterious lady friend in the musquash coat who decoyed Tinker to his doom in Robespierre Gardens?"

Julie looked up with a merry laugh.

"That is just so, Monsieur Blake," she agreed. "It was a shame to lock the poor Tinker in the cellar. But it had to be."

Blake glanced at the silver sandals that were showing beneath her dark mantle, and continued.

"And it was you also, mademoiselle, who danced so beautifully in the mosque tonight and sang that little French song?"

"It was, Monsieur Blake!"

The detective looked at her appraisingly.

"You are a very wonderful young woman, mademoiselle," he said quietly.

The young woman rose to her feet and glanced at the detective with a mischievous look in her dark, perplexing eyes, then turned to Granite Grant.

"But, Monsieur Grant," she asked, "who was that crazy fellow with the mad, performing dog?"

Both Blake and Tinker joined in Granite Grant's amused chuckle.

"We were both of us taken in there, mademoiselle," he said. "Blake has certainly got the laugh of us over that."

"But, oh, it was so drôle!" continued Julie merrily, "the cold, grave Monsieur Blake rolling over and over like a marabout or medicine man. And then the brave Pedro with his big teeth—but it was so drôle! It makes me think of the big Monsieur Grant dressed as a waiter and with the white napkin on his arm."

Grant became rather flustered.

"All right, Mademoiselle Julie," he said hastily: "you needn't go telling tales."

But Blake took him up good-humouredly.

"What's that about Grant as a waiter?" he asked, "I should think that ought to prove rather a good story."

"He is a very rude waiter, Monsieur Blake," said Julie, with a little disdainful toss of her head.

"So I should think, mademoiselle," answered the detective.

The King's Spy broke in impatiently:

"Blake," he said anxiously, "we've all got lots of things to tell each other. Let's leave them for a bit. I'll tell you the waiter story some other time. I'm anxious about the stolen cipher; where is it?"

Mademoiselle Julie immediately became grave and serious; beneath her gay, charming exterior lurked always the knowledge of the bigger game which she played with such dexterity and cunning. She glanced expectantly at the detective.

"What happened to the wallet, Tinker?" asked Blake, a little anxiously.

"I'd forgotten all about that, guv'nor," said his assistant, and, diving into the inside of his coat, drew out the large leather wallet.

Granite Grant seized it eagerly.

"You don't mind, Blake!" he said, and, undoing the strap, drew out a wad of canvas.

He shook it out with hands that trembled a little, and displayed the oil-painting of the old man in the grey military tunic. Then he turned the picture over and carefully scrutinised the back, while Mademoiselle Julie gazed intently over his shoulder.

"Thank heaven, Blake!" Grant muttered, at last. "It's the genuine Murillo this time."

"And is the stolen cipher there as well, Grant?" asked the detective.

"Yes, it's here right enough, Blake. See! The canvas has a false backing of thin parchment; it is glued securely to the canvas. The cipher is written on the inside. It would have to be very carefully steamed off. That is why they cut the picture from the frame."

"I understand, Grant. And now you've got it in your possession, you'd better look after it well. I must confess that I'm not too anxious to sleep with the thing in my room. It seems rather unhealthy."

Grant smiled grimly.

"I agree with you, Blake," he said; "it's not exactly a life-insurance policy. A certain person in this hotel would give a fortune for this piece of painted canvas. But it will never leave this room again."

He went quickly over to the empty grate.

"Watch me, Mademoiselle Julie," he said. "You can inform your people what has happened."

Thrusting the picture between the bars of the grate he struck a match and applied it to the canvas. The inflammable material quickly caught alight and flared up. In a few moments nothing was left of the Murillo but a few carbonised ashes.

Blake watched in silence until the last flame had flickered out.

"You have just burnt one hundred guineas, Grant," he said.

The King's Spy shrugged his shoulders.

"In the game we play, Blake," he said, quietly, "one hundred guineas is a very small premium to pay to cover such a great risk."

"Then it is rather an expensive pastime," rejoined the detective drily.

"Expensive, but necessary, Blake!" added Grant nonchalantly.

"Well, Grant," said Blake presently, "I suppose it is time I got out of your room?"

"Not tonight, Blake!" said Grant firmly. "You stay where you are, I'll get another room. You'll be quite fit in a day or so."

"Well, I don't mind, Grant. I'm not anxious to move tonight, I must confess. When are you leaving Algiers?"

"Tomorrow morning, Blake!"

"And you, Mademoiselle Julie?"

"I also go tomorrow, monsieur."

"Quick work!" said the detective. "I shall not follow for a couple of days or so. But we sha'n't be able to exchange notes, shall we? That's rather a pity."

Grant thought for a moment.

"If you're in London before the end of next week, Blake," he said, "I'll call at Baker Street and pay you a visit."

"Do, Grant! I shall be delighted to see you at my humble abode."

"But, Monsieur Blake does not invite me!" exclaimed Julie petulantly.

Blake glanced at the young woman with a flicker of amusement.

"I am afraid you will find my flat rather different from your palatial house in the Rue de Ravenne, mademoiselle," he said. "But I give you a standing invitation to my humble quarters."

Julie clapped her hands in glee.

"That will be splendid," she cried. "When I have been to my Paris I will come straight on to your sombre London. Then we will all gather in Monsieur Blake's house in the Street of the Baker. We will have what you English call a fight-bun—is it not so?"

"A fight-bun!" repeated Blake in perplexity.

"She means a bun-fight, guv'nor!" said Tinker.

Blake gave an amused chuckle.

"A bun-fight, mademoiselle!" he said. "Very well, then; I'll ask my housekeeper to do her best to make a good spread. But you'd better have a substantial meal just before-hand."

"And we shall see the room where the great English detective has all his wave-brains?" asked Julie excitedly.

"Brain-waves, mademoiselle!" corrected Blake.

"Well, brain-waves, monsieur—it is all the same!"

"Yes, but I don't leave any brain-waves lying about, mademoiselle!"

"It does not matter," said Julie, "it will all be very jolly. And now, Monsieur Blake, good-night!"

"Good-night, mademoiselle!" said the detective.

He watched her go towards the door—a slender, cloaked figure, with the silver sandals on her dainty feet.

At the door she paused, then came back.

"You were only just in time, Monsieur Blake," she said. "Another few minutes, and I should have won."

"How do you mean, mademoiselle?" he asked, not following her meaning.

"Another few minutes, Monsieur Blake, and I should have obtained the stolen cipher from Kalib Pasha."

The detective eyed her in silence for a moment or two. She looked very dainty and charming as she stood there; he knew only too well the secret of her strange influence over men. He remembered, also, the look of infatuation on the Turk's face when she had held out her arms to him in the mosque.

"I believe you would, mademoiselle!" he said quietly.

Chapter 27
Conclusion

ALL that day Sexton Blake's rooms in Baker Street had been the scene of great bustle and activity. Never had Mrs. Bardell, the housekeeper, made such a thorough spring-cleaning; never before had she exerted such supreme authority.

All Blake's curios and relics, his documents and papers, his pipes and tobacco-jars— the pictures on the wall, the antlers, the tanned hide shields, the rusty, antiquated weapons, the boxing-gloves and foils—all had been thoroughly scoured by Mrs. Bardell's merciless mop, duster, and broom.

She had tipped out the bookcases, pulled up the carpets, turned out the cupboards— rudely pried into his most intimate affairs with scrubbing-brush, soap, and water. She seemed to be a perfect fiend after dust: she hunted it down relentlessly and ruthlessly in crevice and cranny, nook and corner, crack and fissure; and not the smallest particle escaped her eagle eye.

For a while the detective had looked on at this scene of devastation with the utmost consternation. Then he had vainly attempted to remonstrate.

"Don't touch that, please, Mrs. Bardell," he had said timidly; "it's rather important. You might let that remain just where it is."

But Mrs. Bardell was not to be dictated to. For months she had awaited this opportunity; for months her fingers had itched to get going with mop and dust-pan in Mr. Blake's private sanctum. Now the opportunity had come. The detective was expecting visitors, and he had asked her "to tidy up a bit." It was an opportunity that only came once in a lifetime; she was not going to let it slip from her grasp.

She had turned on him with some asperity.

"Do you want me to tidy up, or don't you, Mister Blake?" she asked, with a note of wounded vanity.

"Yes, yes!" said Blake quickly, trying at the same time to propitiate her: "by all means tidy up, Mrs. Bardell. But—er—it looks as if we'd had the brokers in. I'm afraid I shall never be able to find anything again."

Mrs. Bardell gave a sniff of injured pride.

"The brokers in!" she exclaimed. "And me trying to do my best to make the room look respectable! Rank ingratitude, I call it—so there!"

"No, no, Mrs. Bardell," he added hastily, "I am extremely grateful, I'm sure. But—er—please don't strip the paper from the wall; we shall never get it back in time!"

"I'm not stripping the paper from the wall, sir—although, Lord knows, it could do with it! But the place hasn't been cleaned for years! It's perfectly disgraceful—that's what I call it! Why, the dust behind that bookcase has been there for centuries!"

"Come, come, Mrs. Bardell," he said mildly, "that's a libel. You're exaggerating now! Why, the room was swept out last year—I distinctly remember the occasion."

"And what if it was?" she broke in impetuously. "A year, indeed! Why, it ought to have a thorough scouring out every week!"

"Every week, Mrs, Bardell!" Blake exclaimed, in a horrified voice.

"Yes, every week, Mr. Blake! But I'm just tired of all the bother and argument. I won't do a bit more; I'll leave it just as it is—so there!"

"No, please don't say that, Mrs. Bardell," said the detective, in a great panic, hastily getting between her and the door. "It was all my fault; it was very wrong of me to interfere. Please carry on as you think fit, Mrs. Bardell; I'm going out for a stroll. I'll leave you in absolute possession."

And so saying, Blake turned and fled from the room.

He strode down the street in a state of great agitation, muttering to himself all the while:

"It's useless, absolutely useless, to argue with a woman. But what a fool I was to ask her to tidy up! The place is a total wreck. I shall never, never be able to find what I want again. What shall I do—what, in the name of goodness, shall I do?"

But Mrs. Bardell had gained one victory; only a minor tussle now remained for her to establish herself supreme. She turned on Tinker, whose consternation had not been one whit less than his master's.

"And now, Master Tinker," she said, "you just toddle off and follow the master. I don't want any menfolk hanging about and getting in my way while I'm busy. Off you go!"

And Tinker went.

"Who'd have thought it?" he muttered, as he got outside.

He whiled away several hours in a picture palace, but at regular intervals he still kept muttering to himself:

"Who'd have thought it? Who'd jolly well have thought it!"

***

The detective and his assistant both entered the room together; both of them glanced round in blank astonishment at the unfamiliar surroundings; both of them stared at each other in silent wonderment.

"We've come in the wrong house, Tinker, haven't we?" asked Blake, in an awed whisper.

"I think we must have done, guv'nor," replied Tinker, in the same awed whisper.

Blake stared round again at the spotless room the brand-new curtains at the windows, the polished fireplace, the shelves of dusted books, and the table in the centre, with its snow-white tablecloth and its vase of fresh-cut flowers—and then glanced at Tinker again.

"There's something familiar about it, though," he said. "I seem to remember seeing that steel engraving of 'The Blind Fiddler' before—don't you?"

Tinker was about to reply, when Mrs. Bardell appeared at the door. She held her broom in her hand as if it were a trident, and calmly surveyed the results of her handiwork as one who has achieved her life's work, and knows that now nothing remained for her but to enter into immortality.

Blake suddenly concluded that it was up to him to say something.

"I congratulate you, Mrs. Bardell," he said. "It does you credit—great credit. I would never have recognised the place had I not seen you standing there. But we shall have to have the number painted more plainly on the door—it will be rather difficult to find where one lives until one gets more used to the new aspect. However, I congratulate you again."

Mrs. Bardell gave a slight inclination of her head, as one to whom earthly honours were so much vanity and tinsel.

"Tea will be served when you ring, sir!" she said, and stately withdrew from the room.

Tinker looked at Blake, and Blake looked at Tinker. Then they both roared with laughter.

"Never ask a woman to tidy up unless you're prepared for the worst, Tinker," said Blake solemnly, when he had somewhat recovered his composure. "If you give them an inch they're bound to take a mile."

"Thanks for the tip, guv'nor," said Tinker gratefully. "I'll remember that."

Blake looked at the clock on the mantelpiece. It was ten minutes to four; and at four o'clock his visitors were due to arrive. He walked over to the window and stood there gazing abstractedly into the street.

It was just a week since they had embarked on the Marseilles boat from Algiers. In a short three days they were in London again. From the wonderful town of Algiers—with its wreaths of almond blossom and golden fountains of mimosa, bathed in dazzling sunshine—they had been transplanted by boat and train to smoky, foggy, murky London once more. It seemed impossible. The whole thing seemed a dream. Already the mystery of the Veuxpillo Galleries was being relegated to the dim past.

The detective turned suddenly to Tinker.

"Here they are!" he said excitedly. "Quick, Tinker! See if Mrs. Bardell has the toasted fight-buns ready to bring in!"

"The toasted fight-buns, guv'nor!"

"Yes, the fight—er—I mean the wave-brains, Tinker!"

"The wave———"

"Don't argue, Tinker! You know what I mean—the toasted bun-waves! That is, the toasted brain-fights."

"You mean the toasted bun-fights, guv'nor?" said Tinker, in a perfect stew of agitation.

Blake looked at his assistant with an expression of grim determination.

"I don't mean anything of the kind, Tinker," he said slowly. "What I really did mean to say—and what I believe I did really say was the buttered scones. Ask Mrs. Bardell to bring in the buttered scones, And don't stand there with your mouth wide open—you ought to know what I mean without arguing about it in that absurd fashion."

"Crummy!" said Tinker, and rushed to the door just as it was opened, and Granite Grant and Mademoiselle Julie stood smiling at the scene.

The next moment Blake found himself busy shaking hands with his friends with both hands.

"I guess this is where Blake has the brain-waves," said the King's Spy, in his deep bass voice.

And Blake started self-consciously.

Then Mademoiselle Julie, whose quick eyes had roved round the room and taken in every little detail, turned to the detective with an expression of disappointment.

"Monsieur Blake is a cheat!" she exclaimed accusingly.

"Why, whatever is the matter, mademoiselle?" asked Blake quickly.

Julie waved her little hand disdainfully.

"Everything is so clean and neat and tidy," she said. "It is not at all what you English call, a bachelor's den. It is a shame!"

Blake's jaw dropped aghast. This, then, was the recompense for all his self-sacrifice! Mrs. Bardell's strenuous labours had been in vain. He had allowed himself to be turned out of house and home, his room had been ransacked, the ruthless scrubbing-brush had gone into the most private and intimate corners of his wardrobe; and all because Mademoiselle Julie was coming to tea! Now she had turned round and accused him of cheating.

He determined to bluff the thing out.

"Allow me to inform you, mademoiselle," he said stiffly, "that my rooms are always clean and neat and tidy."

At this unblushing falsehood Tinker made a noise like a burst water-pipe. But Blake silenced him with a glassy stare.

"Always clean and neat and tidy, mademoiselle!" he reiterated, with an emphasis on each adjective.

But Julie only gave a silvery peal of laughter, and insisted again:

"Monsieur Blake is a cheat!"

Blake thought it best not to argue the matter further, and gave it up with a sigh of self-pity.

"And where is the brave Pedro?" asked Julie the next moment.

"Go and fetch him, Tinker!" said Blake, only too pleased at this diversion.

Then Pedro came in, and began dancing round his friends in great delight, while Mademoiselle Julie vainly endeavoured to hug the great dog to her.

"How about this bun-fight, Blake?" asked Granite Grant presently. "I haven't had anything to eat since lunch. I've been preparing for it ever since. I'm getting rather hungry now."

"Then take your seats," said Blake, "and we'll ask Mademoiselle Julie to perform on the teapot."

And so Sexton Blake's little tea-party sat down to the buttered scones and the candy cakes and all the other delectable luxuries prepared by Mrs. Bardell.

And there we will leave them to tell their stories in their own way, until we meet them again on some future occasion in Sexton Blake's strenuous and varied career.

A Complete Sexton Blake Story appears every week in the

UNION JACK LIBRARY.   Price 1½d.

Classic Cases from the Sexton Blake Library
TALES FROM THE GOLDEN AGE

THE FERRARO FILES
R. C. Armour

The first of several anthologies
featuring popular Blake foe
Dr. Antonio Ferraro.

Features:
The Episode of the Stolen Voice
The Man Who Forgot
and The Mystery of the Sunken Road

THE THREE MURRAYS

Andrew Murray
Robert Murray Graydon
William Murray Graydon

Three legendary authors
Four classic tales.

Features:
The Masquerader (Starring The Bat!)
The Case of the Suppressed Will
The Black Bat
The Mystery of the S.S. Olympic

ROH PRESS

If you have a moment...

We hope you enjoyed this Sexton Blake Anthology! If you have a moment please help us out by leaving a review.

www.ingramcontent.com/pod-product-compliance
Lightning Source LLC
Chambersburg PA
CBHW081102300726
48976CB00011B/2702